CURSE
OF THE
WOLF
KING

Tessonja Odette is a Seattle-based author of fantasy romance, epic romantasy and fairy-tale retellings. Her different series range from cosy fae romcoms to dark and twisty fantasy. In her books you'll find witty banter, sizzling romance and breathtaking magic. When she isn't writing, she's watching anime, squeezing her pets or dancing to the music only she can hear.

tessonjaodette.com
@tessonja
/tessonjaodette
@tessonja
@tessonjaodette

Also by Tessonja Odette

The Fair Isle Trilogy

To Carve a Fae Heart
To Wear a Fae Crown
To Spark a Fae War

Entangled with Fae

Curse of the Wolf King
Heart of the Raven Prince
Kiss of the Selkie
A Taste of Poison
A Dream So Wicked

Fae Flings and Corset Strings

A Rivalry of Hearts
My Feral Romance

Songs for the Sinless

The Lies That Summon the Night

CURSE

OF THE

WOLF

KING

TESSONJA ODETTE

ZAFFRE

First published in 2021
First published in the UK in 2025 by
ZAFFRE
An imprint of Bonnier Books UK
5th Floor, HYLO, 105 Bunhill Row,
London, EC1Y 8LZ

A CIP catalogue record for this book is
available from the British Library.

ISBN: 978-1-80617-025-8

Also available as an ebook

1 3 5 7 9 10 8 6 4 2

Typeset by IDSUK (Data Connection) Ltd
Printed and bound in Great Britain by Clays Ltd, Elcograf S.p.A.

The authorised representative in the EEA is
Bonnier Books UK (Ireland) Limited.
Registered office address: Floor 3, Block 3, Miesian Plaza,
Dublin 2, D02 Y754, Ireland
compliance@bonnierbooks.ie
www.bonnierbooks.co.uk

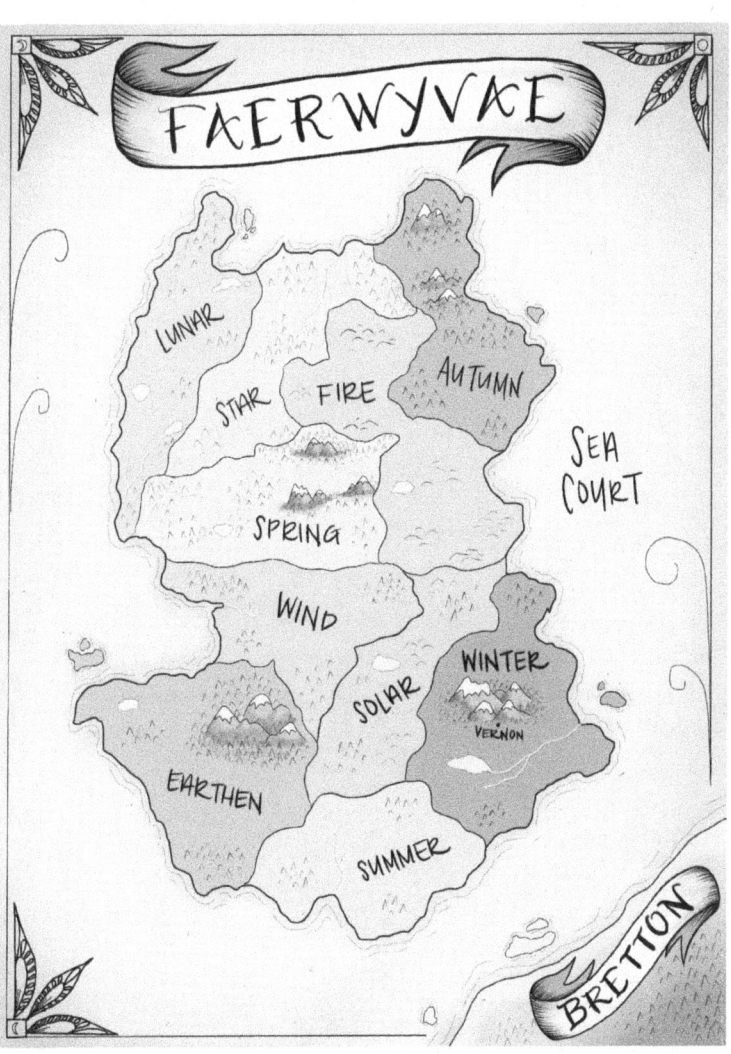

1

J ust breathe. They can't hurt me from here. No one can.

I release a heavy sigh, my breath fogging the window glass and obscuring my view of the enormous snowflakes that fall on the other side, floating from the vast white sky to the streets below. I press my forefinger to the fogged glass, tracing a circle, then several lines radiating out from its circumference. By the time I draw my last line, the image fades, taking with it my temporary sun.

I let out another sigh, my brow pulling into a scowl. I despise snow. Almost as much as this town.

I squint beyond the snowflakes to the bustling streets outside my home. A row of townhouses identical to mine line the opposite street. One family all but spills from their doorway in their haste to get outside, gathering their composure when they reach the cobblestone street. The father straightens his cravat, tips his hat, and mouths what I can only imagine are kind greetings to passing neighbors, who in turn stop to chat. Their words are too distant for me to hear from inside my townhouse's parlor, but the delighted squeals of the children are loud enough to reach me. A boy and girl grin up at the sky as they bounce up and down on the balls of their feet, faces alight at the sight of snow. It's almost enough to make me wonder if the falling flakes of freezing doom perhaps aren't the worst after all. However, all mirth from both myself and the children is stripped away when the mother swats at them, prodding her progeny into silence and well-behaved postures before contriving exaggerated smiles for her neighbors' sake.

"Why, of course, Mrs. Aston," I say under my breath, tone mocking, "you most certainly should strip the joy from your happy children while you can. Wouldn't want their enthusiasm for life's early pleasures to stain your well-kept reputation."

I shake my head and turn away from the window with a huff. Mrs. Aston, like everyone else in the town of Vernon, is yet another simple-minded, judgmental prude. I can't believe I was ever so naive to think this place would be a fresh start. A place where I could escape the rigid structures of human society and just be...me.

But no. There's no room for *me*, not when society has already decided who and what I should be. A daughter. A woman. A wife-in-training. Quiet. Demure. Chaste.

One would think moving to an isle ruled by the fae—magical creatures I once thought could never belong outside mythical stories—would provide a fresh perspective on social norms. When Father announced he was moving me and my youngest sister from Bretton to Faerwyvae, and to the Winter Court of all places, I felt a mix of emotions. Terror. Shock. Relief. And, yes, most pathetic of all, hope. I should have known better. For it turns out, the human towns in Faerwyvae are just as uptight as the cities in Bretton.

If only I could go home. To my *real* home. Not here. Not even Bretton, but to the home of my childhood where the sun shone year-round, browning my skin as I played outdoors with my sisters, not a care in the world to dampen our spirits. That was joy. That was happiness. That was when our family was whole, and Mother was still...

My shoulders stiffen. Shaking the ruminations from my mind, I stride to the fireplace at the opposite end of the parlor. I cross my arms and pop my hip to the side as I glower at the meager flames. An unladylike countenance, I'm sure, but considering I'm alone in my family's parlor, I really couldn't give a damn.

I suppress a shudder, wishing the heat of the fireplace could more adequately warm the room. How is it that I live in a land filled with magic, and yet we're still plagued by the same unreliable hearths I left behind? The Winter Court, more than any other court in Faerwyvae, should make proper heat a priority for its residents. Shouldn't it?

I grit my teeth, releasing a grumble of muttered curses.

Saints Above, why am I so on edge today?

As if in answer, my gaze is drawn to the tea table in front of the couch, where a well-worn book rests, taunting me.

Oh, that's right. Because I'm out of reading material. Again.

I move to the couch and retrieve the shawl draped over one of the pillows, then wrap it around my shoulders. I pick up my book and settle into the cushions, smoothing the folds of my blue satin skirt close to my legs, wishing I'd worn wool hose today instead of silk stockings. Then I pull the cord of the tall floor lamp next to me, igniting a warm, subtle glow that lights my pages.

We may not have leading-edge technology for heating, but at least we have electricity for light—or a form of it, I should say. Unlike Bretton, where light is generated by traditional means, here it comes from strange fae magic, traveling along ley lines, or some such.

I flip past the title page of my book, which reads *The Governess and the Rake*, to page one. The familiar words set my nerves at ease as I begin to read. But as I make it to page three, I find my mind beginning to wander. As much as I love my book, I've already read it three times. I want something new. *Need* something new.

I slam the cover shut and return it to the table. Bringing my thumbnail between my teeth, I make my way back to the window to look out at the streets that have grown even busier in my short absence from my post.

My heart races as the bodies that swarm the streets grow denser, the chatter of excited pedestrians compounding with horse hooves, carriage wheels, and the rare automobile until it becomes an audible roar of sound.

I'm transported to a similar street in recent memory, one crowded with sneers and whispers. Eyes that burn with hate and scorn. All directed at me, as barbed as if they were lashes upon my flesh.

I bite the inside of my cheek, which helps me recover my bearings.

Just breathe. This is here. This is now.

Damn it all to hell, I really need a new book. Otherwise, my mind will be the death of me. But new books mean leaving this room. Walking in the saintsforsaken snow...amongst all those people.

I swallow hard.

We've been living in Vernon for three weeks now. The first week was almost a respite. Being a newly opened resort town near the mountains of the Winter Court, Vernon welcomed us as one of the first families to take up residence. The shops were new and stocked to the brim with untouched goods, which thankfully included a bookshop. That became my immediate haven, and I confess, I spent my weekly allowance during my first trip there. The second week brought more new families settling into the empty homes, including the nosy Mrs. Aston. Still, I continued to escape into my books and replenish my wares as soon as one story was finished. The start of this week, however, brought a flood of residents, some permanent, others visitors. All bursting with anticipation for what is considered a momentous event— the start of the Winter Court's social season.

I once was excited by social seasons, but now I dread them. Dread with a capital D and a string of colorful curses. The kind a lady should never say. Shit. Damn. Hell.

I really, *really* need a new book.

Clenching my fingers into fists, I stare out at the streets one more time and give myself to the count of five to feel afraid.

One.

The bookshop is just a few blocks away.

Two.

No one here knows my past.

Three.

They don't know me at all.

Four.

And if I have anything to do about it, no one ever will.

Five.

With a deep inhale, I straighten my posture, swallowing my fear. Then I suck in my stomach, aided by my tight-laced corset, and throw back my shoulders. I pat my black tresses, ensuring every wavy strand is secured in its fashionable twist at the nape of my neck. Lifting my chin, I press my lips into a haughty smile, the first ingredient that makes up the mask I must wear. The persona I present to the world. The kind that keeps me strong. Confident. Impervious to pain.

A lie, yes.

But one that I, Gemma Bellefleur, wear so well.

2

Head held high, I exit through my front door. The chilly air immediately strikes me, teasing the warmth from my thick wool coat. My sable collar brushes my cheeks as I pull it higher, wishing it were tall enough to cover my ears. At least my wide hat protects me from the falling snowflakes that continue to float down from the sky.

Sound is amplified tenfold from what it had been behind the safety of my parlor window, sending my pulse pounding. And yet, my smile doesn't slip. I give way to not a single flinch as an automobile roars by, sending pedestrians hurtling out of its path. Part of me begs to rush back inside, back to the warmth of the fireplace, to the quiet of the parlor, but I shove that part of me into the recesses of my mind and focus on the task at hand.

Just breathe. Just smile. Just pretend.

With a deep breath, I descend the front steps to the sidewalk below, my low-heeled boots crunching into the dusting of fresh snow. The snow here is always fresh, never accumulating higher than a quarter inch on the streets, no matter how much has fallen the day before. It must be magic that keeps it that way.

"Miss Bellefleur!" a voice calls from across the street.

Mrs. Aston gives an enthusiastic wave, and I curse my reactions for being so automatic. If I hadn't made eye contact, I could pretend I didn't see her. But it's too late. She's already crossing the street toward me. I manage to suppress a groan, although I'm sure I can't keep my full displeasure from my eyes. To counteract it, I force a smile.

"Miss Bellefleur," she says when she reaches me, "is your father home? I was hoping to have you and your sister over for dinner tonight."

Bodies weave around us on the sidewalk, making my breath hitch. I hate standing still in a crowd. Hate it. I can almost hear whispers, jests, snide comments laced beneath the roar of footsteps, pitched within the blare of an automobile horn—

I blink a few times, breathing the memories away. *This is here. This is now.* I refocus on my outer composure and recall Mrs. Aston's question. "No, my father is not home," I say and leave it at that.

"Oh, but I must have you over. You simply have to meet Gavin. He's finally arrived in town." Her eyes are alight with excitement, her smile oozing saccharine sweetness.

"Gavin," I echo flatly.

Her grin falters. "My eldest son. You recall I told you about him when I was last over for tea?"

"Ah." I nod. Now I know what this is about. It's the social season's most heinous of activities. Matchmaking. Time for a swift exit. "My father and sister are in the market square. I'm sure you can speak to him when he returns."

I take a step to the side, but she mirrors me.

"Oh, but did you hear about Miss Weathersbee?" She lowers her voice just enough to feign discretion, although hardly quiet enough to truly avoid being overheard. "I was most surprised when I heard. She'd taken a walk —*unchaperoned*—with Mr. Evans. And—"

"Mrs. Aston," I say, allowing some sharpness to infuse my tone, "I doubt this is any of my business to know, considering I am acquainted with neither Miss Weathersbee nor Mr. Evans."

Heat flushes her already heavily rouged cheeks. She purses her lips, then returns them to her false grin. "Miss Bellefleur, I was simply leading up to tell you that they spotted a wolf. Two of them! Right on Whitespruce Lane at the edge of the woods. I merely wanted to warn you."

I grit my teeth. That's how some of the vilest rumors start, the kind that are cloaked in a way that makes the news seem prudent to share. I've heard it all before. *I'd be a terrible friend if I didn't confess*, or *I only say this because...* There's always a reason. Always a way to rationalize why one must invade another's most private moments.

I curl my fingers into tight fists, feeling the stretch of my kid gloves. It takes all my restraint to maintain my composure. At least my irritation has overridden my fear. I can hardly see the bustling bodies that continue to shove past us. When I speak, my words come out calm. Collected. Just like my outer persona. "We do live in the Winter Court, Mrs. Aston. Spotting wolves at the edge of the forest is hardly news worth spreading, regardless of the gossip you've so neatly tied to it."

I expect another blush, but she's nonplussed. In fact, she seems encouraged, her smile brightening. "They could have been *fae* wolves."

"Here?" I say with mock concern. "At the heart of a fae court? Why, never in all my days would I have thought such a thing possible."

This time, she seems to catch the hint. She folds her hands before her with a huff. "We don't see many fae here, Miss Bellefleur. This is a human town, after all."

"Vernon has only been open for a matter of weeks."

"Which means every sighting of a fae is news!" She places a hand on my arm, her words taking on a conde-scending tone, her cadence slowing. "Gemma, dear, you are new to Faerwyvae and are not yet versed in our ways. The fae may rule us and they may mingle with humans freely in some cities, but very rarely here in the south. The northern cities near the palace of the seelie king are where most high fae live, and the lesser fae, like the wolves and bears, tend to stay away from towns like ours."

I plaster a smile over my lips and tilt my head. "On the contrary, I have been told all of this. I've also been told the fae take offense to the terms *high fae* and *lesser fae* and prefer the terms seelie and unseelie, so I suggest you forgo repeating the former."

She waves a dismissive hand. "That's only if they hear you use such phrasing. It's not likely I'll offend anyone here. As I've already said, there's hardly a fae living in Vernon. Unless, of course, you count Mr. Hamish's new wife. Have you met her yet? She looks like one of us, but they say she's half pixie! Can you even imagine?"

There's really no getting through to this woman, is

there? Then again, based on our previous encounters, I shouldn't have expected this conversation to go any different. "I must be going, Mrs. Aston."

Again, I step away, only for her to shadow me.

"Where are you off to? Perhaps we can go together? We're on our way to meet Gavin. I'm sure an early introduction—"

"What a kind and generous offer," I say without warmth, "but I must be on my way alone. Good day."

She opens her mouth to object, but I'm already taking my leave—with haste this time.

THE BOOKSHOP, LIKE ALWAYS, IS NEARLY EMPTY.

As soon as the door closes behind me, I feel like I can breathe. More than that, I can finally let my guard down. Here I can be myself. Here I can find quiet.

I head for the bookseller, Mr. Cordell, who nods at me with a warm smile as I reach his counter. He's an older gentleman, perhaps twenty years my father's senior. His hair is gray, his eyes a watery blue. I return his smile, this one genuine, unlike the one I wear among the other townspeople.

"How many today, Miss Bellefleur?" Mr. Cordell asks.

"That depends. Anything new?"

He pretends to ponder, squinting at me as he taps a finger to his chin. "Well, I have plenty new. But the kind of books *you're* after…"

"Don't hold out. Tell me!" I say with a laugh.

With an exaggerated sigh, he reaches beneath the counter and takes out a rectangular bundle wrapped in cloth. He barely has a chance to push it across the counter toward me before I gather it up and tear off the wrapping. I can't contain my excitement as I read the title. *The Governess and the Earl.*

My breath catches. This is the newest book in the *Governess in Love* series. And it's here. In my hands. My mouth falls open as I hug the book to my chest and meet Mr. Cordell's eyes.

He gives me a knowing nod. "It's quite good."

"You read it already? That's so unfair. You should have hand-delivered it to me at once."

"Perhaps," he says. "But then how else would I get you in here to brighten up my dreary shop? There are so few others in town with such keen tastes."

I must confess he's right. I've hardly met another soul who appreciates the intricate art of the romance novel more than Mr. Cordell. He's probably the most—if not only—pleasant surprise I've had since moving to Vernon. "You're saving my sanity, you saintly old man."

"I'm not sure if I can be considered a saint after reading chapter eighteen. There are few things that can make me blush anymore, but...just you wait."

My entire being hums with my eagerness to get home and dive into my book straight away. But considering how quickly I finished the last book, I should probably take home more than one. "Is this the only new arrival?"

"Oh, no. There's plenty more. I knew you'd be most excited about that one, and it would be a crime not to reserve your copy at the counter. Go ahead and browse. You know where to find the good stuff." He gives me a wink, and I make my way to the back of the store, *The Governess and the Earl* still clutched close to my chest.

I reach the romance section, a wall of my favorite books spanning before me, most of which I've read once, if not several times. The aroma of paper envelops me like a warm blanket, one that feels like home. Safety. I'm so comforted in this moment, tears begin to prick my eyes. I run my fingers along the spines of the books, reading each title with care as if greeting a dear friend. I am, in truth. For here I am amongst my true peers. Men and women who've been swept beneath the tides of love, overcome by its grief and madness, in all its glorious stupidity. Of course, the characters in these books always end up with their lovers, safe and happy on the other side of scandal, betrayal, and heartache. Unlike myself.

Perhaps that's why I choose to disappear into books. It's a place where I can feel seen for who I am and everything I've been through. Where I'm not judged for the things I've done or the messes I've made. And in these books, I can give myself the ending that was stolen from me. The ending I no longer believe exists in real life.

Love.

Just like my outward persona, it's a lie.

I continue my exploration of my silent companions, adding each intriguing new title to a pile on the floor, until I discover a spine that I immediately know is out of place. I don't even need to read the title to know the book has been misshelved, for its bland color and unwieldy size say anything but romance. Such a crime could never be pinned on Mr. Cordell. No, this is the result of careless shoppers, the kind that make my blood boil. With a grumble, I remove the interloper and place it on top of my books. Seeing how tall my pile has grown tells me my shopping trip should probably be at an end, otherwise I'll surpass my week's allowance and end up owing Mr. Cordell at my next visit.

I gather my merchandise, plus the wayward book, and head for the counter. Only now do I realize how busy the shop has become while I've been enchanted in my quiet corner. Couples stroll arm in arm, browsing the shelves as if they are looking at fragile artifacts and not dear friends. A pair of young women chat near a table of books, idly handling them without so much as looking at what they touch. I've never seen the shop with more than one or two patrons visiting at a time, and now it's downright crowded. If this is what it's going to be like now that Vernon's social scene is in full swing, I must begin my visits to the bookshop much earlier in the morning.

Making a beeline for Mr. Cordell, I quicken my pace. I'm nearly there when—

"*Infinite Suffering in the Garden of Happenstance.*" A young man, perhaps a few years older than I, blocks my path, eyes not on my face but my chest. Or the books that cover it.

I pull my merchandise closer, heart racing at his unexpected proximity. Not out of excitement, but a fleeting terror. I take a few breaths to steady my nerves and back up a step to put space between me and the man. "Excuse me?"

He finally meets my eyes. I admit he's handsome with his dark hair and eyes, his fashionable black jacket, sky blue waistcoat, and matching cravat. But his looks are marred by the condescending grin he wears, and when he speaks, his voice carries a nasal quality that grates on my ears. "The book," he says. "The finest piece of Brettonish literature, and I must say, I am delighted to see one so beautiful as you holding it. I know by that alone that you are a woman of supreme breeding and unparalleled intelligence."

With an inward groan, I realize he's mistaken the misplaced book as something I'm actually interested in. More irksome than that is his assumption that my level of intelligence can be measured by what I read. "Sir, I—"

"Gavin Aston," he says with a bow.

I almost laugh. So, he's Mrs. Aston's son. What a surprise. "Mr. Aston—"

"And you are?"

I clench my jaw. "Gemma Bellefleur. And I—"

He lifts his chin with what he probably thinks is a charming grin. "Call me Gavin."

I narrow my eyes. "Mr. Aston," I say, punctuating each word for emphasis, "I am in a hurry to purchase my books."

"Ah, yes, how foolish of me." Before I can react, he takes them from my arms and hefts the stack onto the counter.

I rush after him. "I can carry my own books."

He pays me no heed. "Allow me to escort you home. You shouldn't walk in the snow with such heavy merchandise."

I straighten my posture, bringing us nearly eye to eye. I'm tall for a woman, with broad shoulders and wide hips. It's what my father calls a sturdy build—an insult, I'm sure, but I take pride in my figure. It helps add strength to my false persona. Compared to me, Mr. Aston is slim and lean. I highly doubt he's much stronger than I am. "Like I said, I can carry my own books."

"Then perhaps you can allow me to carry conversation instead? I daresay I'll find few others in town with intelligence to match mine."

I turn toward the counter and meet the furrowed brow of Mr. Cordell, whose eyes dart from me to my unwelcome companion. "Mr. Aston," I say without looking at him, "you assume too much of my intelligence. I assure you, we are not as matched as you think. There is, in fact, a vast discrepancy between us."

"I appreciate your modesty, but you need not be quite so self-deprecating. It's clear you are at least my half, if not my equal."

My hands tremble from the restraint it takes not to shake the sense into him with a punch to the nose. Instead, I attend to my stack of books. With an exaggerated motion, I push the misplaced book across the counter toward Mr. Cordell. "*This* was misshelved. I will not be buying it, but the others I will take. Oh, and today's paper, please."

I refuse to look Mr. Aston's way, although I can feel his gaze burning into me.

Mr. Cordell nods and begins to draw up my bill, gaze flashing toward Mr. Aston time and again, who still, for whatever saintsforsaken reason, has yet to get the hint and leave. The old bookseller hands me my bill, as well as my books and newspaper, all bundled neatly together with string. "That will be twelve quartz chips, my dear."

I retrieve my purse and shell out twelve pieces of clear, crystalline quartz—the currency of the Winter Court—and collect my books.

Mr. Aston holds out his arm, all smiles. "Shall we?"

Gritting my teeth, I force myself to meet his gaze. "There's a word where I come from, and perhaps I should have used it sooner, for I'm certain it is a word well-known in Faerwyvae as well. The word is *no*."

He throws his head back and laughs. "You truly are clever—"

"Gemma!" a female voice says with a gasp. I don't need to look to know who it belongs to.

Today of all days, I mutter to myself. With all the effort I can manage, I plaster a smile over my lips to conceal the snarl I'd rather show, and face my nemesis.

Imogen.

3

I mogen greets me with a superficial hug, oblivious to the books I hold between us. "Dearest Gemma," she says, her blonde curls bobbing beneath her pink hat. "I was so put out when I arrived at your house and you were not in. Did you forget our plans for tea?"

"I did not forget them, for we never made them," I say. "I recall you *telling* me you'd be over for morning tea, but I do not believe I affirmed I would be home to receive you."

She laughs, but her blue eyes go steely. "You're so funny, Gemma. However, your father wouldn't like to hear of you missing any of our dates."

"No," I say with a sigh, "I doubt he would." Curse my father for setting me up with Imogen Coleman, daughter of the vile woman he's been courting since we arrived in Vernon. She calls herself my friend, but in truth, she's more like my jailer. Here to keep me prim, proper, and well out of scandal's vicious grasp.

"It's a good thing I knew just where to find you." She

then turns to the infernal man next to me. "I see you've met Mr. Aston already. We're old friends."

Ugh, of course they know each other.

"A pleasure to see you again, Miss Coleman," he says with a nod. "I wasn't aware your family would be vacationing here."

She swats him playfully on the arm. "You should know better by now. My family should be expected at all the liveliest social seasons."

"Yes. In fact, one would almost say you *chase* them."

I'm taken aback by the jibe, impressed to hear the first intelligent thing from his lips.

Imogen's face flashes with a scowl, but she quickly replaces her smile. "Mr. Aston, you must escort us home and carry Miss Bellefleur's books."

"No," I say before he can take a step toward me. "I'm desperate for some time alone with my dear friend." Words I never expected I'd come to say about Imogen, that's for sure.

Mr. Aston frowns, hands extended toward the books I hold in a viselike grip.

"Ah, Mr. Aston," comes the bookseller's voice. "I overheard your love for *Infinite Suffering in the Garden of Happenstance*. If you enjoy that, I have a new book all the intelligent young men are raving about."

My companion perks up at that. "Yes! Yes, I would like to see this book indeed. I will leave you two to talk amongst yourselves. I do know how ladies love to gossip." With a wink, he rushes to join Mr. Cordell, giving me a glorious escape.

Well, sort of. There's still Imogen.

We exit the bookshop, which sends my stomach

plummeting. Gone is the comforting smell of paper, the dim indoor light, replaced instead with blinding white snow and crowds. At least my anxiety has all but retreated in the wake of my rage at Mr. Aston. It makes returning to the busy streets much easier to bear than it had been when I first set off. It's always like this when I leave the house these days. Terrible at first, most often from the vantage inside my own head. Then nearly as bad when I first step outside. But I grow used to it as my memories of the past fail to materialize in the present.

This is here. This is now.

Imogen points across the street. "Oh my goodness. Is that...a fae?"

I follow her line of sight to the elegant hotel-to-be still under partial construction. Outside it, a male figure with brown hair and horn-rimmed spectacles confers with a copper-haired woman next to him. While the woman appears human, aside from her odd choice of clothing— a brocade coat in vibrant chartreuse—the male has distinctly pointed ears. The sidewalk around them is nearly empty, with many crossing the road to give them space. As much as I hate to admit Mrs. Aston being right about anything, it is true that very few fae have come to Vernon so far, and when they do, they tend to be a bit of a spectacle. The two figures across the street, however, don't seem to notice, as their attention is fixed on the hotel's facade.

"I can't believe they're still working on the Verity Hotel," Imogen says with a pout. "It's the only one with space for a proper ballroom. How can we have a true social season without a place to dance?"

I internally roll my eyes. "I'm sure we'll manage."

"I wish they'd hurry. You'd think hiring a fae interior designer would make the process faster, not slow it to a snail's pace." Imogen continues to glare at the hotel, as if that alone could speed the construction, until a petite young woman approaches.

She wears an enormous blue bonnet—although she looks old enough to wear much more mature fashions—and a gray wool coat with fraying hems. "I've picked up your ribbons," she says to Imogen.

Imogen doesn't so much as look at her. "Take Miss Bellefleur's books, Ember," she says, pointing at me before she starts off down the sidewalk.

The girl named Ember takes my burden with a warm smile, adding to arms already laden with bags and boxes.

"Thank you," I say to her, then join Imogen. "Is she a new maid? I haven't seen you travel with her before."

Imogen leans in close and mutters, "She's my stepsister. Might as well make her useful."

I nearly trip over my boots as I whirl back to the girl, heat rising to my cheeks. "I'm so sorry. I thought you were a maid. Here, let me take them back."

"Really, it's fine," Ember says.

"Yes, it's fine," Imogen echoes, but with more ice in her tone. She pulls me to face forward, her smile never faltering as she says, "It's improper to carry your own books, Gemma dear. You'll never snag a husband like that."

Her words return my irritation, but they also remind me to replace my mask. My unflustered persona. With more grace than I truly feel, I ask, "And what about your sister? If such a thing is improper for me, is it not improper for her to carry my books?"

She lets out a high-pitched laugh. "Ember isn't on the market for a husband. *We* are. As someone older than you, you must heed my counsel."

I bite back my retort. Oh, what I wouldn't give to tell Imogen Coleman to take her counsel and piss right off. But, of course, my father would kill me. My so-called friendship with the girl is probably the only thing keeping him from breathing down my neck every minute of the day to find me a husband.

So instead, I look down my nose at her. "How do you know I even want to marry?"

She meets my gaze, aghast. "Well, we've already established you have no merits to recommend you to the fae royals, and becoming one of their prized artisans is the only viable option for an unmarried woman without her own wealth. You don't sing, you don't play the pianoforte, and you have no artistic talent. Besides, the Winter Court's seelie king rarely accepts new artisans, and the unseelie king doesn't even hold auditions. In fact, even if the unseelie king decided to finally grace us lowly townspeople with his presence, I'd hesitate to suggest you get your hopes up with him. Hardly anyone knows a thing about him, aside from his disdain for humans. I don't even know his..."

She trails off, her tirade coming to an uncharacteristic pause. I furrow my brow, watching as her eyes glaze over, face blank as if she's suddenly forgotten what she was saying. Maybe I'll get lucky and she'll stop speaking altogether.

Then, just as suddenly as the strange expression came, it disappears with a shake of her head. "No, your destiny lies not with the fae and their elite cities and palaces." The wistfulness in her tone isn't lost on me, and I wonder if she's speaking equally to herself. I've heard her lament time and time again that there haven't been nearly enough fae princes present at any of the other courts' recent social seasons. Apparently, a royal fae husband equates to the ultimate marital success for human girls in Faerwyvae.

Imogen sighs. "Like me, your place is here, amongst the humans. Which means you must have a husband."

I clench my jaw, wanting to scream. How are the people here so...so stagnant? So unprogressive? I never considered my previous homes to be amidst advanced society, but everyone I've met in Vernon suggests this place is several years—if not decades—behind the times.

Then again, personal experience has proven just how prevalent rigid social structures can be...and the cruelty of those who enforce them. The rumors. The sneers. The leering taunts—

"Mr. Aston is a great option," Imogen says, startling me from my thoughts. "I will hate you forever if you snag him. Although, I am sure I have lost all chance with him regardless."

As much as I despise engaging in such trivial conversation, her words have piqued my curiosity. "Why is that?"

"We courted for no more than a week last year, and I'm certain neither of us could stand it. He wanted nothing more than to talk and debate, and I could hardly keep up with the dreary subjects he wanted to chat about. You could tempt him, though. It's clear he's already smitten with you. Besides, you both like...books." She says the last word with a flourish of her hand, her nose wrinkled with distaste.

I lift my chin. "A mutual love for books doesn't mean I can tolerate tedious conversation with an insufferable fool who thinks so highly of his intellect."

I catch a stifled laugh and find Ember feigning a cough behind us. Imogen, however, has stopped in her tracks, eyes wide as her cheeks burn pink. "You should not speak of Mr. Aston like that," she mutters furiously. Gathering her composure, she links her arm through mine, and we begin to walk again. "He could be just what you need, you know."

I frown. "Just what I need? For what?"

She looks up at me, lips twisted into a knowing smirk. "To secure a husband before everyone here finds out."

This time, I'm the one pulling to an abrupt halt. "Finds out? About what?"

"Your father told my mother all about it, and she told me."

A hollow ringing fills my ears, and time seems to slow down and speed up all at once.

When Imogen next speaks, her feigned whisper sounds more like a shout, and it feels like a punch to the gut. "The scandal in Bretton."

The breath is stripped from my lungs, and my heart slams against my ribcage as I'm suddenly back on that street I was on just months ago. Familiar faces of women I'd once called my friends stand around me, hurling insults.

Whore.

He didn't even care about you.

Hussy.

He didn't belong to you.

Seductress.

How could you betray the princess like that?

Temptress.

Did you use witchcraft on him?

I feel a gentle hand on my arm, one that brings me back to the present. It's Ember who stands at my side, looking up at me with concern. "Are you all right, Miss Bellefleur?" she asks.

With terror, I realize I'm shaking, eyes unfocused. My gaze snaps back to Imogen, who watches me with a triumphant grin. I can't let her see me like this. I can't let *anyone* see me like this. For this is how they can hurt me.

With a deep breath, I force the memories to retreat, let my confident mask settle back over me. *Don't be weak,* I tell myself. *If you can't escape their judgments, then be who they already think you are.*

I brush off Ember's concern and return to walking ahead. I wait until Imogen catches up to me before I speak again. "Oh yes, the *scandal*, as father calls it. Or as I like to say, *a good time.*"

Imogen's mouth falls open on its hinge. "You can't act like that here. It may have been acceptable to play the harlot in Bretton, but the people of Vernon will not tolerate such behavior. If you get caught up in something like that again, I won't be able to be your friend."

"Pity."

"Have you no shame? No one wants a ruined woman as a wife. If everyone here were to find out about your...*colorful* past, you'd become a stain on this town and everyone you associate with. It would destroy my reputation."

I turn my head sharply to the side, letting a hint of rage shine behind my eyes. "Then perhaps it's best you keep your mouth shut about it."

Ember masks another laugh behind a fit of contrived coughs, and the rest of our walk passes in glorious silence.

4

Whe we reach my townhouse, I can hardly contain my joy in bidding farewell to Imogen. I'm even more relieved when I enter the front hall and the maid informs me my father and sister are still out. *That means more time alone for me.*

"Delightful," I say, handing her my hat and coat, dripping sheets of icy water from melted snow. "Has the post arrived yet, Susan?"

"No, miss," she says, "but I will bring it to you when it does."

I don't know why I bother being so hopeful. I doubt there will be anything of interest addressed to me in today's post. Invitations to tea and dinner, I'm sure, but the correspondences I'm awaiting are better than that. They could hold the key to my freedom.

Books cradled in my arms, I make my way upstairs to the parlor. Exhaustion, both mental and physical, drags at my bones. It takes a lot out of me to leave the house, more so when I have to deal with the likes of pretty much anyone in this town. Luckily, with the house nearly empty, I can let my mask slip, let my shoulders fall. Let all pretense wash away as I enjoy this moment alone.

Inside the parlor, the fire still quietly roars in the hearth, which feels like an inferno compared to the bite in the air outside. I pull a chair and small table closer to the fire and settle in, and Susan brings a tray of scones and tea. I flash her a warm smile and gush my thanks before turning my attention to my new books. I organize them in a stack in order from most-excited-to read to still-very-excited-but-less-than-those-above. *The Governess and the Earl,* of course, sits at the very top. I shift the order of the bottommost books several times, but once I'm content, I lean back with today's paper and open it straight to the want ads.

Like I do every day, I scan the columns seeking job postings, which are plentiful, since the newness of this town provides a plethora of employment opportunities. But just like every day before, I'm in a rage by the time I'm halfway through my search. Nearly every job posting with even the slightest prestige has the caveat that the applicant be male. *Male.* Why the hell for? And those that allow women to apply pay far less or are for jobs I'm not desperate enough to take. Factory worker. Maid. Secretary. Governess. I'd be happy as a secretary, I'm sure, but for that pay? It would take decades to secure the financial independence I need to free myself from my father's clutches and the need for a husband. And as much as I love reading about the governesses in the *Governess in Love* series, that career is certainly not for me.

Instead, I seek out ads with the words *accountant,
house steward, management,* but all those postings are for
men. The very jobs I have experience with are the ones
I'm excluded from. It makes no sense! Who better to
manage accounts and households than the middle
daughter who saved her family from destitution?

The thought quickly turns my mood from anger to
sorrow, for it makes me think of Mother. With that comes
a tender lump rising in my throat.

It's been five years since her death, and still it pains
me daily. The darkness of the days that followed her
demise cling to the shadows of my family's past, as none
of us were ever the same again. Father was changed most
of all, not the least bit by the fact that she died in a
collapse of one of the mines he owned. The incident
killed more than just Mother, though, and resulted in
several lawsuits—and even strikes at the other mines—
over unsafe work conditions. Our finances crashed, and
the mining operations fell to ruin. It was as if Mother's
death heralded an end to life as we knew it.

We soon left our home, our country of Isola, and all
our happy memories. Seeking to replenish his wealth,
Father moved us to the country of Bretton, settling in its
bustling capital city. With Father constantly away chasing
business and my eldest sister entering society to find a
husband, it was left to me to oversee our accounts.
Because of me, we survived. Because of me, no one knew
we were poor. I managed our accounts so strategically
that only a glimpse at our ledgers could have given our
secret away. When visitors came to call, they saw our
luxurious parlor, not our bare bedrooms. When we went

out on the town, they saw us in fine dresses, not the outfits we'd had artfully repurposed or sold. The facade was so convincing, I eventually caught the eye of a viscount—

Just like that, my rage returns. I fold the newspaper closed, tossing it on my lap, and take a hearty sip of tea, wishing it were wine instead.

Footsteps sound in the hall, startling me and draining my momentary flash of anger. I replace my cup on its saucer and smooth out my skirts as if the motions could brush away my anger too. At the last moment, I stash the newspaper behind me and sit up tall. But when the figure clears the threshold, I'm relieved to see it's just Nina, my younger sister.

"Gemma, you're still here? Did you even leave the house today?" she asks, golden cheeks flushed pink after coming in from the cold. She takes a seat in a nearby chair and holds her hands out toward the fire.

"I left once," I say. "Did Father come home with you?"

"No."

At that, I fall back into a reclined position and retrieve my newspaper from behind me. Nina may be far better behaved than I am, but she's one of the few people I can be myself around.

She spots my pile of books and rolls her eyes. "Oh, I see how it is. I can't persuade you to come out with *me*, but a need for books can. Remind me to start hiding your books when I'm in want of company."

"I don't know why you'd ever be in want of company, Nina," I say with a smile. "You're already engaged and have made friends of half the ladies in town."

"You'd be engaged too, if you'd get your pretty nose out of a book for once." Her tone is scolding, but her expression is warm, reminding me so much of Mother. She looks just like her. Short, plump, with round cheeks, black hair, and dark eyes. My eldest sister, Marnie, is nearly identical, but just a few inches taller. No wonder Father has always liked them better than me. I take more after him with my height and build.

I pour another cup of tea and bring it to my lips. "I don't want to marry. You know that."

She bites her lip for a moment, as if she's fighting what she really wants to say.

I give her a warning glare. *Don't,* it conveys. *Do not bring up the viscount. Do not try to tell me, yet again, that love still exists. I've seen both its pleasures and its demise, and I want none of it ever again.*

Taking the hint, she replaces her smile. "You might still change your mind. If the right person comes along, that is. Just don't do what you always do."

"And what is it I always do?"

She gives me a pointed look. "You always expect the worst in people. If you didn't, you'd notice just how many handsome gentlemen have arrived in town this week."

"Goody," I say. Taking up the paper again, I hide behind its sheets, seeing words but reading nothing.

Nina groans. "You aren't still looking for jobs, are you? You know Father will never allow it."

"I'm eighteen," I say. "I don't need Father's permission to take a job."

"He'll cut your allowance."

"That's the point of getting a job."

"He'll forbid you from living at home."

"Again, the benefits of a job."

Nina stammers. "You...you'll never snag a wealthy husband if you're *employed*." She says the last word like it's dirty.

I flip the corner of my paper down to narrow my eyes at her.

When I flip the page back up, she says, "Well, have you had any replies to your inquiries?"

Heat rises to my cheeks. I know what she's getting at, and no, not a single response has been sent to me from the jobs in town I've inquired about. That's why I've been so eager for the daily post to arrive, despite my hopes proving futile. I've applied for every job I consider myself qualified for, save for those beneath my financial needs, which means most were reserved for men. Not a single employer has sent so much as a thank you, much less an invitation to interview.

"Inquiries about what?"

I jump at the sound of Father's rich baritone coming from the hall and quickly fold the paper away, stashing it beneath the cover of one of my books. I sit upright just as he enters the parlor. He eyes me, suspicion in his dark gaze, lips pursed beneath his black mustache.

"Dresses," I rush to say. "I'm seeking a new gown."

He pauses to consider my answer, rubbing the stubble at his jaw, then gives an approving nod. "That should help your prospects."

I try my best to smile instead of scowl. *My prospects.* That's all he cares about. Now that we're wealthy again, thanks to a change in fortune a few months back, he has no need for me to act as our household manager. He hires men for that role, and I am to return to what I was always meant to be in his eyes—a daughter training to be a wife. Just another one of his properties. Unlike my two sisters, however, I am more like the mining properties that gave Father so much trouble after Mother died.

With a deep breath, I settle once again beneath my mask of indifference, reaching a delicate hand for my teacup and taking a dainty sip. Ever the dutiful daughter. Ever the prized pig at the fair.

He takes a step closer. "Mrs. Aston says you met her eldest son today."

Ah, so word of that has already spread. I shouldn't be surprised. "Yes, he introduced himself to me at the bookshop this morning."

"You refused his offer to walk you home." He doesn't bother hiding his disapproval.

"I did. I desired some time alone with darling Imogen." My words come out with far more sarcasm than I mean to reveal.

"While I approve of your restraint as opposed to throwing yourself at the young man—"

I nearly lash out as my inner rage ignites. By *throwing myself at him*, I'm sure he's referring to what he assumes transpired with the viscount in Bretton. Swallowing my anger, I grit my teeth and take another sip of my tea.

"—I do think your refusal must be far softer next time. Decline such an invitation only once to demonstrate your virtue. If you refuse a suitor's persistence too many times, he's not likely to try again."

"Perhaps a suitor's unwanted persistence shouldn't be praised but condemned." I try to keep my voice as light as I can, but a bitter edge cuts through.

His eyes narrow to slits, his heavy brow pulling down. "I don't recall that being your opinion when we were in Bretton."

My composure shatters, and I slam the teacup on its saucer. No matter how many times I try, I cannot be the daughter Father wants me to be, not even in pretend. Screw the mask. Screw my false persona.

Burning him with a glare, I rise to my feet. But as I face him, my chest heaving, I know not what to say. I've shared my side of the story once before. I've said my truth. I cried, I bared my bleeding heart. And what was I met with? My own family, both my father and my eldest sister, Marnie—two people I loved and expected to love me back—responded with disgust. Not disgust at the situation or the man who brought scandal to my life, but with *me*.

I was abandoned by the one who swore to love me, and yet *I* was at fault for giving away my virtue. *I* was responsible for my demise. My ruin. My pain. *I* was responsible for what the people were saying about me in the streets. *I* shamed the family, destroyed our precious prospects.

Father holds my gaze, lips pulling into a smirk. In this moment, he looks more like a demon than the father of my childhood. Gone is the kind, loving man whose eyes would crinkle when Mother made him laugh. All that's left of him is a cold, unfeeling husk. And right now, he knows I have no defense against him. He knows I can only seethe and glare and squeeze my fingers into fists.

"You'd do well to behave, my daughter," he says, taking a slow step forward. "If you're caught in another scandal, I won't protect you."

I bite out a sharp laugh. "Oh, because you protected me so well before."

"I did, Gemma." His words are calm, quiet. There's so much conviction in them that I know he must believe it's true. "You are too willful to know when gratitude is due. We could have stayed in Bretton. I could have let you be forever known as the harlot who seduced the princess' fiancé. Instead, I brought you here for a fresh start. If it weren't for my change of fortune with the quartz mine, we never would have had the chance."

He's right about the last part, at least. We never would have had the means to relocate if it weren't for the enormous cache of quartz discovered on one of Father's properties mere months ago. It happened just as the scandal reached its summit and allowed him to make a deal with the Winter Court. He gave the court exclusive rights to the quartz in exchange for a hefty salary and citizenship of Faerwyvae—a rare privilege, I've come to learn, for humans must be personally escorted through the magic barrier by the fae in order to set foot on the isle.

Still, he didn't bring us here to save *me*. He did it to save himself. His precious reputation.

"Say thank you," Father says through his teeth, "and return to your seat."

There's something else I want to say to him, and it sure isn't *thank* you. It's a four-letter word and comes with a rude gesture—

"We *are* grateful, Father." Nina leaves her chair and comes to my side, entwining her fingers with mine. "Gemma is grateful." She looks up at me, her eyes round and pleading. She hates when Father and I fight, and I hate that stupid sweet face she makes at me when we do. It always softens my heart and she knows it.

At least it gives me a chance to cool my nerves before I say something I'll regret. Push Father too far, and I have no doubts he'll strip me of my allowance and marry me off to the first taker. Not even the highest bidder.

No, I need to secure my financial independence first. *Then* I can tell him to piss off.

A trickle of sweat slides down the back of my neck as my eyes continue to burn with rage. Schooling my features behind a mask of subservience, I bow my head. In my mind, this is all pretend. I'm not myself but one of the governesses in my books. In the first book of the series, the governess is forced to play the part of the well-behaved pupil to avoid the wrath of her evil schoolteachers. That's all this is. Pretend. I can play pretend.

I keep the story fixed in my consciousness as I say, "I'm so thankful for everything you've done, Father. I deeply apologize that I fail to show it."

When I meet Father's eyes, he purses his lips. I can't tell if he buys my act, but he makes no argument. Instead, he waves his hand at my chair, and I follow his unspoken order. Then, without a word, he leaves the parlor.

I squeeze the arms of my chair, my body quaking with restrained rage as I listen for the sound of his slow, retreating footsteps. Only when I can no longer hear their echo do I meet my sister's gaze. Nina immediately bursts out laughing as if it were nothing more than an entertaining show. "I'm surprised you lasted as long as you did," she says. "That must be a record. What was that...thirty seconds of good behavior?"

I shake my head, unable to match her mirth. Closing

my eyes, I release a heavy sigh that barely reduces the tension built up in every muscle, but I breathe steadily until I manage to cool down some. When I open my eyes, I feel empty. Worn. Tired. Shoulders slumped, I'm about to retrieve my newspaper when Susan enters the room with a tray of letters. "The post has arrived," the maid says.

A rush of hope surges through me, just enough to push my exhaustion away, and I leap to my feet.

"Is there anything from Marnie?" Nina asks, hard on my heels as we race to Susan.

"I doubt it," I mutter as I reach the tray first and gather up the envelopes. Our eldest sister remained in Bretton with her husband when we moved and has yet to send us a single correspondence since. After our last conversation, I can't say I'm eager to hear from her ever again. I can still remember every word she said to me that day.

You brought this on yourself, Gemma.

Can you really blame him?

There's no use crying over something you caused.

Well, of course they're saying that about you! It's true.

I shake the memories away and begin to shuffle through the stack.

"They're all for Father," Nina says with a huff.

She's right. I'm almost at the bottom of the stack, and so far—

My heart leaps into my throat. There, scrawled over the last envelope, is my name. *My name.* With trembling fingers, I tear it open and retrieve the letter inside. I read the words once. Twice. Then a third time.

"What is it?" Nina says, brow furrowed.

It's finally here. My hope hasn't been futile after all. And while this isn't anything close to a guarantee, it's a step forward. My first shot at freedom. My first opportunity to be the person I want to be. Just me. Alone. Free.

I meet my sister's eyes with tears brimming in my own. "I've been invited for an interview!"

5

"An interview!" Nina echoes my words, and I'm forced to hush her. She lowers her voice to a whisper, eyes flashing toward the doorway where Father left moments ago. "You mean, for a job?"

"Of course," I whisper back, voice quavering. I can hardly contain the excitement that radiates down each limb, so intense I feel I could faint.

Susan, the only maid of ours whose discretion I can depend on, matches our volume and takes a step closer. "Would you like me to send back a response?"

"Yes, at once," I say, rushing to the bureau, my skirts swishing around my ankles. With hasty motions, I grab paper and pen and write my reply, affirming that I accept the invitation to interview.

Nina reads it over my shoulder. "But it's tomorrow," she says. "That's so soon."

"Thank the saints above," I mutter. I sign my name at the bottom and can hardly bear to let the ink dry before I stuff it into an envelope and copy the return address onto the front. Thirty-three Whitespruce Lane.

"But...but it's on Whitespruce Lane! And for the position of house steward? Are there even homes on Whitespruce?"

"I'm certainly going to find out." I seal the envelope and hand it to Susan. "See that this is sent at once, please. And...you know."

"With discretion," she says with a nod.

As soon as the maid is out the door, Nina rounds on me, her frown in stark contrast to the smile I wear. "That was a bit impulsive, even for you."

Her tone threatens to drain my triumph. My lips pull into a frown as I cross my arms. "Excuse me? You know I've been seeking a job ever since we arrived. I'm finally invited for an interview, and you think accepting it is...impulsive?"

"There wasn't even a name with the return address. Do you recall the original posting the job came from? Who you're meeting? You should have written for more information before accepting."

I bite my lip, seeing she has a point. "I suppose that would have been sensible," I confess, uncrossing my arms while keeping my head held high, "but it's too late now."

She lets out a growl of frustration. "Gemma, you better hope you don't make a fool of yourself. If the position is for house steward, then it must be the home of someone quite important. You're going to arrive without any knowledge of whom you might be working for."

I shrug and return to my chair, picking up *The Governess and the Earl* to pretend to read. "Perhaps that's how my potential employer wants it."

She stands before me, shaking her head. "No, this cannot be. We must seek more information. Surely, someone knows who lives on Whitespruce Lane." She lets out a gasp, drawing my attention back to her. "We can ask Mrs. Aston! She knows all the town gossip."

"No," I say, closing my book with a thud. The thought of asking Mrs. Aston about anything, much less for gossip, sends my blood boiling. "We must speak of this to no one. I can't risk Father finding out and trying to stop me."

"But Gemma—" With another gasp, she takes a step back, eyes growing wide. "Wait. Whitespruce Lane. Mrs. Aston told me just today that wolves were spotted there!"

I roll my eyes. "Nina, she only said that so she could spread the gossip about Miss Weathersbee without seeming imprudent."

"It could be true. Whitespruce goes through the woods, and wolves can be dangerous."

"Wolves don't just attack for fun," I say. "Everything I've heard about Faerwyvae suggests this is a lush and plentiful land. If there are wolves, they aren't some starving, rabid beasts. If any were spotted nearby, they were probably caught going about their daily business."

Nina doesn't seem at all placated. "But they could be *fae* wolves." She says *fae* in a whisper, as if the word is a curse.

I give her a pointed look. "You know as well as I do that there are severe penalties for fae attacking humans here."

"How are you not afraid?" She stomps her foot in frustration. "We still know so little about this isle and the creatures who rule here."

To be honest, beneath my excitement and relief lies an element of fear. We spent our whole lives thinking the fae were creatures of myth. It wasn't until we moved to Bretton, which is just across the channel from Faerwyvae, that we learned the mysterious isle is as real as the legends said. And many of the legends were terrifying, describing vicious wars, terrible beasts, deadly bargains. But there were a few accounts that seemed far easier to believe, describing two wars between the humans and the fae. The first ended in a treaty long ago, while the second ended just about twenty years ago after the fae protected the humans from Bretton's armed forces. This resulted in Faerwyvae's independence from the mainland, and its perimeter was sealed with magic.

So, yes, I admit I may be a little afraid. And yet, I know the difference between reality and fantasy. From what little experience I've had with the fae so far, I find it easier to believe they're a race of people who ended an unjust war than monsters who steal children in the night.

Besides, at the end of the day, my determination outweighs my fear. It's what draws me outside to get more books when I'd rather remain locked indoors. It's what helps me sneak behind Father's back, sending out job inquiries no matter how much I know he would disapprove. It's what will take me into the woods tomorrow, seeking my freedom.

Nina must sense my resolve, for she clasps her hands together in a pleading gesture. "At least take an escort."

"Are you volunteering?"

She pales. "Of course not! *I'm* not the crazy one."

I open my mouth in a mock gasp. "You'd leave your

dear old sister to face her doom rather than accompany me?"

She rolls her eyes. "At least take Susan."

I release a resigned sigh. "Very well. I'll take Susan."

She gives me a satisfied nod. "Good. That way when the wolves get you, she can tell everyone where to find your body."

I try to glare, but it turns into a laugh as she settles back into her seat. We fall into silence, and I pick my book back up. As much as I want to read it, my mind is brimming with thoughts, hopes, and possibilities.

This time tomorrow, I might have a job. Saints above, please make it so.

～

I LIED WHEN I SAID I'D TAKE SUSAN. I MAY TRUST THE maid's discretion, but that trust only goes so far. I doubt she'd act so strongly against my father's wishes by escorting me to a job interview in the woods. Luckily, by the time Nina discovers my betrayal, I'll be back home safe and sound, hopefully with word of my great success. She and Father are already out for the day, with Nina taking tea with her fiancé's family and Father likely talking business somewhere. Neither are expected back any time soon. It does mean, however, that the carriage is long gone, and I dare not order a driving service. Trusting my family's own driver would be risky enough, so perhaps it's for the best I'm walking.

And when I say for the best, I mean it's the absolute worst. Snow crunching under my boots, soaking the hem of my skirt and coat. I've worn my most modest and austere dress, the gray satin patterned with black roses, the bodice covered with ivory lace that reaches the top of my neck. I only hope I look the part. I still can hardly believe I'm about to be interviewed for house steward. The job is similar to the work I've done before, managing my former household's day-to-day, our servants, and our expenses. But that was for a modest dwelling in Bretton. I'm not sure what to expect at thirty-three Whitespruce Lane.

I reach the outskirts of town, grateful that the streets are nearly empty this far from the market square. Seeing the sparser homes and lack of incessant foot traffic almost makes me wish Father would have chosen a house for us out here, and not mere blocks away from the melee of town. Then again, if we lived on the outskirts, I'd have to walk even farther to get to the bookshop, bypass even more people...

I suppress a shudder.

Then an even more sobering thought occurs to me. If I get this job, where will I live? Will Father kick me out at once? Will the job provide room and board? Is there housing a single woman can afford in Vernon?

It's enough to send a rush of panic to heat my cheeks, but I breathe it away. Such concerns are irrelevant for now. First, I must actually *get* the job.

The trees at the edge of town come into view. The homes grow even smaller, sparser, the snow less trodden through. Paved roads and sidewalks turn to dirt paths. Thankfully there *is* a path, and the one that leads to Whitespruce Lane appears to have had some recent traffic. That comes as a relief, considering Nina's sensible warnings do occupy a corner of my mind.

I follow the trail to the first copse of trees. Only now does true silence settle around me. If I thought the outskirts of Vernon were quiet, then out here at the mouth of the forest is something else entirely. There is some sound, of course, like the crunch of my boots on snow, the pitter-patter of falling flakes, the rustling of trees. But gone are the sounds of wagon wheels, car horns, horse hooves, and stampedes of chatting people.

Out here it's...peaceful.

It reminds me of home. Of Isola, where I was raised as a child. The climate may have been opposite of where I am now, but the peace...it's achingly similar. In Isola, we lived in the country on several acres of land. Mother tended her horses, and Father oversaw the mining operations. Every night, I'd fall asleep to the melodies of coyotes, and in the morning, I'd wake with the silent sun.

My heart clenches, and for a moment, I can almost feel Mother's arms again, warm and strong as they wrap around me while we sit on our front porch together, watching a blushing sunrise climb over the mountains.

I blink, realizing I've come to a halt.

Shaking the memories from my mind, I focus on the present. I've come to a fork in the road where other paths branch off from here. I study the wooden pole adorned with street names and find Whitespruce Lane. It's the largest path to the left.

I take off down it, following as it takes on a slight incline. Here, the snow seems to accumulate a little deeper than it does in town. Unlike the path that led me here, Whitespruce doesn't seem quite as travel-worn, but there are still signs of earlier foot traffic. However, I'm required to lift my skirts and coat to avoid my hems dragging even further into the snow.

With every step, I watch for branching paths, seeking out signs bearing house numbers hidden somewhere among the trees and snow. So far, there's nothing to indicate a ten or twenty Whitespruce Lane, much less a thirty-three. And yet I keep walking, trying to regain my earlier feeling of peace and not the dread that's beginning to claw at the back of my mind. The silence no longer feels nostalgic and welcoming. It feels...ominous. Not only that, but it's colder here, darker beneath the trees that grow ever denser.

And...is that the sound of movement I hear just ahead, rustling in the undergrowth? No, it's to the side. No, behind me.

A wave of panic urges me to stop, and I obey, halting in my tracks. The skin prickles up the back of my neck, and all I can think is that I should turn around and go home, now before it's too late. But too late for what? Surely, I'm just letting my sister's worry get to my head. This fear I'm feeling...it's just like what happens when I leave the house, isn't it? But comparing the two kinds of fear leaves me realizing how vastly different they are. The kind that keeps me often indoors—heart racing when I think of crowds of townspeople—is rooted in memory, in strands of pain laced through my heart and mind. But this...the way my senses grow alert to every sight and sound, skin pebbling over my arms and neck, the calm *knowing* that I am not where I'm supposed to be...it's something else.

But the interview, another part of me says. I'm so close.

So close. This is the first interview I've been offered, and who knows when I'll receive another. I can't give up now.

Swallowing my fear, I take another step forward, then another. I hurry my pace, eyes darting everywhere for —*thank the saints above*. There, just ahead, is a wooden sign that reads thirty-three Whitespruce Lane, nailed to a tree at the mouth of a branching path. I quicken my pace again, pulling my skirts even higher as I close the distance between me and the sign. My heart is in my throat by the time I reach it, sweat pooling beneath my armpits. I want to feel joy. Relief. But all I feel is a warning to get indoors as quickly as I can.

Without a second thought, I turn at the sign and start down the narrow path.

And there I come to a halt once again, the blood draining from my face.

No more than a dozen feet in front of me is an enormous creature with shaggy brown fur, golden eyes, and long, snarling teeth.

"Well, shit," I mutter under my breath. "There really are wolves."

6

All my bravado about how *wolves don't attack for fun* seems like idiocy now that one of the beasts is before me. This creature is nothing like the timid little coyotes from my childhood in Isola. No, this is a towering giant with paws the size of frying pans and a muzzle almost as big as my face. The wolf lets out a growl that reverberates deep into my bones, sending every hair on my body to stand on end.

"Easy," I say, voice quavering as I hold up my hands in surrender. But what do saintsforsaken *wolves* know about human hand gestures?

Wait...unless...

Keeping my voice calm and even, I say, "Are you one of the fae?"

The only answer I receive is a padding step toward me.

I take three steps back. "If you are, I am not here to harm you or your kind, and it is highly illegal for you to attack me."

The wolf's growl deepens, muzzle rippling with a snarl.

Okay, so this is either a normal wolf or a fae who doesn't give a damn about the law. Neither thought is comforting. I take a few more steps back. "Easy. I'm leaving now, so...just go ahead and let me go on my way—"

Another growl, but this time from behind me. I whirl around and find two more wolves coming down the path, blocking my way to the main road.

Saints above, this isn't good. I have no weapon, no skill in fighting off wolves. When it comes to the coyotes, all one must do is stand tall, yell, and act aggressive. I watched Mother do it when they'd try to steal our chickens, but something tells me that won't work on these vicious beasts.

Their growls grow louder as they pad closer, then they begin to circle me. I keep my trembling arms outstretched to the sides, warding them away, although it isn't much of a defense. All it means is they might eat my arms first. And for the love of all things holy, I don't want *any* part of me eaten.

Sweat coats my brow as I whip my head side to side, trying not to let any of the wolves out of my sight for more than a second as they continue to circle me, snarling, growling, and baring their impossibly sharp teeth. My heart beats so hard, I fear it might explode. Perhaps that would be a mercy compared to what these wolves are about to do.

I have but one hope left. "Help!" I shout at the top of my lungs. If thirty-three Whitespruce Lane is somewhere at the end of this path, then someone on the premises might hear me. "Help!" I call again, but the wolves only growl louder. Then suddenly, they stop.

The first one I saw, the shaggy brown, lowers its head, legs staggered, one paw curled under and lifted as if preparing to leap for an attack.

I call for help one more time, but the words dry in my throat.

The wolf leaps for me.

I scream, squeezing my eyes shut as I shield my face.

And...the attack doesn't come. The snarls continue, but they're mingled with sounds of commotion. I dare to open my eyes and find a fourth wolf—just as enormous as the others but with snow-white fur—has tackled the shaggy brown and is locked in combat off to the side of the path. The two other wolves watch the battle, pacing anxiously, ears pressed close to their skulls.

This is my chance to flee.

I turn and take off toward the main road, but a flash of brown darts before me. Another wolf blocks my path, this one smaller than the others, but still just as angry, teeth bared as it closes in on me. Three more small wolves leap from the underbrush and onto the path. I whirl back around and find the fighting has cleared away from the trail and sounds of combat have died down. The three larger wolves remain, however, eyes locked on me as they too begin to approach.

No, not again.

An ear-shattering growl rips through the air, and I turn toward it. From behind the group of small wolves stands the white wolf, hackles raised. It lets out a booming bark, making me nearly jump out of my skin. But it isn't barking at me. It's barking at the other wolves.

The small ones are the first to flee, scurrying off the trail and out of sight. Another bark sends the large ones darting after them, tails between their legs.

The white wolf—a male—locks his gaze with mine, his eyes a startling shade of dark ruby. Then a voice reaches my ears, deep and gravelly. "It seems I have saved you."

The wolf didn't open his mouth to speak, but I know the words somehow came from him. I shudder with an inner chill. So, *this* must be a fae wolf. "I...thank you," I say through chattering teeth.

"Your gratitude is understandable," he says, padding a few feet closer. The movement is less graceful than that of the other wolves, a slight hobble to his steps. "If the wolves had tried to eat you, you would not have survived."

I have no doubts he's right, but I can't bring myself to speak. It's taking everything in me to remain on my feet. He pads even closer, and I take a few stumbling steps away. The wolf fae may have saved me, but that doesn't mean I'm safe.

The wolf speaks again. "Fae aren't required to intervene where humans are concerned. Doing so can risk our lives."

I nod, the motion jarring and shaky. "I understand what you've done for me, and I appreciate it," I manage to bite out.

If I didn't know any better, I'd think the wolf is now smiling. "Ah, yes. I have done a brave thing, have I not? So very brave and dangerous. You must be...overwhelmed with shock that you are still alive."

Okay, what is he getting at? I narrow my eyes. "I am."

"So overwhelmed. So grateful. You must be feeling like you owe me your life."

My blood goes cold, his words chilling me. They reek far too much of the fae bargains I've heard about. The kind I thought were too fantastic to be real. Trying to recall everything I've heard in stories and legend, I choose my next words with care. "I feel like you've done a great kindness, sir...wolf."

"Yes, such a great kindness. I wonder...does it make you want to repay me for my kindness? Of your own free will and volition, of course." He says the last part in a rush.

I frown, taking a step away. "I must be going. I have an appointment at thirty-three Whitespruce Lane. I imagine it is just at the end of this path." I point behind me, taking another step. Another.

The wolf lets out a grumbling sigh. "What a shame you must be going, for I would like to speak with you more." His voice has raised far louder than necessary, tone dry, each word enunciated.

Before I can reply, the shaggy brown wolf from before leaps out of nowhere, charging straight for me. With a shout, I run, but again I'm saved by the white wolf. Rolling in a blur of snarls and teeth, they lock into battle, tumbling off the path and into the underbrush. I find myself alone on the trail; my moment for escape is now or never. But do I run toward thirty-three Whitespruce Lane, where—*hopefully*—shelter awaits? Or do I run to the main road and try to flee back to town before the wolves catch up with me? Both options pose risks I don't have time to consider.

Everything in me shouts to go home, screw the interview and screw whatever maniac invited me here instead of holding the meeting in a safe place. I take off back the way I came, skidding through snow trampled by wolves, and veer onto the main path. I'm half running, half sliding, as I race down the incline. I must be halfway back to the main fork when an enormous white shape comes into view.

I pull to a halt, nearly losing my legs beneath me.

The white wolf limps across the road, head lowered, his tongue lolling from his mouth. His back end is covered in bright red blood. He moans, an agonized sound, as he takes three more steps and collapses on the ground. "Oh!" he cries. "Oh, the pain. The agony. Please, help me."

Trembling head to toe, I approach the wolf. Part of me wants to skirt around him and claim my freedom, but when I see how much blood coats his back end, my heart softens. Besides, this isn't just any wolf, this is a fae wolf. And there could be consequences for leaving a fae to die. With bated breath, I kneel at his side. I extend my hands toward him, but I don't know what to do. I've hardly tended more than a scraped knee. What am I supposed to do with a wound this bad? And—oh, for the love of the saints—is his rear leg *missing*?

"Oh, the pain," the wolf says. "You must be thinking how brave I am yet again. How I have saved your life twice now."

It's a strange thing to focus on when he's clearly bleeding out, but I say, "Yes, again, I'm so grateful."

"Seeing me in such a state...I'm sure your heart is... warm, yes? You must be feeling very much in debt to me now. Your gratitude swells so overwhelmingly large that you want to...sacrifice something? Your greatest treasure, perhaps?"

I ignore him and instead remove my coat, ready to try and staunch the bleeding from his back leg. But suspicion has me freezing in place. As I try to sort out where exactly to place my coat, I find no source of injury, no mangled flesh, no fresh oozing blood. I lean closer, and a familiar aroma tickles my senses. Is...is that...tomato sauce? I lean back and slowly rise to my feet.

"What are you doing? Can't you see the condition I'm in?"

His terrible acting should have given it away at once, but I'd written it off as simply strange fae behavior.

"Don't just stand there," he says, then twists his muzzle into the semblance of a grimace. "My leg. Oh, my poor leg."

"Your leg appears fine," I say through my teeth, keeping as much calm as I can muster. Even though I now know I'm being tricked, my fear hasn't lessened in the slightest. However, annoyance and fury are now mingling with it, giving me strength not to crumble.

"Fine?" he echoes, irritation seeping into his tone. "My leg is clearly missing. How can that be fine?"

"I agree it is missing, but there's no evidence that it's from a recent wound."

He lifts his head, eying me with that ruby gaze. "What about the red stuff?"

I narrow my eyes at him. "Do you think I don't know tomato sauce when I smell it?"

With a huff, he rises to all three legs. That explains why I'd initially thought his movements held less grace than the other wolves. "So," he says, "you don't care to sacrifice your greatest treasure as a demonstration of your deep respect and admiration for me? Of your own free will and volition, that is." Like before, the last part is said like an afterthought.

My mouth falls open as I shoot him a sardonic look. "No."

"Very well." With a shudder, the wolf disappears into a blur of white, only to leave a man in its place. A towering bear of a man with broad shoulders, a wild mane of long, dark, golden-brown hair, and a grizzly beard. The ruby color of his eyes is more subdued, seeming more like a shade of garnet, like the deepest, darkest wines. He hops on his left foot; the right limb ends at the knee and is hidden beneath the pinned-up leg of his brown trousers. Then, keeping his eyes fixed on me, he lets out a low whistle.

At that, several humanlike figures, just as grizzled as the fae man, emerge from each side of the path. Something tells me these were the other wolves I encountered, just in new bodies. The realization is of no comfort. "What's going on?" I ask, hating the quaver in my voice.

No one answers me. A female with a weathered face and frizzy gray hair tosses the leader a long, gnarled staff that he catches midair. The top of the staff ends in a Y shape, which he props beneath his left arm. "On to phase two then," he calls out.

The others nod, then turn to face me. I don't have to look behind me to know I'm surrounded. I can feel it in my bones. Chest heaving, I dare to ask, "What's phase two?"

A corner of the fae man's mouth quirks beneath his bushy beard. "Take her."

7

I can't see a thing, but whispers fall upon my awareness. I stop struggling against the tight bonds that tie my wrists behind my back and secure my ankles to the legs of the chair beneath me. That's all I know for sure—that I'm tied to a chair. I strain myself to lean forward, turning my head to the side as I try and make out the words the voices are saying, muffled as if coming from behind a door.

That's another thing I'm fairly certain of—I'm indoors. Blindfolded, bound, and gagged soon after I was surrounded by the wolf-people, I hadn't seen where I was taken, but it didn't take long to get me to where I am now. Despite my panicked screams stifled by the cloth covering my mouth as I was physically hauled over what felt like a shoulder, I recall the moment when the cool wind ceased stinging my face and the footsteps surrounding me no longer crunched like boots on snow but pounded against solid floor, echoing against walls.

None of that intel helps me now, for I can't make out a single word that's being said. What could they be discussing? How best to tear me limb from limb? My mind drums up vicious images, ones where the fae creatures shift back into wolves and devour my body while I scream at the top of my lungs. Or they curse me to dance until my toes bleed, just like the terrifying legends I'd so stupidly written off as fiction. It's safe to say I was wrong about all prior assumptions about the fae.

Why did I have to come here? Why? All these weeks spent fearing the townspeople, their gossip, their lies, and the true monsters were the ones I should have expected —the ones every other sensible human being expects. The fae, the wolves, and the woods.

A sound, like the creaking of a door, falls upon my ears, followed by footsteps drawing near. Through my blindfold, my vision brightens somewhat, as if a light has been turned on in whatever room I'm being held in. Rough hands come to the back of my head, and I feel the blindfold begin to loosen. My heart leaps into my throat, terror surging through every inch of me. I don't know what I'll find once the blindfold comes off. I could be in a dungeon, a torture chamber, a—

I blink into the light, its glow the same soft quality as the indoor lighting of our townhouse, and find myself in a...bedroom. A simple, modestly furnished bedroom. It looks as if it hasn't been occupied in half a century, but that's its only horror. Well, that and the three figures standing before me.

Still in the form of humanlike beings, the leader—the one who had been that insufferable white wolf and is clearly this pack's alpha—stands front and center, his staff propped under his arm, golden-brown hair in disarray around his shoulders. Slowly, I crane my neck to meet his eyes, surprised to find he appears far younger than I'd originally assumed. Despite his unkempt appearance, his stained linen shirt rolled up to his elbows, and his hideously wild hair and beard, his face is unweathered, devoid of the creases I imagined from afar. He can't be older than twenty-five.

He's fae, I remind myself. Fae don't age the way humans do. For all I know he's ancient. And even if he isn't, his age has no bearing on my circumstance.

I burn the alpha wolf with a scowl, but I'm sure the effect is lessened by how violently I tremble. One of the two fae—a male with black hair and a dark bushy beard —behind him snickers, then moves to the other side of the room where he sits at a dusty bureau. He wipes his hand across the surface before retrieving a few sheets of paper and a fountain pen from one of the drawers. The other fae, the elderly, gray-haired female I saw before, crosses her arms over her chest, shooting daggers with her gaze. Just like the fae Imogen and I glimpsed outside the Verity Hotel, the only thing that gives these creatures away as being anything but human is their pointed ears.

The alpha leans forward, and I flinch back, but he only reaches for my cloth gag. With a grimace, he tugs it down, then takes a hasty step back, wiping the hand that touched my gag on his shirt.

"What do you want with me?" I aim for toughness, but my voice comes out weak and hoarse.

The alpha's eyes flick from me to the wolf-man at the

bureau. The latter, pen and paper in hand, nods. Returning his gaze to me, the alpha asks, "Are you married?"

The blood leaves my face. What kind of question is that? Oh, for the love of the saints, what have I gotten myself into?

The fae lets out an irritated grumble, his tone taking on a sharper quality. "Answer the question, human."

I swallow hard. As much as I want to resist my captors, I imagine my best bet is to cooperate. For now. "No," I finally say, "I'm not married."

"Who keeps you then?" he asks with a flourish of his hand. "I know your kind like to keep their females like property, am I wrong?"

I bristle, wanting to argue, but as much as it incenses me to admit, he *isn't* wrong. "I live with my father," I say through my teeth.

He looks encouraged by my answer, eyes brightening. "Father, yes. What's his name?"

I open my mouth to speak but can't bring myself to answer. Even though Father and I don't get along, I hate to think sharing his name could condemn him to harm. "Why? What in the name of the saints is this all about?"

He leans down, clasping a hand around one of the arms of my chair, bringing us eye to eye. I lean back as far as I can, holding my breath. "I'm asking the questions here," he says. "Now tell me his name. And don't you dare lie. If we find out you're lying about any of these answers, we'll bite off a finger for each false word said."

"Fine," I say, the word coming out at a higher pitch than I intend. "It's...it's Richard Bellefleur."

He straightens and snaps his fingers, then points to the fae at the bureau. His next words ring out strong and firm. "Richard Bellefleur."

The fae puts pen to paper and scrawls something down, then looks back at the alpha.

The alpha speaks again in that same resonant tone. "I have your daughter—" He turns back to me and lowers his voice. "Name, human. What is your name?"

My lips move before I manage to find my voice. "Gemma Bellefleur."

He adopts that tone again, one I can only describe as his *villain voice*. It's a nearly perfect imitation of the one I imagine the antagonists using in my favorite novels. "I have your daughter, Gemma Bellefleur. She is safe and unharmed. For now." He lowers his tone, flourishing a hand at his scribe. "Emphasize the *for now*, part, will you?"

The fae nods and continues writing.

"If you want her back, I will accept..." He pauses, lips pursed as he squints. Rubbing his bearded jaw with one hand, he looks down at me with an arched brow. "What is your father's wealth?"

"His wealth?" I echo.

He gives an exaggerated nod, his features laced with exasperation. "His annual salary, human."

Annual salary. I narrow my eyes, calculating the sum of all this nonsense in my mind. "Are you...holding me for ransom?"

He furrows his brow. "Is that what it's called?"

"Ransom, yes," the female fae says, revealing a few sharp, crooked teeth. "I do believe that's what it's called."

With this knowledge comes a steadying calm in the

midst of my fear. It doesn't take my terror away completely, but at least it gives me an edge. Ransom, I can work with. It's all numbers and figures, things I know well. Taking a deep breath, I attempt to settle beneath my false persona. Having my hands tied behind my back makes that a little difficult, considering I can't sit tall the way I normally do when feigning confidence, but at least I can school my features, ease my breathing, steady my voice.

"I hate to tell you this, but we have no money," I say. "We're poor. We can't afford a ransom. You should let me go."

He barks a laugh. "That's a lie. Just look at that hideous dress of yours."

Heat rises to my cheeks, but I swallow my indignation and don a mask of embarrassment instead. "It's the nicest one I have. I...only wore it because I had an interview today. A job interview. When you found me, I was on my way to thirty-three Whitespruce—" My words dry on my lips as another calculation plays out in my mind. Damn. I squeeze my eyes shut for a moment. When I open them, I burn the alpha with my gaze. "Let me guess. This *is* thirty-three Whitespruce Lane, isn't it?"

The burly fae smirks with pride but gives no reply.

"You tricked me to come here, didn't you?"

"I like the term *enticed*," he says.

My blood boils with rage, chest heaving, but I force my words to come out calm. "I thought fae couldn't lie." I'm testing the waters here. *Can* fae lie? Are the legends correct in that regard?

"I told no lie."

The female fae nods, as if to confirm the validity of his statement.

I lift a brow. "You wrote a want ad seeking a house steward."

The alpha shrugs. "I don't have a house steward, so technically you could say I'm in want of one. Fae may not lie, but we excel at deception. Now, enough chit-chat. Tell me your father's wealth."

I grit my teeth, mind whirling to come up with a solution, one that sets me free and leaves my father out of this. I'm not entirely sure he'd come for me, no matter how much or how little I'm ransomed for. He may have regained his wealth, but would he dare spend it to rescue me from a situation such as this? One that I clearly got myself into while acting against his rules and demands? I don't know how much time has passed since I've been gone, but Nina and Susan could already be telling him where I am and what I've done. He's probably spinning into a rage as it is. If he learns I've not only gone to a job interview, but also been tricked and held for ransom...

"I lied," I say, lifting my chin. "I am rich. But don't take the money from my father, make a deal with me instead. If you let me go, I'll give you twice as much as you're planning on asking from him."

He lets out a low chuckle. "I don't want money."

I blink a few times. "Then why the hell are you holding me for ransom?"

He clenches his jaw. "The ransom, stupid human, is a front. When he comes to do the trade, he'll find you surrounded by brigands." The other two fae nod excitedly. "Then I, a brave hero, will step in and defeat them, handing you off to your father unharmed."

I stare blankly at their proud expressions. "Why?"

"He'll be grateful. When he sees I've saved both his daughter and his fortune, he'll be overwhelmed with gratitude. So much that he'll be willing to sacrifice that which he holds dear. Of his own free will and volition, of course."

So that's what this is about. It's that same riddle he kept spouting off about before. For some unfathomable reason, he seeks a sacrifice from a willing human. But what's even harder to imagine is his assumption my father will...will...

Throwing my head back, I erupt with laughter. "You think my father will be *grateful* to have *me* returned unharmed. Me!"

He frowns, eyes narrowing to slits. "That's the entire point of phase two," he says, although his tone is stripped of bravado. "If phase one fails, we target someone back home who desperately loves our captive."

It takes several moments to sober from my laughter, and when I do, I can still hardly form my words. "That may have worked for you before, but it won't with my father, I promise you that much."

"It's actually never worked before," the fae at the bureau whispers, scratching his dark beard.

The alpha burns him with a glare. "That doesn't mean we won't try. It's a solid plan."

"You picked the wrong girl, wolf man," I say, shaking my head as my laughter renews. "There's no sacrifice small enough that my father would make for me."

Especially if he thinks I've landed in yet another scandal. I keep that part to myself, of course.

His face burns beet red beneath the scruff, lips

peeling back into a snarl. "Then you can simply rot in here forever!" With that, he turns and stalks out the door, hobbling on his staff. His two henchmen follow, eyeing me with disdain before they turn off the light and close me into darkness.

8

I n the absence of my adrenaline, fear, and even my momentary amusement over the wolf fae's ridiculous plan, all I feel is cold. It seeps through my bones, chills my legs where my dress and petticoats have absorbed moisture from all the snow I traipsed through while running from the wolves. Strands of my damp, dark hair have come loose and are plastered to my cheeks. I can hardly feel my sodden feet in my boots, which might be a blessing, for I'm sure they will ache when feeling returns to them.

As my eyes adjust to the dark, I crane my neck this way and that, taking a deeper investigation of my surroundings. There are two large windows, both of which have the heavy curtains drawn shut to block the light, allowing only the palest haze to creep through. At the edge of my periphery, I see a bed, one that was probably once elegant with its four carved wooden posts and its thick brocade blanket. However, I can tell even in the dim light how dusty it is.

I scan the rest of the room, noting the bureau, hearth, wardrobe, wash station, sitting area, all equally as unused and unkempt. It makes me wonder if these wolf fae have broken into an abandoned vacation home and took up residence to plot their vile schemes. I still can't imagine what would possess the wolf creatures to go through the trouble of trying to tease a sacrifice from a human. Is it just for fun? Is this what the fae do when they're bored? Or is there an actual reason?

And don't even get me started on that despicable alpha wolf. Even in this dark room, I can still see that stupid smirk, hear his grating voice when he tried to dictate the ransom note. Fool. They're all fools.

Ugh. I suppose I'm the bigger one for being caught by them.

The door creaks open, making me jump with a start, pulse racing as I steel myself for the next confrontation. Light shines from the hall, casting the figure who enters the room in shadow. I frown, seeing how much shorter this one is than the three I met before. The figure lifts a hand toward the wall, and the lights in the room begin to glow, orbs of light hovering above several sconces that look like oil lamps. But like the electricity in Vernon, I know it comes not from oil but from the ley lines that traverse the land. Fae magic.

The figure shuts the door and leans against it, a tray in his hands, eyes wide and assessing. That's when I realize it's a boy. A young boy, looking no older than eight. Dressed like the street urchins I saw in Bretton, he wears too-short trousers, worn boots, fraying suspenders, and a tan shirt that was probably at one point white.

Upon his head of overlong hair is a gray cap, sitting just above his pointed ears.

I look from him to the tray he carries, which holds a glass of water and a heel of bread. It hasn't been nearly long enough for me to feel any kind of desperate hunger, but the water makes me realize how dry my mouth has become. Pulling my lips into what I hope to be a comforting smile, I say, "Is that for me?"

His brows furrow over his dark eyes as he approaches. "Try to escape, and my packmates will get you as soon as you reach the door. Try anything with me and I'll bite your arm off."

The smile slides from my lips. This must be one of the smaller wolves I met during the feigned attack. Which means, boy or not, he's dangerous.

He sets the tray a few feet in front of me, then skirts around the chair to the back. I feel the ropes begin to loosen from around my wrists. "Remember, I bite," he says with a growl, but I can't help noticing the mild tremor in his voice. As if he's...afraid of me.

With my hands free, I lift my arms, careful to make no sudden movements as I place my hands in my lap. Everything in me wants to shake them out, to stretch, but the wary look in the boy's eyes has me trying to keep as still as possible. If he says he'll bite, I'm partial to believe it.

Giving me a wide berth, he returns to the tray and hands it to me. As soon as I take it from him, he darts back, teeth bared.

For a few silent moments, I hold still, my gaze locked on his. Then, when his posture begins to relax, I slowly reach for the glass of water and bring it to my lips for a hearty

gulp. In this moment, it tastes better than the most decadent wine. With a sigh, I replace the glass on the tray and
return my gaze to the boy. His eyes, however, are no longer
on me but the heel of bread, his tongue visible at the corner
of his mouth. His face looks softer, younger, vulnerable.

Perhaps he isn't so dangerous after all. Perhaps he's...
hungry. Keeping my voice level, I ask, "Would you like to
share my meal with me?"

"No," he quickly says, his look of yearning replaced
with a scowl. "I hate human food. It's dry and disgusting
and a disgrace to the unseelie." Despite his firm tone, his
words sound cold and rehearsed.

I lift the heel of bread, frowning at it. "You're right,
this bread does look dry. Very flaky too. And is that..." I
bring the bread to my nose and sniff. "Is that butter? Oh,
this is too rich for me. I can't eat it. I should simply tear it
up and throw it away—"

"No!" He takes a step forward, hand outstretched,
before he gathers his composure. "I...I'll bring it back to
the kitchens."

I suppress my grin, instead keeping my expression
open and innocent. "Why don't you eat it for me?"

His eyes turn down at the corners as they lock on the
bread. "I'm not supposed to. I'm supposed to watch you
eat, replace your bindings, and return the tray to the
kitchen. That's all."

"At least share it with me." I tear it in half, finding it
still warm, and inhale. "Oh, that's good. You know what? I
was wrong before. This isn't dry at all. It's moist and
buttery and everything bread should be. Here."

He looks at my outstretched hand and the bread

inside it for only a second before snatching it from me and tearing into it with his teeth.

I take a modest bite, finding the flavor surprisingly satisfying. Perhaps my praise hadn't been in vain after all. I watch as the boy scarfs down his last bite, then I casually ask, "How was it?"

"It was all right," he mutters.

"You ate it quite fast. Are you well fed?"

He glares. "I eat just fine. I just...I like bread, is all."

"I thought human food was disgusting."

"It's dry and gross," he says in a rush. "Wolves are meant to eat fresh meat from fresh kills."

"Yummy."

"It is." His expression falters, glare slipping. "When I'm a wolf, that is."

"When you're a wolf," I say, tilting my head to the side.

"My unseelie form," he says. "In my seelie form...well, I like bread better then."

Unseelie. Seelie. I take the words and filter them through everything I've heard about the fae. If what I've learned is true—about the terms being the preferred definition of what some humans call *lesser fae* and *high fae*—then his wolf form must be unseelie, and his humanoid form must be seelie. Until now, I assumed the fae were strictly one or the other, not capable of shapeshifting between the two at will. That goes far beyond the glamours I've heard about. Why wasn't any of this mentioned in the pamphlet I read when we gained citizenship to Faerwyvae?

I take a small sip of water, determined to finish my meal as slowly as possible; I've already learned something from this conversation, which tells me I could find out even more if I keep the boy talking. "What's your name?"

He lifts his chin in defiance. "We don't have names."

I furrow my brow. "Why is that?"

His lip quivers for a moment, before he says, "We don't remember them. His Majesty calls me Scrappy." The last word is muttered so quietly, I almost miss it.

However, I'm fixated on the term *His Majesty*. "And who is this royal majesty you speak of?"

"The king," the boy says like it should be obvious.

"Who exactly is...the king?"

His eyes widen. "You already talked to him. He's the Unseelie King of the Winter Court."

I pause with a piece of bread halfway to my mouth. The boy looks fully serious, but he can't be. This is just another part of the game, a crew of trickster fae with false personas. "Let me guess. The white wolf with three legs? The alpha male who walks with a staff?"

The boy nods.

"He isn't *actually* the king though, right?"

"No, he's the actual king." He crosses his arms, jutting his lower lip. "I can't lie, lady."

The blood leaves my face. I avert my gaze to my tray, taking a keen interest in my next piece of bread while I puzzle over the information I've gained. The fae may not be able to lie, but does that count if one believes false information? Surely, that grizzled creature is not the king. *My* new king. I go over everything I've heard about the royals of Faerwyvae, particularly the Winter Court. I know each court is ruled by two royals, a seelie and unseelie king or queen, and all humans and fae living in that court owe allegiance to both. Either can be petitioned, but as I understand it, most humans deal with either the seelie ruler or the court's human representative. But even if humans have little to do with the unseelie king, wouldn't the people of Vernon know if he lived nearby? That he's a wolf? Looks like a crazed mountain man? And what about his name? I'm sure it's been mentioned...

My mind draws a blank.

It reminds me of when Imogen and I were talking yesterday. She mentioned that little is known about the unseelie king, but when she went on to say more, she just stopped talking and seemed a bit lost for a moment. I thought nothing of it then, but now...what in the name of the saints is going on here?

I chew my bread and wash it down with more water. "So, when you say you don't remember your names, does that include the king?"

He nods.

"Then how do you know he's truly the king?"

The boy shrugs, unconcerned. "We just know. He's been king forever. Longer than that, probably."

I eye him through slitted lids. "So, you remember he's the king, but not his name. How is that so?"

Another shrug. "It's the curse. Curses are stupid and they do stupid stuff."

I tilt my head back. "Wait, the *curse*?"

"Yeah, are you gonna eat that?" His eyes are locked on the last bit of bread.

Part of me wants to continue eating so I can keep him here longer, extend our conversation. I still have plenty of water left for that purpose, though. "Go ahead."

He takes the remaining bread and stuffs it in his mouth whole.

I lean forward. "So, about this curse."

"I'm not supposed to talk about it," he says, words muffled through bread.

"Surely, it affects you too."

"Yup."

"How, exactly, *does* it affect you?"

He releases a grumble. "It's so boring and dumb."

I bat my lashes. "And yet, I'd love to hear about it."

"Fine." He plops down, folding his legs beneath him. But as soon as he opens his mouth to speak, a knock sounds at the door, sending him scrambling back to his feet. He yanks the tray from my lap and nearly throws it on the ground in his haste, then moves to the back of the chair to replace my bindings. Thankfully, he doesn't tie them nearly as tight as whoever tied them before. Once the deed is done, he gathers up the tray and darts for the door. "I gotta go, bye!"

"Wait!"

He pauses, fingers on the door handle, and meets my gaze with suspicion.

Now that I have his attention, I'm not sure what to say. All I know is this boy could be an ally. And I most certainly could use all the allies I can get right now.

I give the boy a warm grin. "Will you try to get me a bigger piece of bread next time? That way we'll have more to share."

His face brightens as he nods.

"Oh, and if you don't like the name the king calls you —Scrappy, is it?" He frowns. "Yes, I see. Can I call you something else? How about...Micah?"

For a second, his face breaks into a vibrant smile before he steels it behind a mask of nonchalance. "It's okay, I guess. For a human name."

"All right then. Micah, it is. My name is Gemma."

The knock raps on the door again, harder, and the boy rushes out. This time, I'm locked in the room with the lights left on.

Alone, I ponder over the conversation, my mind whirling to make sense of it all. The boy—or Micah, as I've named him—has given me a lot to think about while adding so many more questions. I'm certain if we speak more, I can glean something to use as leverage to get me out of here. Primarily, I need to know more about this supposed curse and if the alpha of this pack truly is the king. Both make for unsettling complications, but ones I must understand if I'm to navigate them. For I *will* navigate them. If I can save my family from poverty using some simple calculations and the execution of a solid plan, then I can escape...whatever this is.

For starters, it's time to get out of these damn ropes.

9

My conversation with Micah was just what I needed to clear my head. Uncertainty still looms over me, and fear continues to rake its claws down my back, but at least the boy has shown me that the fae can be reasoned with. At least a hungry fae who likes bread. That means there's hope for the others, right?

With my determination fueling my resolve, I twist my wrists in my too-loose bindings, shifting my arms, my shoulders, until finally, the ropes fall away. I shake out my arms, massaging my wrists, and then begin worrying at the knots in the ropes around my ankles. Once those are freed, I rise on unsteady feet, my muscles screaming in protest with every move. I wince as pain pinches my toes, and when I try to take a step, my feet make a squelching sound in my shoes.

With a groan, I sit back down and unlace my boots, then peel off my soaked hose. I shudder, the cold further seeping in from my damp dress. Glancing around the room, I find no sign of my coat. Only then do I recall taking it off to stanch the white wolf's false wound.

Well, if these crazed wolf fae are trying to kill me, then this is certainly one way to get the job done. Without a fire and dry clothes, I'll surely get hypothermia. The thought quickens my pulse.

On bare feet, I cross the room to the wardrobe and fling open the doors. I have very low expectations that I'll find anything useful inside, so I'm pleasantly surprised when I find it stocked with a gray wool cloak and three dresses. They smell slightly musty, but upon further inspection, they appear in good condition. The cloak is long and thick, basically begging me to wear it. I remove it from the hanger, then turn my attention to the dresses. My hands fall on the fabric of the first, and I pause, taken aback by the softness beneath my fingers. Perhaps I'm just cold and anything would feel luxurious, but I can't help puzzling over the smoothness of the fabric. The style of the dress is unfamiliar as well, with its long, flowing, multilayered skirts, the long sleeves that flare out at the wrists. The bodice is loose and low-cut both front and back and doesn't seem designed to wear with a corset. Despite its strange and elegant style, the color is a dark green and unadorned with lace or frills, giving me the impression of something meant for daily wear.

A glance at the other two dresses tells me both are similar to the first but in differing shades of green. Without a second thought, I take the first from the hanger and strip out of my wet dress and corset as quickly as possible. My bare skin pebbles as the cool air of the room meets my flesh, but relief comes as soon as the new dress is over my head. Luckily, I don't require assistance to finish dressing, unlike with the gowns I normally wear, and can easily reach the closures at my lower back. Despite the loose design of the dress, the fit is a little tight, but I can hardly find it in me to care. Not when the layers of silky-smooth fabric hug me in a blanket of warmth. Next comes the cloak, which I secure over my shoulders with a gold leaf-shaped clasp.

Fully dressed, I close my eyes and release a sigh. At least now I can panic less about hypothermia. I'm not sure how the wolves will react to me sneaking around and taking liberties with the wardrobe, but that's not my biggest problem right now, is it? Right now, I must take inventory and make note of my assets.

I have a room and dry clothes, I think as I stalk the perimeter of the bedroom. *I've been given food and water. And I'm in the process of making Micah my ally. If they're feeding me, they probably don't intend to kill me. Yet.*

I reach the bureau and rifle through the drawers, hoping for some kind of weapon. Even a letter opener will do, but no such luck. All I find is paper. Not even the pen was left behind.

I abandon the bureau and examine the hearth, which is empty and without any means to start a fire. Then I inspect the bed, looking beneath it and behind the pillows. I can't help thinking about the stories where the captured heroine makes a grand escape utilizing a rope of tied-together sheets. Considering the length and thickness of the two sheets, the brocade-covered down blanket, and the wool throw, I'd have to hope for a very short drop to traverse if I'm to have any luck with that.

This thought brings me to the two windows next. I throw open the curtains of both and gaze out the second.

My first glance through the frosted glass tosses all ideas of escape straight into the refuse bin, for the distance from here to the ground is frightening indeed. I must be up three stories high. There are no ledges or trees to climb upon, and the ground below is solid snow-dusted stone that makes up part of a garden path.

My heart sinks. No fairytale blanket rope escape for me, it seems.

Next, I assess the daylight and try to glean what time it might be. I left my house shortly after nine this morning, but the bright, cloudy sky looks much the same as it did then. Without any outdoor navigational skill, I can only guess it's late morning. Noon, perhaps. I feel a subtle relief at that. If it's still early in the day, then maybe Father and Nina have yet to return home. There's still a chance I can get free of this place before they find out anything is amiss. Before Father learns of my mistake and strips me of my allowance for good. Before he decides to marry me off and be rid of me. Before all hope of getting a job is lost to me forever, as well as earning my independence and freedom. Before—

I shake the worries from my mind. There are more immediate concerns to deal with.

I'm about to turn away from the window when my attention snags on the more distant view. Beneath the cloudy sky sprawl emerald mountains dusted with pure white snow. Closer in proximity, I see the tops of tall, elegant trees. On my walk here, I hadn't realized just how high up Whitespruce Lane had taken me. While I certainly hadn't crested a mountain, I had journeyed far deeper and higher than I realized, providing a startlingly beautiful view of the mountains that normally serve as nothing more than a dull backdrop to the town of Vernon.

Here, it's so much more than a backdrop. It's an all-encompassing centerpiece.

Just like when I first stepped into the quiet woods this morning, the same feeling of peace settles over me. I'm so used to looking out my window and feeling my stomach clench, my heart race, nausea churning my gut when I consider the conversations that are always humming through the streets of Vernon. But here...it's nothing like that. No gossip. No carriage wheels or automobiles. Just vast empty silence. Calm, dense wilderness.

Dangerous wilderness, I remind myself, forcing my wistful feeling away.

I pull my investigation back to the garden, startled when I catch sight of movement. Squinting through the frost, I try to peer closer, then abandon this window for the other. There I'm given a better view, and I see a figure standing at the far end of the garden where overgrown brambles surround a small courtyard. A fleck of red hints at a rose hidden beneath the snow. Near this splotch of red, the figure takes a seat on a stone bench. I can't tell for certain, but the broad-shouldered build and dark golden-brown head of hair make me wonder if it's the alpha—this supposed *king* fellow. Whoever it is sits hunched over, head low, elbows propped on his thighs. Could that be...defeat in his posture?

I narrow my eyes, squinting—

His head swings to the side, toward me, and I quickly dart away from the window and behind the wall. My breaths quicken, pulse racing, although he couldn't have been looking at me, could he? For several moments, all I can do is close my eyes and try to steady my breathing. Once I've recovered my composure, I slowly creep back to the window, keeping most of my body out of sight. But when I return my gaze to the courtyard, there's no one there. I release a sigh, but my relief is short lived. His absence is likely more condemning than if he'd still been there, for it suggests he truly had spotted me and is on his way to tie me back to the chair. Or worse.

I bite my lip, eyes darting around the room. No escape. No weapon. I think of securing myself back in the chair and pretending I haven't freed myself, but my change of clothing foils that guise. And there's no way I'm putting my wet clothing back on.

Sure enough, footsteps sound outside the door.

My heart leaps into my throat.

Left with my only defense, I give myself to the count of five to feel afraid.

One.

I inhale deeply and throw back my shoulders.

Two.

I stride to the center of the room and plant myself there, arms crossed.

Three.

I lift my chin and pull my lips into a haughty grin.

Four.

The door handle turns. I narrow my eyes and hide behind my false persona.

Five.

In storms the alpha, stomping with his foot and his staff, a snarl on his lips. The same two fae as before—the dark haired male and the elderly female—flank him, pulling up close behind.

I march forward to meet him halfway. "You have some nerve locking me in here without a fire. I demand you remedy this at once."

He halts and retreats a step back, nearly stumbling as he eyes me from head to toe. "You dare make demands of me?"

"If you're planning on holding me for ransom, you should probably make sure you stay true to your word."

He blinks a few times as if I've grown a second head. "Excuse me?"

"In the letter you were writing to my father, you stated I was unharmed. But you lied. I was left in a cold room in sodden clothing without a fire. If fae can't lie, what do you call that?"

His hand flies to his chest, and a grimace begins to twist his features. "You are fine," he says through his teeth. "You found dry clothes."

I pop my hip to the side. "No thanks to you. I had to free myself to find them."

He closes his eyes as if overcome with excruciating pain. My confidence falters as I watch him, his face screwed tight as he grasps his chest. Is this what happens when fae lie? They're punished with physical pain? But who punishes them? Some mysterious force...or themselves?

"I didn't send the letter," he says in a rush. "I lied to no one. No one!" At that, his features begin to smooth, his ragged breathing growing even. When he opens his eyes, he burns me with a glare. His words come out like a growl. "You're unharmed."

"Until I have a proper fire, I fail to agree with you. I'm in danger of hypothermia."

"Blackbeard," he says, and the male fae takes a step forward. Keeping his eyes on me, the alpha says, "Do you still have the unfinished letter?"

Blackbeard—a most uncreative name, if you ask me —removes a piece of paper from his trouser pockets.

"Tear it up."

Blackbeard obeys, ripping the paper in half. Then again. And again.

With every shred, the alpha seems to relax more and more, which in turn sets me further on edge. I feel my false persona slipping, the frightened girl in threat of being revealed. Once the letter is reduced to litter on the floor, the alpha's lips pull into a smirk.

I swallow my fear and keep my head held high as he closes the distance between us. I'm surprised to find I must crane my neck to meet his gaze; I'm used to being of equal height to most men, if not taller. It's disconcerting, to say the least.

"Did you mean what you said about your father? That he won't fall for my ruse?"

"If you're trying to trick him into making a sacrifice based on gratitude, there's nothing in the world he'd sacrifice for me. In fact, I'm certain there's *nothing* in this world he'd be willing to make even the smallest sacrifice for." While I'm not sure how much truth lies in my last statement, my tone holds all the conviction I can muster.

He sighs. "A shame. It would seem you're of little use to me then. You're expendable, really."

The blood leaves my face. "No, I—"

His eyes burn into mine, flickering with danger. "Kill her."

10

The two fae charge forth, and before I can react, they have my arms wrenched behind my back. Biting back a squeal, I struggle in their grasp, but they're both so strong, even the elderly female. There's no masking my fear anymore as all my feigned confidence has drained to nothing. "Let me go!"

The alpha does nothing but stand there with his crooked grin, as if my plight amuses him. Behind him, shadows stir in the hall, and curious faces peek inside the door. I catch a glimpse of Micah, eyes wide as he clutches the side of the doorframe.

"What should we do with her?" the gray-haired female asks from beside me.

The alpha looks from me to the bedraggled group gathering outside the door. "Well, let's see. Are you hungry?"

"I could eat," Blackbeard says, and the other fae erupt with excited cheers.

"No!" I shout. "You don't want to do this. Please don't do this."

Ignoring me, my two captors push me toward the crowd, which begins to spill inside the room. Only Micah hangs back, still clinging to the doorframe, his face pale. The hungry fae leer at me, exchanging bets on how my bones will splinter, how warm my flesh will taste.

My head spins, my limbs going numb. The carousing whispers and jests are amplified in my mind, echoing another instance not long ago. That time, it wasn't wild, vicious fae that surrounded me, but friends. Friends whose tongues had turned cruel, laced with venom as they circled me, leering, hurling insults like knives.

No longer here nor there, my vision darkens at the edges and sweat beads at my brow. Every muscle convulses, and only the grip of my captors keeps me upright as the fae close in tighter.

"Let's not eat her!" comes a small, quavering voice. Using it as an anchor back to the present, I seek out the source— Micah. He pushes his way between two fae and stares up at the alpha, who still stands directly before me. "We do not need to. Our stores are full. We hunted yesterday!"

Paying him no heed, the alpha gives him a gentle push back, and his small form is swallowed by the bodies of the larger fae.

Micah's outburst, however, has snapped me out of my stupor, and I'm able to find my voice again, my strength. "Please don't do this. I'm not expendable! We can make a deal."

The crowd continues to cackle and jest, licking their hungry lips, but the alpha's face turns steely and he holds up a hand. The room goes quiet. "I could show you mercy," he says.

I try to stand tall, but the angle of my arms wrenched behind my back makes it nearly impossible. "It's illegal for the fae to attack humans."

He looks down his nose at me. "I'm the Unseelie King of Winter. I enforce the laws. And it looks to me like you've trespassed on private royal property. One would even think you were sent to infiltrate my home and harm me."

Hearing him affirm in his own words that he is, in fact, the king chills me to the bone. If fae can't lie, then it's either true or he and this pack of wild creatures are delusional. Whatever the case, this *king* believes he has every right to do whatever he wishes to me. Which means no fear of the law will stop him. But I've already discovered one weakness. "That's a lie! It's a lie and you know it."

I expect him to grimace, to writhe in pain at my accusation. But he does no such thing. "Not a lie," he says in his low, gravelly voice. The fae around us snicker. "Only a matter of perspective. So don't think for a moment I owe you mercy. It is mine freely to give, understood?"

Gritting my teeth, I force myself to nod.

"Good. Then you should understand that if I grant you freedom to return to your town unscathed, you will be in my debt."

I swallow hard, my chest heaving. "Please, just let me go. I'll tell no one what happened."

"Yes, you would like freedom, wouldn't you? Tell me how much you would like it."

"I would like it very much." My words come out dry, bitter.

"And how grateful would you be if I told my pack to stand down and release you right now so you can be safely on your way?"

"I would be ever grateful."

A corner of his mouth quirks and he takes a step closer. "So grateful that you'd realize you owe me your life?"

My rage and terror freeze, and in their place creeps a chilling suspicion.

The king's expression turns ponderous. "In fact, perhaps you'd suddenly want to bargain something away to demonstrate just how strong your gratitude is. Maybe...that which you most cherish? Of your own free will and volition, that is."

My eyes go wide, and I catch several fae stifling their laughter, while others watch with quiet anticipation. Hope, even. When my gaze returns to the king, my anger reignites like a blaze, boiling my blood. With all my strength, I launch forward, catching my captors off guard. Having loosened their grip during the king's speech, they stumble back, allowing me to wrench my arms free. I use the momentum to shove my hands hard into the king's chest. "You son of a...you tricked me! Again!"

My attack has very little impact on the king, who simply absorbs my punch without falter. Not even his precarious stance between his single leg and staff is compromised. His expression clouds over and all previous amusement leaves his eyes.

My captors regain their hold on me.

"Tie her back up and leave her in darkness," he growls. "We'll draft a new ransom note. One that *doesn't* claim she's unharmed. And if her father fails to comply, then I'm sure we'll find another way. Another family member perhaps." His gaze slides to me, expression triumphant.

Another family member. My mind goes to Nina. "Leave my family out of this!"

The fae begin to funnel back into the hall, and my captors drag me toward the chair. Turning away, the king hobbles toward the door.

"Wait!" I call at his back; he's already halfway over the threshold. "We can talk this out."

He ignores me and disappears into the hall.

My captors push me into the chair, forcing me to keep my seat as they gather the discarded ropes.

I take a deep breath, steadying my resolve, then shout, "Tell me about the curse!"

My captors halt their motions, and all sounds of footsteps cease. For a moment, time seems frozen, until the king stalks back into the room, his staff pounding on the flagstones. His lips are pulled into a snarl. "Who told you about the curse?"

I hear a small gasp and catch sight of Micah peeking into the room, shaking his head vigorously. Averting my gaze to the king, I say, "It's obvious there's some kind of curse at play here. Why else would you be toying with me like this? Trying to trick me time and time again to make some silly sacrifice for you?"

His chest heaves. "Some silly sacrifice?" The words come under his breath, so low they reverberate in my bones. "This *silly sacrifice* could mean my life."

"If that's the case, then you're going about it all wrong. The ransom plot, the feigned attacks, the trickery. What you're doing will never work."

"You know nothing."

"Then tell me. Instead of using me as bait, make me an ally." I keep my expression neutral to hide the truth. That I have no intention of allying with this fae. What I need are more facts. More figures. More to tally up and divide until I can find the right weakness to use against him.

For several silent moments we just stare at each other, the king's garnet eyes narrowed with intensity. It may not be the ruby stare of his wolf form, but there's certainly something predatory about it.

Finally, he speaks. "Out." His voice comes out quiet, then magnifies into a roar. "Everyone out!"

"Even us—" Blackbeard begins.

"Out!" the king shouts again.

Blackbeard and the female release me and hurry out the door.

I catch a final glimpse of Micah's wide eyes before Blackbeard closes the door and leaves me trembling and alone with the king.

11

The silence blanketing the room sends my heart hammering against my ribs. This isn't the silence of peaceful mountains and quiet woods. This is the eerie quiet that comes before the storm.

Eyes locked on me, the king takes a step closer, then another.

I rise from the chair, shoulders thrown back. Everything in me screams that I should run, cower, but I refuse to give in. If this is where I die, then I'll go down with my eyes wide open and defiant. Counting to five, I steady my breathing and curl my fingers into fists to keep my arms from trembling. Then, voice as steady as I can manage, I break the silence. "Are you truly the Unseelie King of Winter?"

He ignores my question, lips curling into a snarl, but his expression falters. He drops my gaze, shoulders drooping. Then with slow steps, he closes the distance between us. I hold my ground, pulse racing, but as he approaches, he waves a hand at me. "Move."

I step away and he takes my place in front of the chair and lowers into it. Slumping to the side, he leans on his elbow, propping his face with his fist. In the other arm, he cradles his staff. "So," he says, his tone cold and distant, "you want to be my ally."

No, I think to myself. *I want to measure your weakness. Strike where it hurts.* Out loud, I say smoothly, "I think there's a chance we could work something out."

"Fine," he says with a dismissive flourish of his hand. "Pitch me this alliance of yours."

With slow, hesitant steps, I move a few paces away and face him. "I have questions first. To start, tell me if it's true. Are you the king?"

"I am," he says with an irritated grumble.

So, he's affirmed it twice now. Can I believe him? Or is he a delusional fae who only thinks he's a royal? "If you're the king, then where is your wealth? Your luxury?"

He lifts a brow as if he can't comprehend my puzzlement. "I am wealthy."

"Then why aren't you dressed like a king? Where is your crown?"

He scoffs. "Why bother? It's like that human saying… how does it go? You can put rouge on a pig, or some such?"

This, I'm confused by, but I decide not to press further. "And this," I extend my arms to indicate the room, "is your palace?"

"It's where I live," is all he says.

In my mind, I draw up a ledger and create an imaginary column collecting his assets. He's supposedly wealthy. Has some rundown manor. Now, what are his liabilities? His weaknesses? He can't lie, but I need more than that to use against him. Which means I need to investigate further. Continue my ruse of an alliance.

Allowing only curiosity to infuse my tone, I say, "I've yet to hear your name. Not here, and not in Vernon. Is it true you do not know it?"

"My name is forgotten, both by myself and anyone who dares to think of me. It's part of the curse, slowly stripping away my memories and those of all fae who remain under my roof. Our names were the first to go."

Now we're getting somewhere. "Why are you cursed?"

He meets my gaze for a moment, eyes flashing with indignation. "I killed a human." He winces, sinking lower in his chair. "Several of them."

My throat feels dry at the confession. "Why?"

His expression darkens. "They hunted and killed one of my fae brethren, so I took my revenge and killed the entire hunting party. I...I didn't know the wolf was killed on approved hunting grounds, so my vengeance was unlawful, especially without consent of the Alpha Council."

I nod, although I feel like I'm barely following. From what I've learned, the Alpha Council is the highest level of government in Faerwyvae, consisting of all ruling kings and queens of each court, and acting in alliance with the courts' human representatives. What I hadn't known is that there's such a thing as approved or unapproved hunting grounds. I suppose it makes sense, though, making specific areas safe for the fae, while opening others so humans can continue their hunting activities for sport, survival, or trade. "Were you not informed where the wolf was killed?"

"I knew where he was killed, I just...I hadn't realized what that land was."

"Was it not in your own court?"

"It was."

I raise a brow. "Do you not know your own lands?"

He burns me with a glare. "I once knew my lands like the back of my paw. I ruled Winter—all of it—for hundreds of years. But when my court moved—"

"What do you mean it moved?"

"Do you not know the history of Faerwyvae?" His words are heavy with condescension. "I admit, you look barely older than a pup, but surely you've heard about the war."

"I have heard about both wars, the most recent one ending twenty years ago. I'm just...not originally from here. I just moved a few weeks ago." I bite the inside of my cheek, hoping I don't come to regret the confession. I see no benefit in hiding the truth, though.

His expression softens, and his voice takes on an almost conversational tone. "Then perhaps you've heard Faerwyvae was once called the Fair Isle and was divided in half. The north was called what our entire isle is named now—Faerwyvae—and the south was called Eisleigh and was ruled by Bretton. When Bretton betrayed the humans and declared war on the isle, it was the fae who saved everyone. We fought the human armies, defeated them, and set up a perimeter wall of standing stones infused with magic. I assume you were escorted between the stones when you arrived?"

"Yes," I say. In fact, there was an entire fae guard awaiting our arrival at the docks when our ship pulled into the port. Myself, my father, my sister, and the few other humans who'd been granted citizenship, were escorted by two armed guards per person, marching us single file between a pair of enormous, towering stones. There was no fiery blast or shimmering lights to signify the invisible magic barrier we crossed, but the hair stood up on the back of my neck just the same. I shudder at the memory.

The king continues. "For a moment, imagine what the isle was like after the war. The southern half that was previously human land now fell under fae rule. It took years for the Alpha Council to rework the divide of property, determine the new boundary lines. Many of us had to relocate our palaces, our homes, our people. After that, the land had to adapt to the magic and climate of each court. I was one of the unlucky ones, a king forced from his lifelong throne to settle in the south, claiming a land still thick with the stench of iron. I refused to have a palace rebuilt and held court in the mountain caves instead. I paid little heed to the humans or the decisions made by the Alpha Council regarding my land, since I clearly had no say."

I frown. "As king, aren't you part of the Alpha Council?"

He grunts a bitter laugh. "I was overruled more often than not. Let's just say there were—*are*—many on the council who are not my greatest fans. I'm sure the feeling would be mutual...if I could remember those fools clearly." He mutters the last part under his breath.

"So, I'm guessing you didn't pay attention to where the approved hunting regions were?"

He shifts anxiously in his seat, refusing to meet my eyes. "Correct."

I purse my lips, finding it hard to pity him when his own negligence brought about his fate. "All right, so you took unlawful vengeance on a pack of hunters and were cursed for it. Is that...normal for fae punishment?"

He shrugs. "Curses and bargains are what fae specialize in, especially when it comes to punishments doled out by the Alpha Council."

"How long have you been under this curse?"

Closing his eyes, he rubs his brow with his thumb and forefinger. "This is the fifth year. The year it will claim my life if it isn't broken." His voice is laced with equal parts exhaustion and irritation.

"How so? Does the curse take more than just your memories?"

He opens his eyes and looks at me from beneath the wisps of his tangled mane of hair, so unlike the white of his wolf form. Barking a laugh, he shakes his head. "Memories," he echoes. "I wish it would only take my memories. The curse can have them all, for all I care."

"What else does it take?"

He rises to stand, bringing his staff beneath his arm, then hobbles to the window. I remain in place, watching as he gazes out the same glass pane I watched him from not long ago.

"Almost five years ago," the king says, "I was condemned to serve a sentence of one year for every life I'd taken, for a total of five. At the end of the sentence, the curse is set to claim me, and I will be permanently stripped of four things: my memories, my magic, my immortality, and my unseelie form. In essence, I'll be mortal, human, and without any idea of who I am. But none of that matters, for when mortality catches up to my age, I will have but seconds to live. I've seen similar curses doled out before. It isn't a kind punishment."

Terrible images course through my mind, of a man aging right before my eyes, the flesh wrinkling and melting from his bones. I swallow hard. "What about now? The curse already affects you, does it not?"

He nods. "During my five-year sentence, I've been forced to suffer a taste of the curse to come. First, I was stripped from both my magic and my unseelie form outside every full moon. During the full moon, I can use my magic to become a wolf again. Every other moment, however, I am trapped in a human body. No connection to magic."

I furrow my brow, recalling the horrifying novels I've read about lycanthropes who shift when the light of the full moon touches them. Could these gruesome tales hold a kernel of truth? "But you were a wolf this morning," I say. "The moon was not out."

"Day or night, it doesn't matter," he says, almost too quiet to hear. "So long as the moon is full, I can shift, but only once. If I don't shift back to my seelie form on my own, I'm forced out of my wolf form against my will once the moon begins to wane."

I study him for a moment, eyes falling on his wooden staff. "Did you lose your leg as part of the curse?"

He shakes his head, still staring wistfully out the window. "I lost it in the war. The second one, that is. Anyway, after I was robbed of my magic and my unseelie form, I began to age like a human. Hurt like a human. Then I began to lose my memories. It started with my name. It continued with small things. Other names. Faces. Sometimes, I can't even recall the way a frozen wind feels blowing through my fur." He grips the edge of the windowsill until his knuckles turn white.

I pause, going over everything he's told me so far. Nothing seems useful as leverage to bargain my way out of here. There must be something. Something he hasn't told me yet. "You said the curse will claim you this year. Do you know when?"

He nods. "The roses tell me it will be soon."

"The roses?"

He presses his head to the glass and releases a grumbling sigh. "Since I had no palace, I was given this manor, abandoned by the humans who once lived here. It acts as my gilded cage, containing me and my pack within the boundaries of the curse. We can only travel within a small radius outside the manor, and any fae who steps within the radius is plagued by my curse, forced into seelie form. For visitors, however, the curse is temporary and allows them free passage in or out of my manor. For myself and all those who remained at my side when the curse was delivered, it is permanent."

I'm not sure what any of this has to do with roses, but I decide to keep quiet. More questions sprout up alongside this new information. Why did some of his subjects choose to stay with him when his curse was delivered? Why didn't everyone flee?

He continues. "Along with this manor, I was given twenty roses, each bearing nearly a hundred petals—some more, some less. One petal has fallen every day since the curse began, robbing one rose of life at a time. As each rose falls, brambles take its place, smothering the life that once bloomed. Today, I watched the second-to-last rose lose its final petal. There is one rose left in the garden. Perhaps one hundred petals. One hundred days at most. Then the curse will take me."

I ponder this. That's approximately three months from now. If he plans on holding me captive until he gets his way, that's the longest I'll have to wait. Then, if what he says is true, he'll die and I'll be free.

"Don't look so hopeful," he says, gaze narrowed at me. "For I *will* break this curse."

I lift my chin, hiding my calculations behind a stoic mask. "And how do you expect to do that?"

He moves away from the window and takes a few steps toward me. "I've been given two ways to be free of this curse. The first way is this: of the four things I stand to lose, if I sacrifice the one I value most, I will be returned those which I value less."

My eyes go wide, my mouth falling open. "Wait, you're telling me you have the power to break your own curse? And instead, you're kidnapping people and holding them for ransom?"

"Did you not hear a word I said? To break the curse myself, I must sacrifice that which I value most to gain what I value less. Besides, it is but a partial breaking, not a true one."

I burn him with a glare. "And what is this great value of yours that is so much more important than breaking your curse?"

He gestures toward himself. "Isn't it obvious? My unseelie form. To break the curse myself, I'd have to sacrifice my wolf body and accept a human form for the rest of my life, just to reclaim my immortality, magic, and memories."

"And that's somehow a bad thing?"

"Life isn't worth living—especially an immortal one —if I'm stuck in this hideous human body," he says with a sneer. "Not even my magic will matter to me if I can't use it to shift forms."

Hideous human body. Could he truly be so vain? I assess the king and his wild hair, his unruly beard, trying to find the youthful male buried underneath. While he claims to have begun aging when his sentence began, it's only his unkempt appearance that makes him look that way. And even though I wouldn't call him handsome by any means, he certainly isn't hideous. On the outside, that is. His personality leaves much to be desired. "You could be...decent looking if you tried, you know. Perhaps you could even come to like yourself the way you are."

He tilts his head back as if I'm spouting nonsense. "Impossible. Do you see me? I'm...disgusting. Repulsive." His face twists in disgust. "Human."

"Wait...you think you're hideous because you look...human?"

"Of course."

I almost burst out laughing. What I first deemed vanity is more a matter of prejudice. "Do you find all humans to be as hideous as you assume yourself to be? If so, you must think I am ugly as well."

His gaze roves my body from head to toe. "Why wouldn't I?"

A blush of heat rises up my neck. "I'm almost of a mind to be offended."

"Waste no emotion on me, human. I'll waste none on you, I can tell you that much."

I purse my lips and force my indignation to cool. Why should I care what he thinks of me, anyway? Men finding me attractive has never served me well before. "Fine then. Now, what is this second option to break your curse? The one that must have something to do with a human sacrifice?"

"The second way to break the curse is for a human to hold me in such high esteem that they are willing to sacrifice that which they treasure most, breaking the curse altogether."

I roll the words over in my mind, studying them from different angles. This time, it's impossible to stifle my laughter. "And you think the tricks you've been playing on me are supposed to work?" I throw my head back, tears pooling at the corners of my eyes. "You can't trick someone into holding you in the highest esteem, nor can you expect a feigned rescue after a contrived attack to stir that kind of sacrifice-inducing gratitude you're after."

He frowns, shoulders rigid as color burns in his cheeks. "Oh, and how would you go about it?"

"Have you ever thought of, I don't know, actually befriending a human to gain their esteem?"

"Would that work?" His tone is skeptical, but there's a note of hope in it too. "Even if I were to befriend a human, as you say, would such a friendship engender someone to make such a sacrifice for me? Would *you* do as much for your dearest friend?"

The question quickly sobers me. While I no longer count anyone as a close friend these days, I can still imagine facing the choice. For someone I loved, would I sacrifice that which I treasure most? I consider my great treasures, drawing a blank. Then it comes to me. My greatest treasure is that which I do not have—freedom, independence, a life of my own. There's no one I'd be willing to sacrifice that for, no matter how dire their circumstance. For where would such a sacrifice leave me? If I am to assume the opposite would then manifest, I'd be...

Trapped. Captive. Controlled.

The thought alone drains the blood from my face.

"I suppose you're right," I admit. "Not even friendship would make such a sacrifice easy. You need something stronger."

He nods. "Which is why I invoke an element of fear, something to set one's mind at unease, make one more apt toward impulsive decisions beneath the weight of their gratitude."

"But that isn't working either," I say. "You need something else. Something that makes someone stupider than fear, but more invested than friendship."

"Well, if you have any bright ideas," he says, voice heavy with sarcasm, "I'm all ears."

I freeze as an epiphany strikes me.

I tally up everything he's told me. His assets. His liabilities. I see his needs, his hurdles, his struggles.

And right there in the middle is an opportunity. Not just for him. For *me*.

I turn away, a plan forming in my mind. I go over it again and again, checking it for weaknesses. Then finally, I say, "I have an idea."

His voice comes out heavy with suspicion. "About what?"

I turn to face him, a smile tugging my lips. "We're going to make a bargain."

12

When we moved to Faerwyvae, I may not have been given a complete education regarding the fae, but I was told the same rule by pretty much every human who welcomed us to Vernon: never bargain with the fae.

I had every intention of keeping to this rule. Additionally, when I began my conversation with the king, I had absolutely zero intentions of actually allying with him.

The thing is, when people mention fae bargains, they describe terrible bonds, blood-curdling curses, and deadly punishments. No one ever mentions a bargain that benefits the human involved, perhaps more so than the fae.

And that's exactly what I've crafted in my mind.

Excitement bubbles in my chest at the possibilities, but I do my best to maintain my composure, keeping a straight face before the king.

"What kind of bargain?" he says, taking a hesitant step back.

I clasp my hands at my waist, standing at my full height. "Like I said, to get a human to break your curse, you'll need something that makes them stupider than fear, but more invested than friendship."

He narrows his eyes. "Go on."

"And if the person must sacrifice that which they treasure most to break the curse, then you need to find someone who has only trivial treasures. Material things. For that, you need to know the right person."

Quirking a brow, he says, "And you happen to know the right person?"

I can't fight the smile that stretches my lips, and it's all I can do to suppress the devious laughter that begs to erupt from inside me. "I do. Her name is Imogen Coleman."

"All right," he says slowly. "How do propose to get this Imogen Coleman to break the curse? The sacrifice must be made of their own free—"

"Their own free will and volition, I get it. Trust me, subtlety is not your strong suit." I take a few steps closer to where he stands. "That is where *my* phase two comes in. Where you make her both stupid and invested."

"You say it like it's simple."

"It is. Because you're going to make her fall in love with you."

"Love!" He scoffs, lips pulling into a grimace. "I'm going to make a human fall in *love* with me?"

I purse my lips to keep my grin from spreading wider. "Precisely. Love is that which makes humans absolute fools while making them equally and irrationally attached to another person. You were right when you said you needed to entice the sacrifice during feelings of great impulse. That's exactly what love does. It turns people into reckless idiots, both blind to reason and ignorant of their own folly, even as it stares them in the eyes."

"You sound like someone with personal experience."

That wipes the grin clear off my face, but I don't let it hold me back. "I do have experience in this department, which makes me the perfect ally. While I am no longer susceptible to the guiles of love, I can still recognize them. Better yet, I know Imogen Coleman and her petty wants and needs. I know what powers love and matrimony have over her, and I know exactly what kind of man will tempt her into the pits of stupidity."

He studies me with that intense, predatory stare, one that tells me he knows very little about propriety and interacting with humans. It makes my pulse quicken, and a wave of panic rises within me. What am I getting myself into? Do I honestly believe I can get anyone, much less Imogen Coleman, to fall in love with this untamed creature?

He has money, I remind myself. Plus, he's a king, for saint's sake. That alone should have Imogen desperate for his favor sight unseen. But for her to sacrifice her greatest treasure for him...for that, she'll need to truly fall in *love* with him.

"We have a lot of work to do," I mutter.

"*We* have no work to do, for I am not going to agree to such nonsense. I will not have you pairing me with a human mate. I have no use for a lover, much less a human one."

"Oh, you're not actually going to take her as a lover," I say. "You will make her fall in love with you, in the same way you tried to trick me into breaking your curse. But we'll do it my way, using deception mingled with truth. After she breaks your curse, you can send her off and never see her again."

The king glowers for a moment, then his eyes widen in something like...admiration. "What did this human girl do to you?"

His words stun me silent, my stomach sinking. I consider my scheme anew, thinking about it from Imogen's side. I know how eager she is for a husband, how desperate she is for a favorable match that will bring her wealth. For a royal title, I'm certain she'd jump through hoops and flip backward. But how will she feel when all of that is stripped away? When she sacrifices her greatest treasure for someone who abandons her?

I know how that feels. I know what it's like to give a man everything only to have him take it away. Every promise. Every kiss. But instead of sparking empathy, it hardens my heart, for I can only recall the words she said to me when we left the bookshop yesterday morning, her tone all but a threat.

It may have been acceptable to play the harlot in Bretton...

No one wants a ruined woman as a wife...

You'd become a stain on this town...

My fingers curl into fists, my resolve turning to steel. "Imogen could use a lesson in humility," I say, surprised at the ice in my tone. "Besides, it's like I said. You need someone who cherishes trivial things. I'm sure her greatest treasure is some fancy dress."

He puts his free hand on his hip while the other rests on his staff. "You've mentioned a bargain," he says, "but you've yet to say what you get out of this."

Just like that, some of my excitement returns, and I

have to bite the inside of my cheek to conceal my grin. *Play this well, Gemma. Don't act too eager.*

"Did you mean it when you said you're wealthy?" I ask.

He shoots me a glare. "What does that have to do with anything?"

"We're going to need some funds for our scheme to work. You can't leave the manor, which means I'll have to tempt Imogen here. And there's no way she's going to fall in love with you if the entire place looks like this." I gesture toward the dusty furniture.

"I'm not wasting my money on frivolous decor for a manor I have every intention of vacating when the curse is broken."

"I won't waste it, trust me," I say. "I know how to handle finances in just the right way. That is why I applied for the job, you know."

"The job?"

"Your want ad for a house steward. I have experience running a household on a very tight budget. And my need for that job hasn't changed."

"Your point being?"

My eyes lock on his. "You're going to offer me employment."

He barks a laugh. "I don't actually *need* a house steward."

"You do now," I say. "If you want this bargain and my assistance in breaking the curse, then you'll appoint me your house steward, provide a handsome weekly salary as well as room and board—"

"Room and board? You want to *stay* here?"

"Yes. That's a non-negotiable part of the bargain." In

truth, it's the answer to all my prior concerns regarding getting a job—whether Father would strip my allowance, turn me out of the house. This way, I'll have it all. A salary, work I'm suited for, a place to live. "In addition to these terms, once the curse breaks, you will reward me with a hefty sum of money."

"In addition to a weekly salary?" He throws his free hand in the air, shaking his head.

"What do you care for money, anyway? You clearly aren't spending it. Besides, you said you value your unseelie form more than anything. Would you put a price on that?"

"I may not spend my fortune now, but I like spending it when I'm a wolf, human."

I take a firm step forward. "My name isn't human, it's Gemma. And if we are to work together, you will call me Miss Bellefleur."

He takes a forbidding step closer to mirror mine, his eyes glinting dangerously. "Then you will cut that tone and call me Your Majesty."

I refuse to falter beneath his glare. "Fine, Your Majesty. What's it going to be? Do you agree to my terms?"

A corner of his mouth lifts. "You're *my* prisoner and I am your king. I could kill you for insubordination, you know."

I cross my arms, pulling my lips into a forced smile. "You could, but I doubt that would go over very well with the Alpha Council, especially after they find out you abducted me. Besides, I'm probably the closest thing you have to a shot at breaking this curse. Kill me if you want, but if this curse is meant to claim your life at the end of your sentence, then I'll see you in hell in three months' time."

His eyes widen. "I don't need you."

"No, you could keep trying to trick unsuspecting townsfolk using fear and false heroics." I flutter my lashes. "But...how has that been working so far?"

He releases a grumble. "How much money are we talking about?"

I pause, running some calculations in my head. "One thousand quartz chips per week."

He moans.

"And twenty thousand quartz rounds once the curse has been broken."

His mouth falls open, but no sound comes out. Eyes bulging, he finally speaks. "Twenty thousand rounds! You're out of your mind."

"Do you have it or not?"

"Of course I have it," he says.

With slow, steady steps I close the distance between us, stopping only when we're mere feet away. "Then do we have a deal? I'll help you break the curse by getting Miss Coleman to fall in love with you. In return, you will provide room and board and pay me the agreed upon salary and follow my plan. Give up your ridiculous schemes of kidnapping and ransom notes and do what I say instead. When your curse breaks, you pay me the rest. Afterward, we never have to see each other again."

His jaw shifts side to side, and he brings his hand to rub his beard. "The fae are supposed to be the ones to craft the bargain," he mutters, a hint of petulance in his tone.

I hold out my hand.

His predatory gaze burns into me, brow furrowed as if he's puzzling over a complicated mathematic formula. One only I know the answer to. Then, with a reluctant sigh that turns into a grumble, he places his hand in mine. "I agree to this bargain."

13

J ust like when I walked between the standing stones to enter Faerwyvae, this bargain conjures no outward sign that magic is taking place. But as before, I feel the hair rise on the back of my neck. Is it a coincidence? A matter of my own physical response to knowing I've just sealed a bargain with a fae? Or is this what magic feels like?

Whatever the case, the king seems none too pleased about it. Releasing my grip from our handshake, he can barely meet my eyes. "I can't believe I just put my fate in the hands of a human."

I can't believe I have a job, I want to squeal in response, the reality of our bargain just beginning to sink in. He has no idea how greatly I've desired this. How badly I've needed this. Not our bargain, per se, but the first step toward freedom that employment brings. Squaring my shoulders, I allow only a hint of mirth to infuse my tone when I say, "I can't believe it's taken you five years to even try."

"What, an alliance with a human? I'll have you know, it was quite peaceful around here up until that appalling town began construction. Not a human in sight for almost five years. Yet another proposal passed by that filthy ferret..." He trails off, running a hand through his wild hair.

I furrow my brow. "A ferret?"

"Fine, he's an ermine. But even in his seelie form, he's nothing more than a weasel to me. Claiming his place as Seelie King of Winter when I'm stuck here and unable to challenge him. I used to rule all of Winter alone, you know."

"Isn't there a seelie and unseelie ruler in every court now, though?"

"Yes," he says through his teeth, "but if I hadn't been cursed and trapped in this manor, I could have held onto the kingdom far longer."

"Surely, you have some ability to counter the proposals passed by the seelie king, don't you?"

His eyes flick to me then away again. "I can, but it's a bother."

"A bother?" I snort a laugh.

Indignation reddens his cheeks as he fully meets my gaze. "Yes, it's a bother. If I want to counter the proposals he passes, I must either meet with my ambassador and send her off to speak in my stead or call him here to discuss it."

I lift a brow. "And that's...hard?"

"It's...you wouldn't understand. There aren't many who know about my situation, for the curse keeps me from others' minds and makes me easy to forget. And of the fae who do know about the curse, very few are willing to suffer it by visiting. While my ambassador doesn't mind...well, I'd rather others not see me like this if I can avoid it." The last part ends in a mumble as he turns away from me, facing the windows. His wistful expression returns as he stares out at the scenery. "Besides, when I read the proposal for the new town, I didn't understand the location it described. I didn't grow up in the Chamberlain Mountains or the Holbrook Pass. These are names leftover from a human reign, not the ones embedded in my very bones since birth."

My chest squeezes as I find his words resonating against my heart. I too know what it's like to be taken from my home, thrust into a new place. It's happened twice now, and each new town, new country, feels like an entirely new world. The king, however, isn't just living in some foreign place; he's ruling it. And considering how old I imagine he must be, the time he's spent adapting to the changes since the end of the war must feel like a blink compared to his immortal lifespan.

The thought threatens to shatter my mask, and before I realize it, I open my mouth to speak. But what is it I want to say? My heart begs to relate to him, tell him I understand. Say that perhaps humans and fae aren't so different after all. Instead, I swallow those words, reminding myself I didn't seal this bargain to make friends with the king. Friendships are no longer something I care to invest in, and certainly not with a fae who tried to trick me and threatened to *kill* me. No, he doesn't deserve my pity. We are but cold allies and he is nothing more than my ticket to freedom.

I lift my chin. "If we are to convince Imogen Coleman

to fall in love with you, we'll have to turn you into a more capable-seeming king."

Still facing away from me, he shakes his head and mutters, "Freezing iceforsaken woman."

"Speaking of freezing," I say, taking a few steps closer, "I meant what I said about a fire. I cannot tolerate staying somewhere without proper heat. So, let's talk room and board. Will I be staying here?"

"This room has been set aside for my ambassador," he says, rubbing his chin, "but like I said, I do not call her here often. Even when she does come on business, she does not stay long."

"Which explains the state of the room," I say under my breath. Then my gaze snags on my pile of damp discarded clothing. My hands fly to the skirt of the gown I'm wearing. "Oh, your ambassador. Is that whose dress this is?"

He smirks, eyes trailing the length of my gown. "Might as well claim the wardrobe for yourself too. It's not like she's using any of it."

Something about the smirk he wears, the fleeting heat in his gaze as he continues to eye my dress, makes me wonder if he and his ambassador were—or are— lovers. Because it couldn't possibly be the sight of *me* that put that look in his eyes, not after everything he's said about humans. This, of course, sends my stomach roiling as I consider just how invasive my presence and actions might have been. "I can stay in another room and fetch my own clothes from home—"

"Don't bother," he growls. "I'm not making up another room for you."

"Fine," I say, swallowing hard and hoping my flustered air goes with it. "In that case, I'll need the bedding cleaned, the room dusted. Do you have servants? A cook?"

He shifts his stance, planting his leg more firmly beneath him, and stares down his nose at me. "We keep after ourselves."

"You're a king without servants?" I shake my head. "This won't do. But don't you worry; as house steward, I will see that all necessary positions are filled. It would be best that all daily tasks are given to those you can trust, so we should probably put your wolf pack to work, don't you think? As for the position of cook...who made the bread I was given?"

"That's Bertha," he says with a grumble. "A bear from nearby who insists on feeding us."

"A bear?"

"In her unseelie form," he amends. "But she's seelie through and through, always baking us bread and pies and—"

"Perfect." I clap my hands together. Yet another asset to tally in my imaginary columns. "I'll need her contact information at once."

"Contact information?"

"Address, location, you know. Or the perfect pitch to howl when you need to summon her." The last part is said in jest, but he doesn't seem to catch my humor; he simply stares at me, perplexed.

"She comes along whenever she likes, uninvited like the wind," he says.

"Great, then I'll speak to her at her next visit. Come." I turn and head for the door.

"Did you just...order me to follow you?"

For a moment, a wave of fear strikes me. Beneath the false confidence of my outer persona, it's easy to forget when I'm getting carried away with the act. Still, I maintain my composure as if no misstep was made. "This is a business partnership, Your Majesty," I say as I reach the door handle. "I'm simply continuing our business. And now I'll need a tour of the manor. I must have an understanding of what I'm working with here."

"You have some nerve," comes his gravelly voice, followed by the sound of his footsteps and staff pounding behind me.

I pull open the door and bite back a yelp as a cluster of bodies all but tumbles through the threshold, their pointed ears having been pressed to the door. Leaping back, I nearly lose my footing beneath me before a strong hand closes around my arm at the elbow. I meet the king's gaze as I regain my bearings, surprised at finding him so close, his face just inches from mine. My breath catches, my heart racing at the sudden proximity.

He releases me, shaking out his hand as if touching me had scalded him, then charges toward the group of fae who eagerly shuffle away from the door, feigning nonchalance. "Don't bother pretending you didn't listen in on the whole thing."

I recognize Blackbeard leaning against the opposite wall, scratching the side of his head while the elderly female examines her nails with keen interest. Finally, I catch a glimpse of Micah, peeking between the legs of two unfamiliar fae. "She's staying?" the boy asks. "We don't have to eat her?"

"Not today," the king says dryly. "Meet our new house steward."

MOST OF THE FAE MAKE THEMSELVES SCARCE AS SOON AS I enter the hall to follow after the king, while a few others trail behind us. The latter group includes Blackbeard and the female, who the king calls—again, most uncreatively —Gray. The king leads us through the halls of the manor, which unfortunately proves as unkempt as my room, if not worse. Dust lines every surface, cobwebs gathering in each corner. I take note of it all, feeling daunted by both the immensity of the manor and its sorry state.

As I consider the task at hand, my pulse begins to race, but I remind myself I've done this before. I've masked poverty and made it look like wealth. I've hidden darkness and desperation and made others see only luxury and light. I've done it before, and I can do it again. Especially if it ends with my freedom. Independence. A chance at a life of my own.

We reach a platform between several large staircases that branch off in different directions.

The king points to the left. "That goes to the east wing. It's nothing but empty rooms." He points to the right. "There's the west wing, but don't go there."

"Why, what's in the west wing?"

"What's in the west wing?" he repeats in a mocking tone. "What do you think is in the west wing? Dust, spiders, cobwebs. It's nothing but dreary freezing shit everywhere in this manor. Don't go in the west wing, don't go in the east wing, just...don't bother with anywhere."

Blackbeard steps up beside me, leaning forward. "The kitchens are nice, though."

The king sighs, then gives a resigned shrug. "Yeah, the kitchens, those are fine."

"And her bedroom," Gray adds, her voice like a creaky floorboard.

"Obviously," the king says with a nod. "We keep the ambassador suite up to par."

"The parlor has good lighting," Blackbeard says.

The king scoffs. "The parlor is a dump, but you're right, we get by."

"And the library." This voice comes from Micah, who I hadn't realized until now had been following.

The king barks a laugh. "The library. Now that's a joke."

Warmth spreads over my chest, sending tingles down my arms and spine. I almost feel as if I could float on air. It's impossible to mask the longing in my voice when I whisper, "You have a library?"

He nods, oblivious to the pounding in my heart, the yearning in my eyes at that delicious, magical word. *Library*.

"Now, onto the dining room," he says and starts down one of the staircases.

I follow, but my mind lingers on the platform above, waiting, watching, seeking any sign that could lead me to the promised haven of books and paper. Of unread sentences and uncharted worlds.

My body tugs at my mind and orders it to rejoin the tour.

With a sigh, I obey, returning my attention to the stairs beneath my feet and the dust I disturb with every step.

14

Exhaustion tugs at my bones by the time the tour is over. It ends in the parlor, which appears to be the most frequented room in the manor, although the furniture is sparse, faded, and outdated. But just like Blackbeard had mentioned, the lighting is good, with several tall windows lining one wall, inviting a view of the gardens. Daylight streams inside, illuminating motes of dust swirling through the air and laying over every surface.

"This room will be one of the first we make presentable," I say, facing the king and the fae who've continued the tour with us—Blackbeard, Gray, and a few other wolf-people I've yet to know by adopted name. Micah, it seems, had run off at some point.

The king grunts in response and turns away from me to stalk toward the hearth. Unlike my room, a fire has been made. Without a word, he settles into a wingback chair facing the fire. The other fae shift anxiously from foot to foot, glancing from me to the king.

With my bare feet still aching and my body drained of energy, I feel my outward persona attempting to slip away. I breathe in deeply to steady myself. There's still so much more to do. To learn. To plan for. And I've taken it all upon my shoulders.

The latter thought should feel daunting, but instead, it echoes inside me, to the last time I ever felt important. When I ran my family's household in Bretton, there was never a dull moment, and the pressure was fully upon me to keep our lives afloat. In turn, I was given a sense of purpose, appreciated by those I loved.

That all changed, of course, with the scandal.

I shake the thoughts from my mind and focus on the anxious fae before me. "Do any of you have positions in this household?"

They exchange glances, then Blackbeard says, "I used to be on the king's royal guard, but...there isn't much need for that anymore."

"I was once a soldier," Gray says, surprising me. It's hard to imagine the ancient woman as a fighter. "It was long ago, though, in the first war. I simply serve the king now."

"You won't find the servants and staff you're looking for," the king says, eyes on the flames in the hearth. "I lost most of my household staff when I refused to have a palace built in the new Winter Court. Everyone else left when I was sentenced to be cursed."

"Who are the rest of you then?" I ask.

The king says nothing, so Blackbeard takes a hesitant step forward. "We are those most loyal to His Majesty and suffer the curse at his side. We are ready to face death if needed."

"Pah! Don't listen to him," says the king. "Blackbeard may have stayed out of loyalty, but these other wolves were from my pack. The weakest ones. Too injured, too old, or too young to survive in a new pack. They stayed with me out of lack of better options."

Gray rolls her eyes. "That's not all true, Your Majesty."

"Oh?" The king turns in his chair to smirk at her. "How would you have fared in a new pack? They'd have berated you for looking so old."

She puts her hands on her hips. "I'd have done just fine, thank you very much. I'm still spry in my wolf form."

The king shakes his head and returns to looking at the flames.

I am curious why Gray looks old when the others look so much younger. How does aging come into play for immortal beings? And will all of them die alongside the king if the curse isn't broken? The thought sends a pang of worry to my heart, but I force the questions from my mind.

"Regardless of whether you had positions in the king's household before," I say, "we must all take up work from this point on to make the manor presentable."

A few of the fae wear scowls at that, but others, like Blackbeard and Gray, seem encouraged.

"I'll draw up a list of positions and set about filling them. Now, where are the ledgers tracking the king's finances?"

Gray points to a bureau near the wall of windows. "You'll find them in the drawer."

I approach the bureau, which appears far more frequently used than the one in my room, with several papers strewn over the top, two pens, and even an old quill. I see two half-finished copies of the ransom note to my father, both scratched over with a haphazard slash of ink. My stomach drops at the sight, reminding me of the most dreadful task to come—one I must take care of at once.

"How do you send or receive correspondences?" I ask. "If none of you can leave the boundaries of the curse, how do you deliver letters or get want ads in the paper?"

"Bertha takes them to town," Blackbeard says. "And she always checks the post for anything received."

"Bertha...the one who makes the bread?"

He nods.

"But you don't know when to expect her back?"

Blackbeard opens his mouth, but it's another voice that answers, muffled as if stuffed full. "She's already here." I look toward the parlor door, where I find Micah peering around the doorframe, cheeks puffed as he chews what must be an enormous bite of bread. "She came to bake more bread for our prisoner."

The king releases a grumble. "Might as well have her make a full dinner."

Micah's eyes brighten, but he quickly feigns nonchalance. "I'll go let her know." He prepares to take off, but I start forward.

"Wait!" I call after him.

Micah pops his head back around the doorway.

Before I can speak, the king rises from his chair and makes his way to the door. "Just bring the old bear up," he says with an irritated sigh. "I'm sure Miss Bellefleur has a job to offer her, or some such nonsense. In the meantime, I'll go find some new corner of this shithole where it's *supposed* to be quiet."

By the time I have my letter finished, signed, and sealed, Micah returns with Bertha. Even in her seelie form, she's a bear of a woman, with a wide, dense build. Her skin is the color of raw honey and her hair is just a shade darker. She's dressed in a simple brown dress covered in a stained apron. I meet her in the middle of the parlor, which emptied of the other fae shortly after the king left.

"You must be Bertha," I say.

She greets me with a warm smile, eyes crinkling at the corners. "And you must be this *prisoner* I've heard about. Lovely to meet you, my dear." She emphasizes the word *prisoner* as if she's referring to a harmless game played by unruly children.

Come to think of it, that isn't too far off.

"She's not our prisoner anymore," Micah says. "She's our house steward, whatever that is. Is there more bread in the kitchen?"

Bertha nods, and the boy scampers off, leaving me alone with the cook. "House steward, eh?" she asks.

"Yes, and my name is Gemma Bellefleur. I hear you're a cook and provide food for the manor?"

"I do my best," she says. "I know His Majesty likes to say my food is drab, but he never fails to eat less than three bowls of my famous rabbit stew."

The thought of warm stew nearly has my stomach rumbling. "Are you compensated for the meals you make?"

She waves a dismissive hand and lowers her voice to a whisper. "It's the least I can do for His Majesty. Very few fae know he lives here, and I understand why. He's a good soul, the king is. Doesn't want anyone else to suffer his curse."

I have a hard time considering *the king* and *good soul* in the same sentence, but I'll let her keep her opinion of him. It would serve little purpose to correct her and inform her that the king's misconstrued vanity is what keeps others away. "You are doing a great service, Bertha, but I would like to compensate you and ask that you prepare meals for the manor more regularly."

Her eyes widen, and she swats me playfully on the arm. A too-familiar gesture that has me suppressing a blush. "Has the king finally come to his senses?"

"Well, with me living here full time and the manor preparing to welcome human guests, we'll need proper food. Not just whatever it is the wolves eat."

She laughs. "You should see them trying to chew raw meat in their seelie forms. If you haven't yet learned, this lot is as stubborn as rocks."

"I can tell," I say, my lips lifting slightly at the corners. "Does that mean you'll accept the position? We can discuss salary—"

"Pay whatever is fair. I make do as it is. In fact, ever since I started coming around here, I often find quartz chips in my apron pocket by the time I get home to my cabin." She gives me a conspiratorial wink. At first, I think she's suggesting she commits theft while she's here, but the warmth of her expression tells another story. She nods, patting her apron pocket. "He's a good soul, His Majesty."

Words are momentarily stripped from my lips. So...he *does* pay her. But why do it in secret?

"I imagine you'll be wanting dinner tonight, Miss Bellefleur," she says, pulling me from my thoughts. She takes a step back and begins untying her apron. "I'll go to town and pick up what I need."

Remembering the envelope clenched in my fingers, I hold it out to her. Dread sinks my gut as the letter trembles in my hand. It takes me a moment to find my voice. "Will you deliver this on your way to the market square?"

She takes it from me, glancing at the address before placing it in the pocket of her dress. "Of course, dear. Anything else?"

All I can do is shake my head, eyes locked on her pocket, breaths shallow. This is it. As soon as she takes that letter to my father, he'll know. He'll know I'm employed, he'll know I've gone against his wishes, and things between us will be forever changed.

Changed for the better, I remind myself.

"Very well," Bertha says. "I'll be back shortly and have dinner ready by nightfall." Too soon, she exits the parlor, taking the letter with her. Sealing my fate.

Left alone with nothing but the sound of my beating heart, my dread lifts and drifts away like clouds on a windy day.

It is done.

Another step toward freedom.

15

Hunched over a stack of ledgers at the bureau, I take my dinner alone in the parlor, alternating between bringing spoonfuls of stew to my mouth and flipping pages. Bertha's rabbit stew is by far one of the most satisfying meals I've ever had. Or perhaps it's simply from how tired I feel, and how hungry I am after such a strange and eventful day. Even though I started my morning hoping I'd be employed by nightfall, nothing could have prepared me for all that I experienced in between.

By the time I finish my bowl, I've already gone through the most recent ledger three times, disappointed by what little detail has been recorded. The first page bears nothing more than a scribbled summary of deposits regularly made to the royal treasury, ending in an outrageously large sum—one I can only imagine came from the deal with my father's quartz mine. The next several pages are tallies of quartz spent, which hasn't been much. In contrast, the older ledgers—which must have come from when the king had a palace—are far more detailed with numerous lavish expenses recorded. Furnishings. Wine. Servants. Parties. Musicians and entertainment. It seems the king wasn't exaggerating when he said he likes to spend his wealth when he's a wolf. It's strange to imagine wolves having parties, palaces, and servants at all. Surely his musicians and entertainers were nothing like anything I've seen. A howling quartet, perhaps? A four-legged cotillion?

I snort a short laugh, then push the ledgers aside and take out a piece of paper on which I list every room that must be made presentable and the furnishings required for each. Just like our townhouse in Bretton, we need not drape the entire manor in luxury. A few key areas will do —the parlor, the dining room, the front hall, the grounds leading to the manor, the front walk, and the back gardens. Everything else can be cleaned and cared for at leisure.

On another piece of paper, I draft a list of positions that need to be filled, both daily and for special occasions. I already anticipate that the king will need to host at least one luxe occasion—a dinner, perhaps—to secure his standing in Imogen's mind. For that, we'll need a convincing staff of human servants who are experienced with serving during such occasions. For everything else, the king's current household will do.

"Oh, you're still here," comes the king's gruff voice.

I turn and find him hovering in the doorway. "I can leave," I say, preparing to rise from my chair at the bureau.

He waves a dismissive hand and makes his way to his chair by the fire. Hunched to the side, he rests his head on his fist like I saw him do in the chair in my room. A lock of tangled hair falls over his eyes, but he doesn't bother pushing it away as he glares at the flames roaring in the hearth.

Looking at him sitting like this, seeming so old, so worn, I can't help but think...is this plan madness? Is there anything in the world that can make this creature desirable to Imogen Coleman?

His throne, I remind myself. He doesn't have to be handsome, gentle, or kind, so long as he has a kingdom and money. Imogen will be satisfied with that, I know it. But will it be enough to convince her to sacrifice her greatest treasure and break his curse?

I shake my head. That's not for me to worry about right now. Besides, even if my great scheme proves fruitless and the king's curse remains unbroken, I have every intention of benefitting from this arrangement whether he lives or dies.

Speaking of...

I put my list aside and return to the ledgers. Then I make a tally estimating the cost to complete my proposed renovations, purchase the king a decent wardrobe, and hire staff. The sum is nothing better than a guess, and yet even if I were to double it, triple it, it would hardly put a dent in the king's wealth. I clench my jaw, wishing I'd demanded higher compensation from our bargain. How could he have dared complain about twenty thousand quartz rounds when he has a fortune in the millions?

I shake my head and hazard a glance at the king's chair. My heart leaps into my throat as I find his eyes locked on me, and he doesn't even flinch when I meet them. Heat burns my cheeks, my pulse roaring as I slam the ledger shut. "You really shouldn't stare at a woman like that."

He blinks a few times. "I wasn't staring."

"You were."

Averting his gaze, he returns to face the fire. "Oh, and how should I look at a woman then?"

"Not like they're prey." I breathe deeply to steady my nerves and slow my pulse. "I'd say you'd scare dear Imogen off, but she is neither dear nor easily unsettled by the attention of men. She might find your inspection thrilling, but I do not. It's very...canine of you."

He shifts in his seat, muttering beneath his breath. "Freezing woman. I wasn't watching you like you were prey."

Recovering my composure, I say, "There are two ways I suggest you look at a woman from this point on, and it depends on how you'd like your persona to come across."

"My persona?"

"Yes. Think of it like a mask you must wear. In the same way you pretended to rescue me and then feigned injury, you'll need to pretend to be a gentleman around Miss Coleman. And to do it convincingly, you should craft a persona. The way you wish to be perceived by her."

"Like a glamour?"

I'm taken aback for a moment. I've heard about fae glamours but never considered if they were real. "I suppose it's like a glamour. I imagine without your magic, you aren't able to produce one?"

He shakes his head. "I cannot."

My curiosity begs me to ask what a glamour is like, how one is created, what uses it has. But the mournful expression on the king's face has me returning quickly to our prior subject. "For your outer persona, the two options I suggest you adopt are either the rogue or the stoic gentleman."

"What the freezing hell is a rogue?"

"It's...well..." I pause, thinking back to my favorite novels. *The Governess and the Rake* comes to mind. "It's a man who is a bit brash, bold, and charming. A little rough around the edges in terms of manners. He can be quite forward in his attentions and pushes the boundaries of propriety. This, I think, will naturally suit you in many ways. However, a rogue requires witty banter, flirtation, and charming conversation—"

He turns in his chair to face me. "Are you suggesting I'm witless and without charm?"

I blush, realizing my insult too late. I know I should apologize, but the indignation in his tone has me wanting to laugh instead. Sealing my smile behind pursed lips, I shake my head. "I'm suggesting no such thing, only that... I imagine you may not enjoy using your charm on a...*disgusting human*."

He straightens his posture. "I'll have you know I'm a great actor."

"I saw," I say, tone flat. "Anyhow, I also suggest you consider the stoic gentleman. He has the benefit of being quiet and aloof, speaking only when he chooses and coming across as confident and out-of-reach. Imogen will love the challenge of winning over such a man, and you will be able to...well, continue to do what you do."

"And what is it I do?"

"Well, a moment ago you were brooding silently at the fire, which is suitable for the stoic gentleman.

However, you must maintain better poise when in the company of our target. And you must behave with far more propriety to pull it off."

He rolls his eyes and turns back to the fire. "Propriety, my freezing foot."

I leave my seat at the bureau and approach his chair with slow, hesitant steps, careful to keep my voice steady as I say, "You'll need a haircut and new clothes too."

He all but leaps from his chair, rising on his staff to face me. "You cannot take my hair."

I pause, folding my hands at my waist. "If we are to present you as the desirable Unseelie King of Winter to a human prospect, you must look the part."

He takes a step forward, eyes wide with something akin to...fear. "You will not present me as the Unseelie King of Winter. You will present me as no king at all!"

"That wasn't part of the bargain."

"Well, it is now. I will have your promise or be done with you. No one will know I am the king."

"My entire scheme hinges upon you wooing her as a king."

He shakes his head. "I forbid it."

"Why?"

"I don't want anyone—neither human nor fae—knowing where to find me. I told you before, not many fae know about my curse, and humans are kept completely ignorant. They know they have an unseelie king, but not who I am, and the curse keeps them from thinking of me too long. This suits me well, for the unseelie ruler isn't required to interact with humans unless they choose to. That's how I want it to stay. I want no petitions coming my way, no human artisans seeking me as their patron, no fae begging for a place in my household. No...no one shall see that this...that this..." He purses his lips, leaving the remainder unsaid. It isn't hard to guess the rest, for it's written all over his face. *That this is what I've been reduced to.*

This puts a huge wrench in my plans, but I can't say I don't understand. I know what it's like to try and keep others at arm's length, keep them from knowing who I truly am. Who I truly was. It does spark a question, though. "If the curse makes you easy to forget, how is it I haven't forgotten you?"

He waves a dismissive hand. "You know about the curse now. It's the same with the fae. Those who know about it are less inclined to forget me, although my name is lost to all regardless. Can't you see how detrimental that could be? If too many people learn about my identity, my curse, my location...I'll lose all sense of privacy."

"Very well," I say with a sigh. "However, this only makes the need to make you presentable far more important. I'm sorry, but your hair must be tamed."

"But...it's all that keeps me warm." He brings a hand to the tangled golden-brown tresses. "I have no fur on this despicable body."

"That's what clothes are for. When I have your new wardrobe made, I'll make sure it's warm."

He mutters a string of curses under his breath. "Remind me why I'm letting a human girl make demands of me?"

I square my shoulders. "Because we made a bargain and I'm basically your last hope."

"If this scheme of yours doesn't work, I'll have your head."

I ignore that, keeping to myself the fact that if this doesn't work, he'll be dead. "Trust me. I know what I'm doing. Besides, if this doesn't work, I don't get paid."

Silence falls between us, and I'm about to return to the bureau when he says, "What will you do with the money? When the curse is broken and I hand over twenty thousand quartz rounds, what do you plan to do with it?"

I consider lying for a moment but settle on the simple truth. "I want to go home."

He furrows his brow. "Home?"

"To where I lived as a child. Isola. It's a warm and beautiful country, one I was forced to leave when...when my mother died. The money will help me buy passage out of Faerwyvae and perhaps purchase property in Isola."

"What will you do there?"

"Have a farm, like the one I lived on when I was little. Perhaps raise horses."

"Will you take your father? This Richard Bellefleur you so greedily stopped me from trying to con?"

My fingers clench into fists at the mention of my father. "No. He is the reason I seek financial independence. I will go to Isola alone."

He studies me, eyes boring into mine as if he seeks to see straight through them and into my thoughts.

I give him a pointed look. "This is what I mean about staring."

He throws an arm in the air and turns around. "Infernal human."

"No, it's good practice," I say gently. "Here, let me explain how to amend the situation next time."

Grinding his teeth, he turns back to face me. "Amend the situation," he mocks under his breath.

"If you're caught staring by a woman, or you find your gaze locking with someone for longer than, say, three seconds, you have two options. If you play the stoic gentleman, you must turn away at once. Show no embarrassment, but you may allow yourself to seem affected, disconcerted for merely a beat. As if you'd been captivated by her beauty but must turn away, lest your stare burn her. Then go about your business. You know, back to brooding and such."

He shakes his head. "This is stupid."

"The second option is the rogue. When the rogue stares at a woman, he need not look away at once, but he must turn the stare into something else. Not a bashful smile, but a devious hint that you know you've been caught staring and you like it."

"What is this devious hint supposed to look like?"

I shrug. "A subtle smirk, perhaps. It must be convincing, though. It can't look like a sneer and it must not be so obvious that everyone around you catches it too."

"Well, isn't that just simple as a snowflake," he says, tone heavy with sarcasm.

"It's probably not at hard as you think."

"If you're so smart, why don't you show me yourself?"

I open my mouth, feeling heat rise to my cheeks. "Well, I've never played the rogue before."

"Surely, you've been played by one, at least."

The statement strikes me like a blow to the chest. His words were said with no malice, no scorn. It was likely nothing more than a clever turn of phrase, but it is painfully true. Played by a rogue indeed.

He must sense my shift in mood, for he lowers his voice, tone gentle. "What I mean is you must have seen this smirk in action before. I want to see it."

I breathe away the memories that threaten to invade this moment, lock them back where they belong in the recesses of my mind. "Oh, fine," I say. "Now, look away for a few seconds. When you meet my gaze, watch what I do."

He does as told, rolling his eyes as he turns around, then slowly finds my gaze again.

When our eyes meet, I allow them to lock. *One, two, three.* Then, letting just a corner of my mouth lift, I slowly turn my head, breaking eye contact at the last second possible. I look around the room, then drop the act and return to face him. "See?"

His expression is blank, eyes fixated on my lips. Then they slowly rise to meet mine, and once again, he holds my gaze for far too long. I lift my brows as a silent cue, and he sighs. Quirking his mouth in something that looks closer to a snarl than a smirk, he breaks eye contact and looks away.

I'm forced to hide my laughter behind a cough. "It needs practice, but you got my hint at least. For now, I suggest you play the stoic gentleman and simply look away."

"Care to leave my parlor yet?" he says through his teeth.

"I will take my leave," I say. "But first, I want to call you something other than Your Majesty."

"Your Majesty will do. Goodnight."

"Come, now. If I am to hide from Imogen that you're the king, I can't introduce you as such. You need a proper name. One that makes you sound like a refined gentleman."

"I have a name."

"But you do not remember it."

He stalks toward the hearth, pacing before it, brow wrinkled. "I've tried so hard to recall it. Sometimes I think it's there, right on the edge of my mind. I can almost hear it ringing in my ears. Something like... Floyd...Farris...Varis...Elvis..."

I bark a laugh. "Elvis?"

He growls and shakes his head. "Freeze off."

"I'm sorry," I say, smothering my laughter. "Can I give you a name then?"

"I doubt you'll take no for an answer."

"That's true." I take a few steps closer, squinting at him while I try to find a name that matches his face. Not the wild mane of hair or frizzy beard, but the man beneath all that. The one with wine-colored eyes who likes to brood by the fire. "Elliot Rochester," I finally say.

"What kind of name is that?"

"Rochester is the name of my favorite brooding hero from one of my most beloved novels, *The Governess and the Cursed Palace*. And Elliot...well, Elliot just seems to suit you."

He shuffles over to his chair and returns to his seat with a huff. "Fine."

I cross the parlor and stop at the door, looking back at him as he drapes a blanket over his lap and pulls his chair closer to the fire. With the memory of laughter still tingling my lips, I can't help but think perhaps the wolf king isn't the worst after all. Maybe he does have a chance at wooing Imogen Coleman. "Goodnight, Elliot Rochester."

"It's Your Majesty," he grumbles. But as I enter the hall, I'm almost positive I hear him mutter, "Goodnight, Gemma Bellefleur."

16

All sense of ease, triumph, and hope I may have felt last night disappears as soon as the sun rises. I wake with a start, bolting upright in my new bed and my new room with nothing but dread filling every inch of my being.

I know what must be done. It is my own scheme that makes me do it. And yet, the thought of returning to town makes my knees quake.

Throwing off my covers, I force myself out of bed. My bare feet meet the chilly flagstones, and I make a mental note to add several rugs to my list of essential purchases for the manor. I cast a glance at the hearth, finding it has cooled to embers overnight. When I returned from the parlor last night, I was surprised to find a fire had been made and my bedding changed. My sodden boots had been left by the fire and my wet clothes taken away, hopefully to be washed. Even though I've yet to appoint anyone but the cook to an official position, it seems someone has started taking initiative.

I wrinkle my brow at my boots. They are likely dry and warm from being left by the fire, but my feet still ache from running in them yesterday. Thinking better of it, I turn to the wardrobe instead. Last night, I inspected the bottom drawer and found some nightdresses and thick hose, which I now wear. This time, I rifle through the drawer above it and retrieve a pair of wool gloves, a fur capelet, and a soft, close-fitting, fur-trimmed hat. The fur on both the capelet and hat is a rich brown, softer than any fur I've ever felt before. I must admit, the king's ambassador has excellent taste.

Setting aside my new findings, I open the wardrobe and investigate the shelf above the dresses. There I find three pairs of boots. All are far more durable than mine are, made from supple black leather and lined with fur. The soles are wide and textured for traction. I try one on, doubting they'll fit, but I find they are close enough. The ambassador, it seems, has long narrow feet, making them just slightly too long for me. I fetch a second pair of hose from the drawer, which will hopefully help me fill the extra space in the boots, and then take out the same dark green dress and gray cloak I wore yesterday. As I pull the dress over my head, I feel a rush of panic at the thought that my unusual style of clothing could draw even more attention than I like. Luckily, the cloak will cover most of the dress, leaving nothing but the hem of my skirt visible. The capelet, hat, and gloves are modern enough.

Fully dressed and feeling much like an armored soldier ready for war, I do what I do every time I prepare to leave home and enter town—I go to the window. Unlike my view from the townhouse, here I see nothing but mountains and trees. All at once, my anxiety dissolves beneath my awe as I take in the frosted treetops, the gently falling snow, the pale sky brightening beneath the rising sun. Then, just like yesterday, my attention snags on something in the garden.

There, in the same small courtyard I saw him in yesterday, sits the king—my newly named Elliot Rochester. This time, I know it's him, for that hunched posture and unruly mane of hair can no longer be mistaken for anyone else. I peer closer, studying the hang of his head, the slump of his shoulders. His fingers clasp something small and red.

A rose petal.

My mouth feels suddenly dry; seeing him in the garden holds a whole new significance that was not there yesterday. Because today I know the truth—that he holds not a simple petal, but a *day*. Another day ticked off his life. Another day closer to the curse coming to claim him.

It's enough to draw a lump rising to my throat, but I swallow it down. I have enough of my own to worry about.

He turns his head, and in yet another echo of the day before, he seems to be looking right at me. This time, however, I don't dart away. He doesn't avert his gaze either, which doesn't surprise me; I doubt last night's lesson has yet to sink in. So I hold up my hand and offer him a curt wave. He slowly straightens his shoulders, lifts his head a little higher. Then returns the gesture.

Under my breath, I say, "Time for phase one."

∾

THE MORNING IS STILL EARLY BY THE TIME I REACH THE market square, making the sidewalks easy enough to navigate. Luckily, I've yet to be intercepted by anyone I know. However, I'll need to speak to at least one undesirable person before my visit in Vernon is done, but I can't stand to think of that just yet. There's another meeting I'm determined to orchestrate first.

As I near the bookshop, I can almost smell the paper calling to me, hear the books whispering my name. My heart yearns to answer. The pain of turning away from the shop and crossing the street instead feels like the deepest betrayal. But I didn't come to Vernon for books.

Stopping outside the unfinished Verity Hotel, I take a deep breath. I have no clue if this part of my plan will prove successful, but I must try. Wrapping my false persona tightly around me, I open the door and enter. Sounds of hammers immediately fall upon my ears, the ground beneath my feet coated in sawdust and debris. I knew the hotel was unfinished, but I hadn't expected it to be in this much disarray. From the outside, it looks nearly done.

I follow the sounds of construction but see no sign of anyone. "Hello," I call out. "I need to speak with someone." The pounding of hammers is my only answer, so I continue to follow the sounds. Finally, I step into a wide-open space where the work is amplified to a roar. Every inch of the towering perimeter is lined with scaffolding from floor to ceiling, crawling with bodies busy at work. Some are painting while others are finishing trim on elegant walls. Orbs of blue light flutter about, brightening the space and illuminating certain areas for the workers.

My mouth falls open. Those orbs of light...are they... fae creatures?

I've heard of wisps but have never seen them before. Never would I have imagined seeing them working alongside—

"What are you doing here?" I whirl to face the source of the female voice and find a woman with copper hair— the same one Imogen and I saw two days ago. Her vibrant green eyes bore into me, her brow furrowed. "This isn't a public construction site. You must leave."

She reaches for my arm, but I step back, lifting my chin and squaring my shoulders. "I came to speak with someone."

"Do you have an appointment?" she asks, not unkindly.

"No, but I come on behalf of my employer, who is someone of great importance."

She quirks a brow. "Who is your employer?"

I consider my words, wishing the king wasn't so adamant I keep his identity a secret. Still, he never said I had to pretend he was inconsequential. "My employer is a fae royal. I am not at liberty to discuss his identity with you, only to follow his orders. And for that, I must speak with the fae in charge of this hotel's design."

She narrows her eyes and says nothing as she studies me from head to toe. In turn, I do the same. It's then I notice she's wearing the same chartreuse coat as before. Up close, the brocade looks even more elegant than it did from afar, with turquoise skirts of shimmering silk peeking from beneath the bottom hem. Unlike most of the women in town, she wears her hair long and loose like wild copper waves. She may look human, with rounded ears and average stature, but she certainly doesn't style herself like one.

"Who are you?" A fae male comes up behind the copper-haired woman, squinting at me while he rubs the lenses of horn-rimmed spectacles on his burgundy silk cravat. He's perhaps an inch or two shorter than I am with dark hair and a stout build. I recognize him as the fae I'm looking for, the one Imogen had referred to as the hotel's interior designer.

"I've come to speak with you on behalf of my employer."

He replaces his spectacles. "Ugh, let's get away from this infernal racket. My ears are about to melt off my head." Turning on his heel, he stalks off in the direction I came from, and the woman follows after. I make haste to catch up as they weave back into the main foyer then down a hall at the other side. Here, construction appears complete, with plush carpet, intricately painted walls, and elegant light fixtures. The hall opens to a modestly sized room with several round tables and chairs. This must be the dining room.

The woman and the fae head for a table laden with tea and pastries. The fae sinks into a chair, sulking into the backrest. The woman takes the seat next to him and pours a cup of tea.

I stand before them, trying not to feel flustered by their lack of care over my presence. Folding my hands at my waist to keep from fidgeting, I address the fae male. "Are you the interior designer of this hotel?"

He reaches for a decanter of something in a deep violet and pours it into an empty porcelain teacup. From the smell, I imagine it must be wine. This early? He brings the cup to his lips and takes a dainty sip. "I am, but you wouldn't know it by the lack of respect I'm shown around here. Can you believe the decor I've purchased for the ballroom has been denied *again*? They said they didn't want the ballroom to look too fae. Something about propriety and not wanting to stir carnal desires and whatnot. What does that even mean? So I gave them what they wanted. A very human ballroom."

The woman laughs. "Believe it or not, *very human* doesn't equate to doilies lining every surface, Foxglove."

His mouth falls open in mock offense. "Humans love doilies, Amelie. You should know."

"I promise you, they don't love them nearly as much as you think," says the woman named Amelie. She faces me, lips pulled into a smile. "Even after twenty years on the job, Foxglove here hasn't quite mastered the difference between *human* and *hoarder-of-hideous-things* when it comes to decor. To him, they are one and the same. You should see the parlor he made for my sister."

"Evelyn has always loved her parlor! So much so, she asked me to replicate it when she and Aspen moved to Maplehearth palace."

Amelie covers her mouth, nearly spitting tea. "She asked you to replicate it because it's funny."

He huffs. "I fail to see the difference between my artistic interpretation of a human parlor and an actual one."

She leans forward and pats his hand. "Which is why you should listen to me next time. Is that not why you brought me along? For my artistic eye and human sensibilities?"

I clear my throat, reminding them I'm still here. It doesn't do the trick.

"I've had about enough of human sensibilities," Foxglove says. "I swear, this town is probably the stuffiest I've ever had the horror to work in. I'm supposed to design a ballroom that is neither too human nor too fae. And heaven forbid it inspire carnal desires. What else is a ball to do? Better yet, what am I to do with the furnishings the board has rejected *again*?"

"It is a shame," Amelie says. "The furnishing themselves weren't bad. Just the presentation. If you hadn't covered everything in doilies, pocket watches, and rugs, it would have been fine."

My pulse races at their words, and I rush to speak before they can continue to ignore me a second longer. "Mr. Foxglove, I came to speak to you about your services, and they may benefit your situation. My employer would like to...spruce up his vacation manor, and we will gladly take whatever furnishings you can provide, so long as they are fashionable and in good condition. We may also need minor renovations. We will compensate you handsomely, of course. In addition, we require discretion and will pay for that as well."

Foxglove looks me over as if seeing me for the first time. "Discretion? Who is your employer?"

"He's a fae royal, but he prefers to avoid undue attention to his title," I say. "As he will be entertaining human guests, he must have suitable decor as soon as possible. Is there any chance we can steal you away from your work here? Just for a time. A consultation at the very least."

He ponders for a moment, then takes a sip of tea. "I suppose I could take leave while we await the next shipment of furniture. The ballroom is all that's left to furnish."

A flush of excitement washes over me, radiating down to my hands. They tremble as I pull a folded card from the pocket of my cloak and hand it to the fae.

"Thirty-three Whitespruce Lane," he reads, taking the card from me.

"Please call on us as soon as you can. We'd like to have the manor improved at once."

He nods and tucks the paper into his coat. "Very well. Any other demands on my time, tall human?"

"Well...while I'm here," I say, "there's another service I'd like to secure that requires some discretion as well. Is there anyone you would recommend to fit my employer for a new wardrobe? And perhaps a trusted barber willing to travel to perform a haircut and shave?"

"Hair is a little beneath me these days," Foxglove says, bringing a hand to his chest. Then his expression turns wistful. "But I do miss it from time to time. I'll see what kind of magic I can work on your employer."

Little does he know, it will certainly take magic to turn the grizzled king into the Elliot Rochester he needs to become, but I keep that part to myself. "As for his wardrobe?"

Foxglove shakes his head, but Amelie leans forward and lights her hand on my forearm. With a wink, she says, "I'll take care of his clothes. It's sort of my specialty."

My relief at securing my first task is all that keeps my legs from feeling like lead as I drag myself to my next destination. The nearer I get, the more my stomach begins to churn. I can't believe I'm *choosing* to call upon Imogen Coleman.

Think about the money and the freedom, I remind myself. There's something else I look forward to lurking beneath that, something I hardly dare to admit. *Think about the look on her face when she realizes she's been duped.*

I arrive at the door to the townhouse and knock, my carefully curated outer persona firmly in place. A maid answers and invites me inside. I barely take two steps before Imogen all but tumbles down the stairs, eyes wide when they meet mine. She looks me over, then rushes to take my hands.

"Tell me it isn't true," she says, voice low.

"What isn't true?"

Cheeks tinged pink, she looks like she's on the verge of exploding. "I called upon you this morning and you weren't home. Your sister, however, informed me of the most distressing news."

My heart leaps into my throat. That means Father and Nina received my letter.

Imogen squeezes my hands tight in her grasp. "Tell me you did not get a *job*." The last word is said with so much disgust, one would think she was talking about murder.

"I did—"

Before I can say another word, she pulls me toward the stairs, one hand still clenched around mine. I snatch my fingers away and follow her at a more moderate pace. She reaches the top landing and begins to tap her foot while she waits for me to meet her there. With every step I climb, I relish her annoyance.

"My dear Gemma, I am so upset with you I can hardly find the words," she mutters once I reach her. She then leads me to the door I recognize as belonging to their parlor. Strains of piano music float from the other side, a sound so peaceful and elegant, it momentarily roots me to the spot. Imogen, far less moved by the melody, throws open the doors and stalks into the parlor. "Enough, Ember."

The music halts abruptly, and I enter the room, finding her stepsister, Ember, rising from the pianoforte. Like the first time I saw her, she wears a large bonnet that almost obscures her face. She offers me a smile, which I return behind Imogen's back.

"Go away," Imogen barks at Ember. "You too, Clara."

Another girl, one I've only met once or twice, sits up from where she'd previously been lying on one of the couches. Nearly identical to Imogen with her blonde curls and pouty face, Clara whines, "I was here first. Besides, I have a headache."

Imogen strides up to her sister, hands on her hips. "It should be better now that Ember's racket has been cut off. Now, get out so I can speak to darling Gemma alone."

With a huff, Clara stands and drags her feet to the door, giving me not even a moment's glance.

As soon as the door is closed, Imogen rounds on me. "I cannot stand the suspense. Come and explain this nonsense at once, for I feel I might faint." Eyes unfocused, she takes her sister's place, lowering onto the couch and patting the seat next to her.

I ignore the gesture and claim the chair across the table instead. "It is as you already know. I've accepted a job."

She stifles a cry of alarm, bringing a hand to her lips. "Gemma, you cannot. Have you any idea how this looks? No man wants a wife who works outside the home. It makes you seem...poor."

So many arguments spring to my lips, but I crush them with a false smile. I know where my justifications will get me with Imogen. Bloody nowhere. Which means it's time for me to take the lead. Leaning forward, I prepare my lies behind a mask of apology. "Imogen, I know how distressing this must be for you. Seeing me employed wasn't part of your designs for my happiness, and I know my father tasked you with finding me a husband. But I'm not sure anyone could have refused the job I was offered."

"How so?"

"It's just...my employer. He's not a person one can say no to."

She scoffs. "It's easy enough when one is rich like you are. What use could you possibly have for a job?"

There's no answer I can give her that will make her understand, so I'm left with but one thing to say. Lowering my voice, I infuse my tone with a conspiratorial air. "Imogen, dear, why did you never tell me a fae royal lives in Vernon?"

She pales, mouth falling open. "Excuse me?"

"Well, technically, he lives just outside of town. You've met him, though, haven't you?"

Her face flashes between shock and irritation. I can only imagine how incensed she is that I appear to know something she does not. "A fae royal, you say?"

"Yes, and such a refined fae gentleman, at that. I thought for sure you would have met him, considering you are such a popular young lady in town. Then again, perhaps he has yet to make any acquaintances in Vernon. He has just taken up residence here. It's his vacation home that's nearby, and I have been tasked with managing it."

Eyes wide, she shakes her head in disbelief. "He can't be a royal. I refuse to believe it. What is he, some minor nephew of a lesser prince?"

"He is far higher than that, although I've been sworn to discretion regarding his title. But I promise you, your head would spin if you knew just how royal he is."

"I still don't believe you. How did you receive such an offer to begin with?"

"Oh, I saw an interesting ad in the paper." When I see her opening her mouth to continue a similar line of questioning, I add, "Can you keep a secret?"

Snapping her lips tight, she scoots to the edge of the

couch cushion, leaning so far forward I fear she might take a spill to the ground. "Tell me at once, Gemma."

I lower my voice further. "My employer is in want of a wife."

Her expression hardens and a flash of rage sparks in her eyes. Her tone turns cruel, cold. "Oh, and let me guess? That's the real reason you've accepted this job. You're hoping to scheme your way into his bed chamber, then secure a royal husband. You think you're clever, but royals don't marry their servants."

My fingers ache, begging me to curl them into fists, to twist my lips into a sneer. Instead, I plaster on an innocent smile. "Oh, no, you mistake me. I am not asking you to keep this secret on my behalf, but for my employer. That is why he's asked me to be discreet. He wants someone to love him, not for his money and his title, but for himself. And I fear if word gets out that such a wealthy and refined fae royal is seeking matrimony, he'll be inundated with callers and he'll never be able to find true love. And he must find love quickly. He is to be married in three months' time."

All suspicion and scorn dissolve from her face, replaced with hunger. "Three months? Why so soon?"

"Isn't it just as you've told me before? A man with a mind to marry has no time to waste. A woman in search of his heart must act with haste."

"And you honestly don't plan on trying to claim him for yourself?"

I place a hand on my chest. "Saints, no. I assure you, my employer has no desire to make me his wife, and we've already agreed our relationship is strictly business. Like you said, royals don't marry their employees. I am out of the question." I pause, releasing a wistful sigh. "But I do feel like I should help him. If only I could find the right person for him without inviting the attention of every woman in Vernon. It would make things so much easier."

Imogen's lips part, and I know the seed has been planted in her mind. She's all but salivating over the tempting morsel I've laid at her feet. Placing a hand on her heart, her voice comes out soft, controlled. "Oh, Gemma, you are a good soul. I believe you are right in what you hope to do for your employer. It would be cruel to unleash all the women of Vernon on him at once."

"I knew you'd agree with me."

"As his...whatever you are. His...manager?"

I nod. "I am his house steward."

"Well, as his steward, do you happen to have control over, say, his appointments? His trips to town?"

"Oh, he won't be coming to town. Any new acquaintances will be meeting him at his manor. And yes, I will have full knowledge of all appointments, and he has requested my aid in introducing him to the...*right* people."

She shifts in her seat, folding her trembling hands in her lap. "But my dear, you hardly know a soul. You cannot take this task upon yourself."

I pretend to look ponderous. "Perhaps you're right. I am very unfamiliar with the elite families in town. How will I suggest any proper acquaintances?"

Imogen sits upright, nearly bubbling over with poorly concealed excitement. "You are so fortunate to have me, for I am willing to help. Encourage your employer to befriend my family before anyone else, and we will act as ambassadors to Vernon's high society."

As gatekeepers, I'm sure she means. Just as planned. "That's a wonderful idea, Imogen. And, you never know, perhaps once he meets you, he'll have very little desire to engage with anyone else."

My words have their intended effect, sending stars to her eyes. "Wouldn't that be...ideal."

Interrupting what I'm sure are Imogen's daydreams of wedding bells, I rise from my chair. "I must be going. He's expecting me back at once."

She springs to her feet. "Won't you tell me his title? I promise I won't tell a soul."

I shake my head. "I'm sorry, but I am sworn to secrecy. But when you meet him, you'll see just how refined he is."

"And when will I meet him? Will he be hosting any dinners this week?"

"You'll be the first to find out when he does." With a wink, I walk toward the parlor door.

Imogen's steps shadow close behind. "At least tell me his name."

Fingers on the door handle, I turn back to her and smile. "Elliot Rochester."

She visibly swoons, cheeks flushing pink. "Oh, even his name sounds refined."

"Just wait until you meet him." Leaving her wriggling on the hook I've cast for her capture, I exit the parlor, laughter bubbling in my chest.

18

The walk back to thirty-three Whitespruce Lane isn't nearly as bad as the first time, considering I'm not being harassed by wolves. This time, my shoes have managed to stay warm and dry during my entire trek up the hill, although my cloak and skirt could use drying. And my stomach could definitely benefit from Bertha's rabbit stew, if she's made any today.

I make my way down the path that leads from White-spruce Lane to the manor. The view is new, considering I was originally brought to the manor blindfolded. While I had experienced the path from the other direction when I left this morning, this new perspective helps me see it from a visitor's eyes. From *Imogen's* eyes.

On each side of the path lie overgrown shrubs and brambles, which at least need to be trimmed back to allow the width of wagons, coaches, or even the occasional automobile. As I approach the manor, the more serious the landscaping needs become, with downed trees and branches littering the drive, unruly plants obscuring filthy windows, ivy climbing up the walls. It looks nothing like the home of a king. In fact, one look would have me assuming the property was vacant.

At least none would guess the truth—that it houses a pack of cursed fae wolves.

Still, I need this manor to scream *eligible-royal-to-marry*, not *keep out, no one is home*.

I make a mental tally of which landscaping tasks must be prioritized as I approach the front door and push it open. The hall is empty, the manor quiet, so I make my way to the parlor. I'm so lost in my calculations, I don't notice the king until I nearly trip over his staff.

I startle, backing up a few paces, and find Elliot sitting in his chair, facing the fire. "Sorry, Your Majesty. Or, should I say, Mr. Rochester. I wasn't paying attention."

"You had it right the first time," he grumbles.

"Perhaps," I say, making my way to the bureau, "but I should probably become more familiar with calling you Mr. Rochester so that I can address you properly when our first visitors come to call."

He stands, planting his staff beneath his arm, and faces me, brow furrowed. "I didn't expect you'd come back."

I'm about to take a seat at the desk but pause. "What do you mean? Why wouldn't I come back?"

"It's just..." He rubs his jaw. "Well, unlike me, you can come and go as you please. Why you'd choose to ever return once leaving this manor is beyond me."

"We have a bargain, and I'm guessing there are severe punishments should I choose not to fulfill it."

"Our bargain states I must provide room and board. It

doesn't enforce you to accept it. I thought perhaps going to town would shock some sense into you."

I shake my head and lower onto the chair. "All it did was remind me why I despise Vernon and everyone there. It was successful, however. I've made appointments with both an interior designer and a seamstress. They should be paying a visit tomorrow."

"Great," he mutters and returns to his seat.

I find my list of tasks and add my new ideas about the landscaping. Only once I've gotten everything out of my mind and on paper do I remember my conversation with Imogen. I shift in my seat to face Elliot's chair. "Oh, and I spoke with Miss Coleman today. The woman you're going to woo. She's quite intrigued by you."

He doesn't look at me, but I see him stiffen, fingers digging into the cloth of his armrests.

I leave the bureau and cross the room, claiming a chair at the other side of the hearth. Once seated, I study him over the small circular table that stands between us. His face seems to have gone a shade paler, eyes unfocused as he stares into the fire. "Are you nervous about meeting her?" I ask.

Slowly, he meets my gaze. This time, there's no predatory intensity but a hint of trepidation. His voice comes out small, quiet. "Will this...human of yours find me very repellant?"

Something in his tone tugs at my chest, but I remind myself his question comes not from vulnerability but vanity. "Trust me, you find the human form far uglier than we do. Once I have you dressed and cleaned, you'll be quite..." I pause, seeking the right word. "Presentable."

He averts his gaze. "I'm talking about...my leg."

My words are robbed from both my lips and my mind as his question takes on new meaning. It wasn't vanity after all. It was personal.

To be honest, I've already gotten used to the amputated leg, and there's nothing too repulsive about it. I met several esteemed gentlemen in Bretton who'd fought in wars past and wore their injuries like medals of honor. But Bretton is a country used to luxury and war in equal measure. Its king always seems to be battling with one kingdom or another. Here in Faerwyvae, though, where only two wars have ever touched its soil in thousands of years...

"I don't know," I confess, my stomach sinking. "While I think your wealth and status will be enough to sway Imogen's heart, it might be best to fit you with a prosthetic."

He looks at me and scoffs. "You mean one of those fake legs? I have one already. It was given to me early on in the curse by...well, I don't recall. I suppose that's one of the memories that's been claimed. But I do have one."

"You do? Why don't you wear it? Is it uncomfortable?"

He shrugs. "Comfort or no, why bother?"

I wave a hand at the staff cradled in his arm. "It might be easier than walking with that."

"Why should I let it be easier? As a wolf, I can manage having one less leg with very little inconvenience. I can stand, run, leap. Nothing is impossible. But this!" He gestures to his lower half. "Human mobility is a menace with only one leg to stand on."

"I don't understand why that should prevent you from trying to be as comfortable as possible."

"What's not to understand? Haven't I told you already? It's that...rouge on a pig thing."

I narrow my eyes at him. "Let me get this straight. You refuse to be comfortable because you don't think your human body is worth the effort?"

"I'll still be hideous," he growls. "A false leg will only draw attention to this repulsive form."

I rise to my feet and face him, hands on my hips. Torn between indignation and annoyance, I'm at a complete loss for words. I want to rage at him for thinking so rudely about human appearance, for criticizing my entire species based on his perception of how we look. Just as much, I want to correct the errors in his thinking, pull him from this frustrating stance he has about his own looks in particular.

"Your Majesty, I will say this one time and one time only, so listen up."

He leans back in his seat, eyes wide as he meets my furious gaze.

"You are not ugly," I say through my teeth. "You are annoying, smug, and irritating, and you may look like a deranged trapper who hasn't had a bath in a year, but you...*you*...are not ugly."

Silence falls between us, our eyes locked. Then finally, he returns his gaze to the fire. "Come, Miss Belle-fleur. Not even you believe your words. You're the one making me cut my hair."

I curl my fingers into fists, teetering between shouting and laughing. "I'm making you cut your hair because it's a mess. You clearly haven't taken care of it. Besides, your hair isn't *you*. Underneath that hair and beard, you have... tolerable features."

He quirks a brow, an amused grin tugging his lips. "Tolerable? What a compliment. What exactly are these tolerable features you claim to see?"

I fold my arms over my chest and burn him with a scowl. Then, keeping my voice neutral, I say, "Your eyes are an interesting color."

His garnet irises seem to respond, flashing with the light of the flames in the hearth. Slowly, he slides that gaze to me. "Interesting color, eh?"

I shrug. "It isn't a common color in humans. And your...well, your hair isn't completely awful. The color is nice. The way the dark brown melts into gold makes it look like it's been kissed by the sun. It needs to be tamed, yes, but I don't hate it."

"And my beard?" He scratches at the scruff on his chin.

"I don't love the beard, but...I think there's a decent jaw beneath it. You have strong cheekbones. Deep-set eyes and a heavy brow. It makes that rugged look seem not so bad. And your build." I turn my study to his broad shoulders, his wide chest. Beneath the stained linen of his shirt, I can just make out hints of a firm musculature. Further proof is written over his bare forearms, roped muscle exposed by the rolled-up sleeves of his shirt. Strangely, my pulse begins to quicken, and my next words come out somewhat breathless. "Your build is desirable."

He cocks his head, the corner of his mouth lifting into a smirk. "Desirable? That's a strong word."

I take a step away, turning slightly to the side as heat flushes my cheeks. "To most women," I amend. "Your build is desirable to *most women*."

"And do you consider yourself most women?" he asks

with a teasing, rumbling laugh, one that crawls up my spine and radiates down my arms like a caress. If I didn't know any better, I'd think he was a natural at playing the rogue after all. Is he practicing for Imogen...or has he always had this insufferable ability to unsettle a woman like this?

"I most certainly do not," I say and stride to the parlor door. "Unlike Imogen, I know the wolf beneath the façade and he's getting on my last nerve. Good day."

"If that's all it takes to get you out of my parlor, I'll be sure to get on your last nerve more often."

I pause, hand clenched on the doorframe, and look over my shoulder at the king. Clever retorts swarm in my mind, but as I watch him grinning at the hearth, I realize it's the first time I've seen such a smile from him. There's teasing in it, and it's no doubt at my expense, but there's something in his posture that wasn't there before. He sits taller now, straighter. The absence of his brooding slouch lends warmth to his expression. Whether he's taken my advice about adopting an outer persona, or if this new sense of comfort and confidence is genuine, it's not something I can bring myself to discourage.

Without a word, I slip quietly into the hall. As I make my way upstairs to my room, I can't help but note yet another thing I don't hate about Elliot Rochester.

I don't hate his smile. In fact, it isn't terrible at all.

19

T he next morning, I wake to pounding on my door, followed by frantic feet as Micah and three other children his age stream into my room. "Wagons," Micah says before I can ask what the commotion is all about. His eyes are bright, his grin stretching from ear to ear as he skips toward my bed.

I rub my eyes and sit up, meeting the gaze of the other children—two boys and a girl—standing behind Micah. None appear to have the same enthusiasm as Micah, each eying me with suspicion. "Good morning." My voice comes out with a tired croak. "Wagons, you say?"

His head bobs up and down. "Three of them! Full of furniture. And there's this fae wearing spectacles—"

"Foxglove is here already?" When I told the fae to come at his earliest convenience, I didn't expect it to be so soon. Or so early. I spring from my bed and rush to the wardrobe. "Tell him I'll be down at once."

At that, the children skip from my room and slam the door behind them.

Blinking sleep from my eyes, I make haste to get dressed, choosing another gown from the wardrobe and then splashing my face with water from the washbasin. I don't even bother pinning up my hair and simply brush it out to flow loose around my shoulders. If Amelie—the copper-haired seamstress—can get away with wearing her tresses long, then I don't see why I shouldn't. Especially considering the hurry I'm in.

By the time I make it downstairs and to the front hall, I find Foxglove and Elliot facing each other in an icy standoff.

"I was invited here by your steward, sir," Foxglove says with a scoff.

Elliot slams his staff onto the flagstones. "This damn early?"

Foxglove flourishes a hand. "I have another job in town. If you want my services, you'll accept them when I can offer them."

"I don't want—"

I step between the two and silence the king with a glare before turning to the other fae. "Foxglove, so good of you to come."

"Your employer doesn't seem to think so," the bespectacled fae says with a huff.

"My employer isn't used to welcoming newcomers into his manor," I say, then turn to the king with a withering look. "Since he'll be entertaining human guests soon, now is a good time to practice."

"Freezing woman," he mutters under his breath, then turns away to stalk down the hall.

I give Foxglove an exaggerated smile. "Sorry about him. He's not a morning person."

"He most certainly is not. Now, shall we get started?"

THE MORNING QUICKLY SPINS INTO A FLURRY OF ACTIVITY, starting with me giving Foxglove a tour of the necessary rooms and sharing all my ideas for renovations and improvements. Then Foxglove orders the wagons unloaded by some of the manor's residents, including Blackbeard and Gray, and soon the halls are cluttered with items being brought in or taken out.

Elliot is a grumbling, cursing mess when Amelie arrives to fit him for clothes. I send him off to fetch his prosthetic while I situate Amelie in my bedroom. Not daring to subject the woman or her elegant fabrics to the rooms that have yet to be cleaned, mine will have to do. Besides, being so far away from the chaos downstairs will hopefully give Elliot no reason to bite Amelie's head off.

"I'm sorry if my employer is a little rough around the edges," I say, keeping my voice quiet as I lay out an array of suit jackets she's brought while she organizes several swaths of colorful brocade on my dressing table. "Please ignore his crass manner if you can."

She smiles at me. "I'm used to dealing with the fae, Miss Bellefleur. I, myself, am a quarter fae and have been living closely amongst faekind for over twenty years now. Before that, I spent my youth and teen years ignorant of their strange ways, but now I'm used to them. Even the cranky ones."

I pause, my eyes widening. It hadn't occurred to me that the woman had any fae blood at all, much less that she could be older than perhaps twenty-two. But if she were both a youth and a teen before these twenty years she spent close to the fae...how old could she actually be? I've heard rumors that the magic of Faerwyvae has been known to extend human lifespan...but is it only her fae heritage that makes her look so young? Will *I* age slower now that I live here? I try to conceal my overwhelming awe by returning my attention to the jackets I'm supposed to be laying on the bed. "So, there are other fae like my employer?"

"Many, and some are even worse," she says and begins to unfold a dressing screen. "And not just to humans. Some fae can hardly stand to get along with each other. Conflict is often between rival courts, but sometimes it's even within the same household. How do you think the second fae war began? It started with a civil war amongst the fae, you know."

Considering her supposed age, I must take her word as truth, as she was likely alive for it. It leads me to recall what Elliot said about not everyone on the Alpha Council being his biggest fan. At first, the reason was obvious; how could *anyone* like the bristly wolf king? But now I wonder if royal tensions are more political than personal.

"Freezing woman," comes Elliot's voice from the hall outside my room. "Are you trying to make me look like a fool?"

Clenching my jaw, I take back my previous musings. Any royal tensions regarding the king would most *certainly* be personal. "You can do that all on your own, Mr. Rochester. And, if you recall, my name is Miss Belle-fleur, not *woman*."

Amelie looks over her shoulder from where she sets up the dressing screen and gives me an approving smile.

Finally, Elliot appears in my doorway, expression furious as he slowly limps into my room on two legs. "Must I wear this damn thing?"

I stifle a grin. "It's not nearly as bad as you think."

"It makes me walk like a lame animal," he says. "If I were a wolf, I'd be easy pickings for predators."

Amelie quirks a brow. "A wolf?"

"My employer's unseelie form is a wolf," I rush to say.

She takes a step away from the dressing screen to squint at the king. "A fae royal with a missing leg who can shift into a wolf."

Elliot glowers at her scrutiny. "What's it to you?"

She nods. "Ah. I think I know who you are. But why can't I remember your name? It certainly isn't Elliot Rochester..."

The king takes a step forward, brows pulled into a scowl. "Whatever you think you know, mind your own business."

I move to Amelie's side and place a hand on her arm. "Please say nothing. We're paying you for your discretion."

Unflustered, she shrugs. "It's no matter to me. The only reason I made the connection is because of my sister."

"Your sister?" Elliot echoes.

"Queen Evelyn of the Fire Court." She scoffs a laugh. "I stay out of politics, but I get the sense you weren't the best of friends."

He shakes his head. "I don't remember her."

Her eyes widen as she studies him with keen interest. Her words come out awed, quiet. "Is that so? What strange thing has befallen you?"

Elliot growls, and a flash of panic spurs me to speak. "Please ask no more questions."

She nods and the curiosity fades from her eyes. "Very well. It's like I said. I have little interest in politics these days. Your private matters are yours to keep."

My stomach unclenches as relief moves through me. She seems to have uncovered his identity but doesn't appear to know anything about the curse.

Amelie squints, tapping a finger to her chin. "It does tell me what I need to know though..."

My panic returns, speeding my pulse. "About what?"

She grins. "How refined I must make his clothing. Come, Mr. Rochester. My measuring tape awaits and I'm burning with ideas."

ELLIOT AND AMELIE DISAPPEAR BEHIND THE DRESSING screen. Hoping I can act as mediator to prevent any further tensions from arising, I remain in the room, handing articles of clothing over the top of the screen at Amelie's command. Luckily, Elliot seems to obey the seamstress' poking and prodding with nothing worse than halfhearted protests and muttered curses. After several changes of clothing, each one ending in Amelie's *no, no, absolutely not,* I hear her exclaim a hearty, "Yes! This is the right color, and the fit is nearly perfect."

Elliot groans. "I feel like a stuffed turkey, and I must look like a peacock."

Amelie steps out from behind the screen. "Peacocks are beautiful, Mr. Rochester. Now, let's see what Miss Bellefleur thinks."

At that, I rise from where I've been sitting on the bed and move closer to the screen.

For a moment, nothing happens. No footsteps, no grumbles. Then finally, a sigh. With slow, uneven steps, the king leaves his hiding place. I blink a few times, lips parting as I take in the transformation. Dressed in a smart, modern suit, he seems to have grown taller. His slim trousers are of the darkest green with a jacket to match. His waistcoat is gold brocade, and his emerald silk cravat seems to bring out the ruby tones in his eyes.

Amelie comes to stand at my side, assessing the king with a hand at her chin. "Yes, I will customize your new wardrobe with this look in mind." She faces me. "Don't you agree?"

With my eyes still locked on the king, all I can do is nod. "You're...you're amazing, Miss Amelie."

"It helps that my model cuts a nice figure all on his own," she says with a wink.

Elliot rolls his eyes.

"Oh my." I turn to find Foxglove entering the room, eyes roving the king from head to toe. "You've done the impossible, Amelie," he says.

"Are you done treating me like I'm on display? I'd like to change out of this ridiculous frock—"

"No!" Amelie says with horror. "Until I finish your wardrobe, you must wear this. I will not have you insulting my work by changing back into those rags."

"She's right," I say. "You must get used to refined clothing if you are to impress our future...guest." More than that, I just want to look at him in these clothes at least a while longer. Not because he's attractive. No, not that. I'm fully aware he's the same awful wolf I met over trickery and tomato sauce. The new look simply provides a more pleasant view than stained linen and dingy trousers.

Foxglove's lips pull into a grimace. "Ugh, but that hair. It most certainly won't do."

Elliot closes his eyes, teeth bared as he utters a string of curses.

Pounding footsteps draw my attention back to the door where Micah springs forth. "More wagons! A nice one."

"Oh, that might be the paintings," Foxglove says. "I should direct them where to put everything."

"Excuse me," Elliot says, "but this is my manor."

Foxglove puts a hand on his hip. "And what a nice manor it will be when I'm done. Now, Miss Bellefleur, please find someone to brush his hair so I can get started on it when I return. I can only work with a clean canvas." At that, he turns on his heel and follows Micah out the door.

Amelie beams a smile at me, eyes alight with excitement. "I need to grab the rest of my things from downstairs. I cannot proceed without more emerald spider silk."

I shudder at the thought of silk made from spiders but let her go without argument. Aware that I'm now alone in my room with the king, I take a step away and retrieve the brush from my dressing table. Gesturing toward the chair at the bureau, I say, "Sit. I'll try to brush out that mane of hair."

With a curse, he makes his way to the chair—his limp growing less and less pronounced—and sinks down onto it, arms crossed. "Remind me again why I'm doing this?"

I come up behind him and bring the brush to the ends of his hair. "Running on three legs. A body covered in white fur. Eating raw, freshly killed carcasses. You know...that which you value most?"

"Freedom," he says with a sigh. He turns his head to the side and eyes me from his periphery. "Meanwhile, you're torturing me for money."

I attack a particularly stubborn knot, half-afraid the brush will be swallowed by it at any moment. When my own hair falls into my face, I pause long enough to bundle it at the nape of my neck. I now regret not putting it up this morning, but with no pins in reach, it's held in place by nothing more than a prayer. Returning to my efforts, I say, "I'm doing this for freedom too, you know."

He scoffs. "Is that so?"

"It is. You were right when you told me humans keep their women as property. It's one of the most backward and suppressive human traits, in my opinion, and one I want nothing to do with."

"Money is supposed to help?"

I nod. "As an unmarried woman, I have no wealth of my own. And even if I were married, I'd have an allowance like I had from my father, but no wealth would be mine. Perhaps when he died, I could be a wealthy widow. Regardless, marriage is not in the cards for me."

"Why is that?"

I bite the inside of my cheek, my heart plummeting at the question. "I've...given up on love and matrimony. I've had my share of romance. Played the game of courtship. And...I lost."

He eyes me again from the side. "That's why you want to move to your childhood country alone?"

"Yes. I want independence. Freedom, just like you. I want to be free from my father's clutches and his designs for my future. I want to be free from needing to marry just to live a comfortable life. I want a life of my own on my terms."

"Is that your greatest treasure then?"

I pause my brushing. "It is," I whisper. "Which is why you can now understand why your tricks never would have worked on me. There's nothing in the world—no gratitude great enough—that could make me sacrifice my chance at freedom."

"Then in turn, you must see why I can't break the curse myself," Elliot says.

I recall what he told me about the first option to break it. *Of the four things I stand to lose, if I sacrifice the one I value most, I will be returned those which I value less.*

Elliot continues. "Sacrificing my wolf form means losing my freedom. There's nothing worth sacrificing for that. Not even if it means my life."

I return to brushing. "I do understand. We...understand each other. Which is why this alliance of ours will work. We both stand to lose on one side and gain at the other." That last part isn't entirely true, but I keep that to myself. For if my scheme fails and the curse remains unbroken, I cannot return to my old life, to my father. I must assure my success either way.

If the king dies, I'll still need those twenty thousand quartz rounds.

My heart sinks at that. I may not know him well, but I don't *want* the king to die. More than anything, I want this plan to work, for Imogen to break Elliot's curse and give us both the freedom we crave.

But if it fails...

I force the thoughts from my mind, redoubling my focus on his hair. That's more than enough to consume all my attention, for the brush seems to be doing very little to help. I consider giving up on the back and move to the front to assess if it's any better. Leaning forward, I lift a tangled lock from his forehead. "Saints, Elliot, have you ever once brushed your hair?"

"No. I never needed a brush as a wolf."

"But you groomed yourself in your own wolfy way, did you not?"

His frown tells me I'm right. "Yes," he bites out.

Rifling my fingers through his matted strands, I shake my head. "Damn it to hell, this is impossible. I might have to tell Foxglove to just cut it all off at the scalp. In fact..." I smooth his hair away from his forehead, then bend down closer to study how it looks. I squint, trying to imagine him with such a short style. It would be ideal if he could keep the top long while trimming the back to his nape so at least some of the sun-kissed gold at the bottom half remains. I lean to the side and gather the back of his hair, then assess him again. Cocking my head to the side, my haphazard updo tumbles loose over my shoulder. I release the king's hair, preparing to collect my own, when he leans slightly forward.

And inhales.

I freeze, caught off guard as he breathes in deeply, lips just inches from my neck. Then, like it had been the most normal thing in the world, he leans back in his chair.

My heart hammers in my chest as I struggle to compose myself. Straightening, I say, "What was that?"

"What was what?"

I give him a pointed look. "You can't go round smelling people like that."

His eyes take on a distant look. "Your hair smells like the wind. Mountains, snow, and trees."

A blush burns my cheeks, and I can only pray he doesn't notice. "Well, I was outside much of yesterday," I mutter. "But you must take better care next time. That isn't proper. Perhaps with Imogen...during courting...but with me...well, it's like I said about the staring."

His gaze slides to mine and there it locks, burning like the heat flooding my face. A corner of his mouth quirks into a smirk, but he doesn't avert his gaze the way I taught him.

"Damn it, Elliot." My voice comes out breathless. "You're doing it wrong."

For several moments, all I can hear is my raging heart, unable to look away as his gaze traps me like prey. Something moves inside me, but I can't identify it. Is it fear? Panic? No, neither of those. Excitement? My pulse speeds even faster at the thought. *No, it most certainly isn't that. Not over the wolf king.*

"Miss Bellefleur, that's hardly what I'd call brushed," Foxglove says from the door, freeing me from the king's gaze.

I slam the brush on the bureau and stalk away from Elliot, arms crossed. "I've given up. Shave it clean off if you must."

Elliot groans a protest, and I answer him with a glare.

"I'll do whatever I can," Foxglove says. "Oh, and by the way. The coach that arrived was not here for me after all. It brought humans and they refuse to leave."

My eyes go wide. "Who are they?"

"Some Richard Bellefleur," he says with a shrug. "A relation of yours, I presume."

The blood drains from my face, and my heart hammers for a whole new reason. "Shit," I say. "My father's here."

20

I t takes me several minutes to compose myself in the hall as I gather the nerve to meet my father. I've known in the back of my mind that I'd eventually need to confront him, but I hadn't been prepared to do it this soon. How did he even find me, anyway? When I sent Bertha with my letter informing him of my new employment, I gave no indication where said job was, only that I was being provided room and board and would not be returning to the townhouse.

Then it dawns on me.

Nina. My sister saw the address when I received the invitation for the interview. She warned me not to come here. Torn between feeling betrayed and guilty that I hadn't sent an additional letter just for her, I take a deep breath and force myself out the front door.

Once outside, the first thing I see is Gray and Blackbeard standing guard before the door, their stern expressions a silent threat barring entry to the manor. Both fae appear to have been gifted new clothes. Neither are outfitted as elegantly as the king, but their linen shirts are clean and their trousers well-fitting. They give me curt nods as I pass, but keep their gazes fixed ahead.

That's when I see Father pacing alongside the rows of wagons in the drive, his coach-and-four at the very end. His face is beet red, and upon seeing me, he halts his pacing, eyes bulging with rage. "What is the meaning of this, Gemma?"

I stop several feet before him and fold my hands at my waist. Lifting my chin, I wear not the mask of the dutiful daughter, but the one I don for the townspeople. Confident. Cold. Haughty. "If you got my letter, then surely you know exactly what the meaning of this is."

He bares his teeth for a moment, fingers curling into fists. "You have no right to send me a letter informing me you've taken a position of employment. I forbade you from seeking work the first time you brought it up."

"I'm eighteen," I say. "You cannot forbid me from taking a job."

"I can so long as you live beneath my roof."

"That's just it, Father. I no longer live beneath your roof, for my new position provides room, board, and ample salary. Your threats to disown, disinherit, and displace me will now fall on deaf ears, should you choose to repeat them."

"Was one scandal not enough?" he growls.

I narrow my eyes. "I fail to see how me gaining employment is worthy of the term *scandal*."

"It is when your employer is a stranger whom you take room and board from. Who is he?"

"How do you know my employer is a *he*?"

"Are you his mistress, hiding out at his country estate?

Is that what this is? Another case of the Viscount of Brekshire?"

The Viscount of Brekshire. The name crushes my chest, making my lungs feel too small, sending my head spinning. My mask falters.

"When will you learn, Gemma? You will ruin yourself once and for all if you keep throwing yourself at the feet of taken men."

I bite the inside of my cheek, seeking the sting of pain. Anything to free myself from the whirl of sound that beats at my mind, invades my senses.

Seductress.

Harlot.

He didn't belong to you.

Father takes a step closer, his voice a barbed whisper. "Get in the coach."

I close my eyes and breathe the memories away. When I open them, I form a word with all the strength and calm I can manage. Even so, it comes out with a tremor. "No."

He crosses the remaining distance between us, bringing his face inches from mine. Expression twisted with rage, he shouts, "Get in the coach!"

I clench my jaw. "No!"

At the same moment, Father lurches back, and in his place stands a towering Elliot, his hand locked on my father's shoulder. The king's voice comes out low, dangerous. "Are you harassing my steward?"

Father shrugs roughly from Elliot's grip, face crimson as he adjusts his jacket. His eyes fall on the king's pointed ears, and his lips pull into a sneer. "Who do you think you are to lay your hands on me, you filthy fae?"

Elliot takes a slow, swaggering step, shoulders rigid as he stares down at my father. "I'm the filthy fae who pays your salary, human."

Father's chest heaves as he stands his ground beneath the king's seething stare. Then, in a rush, the redness melts from his cheeks, eyes widening. "Who are you?"

Elliot's words come from between his teeth. "I will forgive you this once for not knowing the face of your king, for I am not here for recognition. In fact, if I hear word has gotten out that I am here at all, I'll know exactly who to punish. As king, I have a right to live where I please, seek discretion when I please, and employ whom I please, and that includes your daughter. Any questions?"

Father seems to shrink as he takes a step away. His voice comes out tremulous. "Your Majesty—"

"So long as my presence remains outside public knowledge, you will refer to me as Mr. Rochester."

"Mr. Rochester," he says in a rush, "might I ask what your intentions are with my daughter?"

"What the freezing fuck do you think?" Elliot puts his hands on his hips. "To pay her for her duties as my house steward. If you're suggesting—"

Father lifts his hands and retreats a few steps back. "No, Your Ma—Mr. Rochester. No. I meant nothing like that."

A low growl rumbles in Elliot's chest. "Get off my property at once."

Father nods and starts to turn around, pausing only to meet my gaze for a few tense seconds. Then, with a departing glare, he stomps down the drive toward his coach.

Elliot faces me, teeth bared in a snarl. "No wonder you seek freedom from that wretched human."

Taking in his face for the first time since he came to my rescue, I'm rendered mute. In the time I spent preparing to speak with my father, the king's beard has already been trimmed close to his jaw and his mane of hair pulled back from his face with a leather strap. While the job isn't nearly complete—in fact, upon further scrutiny, the beard trim is haphazard at best—I'm given my first look at the *decent jaw* I claimed to believe he has. Seeing the shape taking place beneath the grizzly hair, I must say his jaw is decent indeed. More than decent, maybe.

"Don't look at me like that, Miss Bellefleur," he says. "Have you no manners? It isn't proper to stare."

My eyes slowly lift to meet his, and it takes me a moment to recognize the amusement in them. I blink a few times, shaking myself from my stupor. What's wrong with me? My encounter with my father must have me truly flustered.

I grin. "Elliot Rochester, was that...humor coming from your lips?"

"Certainly not. All I do is brood." His mouth curls into a sly grin. It's not quite the smile I glimpsed last night when he was sitting by the fire, but this one isn't too hard on the eyes either.

"Gemma." The voice comes from the back of the drive near Father's coach, but it isn't Father who speaks. It's Nina.

The king takes a forbidding step forward, a growl beginning to reverberate in his throat, but I put a hand on his chest to still him. His eyes fly to my hand, and I snatch it away, blushing at the contact. I try to erase my mental note regarding how firm he'd felt beneath the brocade waistcoat. "It's all right," I say. "I'll speak with her."

With a nod, he gives my sister a warning look, then makes his way back to the manor. Not daring to get too close to Father's coach, I motion Nina to me. Her eyes are red and glazed with tears when she stops before me. "A letter, Gemma? Was there ever going to be a real goodbye?"

My heart sinks, and a lump rises in my throat. "I had to take this opportunity, Nina. You know I couldn't come back to the townhouse if I got a job. Not if I found a suitable arrangement."

"That's not an excuse," she says. "I understand not telling Father, but...you could have come back to see me."

"I was going to," I say, and it's true. I would have come to see her alone, once she could assure me Father wouldn't be home. Eventually. "I...needed a couple days."

My sister's lower lip trembles and her resemblance to Mother is enough to take my breath away. I rarely saw Mother cry, but when she did, she looked just like Nina does now. "I'm not ready to lose you, Gemma."

Blinking back tears, I pull my sister to my chest. One of her arms circles my waist. "You haven't lost me."

"But I will," she says through her sobs. "I lost Mother and Marnie already. I'll be married to James soon and then...and then what, Gem?"

Another painful lump rises in my throat, one bearing the secret I haven't dared share with her—about my plans to leave Faerwyvae and return to Isola. So I tell her the only honest answer I can give. "I don't know, Nina. I really don't know."

Once our tears have somewhat dried, we manage to extricate ourselves from each other's grasp. Only then do I see what kept my sister from hugging me with both arms; against her side she carries a book. With a sniffle, she holds it out to me. "I thought you might want something to read."

I take the book gingerly in my hands, caressing the cloth-bound spine like the body of a lover. My lips curl into a smile as I read the title. *The Governess and the Earl.*

My sister straightens, composing herself and clasping her hands at her waist. "If you want the rest of your books, you'll have to visit me."

"You're holding my books for ransom?" I laugh, then give her arm an affectionate squeeze. "Thank you."

With a sad smile, she nods and returns to Father's coach. I remain in place, watching as the horses take the black coach away, then stare even longer after they're gone. Only then does my heart feel lighter, relief settling over me. With a sigh, I hug my book to my chest and turn back toward the manor. I'm halfway to the door when I recall how Elliot had stepped between me and my father. The way he revealed his identity just to get him to stand down. It was unexpected to say the least. And I'm grateful for it.

A smile tugs my lips, but I force the thoughts from my mind. For just beneath them lies my poorly discarded mental note, one involving a brief touch and the king's chest. I squeeze my book tighter to stop the tingling that dances over the surface of my palm.

21

I 'm surprised how quickly the manor starts to improve. Walls are scrubbed, some are repainted or repapered. With the help of the manor's residents, the floors are cleaned, corners dusted, and windows polished. As the week goes on, I continue to dole out tasks, helping with some myself, and assign official positions to the king's pack of wolf people. I'm impressed with how amenable they are to work, as if the prospect of keeping busy is a tantalizing thing. I suppose five years trapped in one place without task or purpose will do that to a person, whether human or fae.

By the end of the week, Foxglove has brought all necessary furnishings and the old items have been stored in vacant rooms. Most of the work that remains are finishing touches, which results in several talks with Foxglove about the number of doilies each room should have.

"Are you sure you like the fae style of this room?"

Foxglove asks as he takes me on a tour of the newly finished parlor. "We could try the human style instead, if you like. I have several hat stands and grandfather clocks that were rejected from the Verity Hotel's design proposal."

I take in the freshly cleaned walls, the gleaming floors covered in plush, elegant rugs, the fashionable furniture. "No, Foxglove. This is perfect as it is."

"I'm so glad you like it." He grins, but it soon turns into a grimace. "Hopefully the bristly Mr. Rochester won't have too many complaints."

"I'm sure he'll find it lovely," I say, although I can't be certain what he'll think of it.

I've hardly seen him since his confrontation with my father. Once work began on the parlor, he made himself scarce. I imagine he's been holed up somewhere by the fire in a quiet wing of the manor, far from the noise. I can't say I blame him. It's been chaos around here, with hardly a place to sit and ruminate like he's so fond of doing.

Foxglove extends his hand toward the wall of windows at the other side of the room. "Come see the work in the garden."

I follow him to the windows, the afternoon sun streaming in from outside. Today, the sky is bright and clear instead of cloudy, a light dusting of snow coating the leaves of plants and shrubs like powdered sugar. It's been interesting to watch the weather patterns from the manor. There's always snow on the mountains, but just like in town, never a massive accumulation of it on the property. And unlike Vernon where foot traffic makes the snow slushy and brown by the end of each day, it's always pristine here.

I study the swarm of activity in the gardens as the landscapers Foxglove helped me hire set about their tasks. Hedges are trimmed, shrubs are shaped, and debris is hauled away in wheelbarrows. "It's turning into an elegant garden indeed," I say.

"They're working on the front too. Although," Foxglove points out one of the windows, squinting, "any idea why your employer refuses to let us enter that court-yard? It's a mess. Brambles and thorns everywhere. And one single rose, nearly smothered by thorns."

My heart leaps into my throat, knowing exactly what part of the garden he's referring to. That's where I've caught Elliot sitting, watching that very rose. The one that counts down to the day the curse will claim his life. I shudder at what could happen if anyone were to acciden-tally brush up against it, dislodge its petals. "It's a sacred place, Foxglove. Do not let anyone set foot in it."

He frowns, releasing an irritated sigh. "Fine, fine. Mr. Rochester said as much."

"Thank you," I say. "It's very important."

"Very well." He turns to face me and reaches inside his jacket to retrieve an envelope. "Here's my bill for this week. There won't be much more to do next week, so whatever grand event you're preparing for can probably commence."

I take the bill from him, my pulse quickening at the mention of the *grand event*. In other words, phase two. Everything has happened so fast, I've hardly had time to plan Elliot's first meeting with Imogen. "Wonderful," I say. "I'll see that you are paid as soon as possible."

He nods with a warm smile, then takes his leave. As soon as he's gone, I rush to the new bureau—one of rich mahogany—and take out a new piece of paper. There I start my list of ideas and tally everything I'll need to execute my phase two plan. I'm so engrossed in my work, I don't even notice the figure that stalks into the room.

"Where is my chair?" asks a gruff voice.

I whirl to find Elliot standing before the fire, glaring at the elegant furnishings that have been placed around the hearth.

It takes me a few moments to compose myself, blinking away the numbers and calculations that dance over my eyes and turn my attention to the king. He's back to walking with his staff instead of his prosthetic, but his clothing is new. Unsurprisingly, he doesn't wear a full suit, but at least he's chosen a nice pair of trousers, the leg neatly folded and pinned on his amputated side, as well as a crisp white shirt and open waistcoat. "Take your pick," I say, recalling his question.

He frowns at the two new chairs, then his gaze flicks to mine. I'm surprised how much more prominent his eyes are now that his hair has been trimmed. Luckily, Foxglove was able to salvage far more hair than I expected, with the back falling to the nape of his neck and the top a little shorter, parted to the side where it sweeps away from his face in a light wave. Most of his hair is dark now with just a hint of gold at the ends. The close trim of his beard reveals all the angles of his striking jaw and cheekbones. "Where's my *old* chair?"

I grit my teeth. He may look something like a gentleman, but he's the same old wolf on the inside. I rise from the bureau and approach the sitting area, quirking a brow. "Have you even bothered to try any of these chairs? I asked Foxglove to keep your comfort in mind when selecting these furnishings."

"What was so wrong with my chair that it needed replacing?"

"Oh, I don't know. Perhaps it was the fading, the stains, the tears, and—oh, yes—the white fur coating the seat."

"I liked sitting on it as a wolf!"

"And you'll like this one too," I say, extending my hand toward one of the chairs. "Although, next time you're a wolf, we must have the seat brushed of fur afterward."

He furrows his brow, a hint of worry creeping into his tone. "Do you think your scheme to break my curse will take longer than the next full moon?"

"It's hard to say. I doubt it will take much to get Imogen to fall in love with you, or at least be desperate enough for your hand that she thinks she does. But these things can still take time. Plus, there's the matter of getting her to actually make the sacrifice that will break your curse. We can't broach the subject until we're certain she has her whole heart set on you."

His jaw shifts back and forth, shoulders tense. "What if it takes too long?"

I skirt between the couch and table to bring myself closer to the king. Infusing my voice with as much calm as I can, I say, "It won't. We have almost three months. This will work."

"What if it doesn't?"

"It will." My words come out firm, hiding the flicker of doubt that's never far beneath the surface whenever I consider this plan. As much as I want my scheme to come to fruition, there's a chance it will fail. If life has taught me anything, it's that even the best, most certain things can go horribly wrong. Painfully wrong. Life has a way of pulling the rug from under my feet just when things seem perfect. It happened with Mother. Then again with the viscount—*no*. I will not think of him. What matters is that any good accountant must know how to prepare for losses. How to counteract them and not be blindsided by them. Thankfully, I know how to protect myself in this situation. As for Elliot...

I shake the thought from my mind and pull my lips into a warm grin. "Try one of the chairs, Mr. Rochester. Please."

He grumbles but finally relents, choosing the seat closest to the fire. It takes him a few moments to settle in and find that slouch of his. Once he does, there's no denying the truth; it's written all over his face. "Fine," he says. "This chair is adequate."

I clap my hands together in triumph and take the seat opposite him. His gaze turns to the flames and I suddenly can't recall what reason I'd had for sitting down in the first place. Surely, I should leave him to enjoy the first peaceful moment he's had in the parlor all week.

I'm about to rise when his eyes flash to me. "Stay," he says.

I settle back in, expecting conversation, but his gaze returns to the hearth, and we fall into silence. I've never been too comfortable with being still, not without a book at the very least. It doesn't take long before words reach my lips, begging to be free.

"I never thanked you," I say.

"For what?" he says, not looking at me.

"For standing up to my father. I appreciate what you did—confessing who you are, despite your desire to remain anonymous."

"He was stinking up my property," he says flatly, but there's a gentleness in his tone that betrays his act of disinterest.

I study him for a few moments, replaying the event in my mind. There's one thing I haven't quite figured out. "How did you know to tell him you pay his salary? Surely, the king isn't personally responsible for paying every citizen. But when you said that about my father, it was true."

"I know who he is," Elliot says. "He's the owner of the quartz mine my court recently acquired rights to. The quartz from that mine has filled my own vault. In turn, his contract with the Winter Court has made him a wealthy man."

I furrow my brow. "Did you know all along? When you captured me? When you planned on holding me for ransom?"

He shakes his head. "Bertha told me the day after I brought you here. Before that, I only knew what I'd read in the documents I'd been delivered to sign, that my court had acquired new quartz and that the seelie king and I would be paying the salary of a man who had brought it."

"Wait, how did Bertha know who my father is?"

He barks a laugh and meets my eyes. "Apparently, your father is a popular specimen amongst the people of Vernon. She'd already heard your family name weeks before she met you."

"How? She's...fae. Doesn't she live in some cabin out here in the woods?"

"She may be fae, but she loves gossip nearly as much as those wretched humans do. When she goes to town, she hides her ears, and the townspeople share all the latest news. Luckily, I trust her not to ever mention me."

I can imagine the easy-mannered Bertha charming gossip from the people of Vernon, leaving them no clue that she's actually a fae bear shopping for dinner supplies to feed a pack of cursed wolves. Which reminds me...

I sit up straighter in my chair, my stomach buzzing with excitement. Or is it trepidation? "Mr. Rochester, I think it's time."

"For what?"

"To invite Imogen Coleman to meet you."

He blinks a few times, then frowns at the fire. "All right. That's your phase two, isn't it?"

"Yes. I was just planning it out when you came in. I think we should host a casual dinner party."

His head swivels back to me, eyes wide. "A dinner party? Does that mean...more than just the human girl?"

"Trust me, I'm not any more pleased about that than you are, but yes. I think, to impress her, we should host a dinner with a small selection of important families. I'll ask Imogen to decide who to invite, so that she feels like she's been given a distinguished task. What it will really do is make her recognize her own desire and possessiveness when she finds herself excluding any eligible young women to compete with."

He groans. "How many guests are you subjecting me to?"

I lean forward, my tone placating. "I'll tell her no more than three families. She'll bring the most tiresome and uninteresting people in town, only to make her own family look better. It will be the most boring dinner imaginable."

"Boring. Well, that's selling it."

"Boring is good. It will allow you to dazzle Imogen with very little effort."

He releases a sigh. "Fine. I take it you've already considered cost—"

"Don't worry. I won't go overboard with the budget. Like I already told you. I know how to handle these things. We'll utilize minimal staff, have Bertha cook, and none will be the wiser. Oh, and speaking of budgets." I rise from my seat and fetch Foxglove's bill from the bureau. When I return to the sitting area, I stand before him and hand over the envelope.

"What is this?" he asks, tearing open the seal.

"That's this week's bill for the renovations and decor. Do not be alarmed. This will be the highest bill of all. After this, very little expenses will be required to maintain the manor."

"Freezing hell," he says, tipping his head back. "How many rooms did you have him redecorate?"

"Not many," I say with a grimace. "I'll show you everything. You'll appreciate it once you see it."

He rises, securing his staff beneath his arm, and heads for the door. "I doubt that."

"Where are you going?"

"Where do you think? If I'm supposed to pay this ridiculous sum, I'll need to fetch it from the vault."

I follow after him. "I'll come with you."

He stops and whirls to face me. "No."

I'm surprised by his reaction. "Mr. Rochester, it makes sense for me to know where your vault is. Since I'm in charge of your ledgers, I should also be in charge of auditing the vault and paying the staff."

"I can handle that just fine."

"But you don't have to. That's what I'm here for."

"Oh, is it?" He laughs, but there's no amusement in his eyes, only scorn.

"Yes," I say. "I bargained to be your house steward because it's a job I'm good at. I'm—"

"Don't think I haven't figured it out," he says, voice firm, cold. "Don't think Gray hasn't told me how many times you've asked where my vault is. I'm sure you've noticed by now that neither she nor anyone else in the manor will tell you."

My pulse begins to race as a creeping dread churns in my stomach. "I don't understand."

"I think you do, Miss Bellefleur. I know you seek to assure your success, but you should also know that I will do the same."

"Speak clearly, Your Majesty," I say through my teeth. "What exactly are you accusing me of?"

He takes a step closer, one that makes me shrink back. "Let me ask you this. If you learn where to find my fortune, what's to stop you from taking it even if the curse isn't broken?"

I swallow hard as a bead of sweat trickles behind my neck. He knows. He knows about my backup plan. Have I been that obvious?

"I'll tell you what will stop you. Me. I will put every preventative measure in place to ensure you don't get a single quartz chip if you fail your side of the bargain and let the curse claim my life."

"Is that a threat?" I try for fierce, but my voice comes out with a tremor.

His, however, is calm, confident. "Yes, Miss Bellefleur, that's a threat. I know better than to put my full trust in a human."

Guilt sends my knees quaking. I hate that he's right about my intentions. But he doesn't have the whole story! He doesn't know me or the pressures I face. He doesn't understand that I don't seek a backup plan because I *want* him to die. I seek it because...because I'll have nowhere to go if this fails.

I push my guilt away, burying it beneath mounds of indignation. Folding my arms over my chest, I burn him with a glare. "How dare you threaten me? How dare you act like you know my mind? You know nothing."

"I know what humans are like. I've been living amongst them far longer than you've been alive. I've seen their follies, and trust me, your kind have no redeeming qualities. Each human I've met has been a thief, a liar, or a murderer to some degree."

"You're wrong. Not all humans are like that."

"No? Can you honestly say you've never lied? Not once?"

Heat rises to my cheeks. "Of course I've lied before."

"Well, I haven't. I'm incapable of it."

"And yet you were perfectly willing to deceive me. You tried to trick me into sacrificing my greatest treasure to free you from a curse you brought upon yourself. Don't try to act like you're so high and mighty. If you were able to lie, you'd do it all the time."

His expression darkens, eyes flashing with rage. "I

haven't tried to deceive you once since we made our bargain. I've respected our arrangement. But have you done the same for me?"

My chest heaves, and I curl my fingers into fists. "What do you think I've been doing all week, if not respecting our bargain? Do you think I went through the tedious process of redecorating your manor because it's fun? Do you think I relish the thought of having to interact with Imogen Coleman at a saintsforsaken dinner party? No! I do it because it's necessary for our plan to work. I could very easily put far less effort into our arrangement and still fulfill my end of our bargain. But, no, I created a solid plan because I want this to work."

He shakes his head, a snarl curling his lips. "That's so human of you to evade my question and make yourself seem honorable instead."

"I'm telling the truth. I don't want you to die."

He goes still, silent, gaze boring into me for several tense moments. Then, finally, his voice comes out cold and quiet. "Look me in the eye and tell me I'm wrong. Tell me you wouldn't take my money if I died."

I hold his gaze but can't find my voice.

"You can't say a thing because you know I'm right."

Yes, he's right. He's so right that I hate myself for it and hate him even more for confronting me about it. He has no right to make me feel this way! I'm certain that if our roles were reversed, he'd do the same thing. Worse, even. There's no doubt in my mind that he would betray me simply for the sake of his vindictive pleasure alone. All because I'm human. A disgusting creature in his eyes.

I take a step closer, rage dripping from my tongue.

"You know what? You and Imogen deserve each other." Then, turning on my heel I storm from the room, blinking away angry tears with every step.

22

I spend much of my time the following week alone in my room. With the majority of the remaining work on the manor well under Foxglove's control, my presence is not as vital to operations as it was before. More than that, I'm avoiding Elliot. I still can't shake our conversation, with equal parts rage and guilt taking up residence in my heart. Just when I started to think the wolf king was a decent creature, he ruined everything.

Or did I ruin everything?

The day of the dinner arrives, sending my nerves into a roiling mess. All duties of preparation must be overseen by me, so I can no longer hide out in my room. Our meager event staff arrives, and I walk them through their tasks. Bertha begins her work in the kitchen, grateful for the extra assistance I've hired for her today. I remind the manor's residents to remain on their best behavior, which includes general hygiene and politeness. Most will make themselves scarce when our guests arrive and will be rewarded by a hearty dinner of their own in the kitchens.

The thought of guests fills me with dread. I already know I'll be forced to endure Imogen's company. We've corresponded a few times since I sent the invitation, with me planting all the right seeds to bloom unwittingly inside her. Her last letter assured me she's selected the most important families in town for Mr. Rochester to get acquainted with, which I know is code for *the families in town who pose the littlest threat to her marital schemes.*

Which might also translate to *people in town I desperately dislike.*

With the latter in mind and all preparations underway, I get dressed for dinner, attending to my own clothing and hair. I haven't gathered the nerve to return to Father's townhouse to fetch any of my belongings, so I've continued to rotate through the dresses in the wardrobe. Today I choose one in a sage color, the design similar to the others with its simple, unadorned style and plunging neckline and back. I've grown used to the soft material and layered skirts, almost regretting that I never had Amelie make me any new dresses while she was fitting the king.

Ugh, the king. That infernal wolf-man.

My stomach churns with the knowledge that I must see him tonight. See him, sit at the same table as him, and scheme with him. There's no way I can leave the dinner's success riding on Elliot's shoulders. Surely, he'll say the wrong thing if I'm not there, act the wrong way, bark at everyone to get out before the first course is served. I had Blackbeard bring him a list I'd made regarding dinner party etiquette, but who's to say he even read it?

For the love of the saints, I think, the blood leaving my head, *why didn't we have a practice dinner?*

The answer is obvious: I've been avoiding Elliot, refusing to even step foot in his parlor, and he's clearly been avoiding me too. If this dinner goes terribly wrong, I'll have only myself to blame. Or him. No, definitely him.

I study my reflection in my bedroom mirror and give myself to the count of five to feel anxious.

One.

I gather my mask of calm and watch it settle around me.

Two.

My brow loses its furrow, my shoulders grow squared yet relaxed, and haughty confidence settles over my lips.

Three.

It's just one dinner. I can handle a dinner.

Four.

I won't need to talk much. Imogen will do most of it. I'll simply steer the conversation when needed.

Five.

Elliot and I will hardly need to exchange more than a word.

A rapid knock sounds at my door, and Micah barges in a second later—something I've learned he excels at. "People!" he shouts. "Really fancy people."

My heart pounds. They're here.

With a deep breath, I secure my persona firmly in place.

～

I ENTER THE PARLOR, RELIEVED AT FINDING IT EMPTY. OUR guests are still coming in from the drive and Elliot must be doing as he should—drawing out suspense with his absence. Along with my list of dinner etiquette tips, I included a note about what he should specifically do tonight, starting with a grand entrance in the parlor once all guests have arrived.

The Colemans are the first to enter the room, escorted by our hired footman-for-the-day. Imogen leads the way while her mother, Mrs. Maddie Coleman, follows just behind. Clara and Ember bring up the rear. Once again, Ember wears a bonnet that nearly dwarfs her face. She smiles at me when she meets my eyes, and I return the grin before fixing my attention on Imogen.

She assesses the room with feigned disinterest, then settles her gaze on me. Her eyes quickly flick to my bosom. "What are you wearing, Miss Bellefleur?"

A blush heats my cheeks. I've been so used to being around nobody but the manor's residents, who never comment on my clothing, that I've slipped into ignorant bliss. Even though my dress is plain, the low-cut neckline and lack of corset is a bit racy for modern fashions. Hiding my momentary embarrassment beneath my confident mask, I wave a dismissive hand. "Just some old thing assigned to me when I took the job. A fae fashion worn by servants."

Her lips pull into a satisfied grin. "Ah, servant's garb. No wonder it's so...indecent."

"Indecent is one word for it," Mrs. Coleman says with a sneer. I can't help remembering what Imogen said, that her mother was the one who told her about...about what happened in Bretton. Thanks to my father, of course. Why he thought it necessary to share such private information with a woman he's courted for not even a month, I can hardly guess. At least I can be thankful he did not receive one of Imogen's invites.

Imogen looks around the room again. "Now, where is the mysterious Mr. Rochester I am to play hostess for tonight?"

"He'll be in shortly," I say, just as another party enters the room. It's a couple I only know in passing—the Davidsons—a middle-aged husband and wife. Imogen, Clara, and their mother go to greet them, and they fall into hushed conversation. I catch the Davidsons' burning stares, followed by Mrs. Coleman's poorly concealed whisper of *fae fashions*.

I grit my teeth.

Ember sidles up next to me, so quiet I almost startle when she speaks. "I think the dress is lovely," she says, her voice quiet and refined. Despite the way she's dressed, she seems to be a mature young woman of fine breeding. "Fae fashions are my favorite, although you won't find them here in Vernon."

I face her with a grin. "It's a shame."

"Perhaps with your employer in town, Vernon will become open to more fae influence, like some of the other cities," she says.

"One would hope," I mutter, glancing back at the gossiping crowd.

Footsteps sound in the hall, and our final guests enter the parlor. It takes all my restraint not to moan. Mrs. Aston enters the room, eyes wide with wonder as she takes in the furnishings. Her husband is far more stoic as he assesses his surroundings, but their third member has his gaze locked on me.

For the love of the saints. It's Gavin Aston, the despicable man I met at the bookshop. He strides over to me with a wide grin. Before I can react, he takes my hand and plants a kiss on it. "Miss Bellefleur, it's been too long."

His mother approaches just behind. "I can't believe I'm in the home of a fae. I had no idea they were so civilized. I suppose we could have brought the children after all, Edward."

Her husband huffs. "I daresay they would not behave."

"Oh, you're quite right," Mrs. Aston says, then turns to me. "It's so good of you to have taken employment from a fae creature, although I can't imagine why you would have. I thought for certain you were heading for matrimony, not spinsterhood."

Gavin releases my hand and pats his mother's shoulder. "A woman can have a mind for both matrimony and employment, Mother. This is the modern era, after all."

Mrs. Aston attempts a smile that looks more like a grimace. "I suppose that could be true, dear."

Gavin turns his eyes back to me. "I, for one, think it's marvelous you've sought employment. I find it encouraging when a woman proves herself my equal through hard work."

A flicker of surprise ripples through me. That was actually...intelligent. Complimentary, even. Could I have been wrong in my first impression of Gavin Aston?

"You won't have to work once you're married, of course," he adds. "But I think employment is a most attractive pastime for a young lady. A way for her to gain experience of the world outside of dresses and dances."

Just like that, my fleeting reassessment wanes. I was right the first time. Gavin Aston is a moron. "You mistake me, sir. My work is not a frivolous pastime to dally with on my way to the altar but a legitimate alternative to marriage."

Mrs. Aston gasps. Her son, however, shakes his head with mirth. "Clever *and* funny. Miss Bellefleur, you are a prize."

I open my mouth, my shoulders tense with rage, but am saved from doing something marvelously stupid when a domineering figure appears in the doorway. My breath catches, draining both the rage and blood from my face.

It's Elliot.

The footman stands at his side and announces him. "Mr. Elliot Rochester."

The parlor falls into silence as Elliot takes a few slow steps into the room. His pace makes him seem confident and calculated, his limp barely distinguishable as he walks with his prosthetic. His hair has been combed in a neat, modern style. His dark green suit and gold waistcoat are impeccable, setting him apart from the black and white the men wear and giving the distinction that this creature is fae. The cut of his jacket accentuates his broad shoulders while his slim trousers reveal the musculature of his thighs.

"Good afternoon," he says, his voice low and deep, yet far gentler than I've ever heard it. His gaze slides over his rapt audience, then locks on me.

My heart hammers against my ribs beneath that stare.

It's enough to empty all thoughts from my mind, making me forget why I started this night angry at him. Although, clearly he still hasn't mastered his lesson about not staring—*Oh!* Remembering my duties, I shake my head and rush to his side. "Mr. Rochester, please meet your gracious hostess, Miss Imogen Coleman."

Imogen's eyes are wide, nearly glittering with stars of smitten attraction as she approaches Elliot and dips into a curtsy. "Mr. Rochester, thank you for trusting me with inviting tonight's dinner guests. I am so pleased to be of service to you."

For a few tense moments, Elliot does nothing but stare at Imogen, his expression unreadable. Then his lips twitch. Once. Twice. Finally, they pull into a modest smile. His words come out smooth and practiced. "Thank you for being so generous in helping me host my first dinner with Vernon's prime residents."

Imogen beams, then stands at his side, all but pushing me away to take my place next to him. "Allow me to introduce my mother, Mrs. Maddie Coleman, and my sister, Miss Clara Coleman." The two curtsy, then Imogen introduces the rest of the guests, leaving Ember for last. "And this is my stepsister, Miss Ember Montgomery."

I'm taken aback that Ember has a different surname from the rest of her family until I remember something Imogen once told me. Mrs. Maddie Coleman is thrice a widow, and after the death of her last husband—who I assume was Ember's father—she and her daughters reverted to Maddie's maiden name. It makes sense that Ember wouldn't have followed suit.

Ember curtsies, keeping her eyes downcast, her face passive, and quickly moves to the side.

Imogen turns to face Elliot. "Shall we continue to dinner?"

His gaze flicks to me, and I give a subtle nod, hoping my eyes convey what I wish I could say. *Offer her your arm!* If he read my instructions, he should know it is now time to escort Imogen to the dining room.

To my relief, he holds out a stiff arm, bent at the elbow. "Allow me to escort you, Miss Coleman."

Fluttering her lashes, she places her hand in the crook of his elbow, then looks at the other guests expectantly.

As they begin to pair up, I'm horrified to find Gavin heading straight for me. "May I?" he asks, arm extended.

Before I can refuse on my own, Imogen pipes up, her tone astonished. "Don't be silly, Mr. Aston. You shall escort my mother. I told you already that Miss Bellefleur works here. She isn't a dinner guest."

Although her tone has me bristling, she's right. Even though house steward is normally considered an esteemed position in a grand house, the dinner guests don't see me that way. To them, I'm a lowly servant who should not be invited to join such an event as a guest. With the rift between me and Elliot, I'm almost certain he'll take the opportunity to exclude me. If he does, I'll accept it and trust he can handle his own for the remainder of the night.

"On the contrary," he says, tone firm, "my steward will be joining us for dinner."

Equal parts surprise and relief wash over me. "Thank you, Mr. Rochester. It's an honor."

Imogen purses her lips. "Do you treat all your staff so kindly?"

Elliot's jaw shifts back and forth. "Gemma is—"

Imogen's eyes widen. "Gemma? Are you also on a first name basis with your staff?"

I feign a casual laugh. "I'm always trying to remind Mr. Rochester that humans aren't as casual with first names as the fae are. It's a strange custom to him, and he's still getting used to it."

"Well, in that case, please call me Imogen." She looks up at him, her expression making it clear that she awaits the invitation for her to use his first name in turn. But it doesn't come.

"Shall we proceed?" Elliot asks.

Again, Gavin offers me his arm. Not wanting to draw further attention to myself, I accept.

Elliot leads the way with the rest of us following in pairs, aside from Ember, who walks alone. Why is she always so coldly excluded? Then again, if it weren't for my presence bringing our party to an odd number, she'd have an available escort.

We enter the dining hall, a spacious, elegant room with marble floors, tall windows revealing the night sky, and a long table at the center.

Imogen tuts as she approaches the table. "No place cards? Miss Bellefleur, if you needed further help, you should have invited me to arrive earlier. But never mind that. As honorary hostess, I shall make it up on the spot. You, Mr. Rochester, should sit at the head of the table. We may be guests at your party, but I can't help considering you the guest of honor tonight."

He meets her fluttering lashes with a tight-lipped smile that doesn't reach his eyes. "Very well."

Imogen orders the rest of us around the table with

her and her mother sitting on either side of Elliot, followed by the Davidsons, then Mr. and Mrs. Aston, Clara and Ember, and me and Gavin at the very end. Clara mutters about being stuck on the boring end, tossing a sneer across the table at her stepsister, while Gavin seems to relish the honor of pulling out my chair and settling in across from me.

"Have I told you how delightful you look this evening?" he asks.

"No, but thank you," I say coolly, then turn my attention to the head of the table. Imogen says something quietly to Elliot, leaning toward him as if she wishes to crawl into his lap. His expression remains neutral, his tone even when he replies. It seems he's chosen to play the stoic gentleman tonight, and he isn't doing half bad. I'm truly impressed.

As the servants step forward and begin ladling food on plates, Mrs. Aston says, "I must say, Mr. Rochester, I had no idea such a lovely manor existed way out here in the woods. However, I've heard the most unsettling stories about wolves in the area. Have you seen any?"

Elliot's eyes meet mine for a moment, the ghost of a grin tugging the corners of his lips before he composes a blank face. "Yes, Mrs. Aston. I have seen wolves."

I suppress my smile. It's a good answer for one who can't lie.

Mrs. Aston gasps. "Have any attacked? Or...or are they," she lowers her voice, "your kind?"

He opens his mouth, but a look of alarm sparks in his eyes as they flash again toward me.

Saints, I doubt he can find a way to truthfully evade that question.

"The wolves around here are nothing to worry about," I say. "They rarely show up and have yet to hurt anyone."

Imogen burns me with a glare. "How would you know, Miss Bellefleur? It's not like you're an expert on Vernon. You only arrived mere days before my family did."

Mrs. Aston nods gravely. "That's true, Miss Bellefleur. None of us really know what they're capable of."

Mr. Davidson faces Elliot. "Have you considered hiring trappers to take care of the wolf problem? It's a shame your property should be overrun by them."

Elliot's façade falters, his irritation evident in the pulsing at the corners of his jaw. "No, I have not and will not consider such a thing, nor do I recall stating the wolves were a *problem* to begin with."

Mr. Davidson blanches at the venom in Elliot's tone, exchanging a glance with his wife before turning his attention to his plate.

"My employer has a soft spot for wolves," I say. "As you can imagine, the fae differ from humans in their feelings about nature."

"Oh, that's right," Mrs. Aston says with a chuckle. "It's so hard to remember these things, Mr. Rochester. When I'm not looking at those ears of yours, you appear nothing but a gentleman."

He grunts a reply, regaining a handle on his composure.

Mrs. Coleman leans toward him. "It hasn't slipped *my* mind once," she says, then addresses the rest of the table. "It's easy for me to recognize the fae and understand their ways. My first husband was fae, after all. And a king at that."

From her seat next to me, Ember snorts a quiet laugh.

Mrs. Aston puts a hand to her chest. "Is that so? Which king?"

Mrs. Coleman's proud smile falters. With a flutter of her hand, she says, "Oh, it was long ago, well before the unification. He died in the second war."

Mrs. Aston and Mrs. Davidson offer sounds of condolence.

Maddie Coleman turns back to Elliot. "I know many fae of great importance. Queen Evelyn and I are practically family. I was childhood friends with her and her sister, the renowned seamstress and fashion designer, Amelie Fairfield."

I'm surprised by her mention of Amelie. I can't imagine the two ever being acquainted. "You must have spoken to her since she's been in town, then?"

Mrs. Coleman's face whips toward me. "Pardon? Who do you mean?"

"Miss Amelie," I say. "She's currently in Vernon."

She pales, then wordlessly sips her wine as if I hadn't spoken.

Ember lets out a quiet giggle. "I guarantee they are *not* dear friends," she whispers to me.

Mrs. Coleman turns back to Elliot. "Speaking of important fae, my daughter says you are of noble fae blood. Might you oblige us with insight into your lineage?"

Imogen burns her mother with a scowl, but the older woman pays her no heed and simply grins at Elliot over her dinner plate.

Elliot is silent for a few moments, eyes unfocused

before he calmly states, "No, I will not share that information."

Not getting the hint, Mrs. Coleman places a hand on Elliot's forearm. "Oh, come, Mr. Rochester. I hope you can trust us to keep whatever secrets you may carry. Remember, I am much acquainted with the ways of fae."

Elliot snatches his arm from her touch, eyes going steely.

Saints, this is what I was afraid of. "Mr. Rochester is here on private matters and intends to keep them that way."

Imogen swivels toward me, eyes narrowed to slits. "Why is it you keep answering for him, Miss Bellefleur?"

"As his steward, I have his best interests at heart."

"At heart, you say?" Lifting her wine glass to her lips, she takes a dainty sip. "If you aren't careful, one might get the impression you know him better than you ought."

I open my mouth, but Elliot speaks first. "And how ought she know me?"

Imogen's lips curl into cruel grin as her eyes lock on mine. "Far less intimately than she'd know a viscount."

Silence and sound crash over me at once, the word *viscount* echoing in my head.

"Viscount?" Mrs. Aston says, turning to look from me to Imogen. "Does Miss Bellefleur know a viscount?"

Imogen's gaze continues to burn into me. "Sometimes I wonder if she's known many."

The eyes of the dinner guests slowly turn toward me, and in them I feel the eyes of others, those not present but in my mind.

The leers. The jests.

I grip the arms of my chair to steady myself, but

already my breaths are growing ragged, the room beginning to tilt. *This is here. This is now,* I try to remind myself, but the here and now is far too unpleasant to provide much comfort.

Elliot's low rumbling voice is all that anchors me and clears a portion of the chaos from my head. "Miss Coleman."

I slowly turn to find him slouched to the side, leaning away from Imogen, his eyes as sharp as daggers. She meets his gaze, and her grin melts from her lips.

His next words come out slow, cold. "Am I to understand your comment was made at my steward's expense?"

She blinks a few times, her cheeks flushing pink. Then her gaze turns to scorn, her lips pressed into a tight line as she stabs her fork at her plate.

Silence falls over the table like a shroud, the tension more chilling than ice.

Oh no. This isn't good. But as much as I want to remedy it, I can't fully shake what Imogen has conjured within me. The eyes from my past continue to glare at me from inside my head, lips hurling insults as sharp as broken glass.

Rising from my seat with all the grace I can manage, I address the table with a weak smile. "I apologize, but I must take my leave of you early. I am not feeling well."

Gavin rises from his seat. "May I—"

"No," I bark, then soften my tone. "I will disrupt this dinner no more. Please proceed without me."

As I rush to the other side of the room, Elliot's eyes follow me, brow furrowed. "Gem—Miss Bellefleur," he whispers, then shifts in his chair as if he's about to stand.

I pause in time to catch Imogen shooting her mother a knowing look.

"Mr. Rochester," I whisper back. "I'm fine."

He opens his mouth, but I give him a subtle shake of my head.

"Don't. Please." With that, I flee, feeling a thousand eyes burning into my back long after I close my bedroom door.

23

I lay in bed reading *The Governess and the Earl*, but despite having done so for at least an hour, I don't think I've made it past a single chapter. Every paragraph or so, my mind returns to the dining hall, to Imogen's cruel smile and Elliot's cold response to her teasing. And every time I read about the brooding earl in my book, I can't help replacing his imagined description with the countenance of a certain fae king.

It's been two hours since I fled the dining room. Now that I've regained my composure, all I can think about is whether I've doomed Elliot's dinner by leaving him alone with his guests like that. Then again, I think it took such a poor turn because of me. Or Elliot's defense of me. While I appreciate the king standing up for me, he shouldn't have. He should have done everything in his power to please Imogen. Now I can only hope he managed the rest of the meal without getting trapped in any uncomfortable truths.

I try reading for another hour with very little progress

and then push back my blankets with a groan. Rubbing my hands up and down my chilly arms, I go to my window and lean my shoulder into the frame. Below, the gardens are quiet with no movement but the swirl of falling snow, the dainty snowflakes blanketing the night in silence. All at once, my mind goes still and my pulse evens out. The peace of the mountains traps me in its spell. Yearning creeps into my soul, a desire to breathe that forest air.

I glance at the clock on my dressing table, its hands telling me it's almost midnight. Surely, our guests have departed by now. I return my attention to the window and that yearning returns, calling to me.

Without a second thought, I pull on my hose and boots, then drape my warm cloak over my nightgown. A hat comes last, then I rush out the door before I can stop myself.

The halls of the manor are quiet, empty, as I creep across the floors. Downstairs, there's no sign of guests, none of our hired servants, no residents. I release a sigh of relief and continue toward the back of the manor to the doors that lead out to the gardens. Once outside, the cool night air greets me. Never before has this sensation felt so welcome. It was always warmth and sunshine I've craved before, but the peace of a snowy night brings such a similar feeling that for once, I don't mind the cold.

I walk down the garden path, emptying my mind as I focus on nothing but the pitter patter of falling flakes, the crunch of my boots in the snow. After a time, a new sound falls upon my ears, footsteps that are not my own.

I whirl around, finding Elliot on the path behind me. His breath comes out in puffs of white while snow falls over his hair. No longer combed and styled like it was at dinner, it falls around his face in disarray—yet, somehow, still makes him look somewhat handsome in a rugged, roguish way. His hands are tucked into the pockets of a long wool overcoat in a deep green. Beneath it, I see the hint of trousers and an untucked linen shirt but no waist-coat, no cravat. I wonder if he too got out of bed to come here.

Without a word, he slowly crosses the distance between us, and I realize he's still wearing his prosthetic. Stopping a few paces away, he offers me a tight-lipped smile. His expression flickers with something I can't quite place. Is it worry? Fatigue?

Finally, he speaks. "I'm sorry."

His words shatter my peace, reminding me of that awful dinner. I release a sigh. "It wasn't your fault. It...it's just how Imogen is."

"Not about that," he says, his voice a low rumble. He shifts his stance as trepidation clouds his face. "About... before. About the money and my vault."

Guilt sinks my stomach, making it churn. My words come out with a tremor. "Please don't apologize for that."

He averts his gaze from me, opening and closing his mouth a few times before he speaks again. "I shouldn't have been hurtful about it. I meant what I said, that I must protect myself in case—"

"Please don't, Your Majesty. I don't want to talk about that."

His eyes return to mine, and his expression softens. A corner of his mouth quirks into a halfhearted grin. "First of all, enough with that Your Majesty nonsense. Call me Elliot. I learned today that first names are considered quite an honor." A smile tugs my lips at the jest in his voice. "Second of all, do you mind if we talk about something else?"

I furrow my brow. "Like what?"

"Anything," he says with a shrug. "I can't sleep."

"Neither could I."

"Well, then." He straightens his posture with a hint of lighthearted mockery and offers me his arm. "This is another thing I learned tonight, thanks to your comprehensive list of dinner etiquette."

I place my hand at the crook of his elbow, and we begin to walk, our steps slow and leisurely. "I'm pleased to discover you read it. Speaking of, how did the rest of the dinner go?"

His lips twist with a scowl. "It was the most unenjoyable thing I've ever been forced to endure."

"But you endured it? Everyone made it out alive?"

"Barely. I followed your list. Finished dinner, adjourned to the parlor. I took my place by the fire, and most of the talking was done at me, more than with me, which I suppose I should be grateful for."

"And Imogen?" I can't say her name without another churn of my stomach. "Were you able to regain her favor?"

"She seemed to light up as soon as you left the dining hall. Hardly a moment passed before she recommenced with batting her lashes at me. I could barely stand to look at her after how vile she acted before you left."

I shrug. "Well, now you see why I chose her for our scheme. I wouldn't select just anyone to trick into sacrificing their greatest treasure."

"No, I can certainly see why she is the one. All the

guests were despicable, of course, but she more than the rest, followed by her mother. How many times must one touch another's forearm when speaking?" He grimaces.

I let out a laugh but sober from it quickly. "You shouldn't have defended me with Imogen, Elliot. You mustn't come to my defense next time it happens."

"Are you telling me I should expect more disrespect from her?"

"Not to you, which is all that matters. You must woo her, remember?"

He scoffs and looks away. "Woo her. Ha! Shouldn't she be trying to impress me? Not...mocking my staff?"

"She probably thinks her cruelty is impressive. There are many stories about fae who value such a trait."

"Cruelty is only admirable when it's either humorous or deserved."

"Is that so? And how do you know I don't deserve her cruelty?" I mean it to come out cajoling, but he must sense the way my heart clenches hard in my chest.

He stops and faces me, tone firm. "You don't." Then, after a pause, he asks, "What did she mean, anyway? About the viscount?"

I shake my head. "It's nothing."

"It's not nothing. Clearly, it's something. If you want my promise that I won't confront Imogen next time she says something vile, then you damn well better let me in on what exactly she lords over you. Perhaps I can steer the conversation better with that knowledge in mind."

I study his face for a few moments, surprised at the sincerity I find there. Perhaps if he knew the truth, he'd understand. Just like everyone else who's heard about it —my father, my former friends in Bretton, my older sister

Marnie—he'll deem me at fault for the mess. Then maybe he'll be more amiable with Imogen.

I lift my chin. "If I tell you, promise you won't scold me or school me in the importance of feminine virtue. I've had enough of those conversations to last a lifetime."

"Why the freezing hell would I give a snow troll's ass about feminine virtue?"

"Fine," I grumble, then begin walking again. Elliot keeps pace at my side, our shoulders brushing now and then. With a deep breath, I begin. "As you know, I was raised in Isola. But after my mother died, Father moved us from there to the capital city in Bretton. There we lived for five years, and my sisters and I entered society as each of us came of age. After my eldest sister was married, it was my turn to secure a husband. So began the games of courtship, culminating in my meeting with the viscount." My voice trembles on the last word.

I sense Elliot's eyes on me but can't bring myself to meet them.

Steeling my nerves, I try to imagine I'm simply narrating a story, something not about me but one of the fictional governesses in my books. This helps me continue with far less attachment to my words. "The Viscount of Brekshire—Oswald—pursued me more than any other man, and it didn't take long for me to return his affections. We were in love, and he promised marriage would follow. There was just one complication."

"What's that?"

I meet his gaze for just a second. "Oswald was already engaged to the Princess of Bretton."

I expect a judgmental hiss, a gasp, a halt in his steps. But he remains steady, not faltering for a single beat.

So I proceed. "It was an arranged marriage for political reasons, something orchestrated by Oswald's father and the king years before. My beloved promised me that he had every intention of breaking off the engagement. He only needed some time to convince his father to allow him to marry someone like me. You see, Oswald knew the truth, that my family was on the verge of poverty, hiding our dire situation behind my expert management of our assets. Even so, he loved me anyway. He assured me his father would understand and give us his blessing when the time was right. Until then, we would need to continue our courtship in secret. As soon as his betrothal was broken, we'd go public with our love. Everything he said to me, the way he treated me, had me convinced it was the truth. I knew it as deeply as my own skin. But months went on and still, he needed more time. More time. More time. I waited. And then I stopped waiting."

I clench my fingers into fists to distract myself from the heat that rises to my cheeks. It takes all my will to voice the next part. "I wasn't chaste with him, and I'll make no excuses for that. I'd never felt more beautiful or loved in my life. But the euphoria of our coupling made us reckless. Or it made me that way, at least. We stopped being as careful to conceal our courtship, dancing together far more than is considered proper at balls, dining together, walking together, stealing kisses in public. Then more than kisses."

My throat closes up, nausea wrenching my gut. "We drew enough suspicion to attract the attention of a reporter running the city's gossip column. She...followed us one day and caught us in the middle of..."

I swallow hard.

Elliot stops and places a hand on my arm, gently turning me to face him. "You don't have to explain more than that," he says. The steadying warmth of his palm makes me realize how badly I'm shaking, and it isn't from the cold.

"Everyone found out," I whisper. "All my friends, my family, Oswald's father. Oswald promised to fight for me. But...he didn't."

The king's brows knit together, and I realize his hand is still on my arm. It keeps me rooted to the moment while memories of the past rush through my mind. I can still see the words I found in the gossip column a week after it had already revealed my tryst with the viscount. Just when I thought rumors couldn't hurt me more, this one made the killing blow, for every letter spelled out a vicious lie.

"The viscount decided to save his reputation instead," I say, anger heating my core. "He spread word that I had tempted and seduced him. That our dalliance meant nothing and his heart belonged to the princess. He married her at the end of the month and his sins were quickly forgotten. Mine, however, lasted long after. My reputation was ruined, my family scorned, and suitors stopped courting my little sister. Friends verbally attacked me, publicly humiliating me one day when I was walking through town." I seize up for a moment, remembering the way the girls circled me, shouting insults that anyone passing by could hear. There was no fight in me then, just frozen terror. The eyes of those girls are the ones I see when I'm dragged back to my memories. Their voices are the ones that resound in my head.

Breathing deep, I focus all my awareness on Elliot's

hand, letting the past disappear into the recesses of my mind. "That's why we moved here as soon as Father got the chance."

Elliot is quiet for a few tense moments. "I'm glad you were able to get away from that."

"But I didn't, did I?" Tears well in my eyes at the words. "Imogen knows. Her mother knows. My father knows. Nina is kind about it, but everyone else makes sure to remind me of my follies time and time again."

He clenches his jaw and I wonder if he's fighting the urge to do the same, to tell me I've brought ruination upon myself. That I should have known better than to lift my skirts. Just like Marnie said. Just like Father said. Just like all my so-called friends said. "How badly do you wish to scold me?"

His grip grows firmer, his shoulders rigid. "Scold you?" He retracts his hand and turns away from me, running his fingers through his hair with a growl. There he stands for a few silent moments, hands on his hips. When he whirls back to face me, his eyes are wide, cheeks blazing crimson. "*Scold* you? Why the freezing hell would I *scold* you? I'm...furious at those...those stupid humans. You're a woman in your own right. No one else has any say in judging you, least of all what you do with your passions or your body."

I'm taken aback. No one has responded to my story this way, no matter how much I cried genuine tears or expressed the depth of my heartache. Not even Nina reacted like this. She showed pity, yes, but not anger on my behalf.

As my eyes lock on his, taking in all their fury and

indignation, I feel seen in a way I never have before. "You really believe that?"

"Of course I do." He pulls his gaze from mine and begins pacing back and forth, his gait uneven from his frantic movements. "Humans and their pathetic ways, always trying to lord over everyone else's private business with inane rules of propriety. It's mating, for ice's sake. Mating! That involves *two*. Well, several, for some fae, but it certainly doesn't involve an entire town nor require anyone else's permission or approval. I'll never understand your kind."

With every word, the warmth of having been *seen* melts away. Not that his rant invalidates his irritation; I just now realize it isn't personal. He may be angry over my situation, but it's less about empathy for me and more about his disdain for humankind. And he has a point, one I can't argue with. Why should I, anyway? Why should I expect him to be anything other than he is? He is fae, after all. A fae who hates humans. Still, I can't ignore the twinge of disappointment that tugs at my heart.

Elliot stops pacing and shakes his head. "You expect me to be cordial to Imogen after telling me all that? She should rot for bringing up such a distressing topic."

Warmth threatens to return to my chest, but I breathe it away and square my shoulders. "Yes, Elliot. Defending me will only get in the way of our plan. Don't worry about me. I can take care of myself. Focus on wooing Imogen."

"Wooing Imogen." He scoffs. "You know what? This plan is absolute puppycock."

I'm about to argue when his choice of swear echoes in

my head. Then a bubble of amusement rumbles in my chest. "Elliot, did you just say *puppycock*?"

His lips pull into a frown and he crosses his arms. "So what if I did?"

"Let me just make sure I heard you right. You said... puppy-cock."

He shrugs, his face flickering with a hint of embarrassment. "It's a human swear. I heard it used tonight by that awful Mr. Davidson. A vile swear, too. No one has any right to take a young wolf's genitals in vain, but I figured I'd give it a go."

I cover my mouth but my laughter only grows.

His eyes deepen into a glare. "What's so funny?"

"It's poppycock, Elliot. *Poppy*."

"Well, that makes no sense at all! Since when does a poppy have a—never mind. Don't tell me. Humans can keep their freezing swears all they like."

His annoyance only makes me laugh harder, and soon I'm doubled over with it.

"Go on, keep laughing at my expense."

I manage to recover my posture and risk a glance at the king through my tear-filled eyes. Expecting to find him glowering, I'm surprised to see the corners of his lips twitching as if my laughter is becoming contagious. I cover my mouth and try to hold my breath, but my next laugh comes out with a snort.

That is what breaks him. His eyes crinkle at the corners, mouth open wide as a deep, bellowing laugh erupts from him. This, of course, only undoes all my work at trying to settle down and has me in a fit again. The next thing I know, Elliot has closed the distance between us, standing just a pace away. "I don't know what we're laughing about," he says, his voice rich with mirth.

"I barely recall the reason myself." My tone comes out light and high, something I rarely hear from my own lips. It reminds me so much of happier times with Mother. My heart squeezes, but it isn't painful; it feels more like a bittersweet parting hug than a clenching fist. Finally, I begin to sober.

Elliot's eyes are still crinkled when I meet them. When he speaks, his voice is quiet, with just a hint of frivolity. "I like the sound of your laughter."

My pulse quickens at that.

"It reminds me of wolf pups playing."

Of course it's wolves. I grin, but my bittersweet feeling remains. And if I'm being honest, the bitter has overtaken the sweet. Is it that I resent his hate for humans and his preference for wolves? Why should I? A wolf is his true unseelie form. It's what he's fighting for. What I'm *helping* him fight for. Why does that give me a sinking sensation?

"Come," Elliot says, shaking me from my thoughts. "There's something I want you to see."

lliot leads me back toward the entrance to the garden, then down a path that takes us between a row of neat hedges. A few more steps and we enter a small courtyard I've only glimpsed from afar. It's the king's rose garden. I turn in a circle, taking in the poorly manicured shrubs that line the courtyard, brambles weaving through each bush. Finally, my eyes land on a blush of deep red—the final rose.

He extends his hand toward the flower, expression grave. "This is the rose that will either allow me to break the curse or kill me."

What a morbid thing he's brought me to see. And yet, I can't deny I have questions about it, as his statement has left me a bit puzzled. I bite the inside of my cheek before I ask, "If the rose counts down the days until the curse claims your life, why do you say it could also allow the curse to break?"

His tone is deep and somber. "When the sacrifice is ready to be made, the one making it must pluck the rose

and state aloud that they willingly and of their own volition sacrifice their greatest treasure. If there were more
roses left, it could have been any of them. But now," he
glances again at the rose, "this one is my final hope. And
my final doom."

My stomach feels heavy, weighed down with dread.
"Why did you bring me here?"

His eyes flick to mine, a frown tugging his features.
"You shared something painful with me, so I figured I'd
return the favor."

That brings a sad smile to my lips. "That's kind of
you."

With slow steps, he approaches the stone bench.
Then, after bending down to brush a layer of snow off the
surface, he takes a seat to one side. "I come every day to
find my fallen petal, and each day I take my petal with me
and keep it in a glass in my room."

After a moment's hesitation, I take a seat next to him.
"Why? Isn't it painful to watch the days count down like
that? To collect them?"

"It is," he says. "And yet every day I return, hoping
that the countdown will slow and give me more time to
break the curse. By some magic, however, the daily petal
always seems to know when I'm here and is sure to fall
right before my eyes, taunting me."

"That must be very difficult for you."

"Not as difficult as being in this body."

Once again, a bitter ache floods my chest. "Why do
you hate humans so much?"

He looks at me with a smirk. "You mean, aside from
the obvious reasons you'd agree with?"

I give him a pointed look. "Yes, Elliot. Aside from

those things. Why do you have such a strong prejudice against my kind? I'm sure humans have given you ample reason, but I want to hear what exactly those reasons are."

His eyes fall back on his rose, then grow unfocused, his lips turning down at the corners. "I was but a pup when humans first came to the isle," he says. "Back then, humans were visitors on our land, and they acted accordingly. They respected my kind. Revered us, even. But as time went on, more and more humans came, and they shifted from awed visitors to determined settlers. They built homes, claimed lands that were never theirs. Tensions grew more dangerous until they resulted in the first war."

The first war. That was over a thousand years ago, from what I've heard. And to think Elliot was alive back then! This youthful man sitting at my side—but no. Despite how human he looks in his seelie form, he *isn't* a man at all, but a separate species. As much as I know the reminder should unsettle me...it doesn't. It amazes me.

Elliot continues. "I was what you'd call a teen back then. Somewhere between a pup and full-grown. My parents fought in the war, which spanned—" He pauses, blinking a few times.

"What's wrong?"

"It seems that's one of the memories that has been taken from me by the curse. I can no longer recall how long it lasted nor how it ended. And yet, right in the middle lies a memory as clear as yesterday."

"Are all the memories the curse has taken like that? In random order?"

"As far as I can tell. Of course, I only realize what I've

forgotten when I try to summon the memory. I can't even imagine how many things have fled my mind without notice." He shudders.

"Go on," I whisper, more to distract him from his chilling train of thought than anything.

"The thing I do remember that happened in the middle of the war solidified my opinion of humans for good. I already considered them my enemy, but I respected them, recognizing their drive for survival and proliferation of their species. That, at least, I could understand." His hands, propped on his thighs, balled into tight fists.

"What happened?"

"Iron," he mutters like a curse. "Humans discovered the fae weakness for iron and began using it against my kind in the battles."

So, the stories are true. Fae are vulnerable to iron. I know pure iron is forbidden in Faerwyvae, but until now I hadn't known if it was due to superstition or truth.

"My parents were killed in one of those early battles with iron before we knew just how devastating an injury from the metal can be. You see, short of beheading or the removal of our hearts, fae can survive almost any injury and eventually heal from it. Iron injuries, however, are far more devastating. If iron is embedded in our flesh too long, it will poison our blood and kill us."

I glance down at his leg, his trousers hiding all signs of the prosthetic he wears. "Is that what happened to you?"

"I've been injured by iron several times, and yes, the bullets that tore through my leg were iron. But I fear not even a lesser metal could have saved my leg. There wasn't much left when—when—"

Again, he blinks.

"Another memory forgotten?"

He nods. "Someone tended my leg and I remember being furious about the amputation. That's all I remember."

I furrow my brow. "Fae healing doesn't include regrowing limbs?"

He shakes his head, and a lock of hair falls over his eyes. "Anyway, my parents were killed in battle. Many lives were lost, so I am not unique in that. However, when I found out about their demise, I sought to avenge their deaths. I hunted down the hands that made the killing blow and I...I found them."

He brushes a hand through his hair, moving it from his forehead to reveal the haunted look in his eyes. Everything in me wants to lay a comforting hand on his arm, the way he did for me, but I can't bring myself to move.

His next words come out quiet. "I knew they were my parents' killers because...because they were wearing their skins."

Bile rises in my throat. "Their *skins*?"

"To a human, I'm sure it looked like nothing. Two men with wolf pelts draped over their shoulders, lifeless canine heads still intact, worn like hoods to rest upon the humans' brows. But to me..."

It isn't hard to imagine the revulsion I'd feel if I saw someone parading around with my dead mother's skin like that. A lump rises in my throat, straining my words. "Saints, Elliot, that's awful."

He meets my eyes, and I see his are glazed with a

sheen of tears. "Humans are unable to distinguish between unseelie fae and a regular animal. And part of me understands, I honestly do. I too must hunt and eat and survive. I can't expect humans to have the same ability the fae do, to know at a glance the difference between people and prey. But then there are times when a human *knows* a fae creature is a person...and still fails to see us as such. And after tonight's display at dinner, I know that disrespect extends even to the seelie fae. In this form, I am but a prize, a spectacle."

His words strike me like a blow to the heart. They're too potent. Too accurate. I hastily wipe my cheeks, catching a few errant tears. "You're right," I say. "In fact, humans treat each other like prizes, property, and spectacles maybe just as often. Perhaps that will make you feel better."

"It doesn't make me feel better." His voice is cold, flat. "It makes me angrier."

My heart sinks as I search for words. While I deeply understand his stance and relate to it personally, I'm also desperate to alleviate his disgust in my kind. In...*me*. I angle myself toward him. "Elliot, you're right about humans. We are at times just as you've witnessed. But there's so much more to us, and not everyone carries my species' worst traits."

He shakes his head with a bitter laugh. "Even after being on the receiving end of humankind's vilest ways, you seek to defend them? You seek to convince me human society isn't as bad as I think?"

I study his face for a moment, recalling everything we spoke of tonight. My mind drums up images of dinner, Imogen's smug grin, and painful memories of my past.

For a moment, I want to take back my sentiment, tell Elliot he's right. But that would be a lie. For alongside these darker aspects, I know brighter ones exist. I find them in my sister Nina, in the kind bookseller, Mr. Cordell. There's even potential in people I don't know well, like Imogen's stepsister, Ember. As much as I desire to rid myself of Vernon and escape the clutches of its society, there's a part of me that knows—if I tried—I could find admirable people here.

I place a hand on Elliot's clenched fist. Holding his gaze, I say with all the conviction I can muster, "Yes, Elliot. There is good in humankind."

For several moments, we fall into a frozen silence. As each second wears on, heat begins to flood my cheeks, the realization of my hand on Elliot's striking me harder and harder. It seemed vital in the moment, a way to drive the strength of my statement, but as his fist remains firm beneath my palm, I can't help but recall how revolted he was at Mrs. Coleman's incessant touches. Terror sends my pulse racing, but I'm too embarrassed to make any sudden moves.

I'm about to slowly pull away when his fist turns suddenly soft, his fingers yielding as they turn upward to lace through mine in a gentle hold. A sad smile tugs his lips. "I'm starting to think it's possible that what you say is true."

My heart hammers against my ribs as his eyes burn into mine. Where once his stare felt invasive, it now feels...different. Still dangerous, but in a new way I'm not sure how to explain. It sends a flurry to my stomach and makes me forget how to breathe. Yes, this is a dangerous feeling indeed.

He runs a thumb over the back of my hand, and the caress seems to radiate up my arm and down to the rest of my body. His lips part, but no words come out.

Like a magnet, I find myself leaning closer, as if that could draw out what he's neglecting to say. Or perhaps it isn't words I'm drawing forth but something else. Something about his lips—

A flutter of movement has our eyes darting toward the rose. There, drifting in a slow, sinuous arc back and forth, a red petal falls to the snow-covered floor of the courtyard.

Elliot grows rigid. Slowly, he rises to stand, his hand slipping from mine as he walks toward the rose. "That's...unusual."

"What?" I stand and come up beside him, finding my knees wobbling like jelly. I'm grateful for the chilly night air, as it helps cool the fire that's invaded my cheeks after our...whatever that moment was.

"I already saw a petal fall today."

My mind is slow to comprehend the significance of his words. When I do, a flash of panic washes over me, but it's quickly replaced with logic. "I'm sure it's after midnight by now," I say calmly. "Technically, it's a new day."

He releases a relieved sigh. "You're probably right."

Remembering he likes to take each fallen petal with him, I crouch down to retrieve it. With careful, reverent moves, I lift the petal, its texture smooth and silky beneath my cold fingers. It's unsettling to think I'm basically holding a day of Elliot's life in my hand. A day that could be one of his last if his curse isn't broken.

Ever since we made our bargain, I've been determined to try my hardest at making our scheme work. Even when I had my backup plan—however ill-conceived it was—my main intent was breaking Elliot's curse. All because it would serve me well in the end, those twenty thousand quartz rounds buying my freedom and independence. But now...now something has shifted inside me. I'm still eager for the financial benefits our bargain will bring, but almost as much—no, equally so— I want to save Elliot's life.

A fire burns inside my heart, my determination fusing with my desires. I'll make Imogen break this damn curse if it's the last thing I do. I'll see Elliot regain his life, his freedom, his wolf form. And I'll claim my freedom too. For the first time since we made our bargain, I truly *feel* its importance from both sides.

I'm about to stand and hand the petal to Elliot when I notice a hint of red peeking from beneath a light layer of snow. I brush it away, revealing another petal. My blood goes cold. I continue dusting away the snow until I reveal the cobblestone floor. And five petals along the way.

I spread them out in my palm, then look up at the king. His face is pale, his eyes wide and distant. "I thought you said you collected each petal daily?"

"I do," he whispers.

Rising to my feet, I drop the petals in the king's trembling palm. Ice fills my heart. "What does it mean?"

"The petals are falling faster." He meets my eyes. "I'm running out of time."

25

I hardly sleep that night, and the slumber I do find is fitful at best. My dreams are laced with vicious, falling rose petals and Elliot's horrified expression.

As soon as the rising sun begins to brighten my curtains, I give up on rest and go to my window. Drawing back the drapes, my eyes immediately seek the rose garden. I'm not surprised when I find Elliot there, sitting on the bench with his shoulders slumped. Did he even try to sleep? Has he been out there all night?

When we parted ways, I begged him not to dwell on the five fallen petals too much. Until we can establish a pattern over the next couple days and analyze it with a mathematic equation, we can't be certain this isn't just a fluke. But, judging from the amount of red I see spread over the king's palm, a few petals have already fallen anew.

With my newfound determination steeling my resolve, I hurry to dress and rush from my room. As I head downstairs, I'm surprised to find several of the wolf-people loitering in the hall. All are dressed in their new clothing, and some appear to even have taken Elliot's lead in getting haircuts, but they seem stifled by an anxious energy, their normally fierce expressions now so subdued. In the corridor leading to the garden doors, I find Gray and Blackbeard leaning against the walls, whispering to each other. They straighten when they see me.

"Have you any idea why His Majesty insists on staying outside all morning?" Gray asks, her brows weaving together. "He won't speak to us or allow us to enter the courtyard."

"I do," I say, "but I don't think—"

"If it's about the curse," Blackbeard says, "it involves us too. We deserve to know."

I sigh. Maybe he's right. "Just after midnight, the king found five petals had fallen instead of just one. I...I think he's watching to see how many fall today."

The two fae exchange a glance. "It's coming to claim us," Blackbeard whispers.

Curiosity buzzes inside me, and I realize there are still a few things regarding the curse that haven't been made clear. This might be my chance to understand the rest. "The residents in the palace chose to stay with the king when he was cursed, right?"

They nod. "Most fled right away," Gray explains in her old, creaky voice. "Especially the young and strong, and any wolves who didn't consider themselves part of the king's pack. The old and injured—those who aged from severe war or iron injuries, like me—had no choice but to stay."

"*Some* may not have had a choice," Blackbeard says, "but others stayed out of loyalty to our king."

"Yeah, yeah." Gray waves a dismissive hand. "Would you like a medal for that?"

Blackbeard ignores her. "Then there were those who had a choice, those who had been loyal to the king all their lives and still chose to leave him behind. A few mothers even left their pups, as I'm sure you've seen."

My heart squeezes with the realization that Micah and the other children were abandoned. By their own mothers, no less.

Gray must see the horror on my face. "Not all unseelie are fit parents," she says.

"Not all humans are, either," I mutter, thinking of the man my father has become since Mother's death. Returning to my original subject, I say, "The king told me that if the curse isn't broken, it will claim his life. His age will catch up to the mortal body he's left with and he will die within seconds. Will the same happen to everyone else?"

"Most of us," Blackbeard says, rubbing the dark scruff on his chin. "The only ones who will have years ahead of them will be the children. They are still pups in both human and fae years."

The consolation that brings is very small. Especially since they'll be orphaned worse than they already are. With their caretakers dead, they'll be left to fend for themselves. And everyone else will be...

"Are you not upset at the king for refusing to break the curse himself?" I ask. "You'd all be free if he'd sacrifice his unseelie form."

Blackbeard shakes his head. "If he sacrifices his unseelie form, the same goes for the rest of us. We'd lose a vital piece of ourselves. The only true way to break the curse is to break it completely."

Gray nods in agreement. "We knew what we were getting into when we stayed. If the curse isn't broken by a human, then it's death we face and death we choose. We've made peace with that. Most of us, at least." Her craggy face softens as she lowers her voice. "Will you keep a promise for me?"

A chill of suspicion crawls up my back. I've heard how seriously fae take promises. "What would you have me promise?"

"If this all goes wrong, if the curse isn't broken, will you see to the children? I'm not asking you to take them in yourself, but will you see they are cared for? Given homes amongst your kind, perhaps?"

Tears prick my eyes at the sincerity in her voice, the pleading in her gaze. "Gray, that's not even up for debate. Nothing could stop me from caring for them if such a terrible thing were to come to pass."

Blackbeard gives a dark chuckle. "Be careful thinking too sweetly of them. Some of them bite."

A corner of my mouth quirks, but my mood is too somber to feel any true mirth. "I can handle a couple bites."

⁓

ELLIOT REMAINS WHERE I LAST SAW HIM OUT MY WINDOW, eyes trained on the rose. He must have returned indoors at least once since last night, for I see he's traded his prosthetic for his staff. I enter the courtyard, the king not bothering to look up. Seeing him like this makes a part of me yearn to rush to his side and sit next to him, to take his hands in mine and offer comfort. But I don't think that's what he truly needs right now.

Standing tall, I put my hands on my hips. "Get up, Mr. Rochester."

Slowly, he slides his eyes to mine. "Why?"

"Why? What do you mean, *why*? Because sitting around here watching petals fall won't help you. Action is all that can. So, come on. We're advancing our scheme to the next level."

He sits a little straighter. "How so?"

"It's time for phase three," I say. "We've snagged Imogen's interest. She's seen what you have to offer— your display of wealth and gentlemanly behavior. By now, you're locked in her sights. Next, we need to encourage a deeper feeling. It's time to tempt her from interest to love."

He scoffs. "How do you suggest we do that?"

"Courtship." I can't say the word without a hint of disgust. "It's time to do all the stupid little things that will encourage her attachment. Starting with an invitation to tea."

He quirks a brow. "Tea?"

"Yes. I'll send her a letter today and invite her to have tea with me."

"Why you? Shouldn't I be the one to invite her?"

"Of course not," I say. "That would be highly improper. Normally, the expected response would be for you to call on her family at their townhouse and thank them for attending your dinner. Since you can't stray too far from the manor, we need a creative alternative. You could invite her family over, but we'd have better luck advancing our timeline if we got Imogen alone. And that, Your Majesty, is why *I* am inviting her to tea."

"I still don't see how that is supposed to make her fall in love with me."

"You'll happen by, of course," I say with a conspiratorial grin. "Just going about your business, you'll see us, stop to pay your respects, and then I will suggest the three of us take a walk in the gardens together. You'll escort Imogen, and I'll remain nearby as a chaperone. I will, however, make myself scarce so Imogen feels she has your full attention."

His lips pull into a snarl. "She better not say a damn word—"

"I don't care what she says. Don't you dare come to my defense, do you hear me? We don't have time for that."

He glances back at the rose and gives a resigned nod. "Fine, but I won't like it."

"I'd respect you less if you did. Now, are we in agreement? I will write the letter now, send it with Bertha this afternoon, and invite her to call tomorrow."

Elliot says nothing for a few moments, his shoulders suddenly tense. Finally, he quietly says, "What am I to do with her when we walk in the garden? Shouldn't I...say something to, as you say, encourage her attachment?"

I furrow my brow. "Well, yes, you must speak with her, have casual conversation. You needn't be too forward in your intentions, but a compliment or two will suffice. A kiss on the back of her hand, perhaps."

He pales, a grimace forming on his lips.

I sigh. "Fine. Let us practice. Come with me." I wave at him to join me. To my relief, he obeys. My main objective in speaking with him had been getting him out of the courtyard anyway, just so he'd stop sulking in despair.

When he reaches my side, he hesitates for a few moments. "I'd offer you my arm, but I'm walking with my staff. My free arm helps for balance."

"It's fine. You already proved last night to be proficient at the art of escorting a lady by arm. Today, we'll walk side by side."

The ghost of a smile flickers over his mouth.

I avert my gaze, ignoring the flutter in my heart. Although, despite my efforts, I can't seem to find my words. So instead, we start our walk in silence, making our way along the garden path. When we reach the place we stood during our conversation about the viscount, I can't help but blush at the memory. The way he placed his hand on my arm. This, of course, only brings thoughts of what happened after, when he took me to the court-yard and we sat together on the bench. How embarrassed I was when I touched his fist, then how stricken I became when he laced his fingers with mine and leaned closer...

I shake my head, realizing we've come to the end of the main path. "Let's follow the trail to the front gardens. I've yet to walk in them."

Elliot nods, and we turn course, making our way along the side of the house.

"We must practice your conversation skills," I say. "I know you're familiar with proper greetings, so let's carry on with what should happen from there. Pretend I'm Imogen and offer me a compliment."

"A compliment?" He sneers. "What about that wretched human am I supposed to compliment?"

I roll my eyes. Again, with the *wretched humans*. "It doesn't have to be something true."

"It does," he says. "I can't lie, remember?"

"Oh, right. Well, then you will have to look at her and find something true to say. Perhaps you can find beauty in the color of her dress, or the shade of blonde in her hair. Even something like you said to me last night, about liking my laugh, will suffice. Although, I don't suggest you add anything about wolves. Now, come on. Try it with me. Make believe I'm Imogen."

He turns his face to me, and I try not to blush beneath his gaze. "Your shade of hair is quite nice," he says, words stilted.

"Good, that's a start."

He's quiet for a few moments, eyes still locked on the side of my face. "It's like raven feathers or an obsidian night sky. Your eyes are nearly the same color, a stunning shade of the darkest umber."

My pulse begins to quicken as heat climbs up my cheeks. "Yes, you do seem to have a handle at compliments. She will like that very much indeed."

Finally, he averts his gaze, allowing me to gather a deep inhale to cool my rising temperature.

"Now, I'll go," I say. "What nice weather we're having today, don't you think, Mr. Rochester?"

He glances around, brow furrowed. "Nice? Why would you say it's nice? It's stopped snowing."

I chuckle. "For one, that is not how you should answer Imogen. For another...you truly like the snow that much?"

"Of course I do. Who wouldn't?" When I narrow my

eyes at him, he pulls his head back. "Are you telling me you *don't* like the snow?"

I'm about to affirm my answer, but a deeper truth reaches my lips. "I hated it when we first arrived in Vernon. Growing up in Isola, I was raised under a constant supply of sunshine. Then Bretton brought nothing but cloudy skies and rain. So, when I arrived in the Winter Court, snow was brand new and something I'd never had experience with. To be honest, I didn't stop detesting it until...well, until I started living here at the manor."

His eyes take on a distant look. "I can't imagine anyone disliking the snow. The smell of it, the feel of it. The almost imperceptible sound it makes as it falls. The feel of it crunching beneath my paws." He looks down at our shoes, brow wrinkled. "Or feet, I suppose."

"I can admire snow's finer qualities," I say, pulling my cloak close to my body. "I'm even getting used to the cold a little. Sometimes it feels cozy to be so bundled outdoors."

He meets my gaze with trepidation in his eyes. "But you'll never like this climate as much as a warmer one, will you? That's why you want to move back to Isola."

I don't know if I'm imagining the sadness in his tone, but I hate what it does to my heart. It hammers in response to the idea that Elliot could be unhappy with the thought of me moving. *It can't be that,* I tell myself, forcing my heart to calm. He's the King of the Winter Court. If he's upset with my preference for Isola, it's because he has a vested interest in this snowy land. He'd be upset if *anyone* found the Winter Court less favorable than anywhere else.

Still, when I open my mouth, I don't know what to say. I find that we've stopped near the front of the manor and are now facing each other. When did that happen?

Elliot takes a step closer, shifting his stance with his staff. His brows knit together. "Do you think you could ever be happy here in Winter?"

My heart causes a ruckus yet again, warring with my mind to form an answer. Our eyes lock, and I take in the deep ruby hue of his irises. I can almost see his question swimming in them, but am I imagining the significance attached to it?

The sound of horse hooves saves me from delving further, and we turn to face the drive. At the far end is a black coach coming this way.

Panic and realization strike me at once. "Get inside. Now! Hurry!" I rush to the front doors of the manor, hoping they aren't locked, and Elliot follows quickly behind. Luckily, the doors open with ease and I slam them shut behind the king.

"What's going on, Gemma? Who do you think is in the coach?"

I can't know for certain, but it isn't hard to guess. "We aren't the only ones advancing our schemes. Now go get dressed at once."

26

I only have a few seconds to spread word through the manor that a guest has arrived. The residents are quick to comprehend what this means and what's expected of them. Just as the coach pulls in front of the manor, I catch my reflection in the hall mirror, finding my cheeks flushed and my hair in disarray. I tuck the errant strands beneath my hat and take a few deep breaths. Then, with all the composure I can gather, I step calmly out the front doors and down the stairs to the drive.

A well-dressed footman opens the carriage door and offers its occupant his hand. Just like I'd suspected, Imogen steps out of the coach, all smiles and grace. Who I hadn't expected to see, however, is Ember. Imogen strides toward me, and the bonnet-clad girl follows just behind.

"Dearest Gemma," Imogen says. "I do hope you aren't too busy working today. I simply had to call upon you for a visit."

Seeing her false, smiling face sends waves of anger through me as her words from last night's dinner echo through my mind. Mirroring her expression, I squint my eyes and stretch my lips into an exaggerated smile. "I can always make time for you, my dear Imogen. And Ember, it's lovely to see you again."

Imogen doesn't give Ember a chance to respond to my greeting. "Your employer doesn't mind me calling on you here, does he?"

"Of course not," I say. "Since I take room and board here, he knows to expect visits and allows me plenty of leisure time."

"Oh, how good of him! But he's not around, of course." She does a poor job of pretending she isn't looking over my head and around me before returning her eyes to mine with a look of disappointment. "Surely, he's too important and busy to be present."

"No, he's present," I say, watching as her expression regains its glow. "We may even cross his path."

"How wonderful! Shall you invite us inside then?"

I hesitate. While I asked several fae to tidy up the parlor and main hall, I'm not certain they've had enough time to do a thorough job. I haven't seen the state of the parlor after last night's dinner. "I had actually just come out for fresh air when you arrived. Why don't we linger out here a few minutes more?"

"Very well." Her expression falters for a moment before she replaces her false smile. "Oh, dearest Gemma, I did want to apologize if I had you flustered last night. You must know I had no intention of doing so."

It takes all my restraint not to turn my smile into a snarl. "No, of course you didn't."

She takes a step closer, lowering her voice. "I only wanted to help you, you know. As your dear friend, I want what's best for you. I was simply drawing attention to something I felt needed a little more awareness on your part."

This time, I can't stop my smile from melting from my lips. "How good of you."

Imogen doesn't seem to notice. "I'm so glad you understand. You know I will always be an honest friend, even if it sometimes hurts."

My fingers curl into fists, jaw clenched. *I know something I'd like to make hurt...*

The sound of the front doors opening distracts me from my violent thoughts, and the three of us turn to face the manor. Back in his prosthetic and dressed in one of his sharp suits, Elliot emerges from the doorway and pauses at the top of the steps. A look of uncertainty clouds his face before he says, "Good day."

"Oh, Mr. Rochester!" Imogen says with a gasp before dipping into a curtsy. "I had no idea I'd be graced with your presence today. I came to visit my dearest friend."

"Your dearest friend," he echoes, a sarcastic bite in his tone.

Thankfully, I must be the only one who catches it, for Imogen only smiles brighter as she links her arm through mine. "Yes, I do adore your steward."

I widen my eyes to keep from rolling them. It isn't hard to grasp the truth of the situation. What I'm sure really transpired is she woke up this morning with the realization that I am her only direct link to Elliot. The thought gives me some semblance of vindictive pride, knowing I have such a power over her.

Elliot grimaces and says nothing in reply, but when his eyes flash to me, I give him a warning look. With a subtle flick of my hand, I gesture him forward. Catching the hint, he releases a sigh and descends the front steps at a slow, leisurely pace. I must say, he's getting quite adept at walking with his prosthetic. Imogen beams as he stops before us, but Elliot says not a word.

Damn it, Elliot! I clear my throat. "Nice weather, isn't it?"

Elliot furrows his brow, eyes sliding to mine.

"So nice, I imagine the back gardens are just lovely." I enunciate each word for emphasis.

He frowns, jaw clenched, then faces Imogen with a poorly developed smile. His motions are stiff as he extends his arm. "Would you like to take a walk with me?"

Imogen takes his arm with enthusiasm, lashes fluttering like butterfly wings as she presses close to his side. My breath catches at the sight of them touching, seeing her hand placed exactly where mine had been just last night. But why should that bother me? It's just a hand. An arm. Simple contact.

Simple. Until it's not.

"I most certainly would!" Imogen says. "Does your garden have any of the Winter Court's famous snow-loving flowers? I have yet to see a single fae garden planted in Vernon."

"It's mostly hedges," he says flatly. "There is very little magic at the manor."

Her face falls a bit. "Oh. Well, I do love a well-manicured hedge. Will you show me?"

His eyes flash to mine, and I can almost see the word

help pulsing within them. However, I've learned my lesson about interfering when Imogen is around. He's on his own.

He holds my gaze a few seconds longer, then it's as if a shroud is lifted from over his face. In the blink of an eye, his expression transforms from dour to radiant, and he turns a warm smile to Imogen. "Yes, I will show you."

Side by side, they turn around and head for the back gardens.

"I suppose you're stuck with me now," Ember says.

I turn to face her with surprise, having almost forgotten her quiet presence. Something about her gentle manner calms my nerves, stills my aching heart. "Come, we must not fall too far behind."

"No, of course not. For that would be highly improper." Her tone is sweet yet subtly mocking in a way I don't think I could ever pull off myself.

I look at her with fresh eyes. In the short time I've known her, I've found her far more likable than her stepsisters. And the more I'm in her company, the more I recognize the silent rebel hiding inside.

Linking arms, we trail behind the couple, keeping them in sight but not sound, just how I'm sure Imogen prefers.

"This is the only reason she brought me," Ember says. "Well, two reasons. First, so I would be paired with you if her grand scheme were to come to fruition and she managed to snag an invitation to converse with Mr. Rochester. Second, so I would pose no threat in attracting your employer's attention."

I frown, assessing the girl at my side. She wears a heavy overcoat in a pastel pink, fraying at the hems.

Today's bonnet is white patterned with daisies. "How old are you, Ember?"

"Seventeen."

So she's a year younger than Imogen and a year older than Clara. "Why does your family treat you so poorly?"

"Well..." She hesitates, as if searching for words. Then a crash erupts behind us, and Ember surges forward, almost falling. I startle, pulling away from her. She whirls around and I do the same. But just as I do, a weight strikes the front of my cloak. Chunks of snow slide off the wool and fall to the ground at my feet.

I lift my eyes to find Micah, head thrown back with laughter. Two other heads, then a third, peek from behind the coach, a tree, and a hedge. "Attack!" shouts Micah.

All four children spring forward, grinning wildly while they hurl balls of white ice. With a shout, I scurry back, panic heating my cheeks. Ember, however, dives to the ground and gathers snow inside her gloved hands.

"What are you doing?" I ask her, barely dodging in time to avoid an icy missile thrown by one of the boys.

Ember hurls her makeshift ball of snow and strikes Micah in the chest. I expect him to react with anger, but he...laughs. Ember squeals as another child—the girl—hits her with a ball to the shoulder. "You've never had a snowball fight?"

"No." I dodge another ball. "What in the name of the saints is it?"

Ember hurls another ball. Then another. "It's fun, Miss Bellefleur. My parents and I always did this when we went on holiday here in the Winter Court when I was little. Try it!"

I glance from her, expertly shaping fluffy snow into a solid orb, to the children, unrestrained joy lighting their faces. With a grimace, I crouch down and try to mimic Ember's motions in creating a ball, grateful I wore gloves today. I'm surprised to find it's easier than it looks, requiring nothing more than pressure to get the snow to clump together. Ember and I rise to our feet at the same time. Her arms are loaded with several balls, and she laughs with every hit she both gives and receives. I throw my first ball, which lands at one of the boys' feet. He sticks out his tongue in a teasing gesture, then throws a ball that barely misses my face.

I crouch back down, my lips spreading wide as I create more ammunition. Ember bends down to do the same, only to get struck in the head. She laughs as she falls to the side, then quickly returns to her efforts. When we stand, arms laden with snowballs, something unusual catches my eye. I glance at Ember, finding streams of long, lustrous, turquoise hair streaming around her face. Her bonnet appears to have been knocked away. When her eyes meet mine, I see their color for the first time. No longer shadowed by the bonnet, they too reveal the most striking shade of aqua.

I'm so surprised, I'm not able to dodge the next strike, and a snowball hits me in the neck, sending icy moisture dripping down my front. With a yelp, I return the attack, and soon we're all dusted with snow and ice, our laughter ringing over the front lawn as we continue our battle.

"Ember!" A shocked voice comes from behind, startling me and my blue-haired friend. We turn to find Imogen, still clasping Elliot's arm, eyes wide and furious as they shoot daggers at her stepsister.

Ember stops and holds Imogen's gaze for a few moments, defiance flashing in her turquoise eyes. Then, with a sigh, she fetches her bonnet from the snow and replaces it on her head, tucking every strand of hair out of sight. The mood is clearly broken, and the children disperse, none daring to continue our battle.

Imogen gathers her composure, plastering a fresh smile over her lips. "Oh, Gemma, I must tell you the great news."

"What is it?" I ask as they walk toward us.

She removes her grip from Elliot's arm to clasp her hands excitedly at her chest. "Mr. Rochester has agreed to host a ball. Here at the manor!"

My eyes widen. "Is that so?"

"Apparently," Elliot says through his teeth, lips stretched into a grin that doesn't match his eyes.

"He's so gracious," Imogen says. "With the Verity Hotel's ballroom still under construction, Vernon's social season has yet to truly begin. But this—*this*—will be perfection. We mustn't invite the whole town, of course, for I assume the ball will be held in the dining room. It's spacious enough, but certainly won't suit a large crowd. Besides, do we really want *everyone* there?"

"Certainly not," I say dryly.

"I cannot wait. I'll draw up the invite list this after-noon and send it back in the evening. Then we only have to wait for Friday."

"Friday," I echo. That's five days from now. Five days to plan a ball. I glance at Elliot, seeing the resignation in his face. That's when I remember the rapidly falling petals. Perhaps a ball is exactly what we need to secure Imogen's attachment. There's nothing more romantic than dancing. Which is, of course, why I've sworn never to attend a ball again. Good thing I'll be working this one and not dancing at it.

"If it's too soon to hire proper musicians," Imogen says, "we can just have Ember play the pianoforte. She's tolerable enough."

I frown. "Won't Ember want to dance?"

Imogen turns her nose to the air. "Of course she doesn't."

I meet Ember's gaze with a raised brow. She in turn gives me a crooked grin and a quick roll of her eyes that Imogen is too busy staring at Elliot to notice. "I'll be happy to play, should you want me," Ember says.

"See, it's settled," Imogen says. "Now, there is much planning to do. I'll need a new dress and shoes. Oh, and the guest list, of course. We should be going so I can get started."

"It was so good of you to call on me today," I say.

Imogen's brows knit together, as if she can't comprehend my words. Then, as if seeming to recall the false pretenses she visited under, she smiles. "Yes, so wonderful it was to see you today. And you as well, Mr. Rochester." She faces him with a curtsy, then stands before him, the hem of her skirts and coat swishing as she sways expectantly side to side.

Elliot looks to me for help, so I tap the back of my hand, then pucker my lips slightly. His gaze rests on my mouth for a beat too long. Then, with a shake of his head, he returns his attention to Imogen. Gently taking her hand in his, he lifts it slowly, then bends down to plant a soft kiss on the back of it.

A flash of anger strikes my core at the sight of his lips brushing her flesh. I breathe it away.

"I shall see you Friday," he says, then releases her hand.

"I'll dream of it every waking moment," Imogen says wistfully. It seems to take some effort to pull her gaze away from him, but she eventually does and then stands before me with a nod. "Gemma, you can expect my lists tonight."

I return the nod, and Imogen takes Ember by the arm. Their footman helps them into the coach and closes the door behind them.

I exhale a heavy breath and watch as the carriage drives away. "That went well."

Elliot comes up beside me. "That went terribly."

I turn to face him. "How so? This ball is exactly what we need. By the end of it, she'll be so smitten, she'll never want to let you go."

His jaw shifts from side to side. With one hand on his hip, he runs the other over his jaw. Finally, he says, "I don't know how to dance."

I'm taken aback for a moment. Such a fact never occurred to me, but I suppose a fae wolf would have very little need to learn human dances. "That is a problem," I confess. I turn my gaze back to the departing carriage, an idea forming in my mind. "I think I have a solution for that."

27

Two days pass, and another five petals fall each day. This makes the math easy, and if the pattern continues without further increase, then we have approximately sixty petals and twelve days left to break the curse. Feeling the strain of our ticking clock, I've poured all my efforts into preparing for the upcoming ball. If I have my way, it will mark the night Imogen falls firmly in love. And if things go even better than I hope, it will be the day I move onto phase four—telling Imogen about the curse and what she must do to save her beloved.

The thought sends my mind reeling. Will the ball truly be enough to make Imogen willing to sacrifice her greatest treasure? I know the exhilarating effects dancing can have. I also know Imogen's desperation for matrimony will amplify her romantic feelings, but...for the love of the saints, is this scheme crazy?

No, it will work, I remind myself. Imogen will do

anything if she thinks it might secure her a royal husband. She *will* break this curse.

I repeat it like a mantra as I head to the dining hall, buzzing with a mixture of anxiety and excited anticipation. The next few hours could make or break the success of the ball and Elliot's ability to impress Imogen.

I enter the dining room, finding it bright and open with the late morning light streaming through the windows and illuminating the marble floor. The table and chairs have been pushed to the far wall, leaving the space open and ready for the dancing that will commence in three days' time.

In one corner of the room, I find Foxglove standing before a grand pianoforte in a rich mahogany. Ember sits at the stool, turquoise hair streaming down her back while her fingers fly over the keys to create the loveliest melody. Her bonnet lies discarded on the seat next to her.

As I approach, the music wraps around me and I feel some of my anxiety begin to wane. Hope takes its place and I feel my shoulders relax, the corners of my lips twitching upward.

When Foxglove catches sight of me, he extends an arm toward the instrument and waggles his brows. "Do you like it?"

Ember ceases playing and turns on her stool to face me, her face bright. "Miss Bellefleur!"

"Please, call me Gemma," I say, then grin at Foxglove. "I love it! It will be perfect for the ball."

"Yes, well, since the hotel decided to go with a white pianoforte instead, I was happy to see this one put to use."

"I'm so grateful you had one on hand. And I'm happy

you both could come today. Ember, I was worried you wouldn't have any luck getting away."

"Mrs. Coleman and my stepsisters are shopping for dresses today," she says. "They will be gone until evening, I'm sure."

"And I'll have her brought home well before anyone notices," Foxglove adds. "So long as we can get started soon. Where is Mr. Rochester?"

"I believe Amelie is still helping him choose what to wear to the ball," I say.

He scoffs. "Surely, it shouldn't take him *this* long. Ah, there he is."

I turn to find Elliot entering the room with Amelie. He's in his shirtsleeves and trousers, and his grimace tells me just how much he dreads what I'm about to make him do.

Foxglove assesses Elliot from head to toe, a frown tugging his lips. "Mr. Rochester, I thought you'd want to practice in full attire."

Amelie crosses her arms. "He refused," she says, "but he did allow me to pick out what he should wear to the ball."

"Very well," Foxglove says, waving him over with no small amount of impatience. "Come on, then. Let us get started."

Amelie comes over to the pianoforte and props her elbow on the side. Ember offers me a smile before facing the keys. "You can sit next to me if you'd like," she says.

I take her up on that, picking up her bonnet and setting it in my lap as I take a seat. Foxglove and Elliot move to the middle of the room and face each other.

Elliot pales, looking like he'd rather be anywhere else than at a dance lesson.

Ember starts right into a song, her fingers dancing expertly over the keys, and Foxglove begins demonstrating some basic steps. Elliot stumbles to mirror his moves, every motion stiff and awkward. While he's become quite graceful walking with his prosthetic, the unfamiliar dance moves seem to set him back to limping. But as the music lingers on, I find Foxglove to be a most forgiving instructor. Ember continues to play, restarting the song when Foxglove asks her to or switching to new ones as Foxglove tries to demonstrate other dances.

I watch the dancing pair with a smile, my heart light at the sight. Soon, Elliot seems to forget his apprehension and finds a true rhythm alongside his instructor. I'm surprised to find a smile beginning to tug his lips.

His grin grows wider as his eyes lock suddenly on mine. Blushing at having been caught staring at him for once, I avert my gaze and turn my attention to Ember's fluttering fingers. "You play most beautifully," I tell her.

"Thank you. I do adore music. My stepfamily doesn't allow me to play much, so this is a treat for me." The whole time she speaks, she does so without missing a single beat.

I remember the bonnet resting on my lap and glance at her. "I hope you don't mind me asking, but why do you normally hide your hair?"

She rolls her eyes. "It's what Mrs. Coleman wants. She doesn't like how the color draws attention to my heritage."

"Your heritage?"

She meets my gaze for a moment before returning

her eyes to the piano keys. "I'm half fae. My mother was from the Wind Court."

"Oh! I had no idea."

"And that's how Mrs. Coleman wants to keep it."

I frown. "But why?"

"I'm not sure myself. Shame. Jealousy. She was only married to my father for a year before he died, and the wealth she gained from his death is quickly dwindling away. She resents me for merely existing."

"That's terrible."

"I get by." Her song comes to an end, and her fingers slide from the keys. For a moment, a flicker of sadness tugs at her expression. She brings a hand to a locket I've never noticed before, fumbling with it idly while her eyes unfocus.

My stomach sinks. "I'm sorry. I shouldn't have pried."

She blinks a few times and replaces her smile. "It's not you, Gemma. That song...even the happy ones remind me of my parents. They loved to dance."

I want to tell her I understand, that I too have lost my mother, but Foxglove's voice steals my attention. "I think he's fully learned the gallopade! Come, Miss Bellefleur. Take my place with Mr. Rochester. I need to judge his dancing from afar so I can make any other corrections."

I blush, my pulse quickening. "Oh, I couldn't. It's been ages since I've danced."

"Amelie, then," he says.

I'm almost disappointed when she accepts and strides forward. It's not that I'd hoped Foxglove would have pressured me just a bit more, but now I feel like perhaps I should have agreed. It's to help Elliot, after all.

Foxglove steps away from Elliot and Amelie takes his

place. I watch as Elliot takes Amelie's hand in his, then places his other on her back. She, in turn, places a gentle hand on his shoulder. Foxglove adjusts his spectacles and assesses them, then steps forward to make a few corrections. No matter what he tries to do, Elliot's arms remain stiff. "Whatever," Foxglove says with a huff. "I suppose you will appear more natural with practice. Now, begin."

Ember starts a new song with a similar beat as the last, and Elliot and Amelie begin a sliding skip to the side. Elliot nearly trips, but Amelie helps him return to the beat, ever patient and smiling. Just like with Foxglove, soon Elliot seems to grow comfortable, finding the rhythm and performing the slides and turns with increasing ease. His eyes begin to crinkle at the corners, and the next time he nearly trips, he simply laughs it off and connects to the beat again. Even his arms begin to lose some of their stiffness. I must say, he's really not a terrible dancer.

Imogen will be satisfied indeed.

A sinking feeling comes over me, and I watch the dancing pair with fresh eyes. Where his hand rests on Amelie's back, it will soon grace Imogen's. Where his smile shines down upon Amelie, it will soon charm my nemesis. Rage and revulsion—*and...is that jealousy?*—swarm my heart. But why? Why should I care? Do I wish it were me in his arms? Do I wish it were me he's planning to woo? Of course not! I cannot be the one to break his curse. As determined as I am to save his life, there's no way I can sacrifice my greatest treasure—freedom and independence—regardless of the cost. It must be Imogen, for what could she possibly treasure but gowns and gold and jewels? She'll lose nothing but her pride when this is all over, but me...I have too much at stake.

My heart beats an angry rhythm, disharmonious with the lighthearted tempo of the song.

Why am I even considering these thoughts to begin with? It's not like Elliot can ever mean anything to me. So what if I've had a few tender moments with him? So what if I imagined we may have been about to kiss in the rose courtyard? None of it matters. None. For he doesn't value me but his wolf form. And once the curse is broken, I'll never see him again. Certainly not as Elliot Rochester. He'll be a wolf king, immortal, and brimming with whatever magic powers he had before. I'll be but a flicker within an unhappy event in his long, endless life.

A lump rises in my throat as heat crawls up the back of my neck. The room suddenly feels too small and too warm, the music too loud, the sound of Elliot's laughter grating on my ears. Without a parting word, I rise from the piano bench and leave the frivolity behind.

28

W hen I reach my room, I feel foolish in a way that has only one solution—literary distraction.

Pushing all thoughts of Elliot, Imogen, and ballroom dances out of my mind, I retrieve *The Governess and the Earl* from my bedside table and settle onto the bed, propping my back against a stack of pillows. I already finished the book yesterday, but considering my mind has been so distracted with work, schemes, and preparations, I'm sure there's a lot I've missed. Besides, I almost always read books two or three times each.

The book has just the effect I was after, and soon the words swallow me into a made-up world. One where happy endings are real and love conquers all. It's nonsense, and I know it. But right now, I just want to get lost there. Lost I become, following the governess' journey meeting the handsome earl, a man who's engaged to another woman. A woman far more beautiful and superior than the humble governess. At first, I thought this story would elicit too many feelings of discomfort, considering it hits so close to home, but knowing what I know about this series, how the governess always gets the man she loves, I'm soothed by it instead.

Hours pass. I don't remember turning on the lights in my room, but I must have at some point, for I can see the words as daylight darkens to evening. I'm swept deep into my story, letting it override all sense of reality. It isn't until I'm nearing the end and embroiled in a particularly heart-pounding scene—one where the governess and earl give in to their passions for the first time—that a sense of unease comes over me. I follow the words on the page, images playing across my mind's eye, and realize I've made a mistake in my imaginings of the earl. I did this several times during my first read-through, but not this time. This time, I kept my vision of the earl accurate to the author's description.

Until now.

The earl takes the governess' face in his hands, eyes burning into hers. *Garnet* eyes. And instead of pale blond hair, the earl has brown hair touched with gold at the ends. I try to shake the image away and re-immerse myself in the scene. The earl touches his lips to the governess' lips, then her arms wrap around his neck as she presses herself close to him. But it isn't the red-headed governess in the earl's arms. It's me. And the earl isn't the earl at all but Elliot.

I squeeze my eyes shut and return my imagined characters to their rightful places. Blond earl. Red-haired governess. Then I dive back in, my pulse racing as I read on. The earl pushes the governess against the wall, and she moans against his lips. I bring my fingers to my own lips as they curl into a wicked smile. Love scenes always make me feel so devious.

The earl lifts the governess in his strong arms, cradling her as he walks toward his bed. Well, I'm not sure Elliot could ever do that with me. Or could he? He walks well with his—

I slam the book shut, a blush boiling my cheeks. What the hell was that? Why the damn bloody roaring saintly hell was I considering whether Elliot—no, I cannot even let myself examine what I was thinking or why. Taking a few deep breaths, I fix the proper visions of the characters in my head and open my book again. It takes a few moments to find the right chapter and page, but when I do, I allow no stray thoughts as I pick back up where I left off.

The earl lays the governess gently on the bed, then leans down to reignite their kiss. She moans, arching against him, and I feel a sizzling warmth at the apex of my thighs. I steady my breathing as I read on, my eyes wide as the earl slides a hand beneath the governess' skirt, caressing up her leg. Then he lowers himself over her, and their eyes lock. The governess reaches for the collar of his shirt, pulling him closer. Closer. They kiss again, their bodies moving against one another. She runs her hands through his hair, their brown strands—

I pause and blink a few times. No, not brown. Blond. The earl is blond. I return to the scene, but no matter how much I try, the earl is *not* blond, nor is he the earl at all. It's Elliot. And the woman he's preparing to make love to isn't the crimson-haired governess but a girl with black hair—me.

With a frustrated groan, I close my book yet again and toss it to the side. Only now do I realize how warm I've become, sweat pooling beneath my armpits and behind my neck. I admit, it's been months since I've had a lover... since Oswald...but reading love scenes rarely gets me this hot and bothered. There's only one thing to do now. I need outside at once.

Hastily, I dress in my boots and cloak, then race to my door. Flinging it open, I nearly collide with a wall before I realize the wall is actually Elliot, standing before my doorway with his fist raised as if to knock. I startle and launch a step back. I can only hope he doesn't see how my cheeks blaze as I look at him, guilt tightening my stomach. Can he see the sheen of sweat on my brow? Do my eyes confess the compromising positions I was imagining us in just moments before?

It takes all my will to burn the questions from my mind and act normal. "Elliot," I say, my words far more breathless than I like, "what are you doing here?"

He lowers his fist and takes a step back. He's dressed the way he was at dance practice, in his shirtsleeves and trousers, his prosthetic still in place. "I came to check on you. You left the dining hall so suddenly and I haven't seen you since."

"Check on me? Why would you need to check on me? There's just...so much work to do. I couldn't allow myself to sit idly by and watch you dance." The last few words feel bitter on my tongue.

He looks me over. "Were you about to go outside?"

"Well, I..." I know what will happen if I say yes. He'll offer to accompany me and I'll have to stand close to him. And I cannot stand close to him right now. "I was, but I've changed my mind. I think I'll stay in and go to bed early."

I expect him to take his leave, but he only furrows his brow. As his gaze locks on mine, I can't help but recall my scandalous imaginings of those eyes of his, inches from my own, his mouth pressing against my—

I avert my gaze, pursing my lips as a rush of desire heats my core.

"Something's wrong," he says, his voice a low growl, his posture visibly stiff. "What happened?"

His response takes me aback, and I realize I must remedy this at once. I need a lie. Fast. Glancing over my shoulder, my eyes land on my traitorous book. I let my expression fall when I return my gaze to his. "I'm out of reading material. I left all my books behind at the townhouse and have only had a single title to read since I've been here. It's...very hard for me to wind down without a good book. That's all it is. Nothing to worry about."

His shoulders relax. "I didn't realize you were such an avid reader. I'm sorry. I should have done this before."

"Done what?"

He turns and waves at me to follow. "Come. It's time you met my library."

He says it with a scoff, but to me, his words are an enchantment, one I follow without a second thought. "The library," I echo, my tone reverent. I remember mention of a library when he first gave a tour of the manor, but I've yet to see it for myself.

Elliot laughs. "It's one of the cruelest jokes of the curse."

I have no idea what that means, but I follow him nonetheless, down the familiar halls and stairs. Then we reach a wing of the manor I've never entered, one I'm pretty sure is near the king's private quarters. As we make our way down the hall, our pace slow and leisurely, I'm surprised to find it so clean. It seems the residents I've assigned cleaning duties to have taken their jobs to heart and are expanding far past the public areas we need for our scheme. If I didn't know any better, I'd think Elliot and his pack were beginning to take pride in this place.

The halls grow narrower, and I'm forced to walk a little closer to Elliot. That and the quiet of our surroundings has my awareness of him growing. We're alone in a wing I've never been to, our shoulders brushing as we walk. I clear my throat. "So, how was your dance lesson?"

He glances at me with a wry grin. "How do you think? It was torture, like everything else in this scheme of yours."

Despite his words, his tone is light. It's enough to ease some of the tension roiling in my stomach. "Sounds like it was effective then."

He shrugs. "I learned the gallopade, the waltz, and the polka. We tried to learn something called the quadrille and then the cotillion, but even with the help of some of my pack attempting to learn the dance with us, it ended in a mess."

I try to imagine such a sight and almost wish I hadn't missed it. I can hardly fathom how uncomfortable Gray and Blackbeard would be if they'd been requisitioned for the lesson. Group dances like the quadrille and cotillion are quite complex for novices to perform.

"Three dances should suffice," I say. "That will give you plenty to have with Imogen, enough to make your intentions clear and for her to be swept away by you." I force my lips into a curt smile while I say these words, but the twisting in my heart doesn't seem to match.

Saving me from further conversation on the topic, Elliot stops outside a closed door. "Here we are."

My pulse quickens with anticipation as he pushes open the door to reveal a dark room, then fumbles with something near the wall. A warm glow emanates from orbs of light hovering over sconces throughout the room, illuminating a modest space filled with several seating areas, the walls covered with floor-to-ceiling bookcases interspersed by a few large windows. Each window hosts a padded seat, and everything in me begs to climb upon one with a book at once. I step farther into the room, turning in a circle to take in the vast number of books.

"My library," Elliot says, tone somber as he stands with his hands clasped behind his back.

I meet his gaze with a wrinkled brow. "Why do you sound so displeased, Mr. Rochester?"

His jaw shifts side to side. "Every one of these books is written by a human."

Some of my joy sinks to my toes, threatening to retreat altogether. "Humans. Those you so vehemently hate."

He takes a few slow steps toward one of the bookcases. "These books are fiction, Gemma."

"Oh, so you have a problem with fiction now too?"

His lips melt into a frown, eyes going unfocused as his tone becomes strained. "There's just so much...feeling in these books. I don't like the way my body responds to it."

This surprises me and manages to lessen some of my indignation. I step closer to him. "Does that mean you've tried reading them?"

"I've been bored now and then," he says with a noncommittal shrug.

"And how exactly did your body respond to what you read?" I grow suddenly hot, realizing how improper my question sounds, especially with the wicked fantasies I had about fictional earl-Elliot still fresh in my mind.

He, however, doesn't seem to find anything lewd about it. "I feel things I don't feel as a wolf. Books give me experiences I shouldn't have, emotions that aren't my own. They spell out words that manage to draw tears from my eyes, twist my heart, even though nothing is physically happening to me. It's a human sorcery I don't care to mess with."

His answer both amuses and saddens me. "Elliot, that's called empathy. It isn't sorcery. Surely wolves—and unseelie fae, for that matter—have emotions."

"Not like this. We feel passions driven by our instincts. But the pages in these books..." He shakes his head. "I cannot explain it, but they have a powerful effect on me."

"That's sort of the whole point," I say. "That is why fiction exists. It takes us to places we'll never go in real life, allows us to feel emotions and experiences we might not get the chance to have ourselves. It isn't something to be afraid of. It's a shame you don't see fiction as the blessing it can be."

"Blessing? How so?"

"Well, it's true that books can make you feel things that may not be pleasant. Sad things, losses, grief. But they can make you feel happy things too. Pleasant endings and resolutions you'll never have yourself."

He studies me for a few quiet moments. "Is that why you love to read so much?"

As his eyes bore into me, I realize I've laid myself bare. Shown one of my most vulnerable truths. "Yes," I whisper. "I read to experience resolutions I, myself, have never had."

He walks over to me, his gaze warmer with every inch he closes between us. "Is it worth it?"

My heart hammers against my ribs at his proximity. Memories of the earl-Elliot return to the forefront of my mind, making my lips tingle. "Is what worth it?"

"Experiencing pain that is not your own. Feeling joy and love and a happy ending that's over as soon as you close the book. Is it worth it? Or does it only make reality colder when you're forced to return to it? Would it not be better to feel nothing at all?"

I swallow hard. Why do I get the feeling there's a layer to this question, with something lying beneath his words that I don't quite understand? Whatever the case, I can only give him my truth. "Yes, it's worth it. To feel nothing is not a life worth living. Yes, it hurts to return to the mundane after being swept away in a beautiful fantasy, but at least for a time, that fantasy was mine. It doesn't matter that it wasn't real, nor could ever be."

"It can never be real, can it?"

I study his face, puzzling over his words. I have no idea what weight the question bears for him, but for me, it carries everything I've given up on—the belief that romance is true and men's hearts aren't fickle. A world where I'm not scorned by friends, and the people I love stand by my side. A life where I'm seen for who I am, not for who society wants me to be. The chance to be free. As

I think it, I realize maybe it *could* be true. Maybe I do still have hope. Isn't that why I made this bargain? Why I'm planning on moving back to Isola? If I can believe it's possible to create the independence I need to free myself from social constructs...then could I learn to believe the rest could be true too? Could I...believe in love again?

It's a dangerous thought, one I'm not yet ready to face.

Elliot watches me, awaiting an answer to his question. Again, I get that feeling there's a layer to his words that I can't see. One that feels both firm and fragile at the same time. One that—if I choose to unearth it—there will be no burying it back again.

So instead of facing it, I do something I rarely do in front of him. I put on my false persona.

With a casual shrug and a forced smile, I say, "Who's to say what can or can't be real? Now, show me which books you've attempted to read."

29

I feel much lighter as I return to my room with a new book in my hands. After Elliot showed me the few titles he'd tried to read, he left me alone in the library to enjoy myself. I assessed each of the four books he'd pointed out, and settled on the one with the most well-worn spine. Even though the wear of the book could be attributed to the manor's previous owner, I wanted to select the one Elliot has seemingly read the most.

Back in my room, I climb under the covers and turn to the first page. I enter the story, finding it very unlike what I normally read. There seems to be no pulse-pounding romance, no handsome hero, no heated scandal, which should help save my sanity for the remainder of the night. Instead, I find a bittersweet tale of an orphaned boy who meets an outcast street dog, and the bond that develops between them. I read late into the night, finding myself laughing and crying in equal measure. At the end, the dog saves the boy's life at the expense of his own, and I'm left a sobbing mess.

With the book clutched against my chest, I turn off the lights and burrow beneath my blankets, feeling a deep throb in my heart that's both sharp and warm at once. No wonder Elliot hates books after reading this one. The books I read have happy endings, not...whatever this is. Then again, I could never wish to erase what this story has given me, for alongside loss came growth and love and friendship. Maybe Elliot was right. Maybe books are a strange form of human sorcery. For how else can a story feel so satisfying and agonizing at the same time?

I hug the book tighter, breathing in the scent of its pages—the classic paper smell mingled with another aroma of earth and pine, one that's becoming increasingly familiar and can only be described as *Elliot*—and a calming peace falls over me. Sleep begins to tug at the corners of my consciousness, bringing with it an echo of the king's earlier question. *Is it worth it?*

My answer is the same as it was before. *Yes, Elliot. It's worth it.*

THE DAY OF THE BALL ARRIVES, AND I'M THROWN INTO A flurry of activity no sooner than the sun rises. Just like with the dinner, we've hired staff for the day, and I set about instructing them in their proper places and duties. Foxglove arrives to put some final touches on the ballroom, bringing with him Ember and a violinist he's hired to accompany my friend as our modest orchestra for tonight's music. Amelie comes shortly after to ensure Elliot has no issues with the outfit she picked out for him. Elliot himself is nowhere to be seen, however, and I can't blame him. With the manor thrown into such chaos as the day draws closer to dusk, I too would rather be away somewhere in a quiet room. But as steward, management of tonight's ball is my responsibility. There will be no breaks for me. No hiding.

The thought is my constant companion, nagging at the back of my mind as I go about my work and continue overseeing all preparations. No matter how busy I make myself, I can't shake the fact that, even though I won't be dancing tonight, I will still face public display. As floor manager, I'll have to interact with most of our guests, responsible for introductions and ensuring each dance set is full. And despite Imogen's assertions that this will be a small and private event, her guest list says otherwise. It seems her confidence in Elliot's attention has grown since our dinner, considering she's invited some of the most well-bred men and women in town. Although I know any decent ball requires a vast number of willing dancers, I'm surprised how many young and eligible ladies she's invited. Probably to show off what she thinks she's won.

As much as that makes my stomach churn, I must let it comfort me instead. This is what we've been working for—Imogen's attachment, her pride in Elliot's affections. Internal arguments rail against me, and I try to take additional comfort in Imogen's eventual demise, for once she breaks his curse, the king will turn her away, and her smug grin will be wiped from her face forevermore.

When none of those thoughts help, I remind myself of the five petals that have fallen each of the last few days. Based on my calculations, we have anywhere from one week to nine days left to break Elliot's curse. Imogen *must* be convinced she's in love tonight.

She must.

At least I have true comfort in the few invitees I've added to the guest list, which includes Foxglove, Amelie, Nina, and the bookseller, Mr. Cordell. Unfortunately, Nina's invite requires one for Father as well, so I must steel myself against his forthcoming presence.

The sky is nearly dark and the ball just over an hour away when I can safely say the manor is ready for tonight's event. Standing at the entrance to the dining-room-turned-ballroom, I give it a nod of approval. The lighting has been lowered to a warm, elegant glow, and the marble floor gleams with a dazzling shine, the very essence of the room screaming romance. Ember and the violinist are set up at the far end, practicing for the first few songs, strains of their lovely music floating upon my ears to ease my frazzled nerves.

I sigh. It's perfect. This will work.

"Why aren't you dressed?"

I whirl at the sound of Elliot's voice, my pulse hammering at the sight of him in his shirtsleeves. "I could ask the same of you. What are you thinking, walking around like this?"

"I've been in the garden," he says, voice quiet.

My stomach drops. "Anything I should be concerned about?"

He shifts his jaw. "Nothing but the usual. Four petals have fallen. I'm sure the fifth will fall by the end of the night."

His tone has me reaching for him, and before I realize what I'm doing, I lay a gentle hand on his arm. My palm buzzes at the contact, sending a rush of heat through me, but I don't release him. Instead, I give him a soft squeeze, and he relaxes, shoulders dropping. "It's going to be all right, Mr. Rochester," I whisper. "If all goes to plan, I'll speak with Imogen tonight."

His face flashes with a pained expression. "What if she doesn't—"

"No," I say, voice firm. "No what ifs. Just stick with the plan. Dance with Imogen. Treat her like a queen. Smile at her, converse with her. Use that clever fae deception and pretend she's the most desirable creature you've ever beheld. Can you do that?"

It takes him a few silent beats to answer. "Yes."

I slide my palm from his arm, ignoring how cold it feels hanging loose at my side. "Good. Here's what to expect. The ball will open with a minuet, so you'll need to wait for the second, which will be a waltz. That's when you will ask Imogen to dance. The sixth dance will be the polka, and the tenth will be the gallopade. Three dances with Imogen. Three chances to demonstrate your favor."

He nods along, as if memorizing my verbal itinerary.

"Now, go get dressed. Hurry!"

He takes a step away but pauses. "Shouldn't you get dressed as well?"

The question has me assessing my state of disarray. Even without a mirror, I can tell my hair has gone limp, loose strands hanging around my face. And although my dress is clean, I can't deny I feel less than fresh, considering how much my anxiety has caused me to sweat. "I suppose you're right. The floor manager mustn't appear so ragged as I look now."

He extends his arm with a crooked smile. "Let me escort you to your room, Miss Bellefleur."

I quirk a brow. "Why? Are you afraid I'll ignore your suggestion to change as soon as your back is turned?"

"Perhaps. Besides, we can practice conversation on our way and help me get comfortable."

"Very well," I say with a resigned sigh as I take his arm. Once again, my palm tingles at the contact, but I shove the awareness to the back of my mind.

We leave the bustle of the main floor behind and head upstairs. Elliot turns to me with a haughty, mocking expression. "What lovely weather we had today, wouldn't you agree Miss Bellefleur?"

I roll my eyes and answer him with an equally cajoling tone. "Oh, so lovely, Mr. Rochester. The afternoon snow was quite a spectacle. How uncannily similar it seemed to yesterday's snow."

His lips flicker with a shadow of a frown, making me recall our last conversation about the weather, one that ended with his unsettling question. *Do you think you could ever be happy here in Winter?*

My voice takes on a more serious tone as I say, "The snow truly was lovely today, the few times I looked from the windows. Each snowflake seemed to sparkle as it fell, like a dusting of diamonds."

His expression softens, his smile shifting from mockery to genuine pleasure. "That's how I see it every day."

We stop outside my bedroom door, and I turn to face him. "Thank you for walking me to my door, Mr. Rochester. Now, run along, and don't you dare be late to your own ball."

He lets out a grumbling sigh. "I promise I'll arrive in a timely fashion."

Promise. That's a weighty word coming from a fae, although I see he's given himself room with *timely fashion*. Clever bastard.

"Now promise me you'll wear the dress that's laid out on your bed."

Taken aback, I blink a few times as I try to make sense of his odd request. "What dress?"

His eyes narrow as his lips pull into a devious grin.

Without a second thought, I push open my door and rush inside. An elegant swath of red lace overlaying crimson silk has me halting in place. I look back at Elliot, my eyes wide with equal parts shock, terror, pleasure, and confusion. "What is that?"

He leans against my doorframe, and a hint of trepidation flickers in his eyes. "I had Amelie make it for you. That's the real reason she came so early today. To drop it off."

I look from him to the gown and back again, tears pricking my eyes for a reason I can hardly comprehend. "Why?"

"You didn't have a dress to wear."

"I have plenty of gowns in the wardrobe to suffice."

"Not for a ball."

I open and close my mouth a few times before I can find my words. "Elliot, I don't need a proper ballgown. I'll be managing the floor, not participating in the festivities."

He shrugs. "As my employee, I think I should get a say in what you wear to my events. Think of it as a required uniform."

I cross my arms over my chest. "So, you're saying I'm being forced to wear this?"

"No, of course not," he says with a furrowed brow. "It's just...it's a gift. I wanted you to have it. Wear it or throw it away if you don't like it. I'll take no offense. However, I can't say I won't be disappointed if I am never to see you in it."

My breath hitches, my stomach swarming with a strange warmth at his words, at the look in his eyes. The timbre of his tone seems to reverberate through my bones, relaying far more than his words can. I know it's all in my imagination, but it makes me eager to change into the gown just the same. "I'll wear it," I say, my voice barely above a breathless whisper.

"Wonderful." He pushes off from my doorframe. "I'll see you in the ballroom soon then."

"Wait," I call before he can step away. He meets my eyes, and I find myself reeling to remember what I had meant to say. A flush warms my cheeks and I clasp my hands tight at my waist to keep them from fidgeting. "Thank you, Elliot. For the dress. It's...beautiful."

His face lights up for the briefest moment before he trains his lips into a modest smile. "You're welcome."

Then he's gone, and I'm left with a gift—one more beautiful than all the jewels, roses, and luxuries I've ever been gifted before. Not even Oswald had lavished me with anything like this. And it isn't just what the gift looks like. It isn't about what it *is* at all.

It's about what it does to my heart.

30

Once dressed, I stand before the mirror with my jaw hanging on its hinge. To say the dress is beautiful is an understatement. To say it is proper for a ball amidst the stuffy townsfolk of Vernon would be a lie. And yet, there's no way I can take it off now that I've put it on, for never have I had the pleasure of wearing something so completely and utterly perfect.

The concoction of scarlet silk, chiffon, and lace reminds me of the fashions popular in Isola when I was a girl, and the gold accents give it a regal flair. It fits like a dream, which tells me Elliot must have given Amelie access to the dresses in my room last time she was here so she could take approximate measurements. Additionally, Amelie must have also guessed the necessary adjustments she'd need to make to those measurements, because where my borrowed gowns are slightly too tight, this one fits like a glove, hugging my curves and allowing generous room for my broad shoulders and hips.

The style itself is certainly what I consider fae, with

its plunging neckline, low-cut back, and flowing skirts. The sleeves are close-fitting from my shoulders to my elbows, where they open to sheer chiffon that trails away from my forearms. The bust and waist are snug against my form, then flare out at the hips into layered skirts that sway with my every move.

Saints, Gemma, I say to myself. *You're going to draw way too much attention in this.*

But it's too late for second-guessing, for I've already committed to wearing it. Still, it takes no small strength of will to prepare myself to meet the masses that are sure to be gathering downstairs already. Like I always do when fear tries to get the better of me, I breathe in deep and count to five.

After that, I do it again, because I'm still not ready, nor can I stop my arms from shaking or the nausea churning in my gut. Names of those I know I'll have to face tonight flood my mind. Father. Imogen. Mrs. Coleman. Mrs. Aston. Gavin Aston. Strangers I've yet to personally know. Voices. Whispers. Eyes staring like daggers. Taunting, leering—

I shake my head and try again. *This is here. This is now.*

With a deep breath, I force my mind to empty. Once my breathing grows steady, I conjure images again, but not of those I dread. I think of the people I'm looking forward to engaging with tonight. Nina, Mr. Cordell, Foxglove, Amelie, Ember. And of course...Elliot.

I don't allow my mind to take me anywhere else but here, in this place of warm anticipation. Then, bottling that warmth deep inside, I wrap my false persona around it like a cocoon, building an aura of confidence thicker, higher, until it feels solid and impenetrable.

I'm ready.

Squaring my shoulders and lifting my chin, I leave my room to greet the townspeople of Vernon. With the poise of a military general facing the greatest battle of her life, I make my way to the ball.

EXCITED GUESTS HAVE ALREADY ARRIVED BY THE TIME I make it to the ballroom. The hired footman and other servants expertly go about their tasks, taking coats and cloaks, escorting the guests, serving refreshments, as if they're regular fixtures at the manor. It gives me far less to attend to myself, but also less to worry about. And fewer worries mean more idle time to overthink and notice the way certain people look at me—

No. Not tonight.

I wander from guest to guest, keeping my false persona firmly in place as I engage in small talk and ensure everyone's needs are being met. Some give only curt, polite responses, while others ask me about my employer, keen on drilling me for details about my job, why I was offered it, and furthermore, why I accepted it. These latter conversations I extricate myself from at once, using my armory of prepared excuses with hardly a flicker of anxiety on my part.

My nerves aren't nearly as strong when a familiar head of blonde hair comes bobbing into the ballroom— Imogen. She assesses the room through narrowed eyes, her sister Clara at her side. And on her other side...my heart nearly skips a beat at the sight of my sister. I want to run to Nina and wrap her in a hug, but propriety has me keeping my steps slow and even as I approach.

If propriety hadn't been enough to stop me, the sight of the figure bringing up the rear of the party certainly would have been. I nearly stumble as Father's shrewd eyes meet mine, his expression full of disapproval as he escorts Mrs. Coleman. With a deep, steadying breath, I return my gaze to my sister, her wide smile acting as my anchor, my strength.

"Oh, Gemma," Nina says, coming to the fore of the party to take my hands in hers. "The manor is beautiful! I had no idea to expect such elegance. And a ball! Although," she lowers her voice, her smile slipping, "I must say I am so disappointed you haven't visited, even with the books I'm keeping hostage."

I squeeze her hands in mine. "I'm sorry, Nina. But as you can see, I have my hands full here. Perhaps after the ball I'll have some downtime to visit." I catch Father's scowl over Nina's shoulder and quickly avert my eyes.

"Miss Bellefleur, the ballroom looks sufficient," Imogen says, stealing my attention to her. "I must say, this space serves as an even better dance floor than it did a dining room. It makes me regret we don't have a finer orchestra to go with it. I hope Mr. Rochester isn't too displeased that I encouraged Ember to lead our music tonight."

I glance at Ember and the violinist, playing a slow, mellow tune. "On the contrary, the music is lovely."

"That was poorly done, my dear," Mrs. Coleman says to Imogen, her nose wrinkled in distaste. "If you hadn't already offered your stepsister's services to Mr. Rochester,

I would have forbidden it. You know how much it irks me when she shows off like this."

I turn my gaze to Mrs. Coleman, keeping my smile firmly in place despite my urge to snarl at her. "How fortunate it was that you weren't there to prevent it then. I daresay my employer would be quite put out to have had to deny dear Imogen the opportunity to dance."

"I too am so grateful this ball was able to happen," Nina says, diffusing some of the growing tension with her sweet voice, "for I've yet to dance with James. I'm not sure I can consider myself properly engaged to a man I haven't danced with. What a night this will be!"

"Where is Mr. Rochester, anyway?" Imogen asks, as if my sister hadn't spoken a word. "Is he always late to his own events?"

"He'll be down shortly, I assure you," I say.

"Who might he open the ball with? Does he recall I was in charge of the guest list? One would consider me hostess."

"Oh, he considers you hostess indeed," I say, "and you will open the ball with a minuet. He, unfortunately, will not be participating in the opening dance."

She gasps. "Not participating in his own—Miss Belle-fleur, I know your employer is an unconventional crea-ture, but surely he mustn't be so contrite as this."

I take her arm and gently pull her away from the others. "Can I let you in on a secret, Imogen? Mr. Rochester spent the last several days learning a selection of human dances for this ball. For *you*. Not all fae are versed in these kinds of things, you know."

A pleased smile flutters over her lips despite her attempts to appear nonchalant. "When I encouraged him to host a ball, I confess it hadn't occurred to me that Mr. Rochester wouldn't know our popular dances. And never in a thousand years would I have considered he might have chosen to host a *fae* ball. I am so glad he didn't. Oh, how dreadful would that have been with their wild, unrestrained dances?"

I want to laugh at the look of disgust on her face but keep my expression neutral. "Can you now see what lengths he's gone to please you? You cannot expect him to know our most complicated group dances."

"No, I suppose I should feel honored. But please tell me he isn't an awful dancer."

"He isn't, trust me. Just be patient with him tonight. He will dance, but he may spend a greater amount of time watching *you* dance."

Her eyes widen with delight, and she opens her silk fan to flutter over the bottom half of her face.

The music picks up with a sudden tempo change, a tune I recognize from the musicians' earlier practice. A tune that denotes my employer's entrance at the ball.

My pulse increases, and it seems everyone in the room turns to face the doorway with me. There Elliot strolls in with slow, confident steps, just the slightest hitch in his cadence. There's a collective silence at his entrance, all eyes upon his striking appearance. Dressed in an impeccable black suit with a silver brocade waistcoat and ruby cravat, he stands out as a specimen cut far above the rest. I've grown so used to his company, especially when he's either at ease or sulking, that it's easy to forget just how fae he truly is—a wild, beautiful creature in both looks and poise. For the first time, I can almost see his seelie and unseelie forms as if they were one, the man and wolf united, indistinguishable. He has the same prowling grace as a wolf, the same dangerous stare, the same powerful build.

For a moment a strange sense of thrilling terror washes over me. This is the creature I've allowed myself to bully and argue with? Forced to dance and entertain humans? If he wasn't cursed and had his magic intact, how long would it take him to kill everyone in this room?

A chill crawls up my spine, but it doesn't make me want to run. It makes me want to move closer to him, as if he's a hearth fire on a chilly day, capable of burning those who get too close...and yet doesn't.

He pauses, and the guests offer bows and curtsies. A flicker of hesitation crosses his face until his eyes find mine. His gaze slides over my dress, and his lips pull into the warmest smile I've ever seen him wear, which doesn't help me rid myself of the image of him being a fire...nor the heat that floods every part of my body. Imogen must feel the same, for she fans herself faster as he advances toward us.

"Mr. Rochester," she croons, stepping to the front of our retinue to greet him, "this ball is simply marvelous. You've truly outdone yourself in giving the people of Vernon the honor of dancing in your home."

He offers her an easy smile, but his eyes flick to me. "You can thank my steward, for she's done all the work."

Imogen purses her lips and I give Elliot a warning look.

He returns his gaze to Imogen and takes her hand in his. "I have you to thank for procuring the guest list. This night wouldn't have happened without you." Then, lifting her hand, he brings the back of it to his lips.

My stomach ties itself in a knot, and for a moment I feel paralyzed. Then Elliot releases Imogen's hand and greets the rest of her party, including my father. They exchange tense formalities, and I'm impressed how well he's playing his role as host, his expression betraying not a hint of the disdain I'm sure he still feels toward my father. Finally, his eyes land on my sister, and his tone takes on an apologetic note. "I'm sorry, but we have not been formally introduced."

"Oh, right!" I say, stepping forward, remembering how he'd almost growled at her the day she came with Father. "Mr. Rochester, please meet my sister, Nina Bellefleur."

They exchange greetings, then Elliot straightens his posture. There's a bit of mockery in it, but I doubt anyone but I can recognize it. "I am pleased to see you all again, but as host, I must greet the rest of the guests so our dance can begin. Miss Bellefleur, come make the proper introductions. Miss Coleman, I shall see you lead the first dance." With a bow, he turns and starts off, and I'm forced to follow.

"You should have asked Imogen to make introductions," I whisper furiously once we're out of earshot. "She's your hostess tonight. Also, you should have said you're *looking forward to seeing her* lead the first dance, not simply state you'll be watching."

He turns to me with a sardonic look. "First of all, you're my steward. You have a job to do, and I'm going to make you do it. If you're going to torture me by forcing me to dance at a ball, then I'll torture you right back and have you make my introductions to the people you despise probably more than I do. Second of all, if I were capable of lying, I would have said how greatly I looked forward to seeing that girl dance, but alas, I cannot, so there you have it."

A corner of my lips tilts into a grin. There's the unrefined wolf man I know. "I suppose that's fair enough. Now, come, let the torture commence for us both."

I lead Elliot around the room, making the proper introductions until all required greetings have been made. Then finally, the first song begins. I guide Elliot to stand where he'll be in Imogen's sight for most of the dance, then leave him alone while I survey the room, ensuring everything is running as smoothly as I intend. As predicted, every moment Imogen can spare, her eyes depart from her dance partner to lock on Elliot with a coy smile. Elliot, in turn, does his part to look pleased. As I study his face from the other side of the room, I begin to wonder if maybe he *is* truly pleased watching Imogen's elegant yet controlled moves as she circles her partner on the floor.

My thoughts are interrupted by a figure parting the crowd to approach me. Gavin Aston. Dread and irritation send my feet into a flurry as I shuffle between a group of guests, then weave my way to the other side of the dance floor. Casting a glance around, I see no sign that Gavin has followed. Thank the saints. I'll do whatever it takes to avoid saying a word to that man tonight.

As the song comes to an end, I rush to Elliot's side and mutter, "The next song is the waltz. It's time to ask Imogen to dance." Seeing Imogen's eager face as she leaves her former dance partner to approach Elliot, I move to step away. My breath catches as I find Elliot's fingers suddenly circling my wrist.

"Stay," he says through his teeth, face going a shade paler.

"Mr. Rochester," I hiss, trying to tug my arm away. Luckily, our hands are hidden behind my billowing skirts, but we're standing too close.

His expression softens. "Please, Gemma," he whispers.

"Fine," I say, and he releases me just as Imogen parts through the crowd.

"How did you enjoy watching the first dance?" she asks, angling her back toward me as if to push me out of the way.

I give in, taking a few steps back until Elliot burns me with a beseeching glare. Then, composing his expression, he answers Imogen's question, his words slow and calculated. "It was a lovely song and...and you looked like you greatly enjoyed dancing."

She cocks her head, clearly having expected a more gracious compliment. Then she somehow manages to pucker her lips and smile at the same time, her lashes fluttering like butterfly wings. "Will you be dancing the next?"

Elliot's throat bobs once. Twice. Then a quiet, "Yes."

"Oh, how wonderful!" Imogen sways side to side, eyes wide with anticipation. The music cues the dancers to secure their partners.

I clear my throat, hoping it will convey what Elliot must do. *Ask her to dance, you fool!* Just then, a new figure joins our party, one that has me stifling a groan. Gavin offers Elliot a nod and me a bow. "Miss Bellefleur, would you do me—"

"Miss Bellefleur, may I have the honor of the next

dance?" My eyes flash to Elliot, who has his hand extended to me. I stare at it in stunned disbelief, barely processing what just happened. Did he just...interrupt Gavin to ask me to dance? But no, this is all wrong.

Imogen scalds me with a seething glare, then stalks off with a huff. Gavin glances awkwardly from me to Elliot, who still holds his hand outstretched, then slowly sulks away.

Heat burns my cheeks as I look up at Elliot. "What do you think you're doing?"

"I cannot dance my first dance with her."

"What are you talking about?" I say through my teeth. "This has been the plan from the start. This is why you learned to dance in the first place."

"I can't do it, Gemma." A twinge of panic seeps into his tone. "I'll dance with her, but not the first one. Do you see how many people are watching?"

"That's exactly why you shouldn't dance with me. I'm your steward, not a proper dance partner. We'll draw too much attention. Besides, balls are a thing of my past. I don't dance anymore."

"Well, you do now," he says, his eyes a bit maniacal. He brings a hand to his hair, as if to drag his fingers through it, but seems to think better of it at the last minute. Instead, he tightens the hand into a fist and holds it at his side. "If you expect me to dance, then dance with me. If I dance with anyone else right now, I'm going to be sick."

I furrow my brow. "Why?"

"I might stumble. Trip on this damn leg in front of everyone. I'll look like a fool."

"Since when do you care what the *vile humans* think

of you? Better yet, how exactly am I supposed to prevent you from tripping in the first place?"

His gaze locks on mine. "I'm...comfortable with you."

My irritation softens at his words, but what he's asking is a terrible idea. "Surely, I'm not the only one you're comfortable with. *Anyone* else would be a better choice than me. Amelie, even. Where is she—"

"There is no better choice." He holds out his hand again and offers something between a grimace and a tenuous grin. I've never seen him so flustered, so...vulnerable. His voice trembles with a desperate plea. "Dance with me, Gemma. I'm begging you. I cannot do this without you."

I bite my lip. Oh, for the love of the saints, I'm going to regret this, aren't I? "Only if you promise to dance the polka and gallopade with Imogen."

"I promise."

With a sigh, I place my hand in his, and we step onto the dance floor.

31

We take our places with the other dancers and face each other. One glance around the room shows Imogen has quickly found herself another partner—Gavin, actually—but if her scowl wasn't already enough to tell me she's annoyed, her tense posture is more than evident from here. I'll have to remedy this at my first chance. Right now, I have more pressing matters to consider. Primarily, the fact that I'm about to dance with my employer in a room full of judging eyes.

Sweat beads at my brow and my stomach begins to turn. Oh, for the love of the saints, why did I agree to do this?

"Gemma," Elliot whispers.

I bring my eyes to his and all prior thoughts disappear. My chest heaves as I notice the slim space between us—space that will only grow smaller once the dance begins.

"It's just us, all right? We can do this." I don't know if

his words are meant to comfort him or me, but they somehow manage to keep my head from spinning.

He's right. We can do this. If it means getting to the next step in our scheme, then it must be done. I take a step closer, our chests mere inches apart. With slow, trembling moves, I lift my hand and press my palm against his, ready to weave our fingers together. But no, that's all wrong, too intimate of a touch. It takes us a few awkward moments to get it right, but soon our hands are properly and demurely clasped and I bring my other hand to rest on his shoulder. He closes another inch between us, and I feel his hand come to the middle of my back.

I gasp at his touch, feeling the tips of his fingers meet bare skin where the back of my dress dips low. My heart pounds against my ribs, a melody I'm sure is loud enough for Elliot to hear.

Then the music begins, and it's now or never. Our first few steps are off beat, my legs threatening to give out beneath me. But the warmth of his hand on my back serves as an anchor, guiding me into the next set of steps. After a few measures, we find the rhythm, stepping and turning with far more ease. I keep my face averted slightly to the right while his remains just turned toward my left, our bearing civil yet unfamiliar, as is proper.

With each beat that goes on, my nerves settle more and more. The dance starts to feel natural, like it's a part of me. Ember's piano blends harmoniously with the violin as we step and turn, step and turn. A smile tugs my lips, my feet feeling lighter, and I realize Elliot must be feeling the same. His grip on my hand has loosened, his palm more relaxed against my back. I hazard a glance at him, and he meets my eyes at the same moment. His grin matches mine, but there's an element of shyness to it. The flush in his cheeks only enhances that quality, and I let out a soft chuckle.

"Don't laugh at me," he says, leaning slightly closer so his whisper reaches my ear above the music.

"I'm not laughing at you. I'm laughing at us both." As I speak, I try to keep my face averted away from him, but I find myself returning to his gaze again and again despite my best efforts.

"Tell me honestly, Gemma." As often as he's used my first name in private, hearing it from his lips in a room full of spectators sends a sinful chill through me. Thank the saints no one can hear us. "Am I the worst dancer you've ever been forced to endure?"

"No, Mr. Rochester. Far from it." It's the truth. Despite his reservations, he moves just as well as anyone I've danced with.

He laughs, his breath stirring my hair. "Freezing hell, if that's the case, I hate to think of the sorry souls who have stepped on your toes."

"Oh, come on," I say with a wry grin. "You're too hard on yourself."

"Am I?"

"Yes. I know you don't love your seelie form, but you truly wear it beautifully well."

His expression turns serious, his garnet irises glittering in the dim light of the room. "So, you like my body as it is?"

I swallow hard, my breaths growing heavy. What kind of question is that? A fae one, of course. One where he has no understanding of its implications. And yet, it's an honest question, and I suppose I can answer with equal honesty. "I think I can safely say I'm fond of it."

He smiles, and we continue the next few beats of the dance in silence, our gazes locked on each other. I feel his hand move slightly lower down my back, his thumb caressing the lace of my gown. Does he realize he's doing that? I suppress a shudder and find myself inching closer, my arm growing more relaxed as my hand rests more comfortably on his shoulder, like it's never belonged anywhere else. In this moment, I feel as if we're the only two people in the room. We move on instinct, unaware of the other dancers, the music guiding our every step, sway, and turn.

My lips part, but I don't know what I want to say. Everything in me wants to step even closer, press my cheek against his, feel his breath against my neck as we dance. But I don't. For somewhere in the back of my mind is a piece of me that knows we aren't alone. That we're being watched, judged, assessed. Right now, it's impossible to care, but logic tells me I will when this is all over.

When this is all over.

Yes, this moment will end. The realization has my heart sinking, making me wish this song could last forever. But I know better. Beautiful moments in my life never last. They always end badly. Still, does that mean I shouldn't enjoy them while I can? I think back to the book I read last night, the one with the boy and the dog. *Is it worth it?*

Yes, it's worth it. The good and the bad. It's the story as a whole that matters.

But if that were true, then why have I been running from love ever since the scandal with Oswald? Why have

I been pushing everyone away? Why have I been dreaming of an isolated life in Isola?

Elliot squeezes my hand, his brow furrowed. "What is it?"

I realize my gaze has dropped, and my lips have pulled into a frown. With a quick shake of my head, I return my eyes to his and force a convincing smile. "It's —" I want to say it's nothing, but can't summon the words. Because it isn't nothing. It's everything. Something has changed inside me, and I can't ignore it any longer. The truth is, I've grown to like Elliot in a way he'll never be able to like me back. All he wants is to be rid of his seelie form and become a wolf again. How many times has he reminded me of this fact? When the curse is broken, he'll flee this place, return to the caves he was once so fond of.

And I...I'll lose him.

Like the boy and his dog.

But if I'm the boy in this story, and Elliot is the dog, then perhaps I can accept that my life has become better from him being in it. Maybe it's even true that he's saved me in a way. Reminded me what it's like to open up to someone, trust someone with the pains of my past. Maybe I'm starting to believe in...I can't even think the word. But I know it's there. That tender connection between two people. Maybe it doesn't have to last forever to be real.

The song draws near its end, and with it comes an urge to speak my truth—the answer to his question that still hangs between us. We slow to a stop with the music and pause in place, my hand still clasped in his, his palm still firm against my back.

I take a deep breath. "It's just...I think I'm going to miss you, wolf man."

The crease deepens between his brows. He opens his mouth to speak, but this is where the dancers must part and offer curtsies and bows. I dip low, and he folds into a bow a moment too late. As we rise, his expression remains flustered, but again any potential response from him is cut off as the floor erupts with polite applause. The sound acts as a wall in my mind, one that seals off this moment from the last, between now and the magic of our dance. On this side lies logic, duty, and a scheme that must be brought to completion. On the other is a beautiful memory I'll keep with me always. But in the past it must stay.

The applause dies down, and the couples separate to find new partners. Elliot advances toward me. "Gemma—"

"Thank you for the dance, Mr. Rochester," I say with calm and poise, my false persona wrapped tight around me. My smile, however, is genuine, and my heart is at peace. Or as peaceful as it can be with such a bittersweet ache at its core. "I have much work to do, and I will get on with it now."

Before he can argue, I turn to leave. A lump rises in my throat, but I swallow it down, vaguely aware of the feel of his eyes burning into me with every step I take away from him. Their heat lingers long after I'm lost in the crowd.

32

The night wears on, and I stay far from the dance floor, keeping to tasks that take me to the perimeter of the ballroom or other rooms altogether. I visit the footman, the servants, confirming all is going well for the evening. Then I make my rounds to the refreshments table, the parlor, finding everything in neat working order. Next, I check on Bertha and the cooks, ensuring supper is coming along in the kitchen, then oversee the final preparations for the dinner table. Since the dining room has been requisitioned for dancing, the break for supper will take place in a smaller, adjoining room.

I return to the ballroom only on occasion, to keep tabs on Elliot from afar. Although I'd rather keep my distance for the remainder of the evening, I'm prepared to intervene if needed. Thankfully, he appears perfectly capable of performing his duties without my assistance. I catch him in several conversations throughout the night, but most importantly, he dances with Imogen as planned.

From the far end of the room, I watch as he turns Imogen around the dance floor in an exuberant polka. Her glowing smile shows no hint of resentment over being slighted over the first dance.

Good. Hopefully she's forgotten by now. My eyes flash to Elliot's face, taking in his composure, his smile. He seems comfortable, happy even. Is that how he looked when he danced with me? In the moment, it felt like so much more.

I shake my head and slip into the hall. After this song, it will be time for supper, so I should probably check the dinner table one last time—

Something catches my attention, a soft sound coming from one of the staircases that leads to the upper bedrooms. My first reaction is a spike of panic. If a guest goes exploring and sees the state of some of the unattended rooms...the gossip that could spread regarding Mr. Rochester's secret frugality could be detrimental in securing Imogen's opinion of his wealth.

But my second reaction has me moving from panic to pain, for the closer I get, the more I'm certain the sound is of whimpering. Crying. On quiet feet, I climb the stairs until I see a small shape silhouetted against the dim light from the hall above. As I draw near, the figure lifts its head and I recognize Micah. I all but run up the remaining steps and sit at his side, throwing an arm over his heaving shoulders.

Guilt swarms my stomach as he leans closer to me, his whimpers growing stronger. The children should be in bed by now. Could the music be keeping him awake? Or is he upset that he isn't participating? All residents were invited to both the dance and the dinner, but almost all chose to keep to themselves and take their meals in the kitchen as the food becomes ready.

"What's wrong, Micah?" I whisper.

"It's my mother," he says, voice trembling. "I can't remember what she looks like. I can't remember her at all."

My heart sinks as I recall what Blackbeard and Gray told me about the poor children being abandoned by their mothers when the curse was laid. I pull him closer, and he wraps his arms around my middle. "I'm so sorry. It's been so long since you've seen her, hasn't it?"

"But the memory was there just this morning. It's the only one I have left from...from before. And now it's gone."

I swallow hard, my throat suddenly dry. Could this be the curse at work? I know children rarely maintain their earliest memories, but the way he describes the loss of this one chills me to the bone.

He lifts his head and stares at me through tear-glazed eyes. "What will happen if the curse isn't broken? Who will I be when my memories are all gone? I won't remember I even had a mother. I won't remember you, or why I'm at this stupid house, or what bread tastes like. I won't remember anything at all!"

I hush him, stroking his hair until he lays his head back against me. The front of my gown becomes sodden from his tears, but I don't care, especially when tears of my own stream down my cheeks to meet his. A deep ache throbs in my heart as I hold and rock the boy, feel him cling to me like I'm the last real thing in the world. When he calms and rubs his eyes, I offer to walk him back to his room. He accepts, and we walk side by side, solemn and silent.

As we continue down the hall, my mind swarms with terrible thoughts. I've considered the ramifications of the curse before, imagining what would happen if left unbroken—time catching up to Elliot, Blackbeard, Gray, and the rest of the pack, resulting in skin that grows sallow and wrinkled in a span of a minute, shriveling until it falls off their bones. However, after learning the children would be spared from sudden death, given their younger years, their loss of memories never horrified me the way it does now.

With every step I take with Micah at my side, my resolve hardens, grows firmer, brighter. We are breaking this damn curse. If I could simply hold a knife to Imogen's throat and force her to say the words, make the sacrifice, I would. Considering it must be made of her own free will, I'll have to ease off the knife play, but still... I'm speaking to her tonight if it's the last thing I do.

Micah opens the door to his room, revealing a large space with four narrow beds. I'm surprised to find it so neat and well-kept and wonder what it looked like before I forced the manor's residents to adopt cleaning duties. Three of the beds are occupied with small bodies, filling the room with the sound of their soft breathing. I bend down to bring myself eye to eye with Micah and place my hands on his shoulders. "It's going to be all right, Micah."

His lower lip trembles and he wraps his arms around my waist. I stroke his back until he reluctantly pulls away. "Will you sit by my bed until I fall asleep?"

I know I should get back downstairs and make sure

supper is going well, but...this feels more important right now. "Of course."

He gives me a sad smile, then climbs into his bed. I tuck the blankets around him and settle onto the floor, resting my elbows on his mattress. A tender feeling wraps itself around my heart as I watch the boy fall asleep. I've never considered myself a maternal woman, never craved the joys of motherhood—not even before I swore off matrimony. But as I watch the rise and fall of Micah's chest, sounds of puppy-like whimpers coming from the dreaming children in the room, I think I understand how it must feel to care for someone small and vulnerable. Though I've known these little creatures for less than a month, they've found their way into my affections.

One of the children stirs, then slowly rolls to the side, facing me. It's the little girl. She appears to be a year or two younger than Micah. In human years, at least. She blinks at me a few times, and I give her a gentle smile, hoping my presence won't startle her. Then she sits up and frowns at me.

With slow, cautious steps, I make my way to her side. "I didn't mean to frighten you," I whisper. "Micah had trouble sleeping, so I kept him company so he could fall back to sleep."

She cocks her head to the side, then gives a small nod and begins to lie back down. Like with Micah, I tuck the blankets around her. "The king already did that," she says with words slow and sleepy.

"Oh." My heart leaps in my chest. "Does he...do that often?"

"Every night. I guess you can do it again though. I like my blankets cozy like that."

I finish tucking her in and am about to leave when her eyes lock on mine, a hint of panic in them. "Do you want me to stay until you fall asleep?"

She nods. "The king always does. He tells us stories too. About wolves and mountains."

"I'll stay," I say and sit at the edge of her bed.

She closes her eyes, pulling the blankets up to her chin. A few seconds later, they flash back open and she lifts her head. "Can I have a name?"

"A name?"

Her gaze darts to Micah. "You gave him one. I want one too. The king calls me Tiny and I think I'd like a different one better."

I feel a pinch of regret. When I first gave Micah a name, it was to win his favor, secure him as a potential ally against my captor. But now it seems out of taste to rename the king's household with human names. Then again, it isn't so much renaming them, but giving them something aside from a shorthand title.

"Please," she says. "It isn't fair he gets one."

"Very well," I say with a sigh. "How about...Jenny?"

"Jenny," she echoes, then brightens with a wide smile. "That's pretty."

"Just like you. Now, go to sleep before we wake the others."

"They should get names too, you know."

I reach out and stroke a lock of strawberry blonde hair. "They will, Jenny. Now sleep."

"Will you tell me a story? One about wolves like the king tells us?"

I ponder for a moment. "I'm not sure I know any about wolves, but I know one about a boy and a dog."

"That will do, I guess."

She settles back down, and I tell her an abbreviated version of the story, keeping my voice to a soft whisper. However, in my version of the tale, the dog doesn't die. In my story, the dog lives. They both do. And they live each day happier than the one that came before it.

33

I return to the ballroom the same way I first entered it earlier tonight—like a general at war. With Micah and Jenny, I had my shields down, my armor set aside as I let them climb into my heart. There they remain, alongside Elliot and everyone else I'm determined to save from this wretched curse. But once again, my armor is on, my false persona like an iron tank, my jaw clenched as my lips are armed with the ammunition required to further my scheme.

It appears I've missed the whole of supper, as the ballroom is full again, the dancing back in session. That must mean Elliot has managed to neither offend nor eat his guests in my absence. It takes me a few minutes to spot the king, but I find him standing amongst the crowd, chatting civilly with Imogen. I wait to make my next move, watching for the perfect moment to get Imogen alone. But as the song comes to an end and new couples form, Elliot extends his hand for Imogen's. The next song must be the gallopade.

Sure enough, when the music starts, Elliot and Imogen begin to prance and turn. I edge closer to the dance floor, weaving quietly between chatting bodies. I catch strains of conversation, much of which involves the king.

"Mr. Rochester and the eldest Coleman daughter..."

"They've danced twice now and conversed all evening."

"Do you see the way Miss Coleman looks at him?"

"An engagement can't be too far off."

"...if I had the wealth of a fae royal. What is his royal lineage anyway?"

When I reach the other side of the room, I assess the dance floor again. I'm pleased to find Nina, dancing happily with the man I recognize as her fiancé. Then I spot Amelie, dancing with none other than my beloved bookseller, Mr. Cordell. I'm surprised to find his dance moves so elegant despite his age. Regret tugs at my heart, and I wish I hadn't been so busy all evening. Other than orchestrating a quick introduction between him and Elliot, I haven't had a chance to stop and chat with Mr. Cordell. I've been dying to share my thoughts about *The Governess and the Earl* and hear his thoughts as well. Then again, I'm not sure I have it in me to talk about books tonight. Not when such an important mission rests upon my shoulders.

"Ugh, I wish my mate were here," Foxglove says, sidling up next to me with two glasses of wine. He takes a sip of one, then hands me the other.

I'm about to refuse—I am working, after all—but consider it just might be what I need for my tightly wound nerves. I accept the glass and take a deep sip, feeling the sweet liquid warm my stomach at once. "Your mate, you say?"

"His name is Fehr. A djinn. He stayed behind while I took this job, which is probably for the best. He'd be far too much of a spectacle for this town, if you know what I mean. His forearms alone would inflict carnal desires upon anyone."

I chuckle. "Is that so?"

"Trust me, honey. In fact, you should visit us after I return home. We reside at Maplehearth Palace, on the border between Fire and Autumn. Queen Evelyn would love to meet you, I'm sure."

I can't imagine why the Queen of the Fire Court would be pleased to meet me at all, but the sentiment warms my heart just the same.

"You could get some sun in Fire and then cool off in Autumn. Get a break from this dreary snow."

I'm about to argue that snow isn't so bad, but I stop myself. Since when do I defend snow? Then something else steals my thoughts—the awareness of how many different courts lie just beyond the borders of this one. Although I've only ever been in Winter since arriving in Faerwyvae, I know there are eleven courts in all, each hosting a different climate and terrain. Perhaps I don't have to leave the isle to experience the sunshine I cherish from my childhood. And, considering how Foxglove speaks about Vernon compared to other cities and towns, maybe I don't have to go as far as I thought to ditch the stifling bonds of human society. What if the freedom I've been craving is closer than I think?

Like a magnet, my gaze slides toward Elliot. But there, of course, lies nothing but a dead end. A goodbye. And that's only if I can get Imogen to break his curse. Otherwise, it will be worse than a goodbye. It will be—

I refuse to think about it, pulling my false persona closer.

"Think about my invitation. It shall remain open, both to you and," he grimaces, glancing at the dance floor, "even your prickly employer."

My pulse quickens, and I turn to face him with a frown. The way he said that almost sounds like...like he expects Elliot and I are *together*. I quickly remind myself that the fae have very different ideas about romantic entanglements, and his statement could mean nothing. Perhaps, like Amelie, he's guessed Elliot's secret, nameless identity. If that's the case, of course it makes sense for the king to be welcomed to another monarch's palace. Before I can summon a response, Foxglove gives me a wink and turns away, disappearing into the crowd.

I puzzle over his words but quickly wash them away with a hearty swallow of wine. The song comes to an end, and I drain the rest of the tantalizing liquid. Then, setting my empty glass on a nearby table, I return my attention to the dance floor and join in the applause, my eyes trained on Elliot and Imogen. After they exchange their expected bow and curtsy, he guides her to one of the chairs at the other side of the room. Keeping out of sight, I watch as they share a few words, both bearing smiles on their lips. Finally, Elliot leaves, which seems to surprise Imogen, for she half-rises from her chair before settling back down with a distant look in her eyes.

I don't bother looking where Elliot goes, and instead take my chance to approach Imogen. Her face brightens as I stand before her, then quickly falls again. "Oh, it's

you," she says, clearly still bitter over the dance I uninten-
tionally stole with Elliot.

"Will you walk with me?"

She turns up her nose, refusing to meet my eyes.
"Don't you have work to do?"

"I'm on a break," I say, doing my best to remain calm
and impervious to her bristly attitude. "Besides, I wanted
to speak with you in private. As a friend."

She scoffs. "As a friend, you say?"

I stifle a groan. It seems I'll need to butter her up if I
am to get her alone. Taking a seat next to her, I force
wistful warmth into my voice as I say, "I can't believe how
smitten Mr. Rochester is with you."

"What's not to believe?" she shoots back.

"I've never seen someone go to such great lengths to
win a woman's favor. First, he learns to dance just so he
can impress you. Next, he gets so nervous that he'll disap-
point you that he coerces me—a far less stunning
prospect—into letting him practice on."

Slowly, she turns toward me, assessing me through
slitted lids. "Practice, you say?"

I nod. "You should have seen how terrified he was. He
told me he'd rather get all his worst steps out with me, so
that when he danced with you it would be nothing short
of perfect."

She puts a hand to her chest, her cheeks turning pink.
"Oh, did he truly say that?"

Thank the saints I can lie. "He did. I hope that doesn't
make you think less of him. He's otherwise so strong and
stoic in everything else. But when it comes to you, I
daresay you enchant him."

"Oh Gemma," she says, leaning forward and gathering my hands in hers. "I can keep it to myself no longer. I've fallen very much in love with him. I understand now that you know his inner workings far more than anyone else. At first, this irked me, but now...well, just tell me, please, do you know his heart? Does he feel for me what I'm beginning to think he does?"

The lie is on the tip of my tongue, but my sinking stomach makes it impossible to do anything but nod.

Still, it has its intended effect, sending Imogen swooning so deeply, I fear she might melt off her chair. When she recovers herself, she leans toward me again, squeezing my hands even harder. "Do not keep me in suspense, my dearest friend. He will ask for my hand, won't he? When you first told me about him, you said he sought to be married in a matter of months. Is that still true? How soon will it be?"

My head spins with her questions, and I know I can put it off no longer. It's time for the final phase.

I pull my hands from hers and rise to my feet. "Come, Imogen dear. We must speak in private. Let us collect your coat and take a turn about the garden."

ONCE WE'RE BOTH PROPERLY BUNDLED, I LEAD HER OUTSIDE to the back gardens. We find a few couples strolling along several of the paths, and it takes a while to find an unoccupied one. Steering clear of Elliot's rose courtyard—which has been blocked off by statues and large potted plants to keep out any potential guests—we make our way to the far corner where we link arms and begin to circle a large topiary in the shape of a fawn.

"You've kept me in suspense long enough," Imogen says with a slight tremble to her voice. "Tell me at once what you brought me here to say."

I take a deep breath and slowly release it, creating a white cloud in the chilly air. The cold feels like a comforting caress against my overheated skin. "Imogen, there's a secret I must tell you about Mr. Rochester. He isn't who you think he is."

She nearly trips as her head swivels toward mine. "Oh, no. No, this can't be—"

"He's so much more." This quiets her, creates the suspense I need to build the final piece of my scheme, the one that will topple her over and pin her in its clutches. I pause and face her, taking her hands in mine as I prepare to deliver my next words. Guilt tugs at my heart, for what I'm about to say goes against Elliot's wishes. At least they weren't woven into the terms of our bargain. "Imogen, Mr. Rochester is the Unseelie King of Winter."

She gasps, her face going pale. For a few seconds, she simply stares at me in disbelief. When she speaks, her voice is strained, quiet. "This can't be. The Unseelie King of Winter? I mean, I've never seen him in person, but... but...his name isn't Elliot Rochester. It's...it's...."

She blinks a few times, then shakes her head.

Now it's time to spin a thread of lies to mingle with the truth. "Elliot Rochester is his seelie name. His unseelie name—his *fae* name—is lost."

"Lost?"

I nod gravely. "Lost inside a treacherous curse."

She brings a hand to her lips. "He's...cursed?"

"A wicked fae cursed the king so that all would forget his name."

Imogen lowers her hand. "How cruel."

"It gets worse." I pluck another strand of lie from my mind and weave it with the ammunition of truth. It feels treacherous, but I can't think of that right now. This is what I've been working toward for weeks. "Mr. Rochester recently learned that his curse is coming to claim his life. As far as he can tell, he has barely more than a week left to live, if even that."

A sharp cry escapes her lips, and she clutches her heart. "Mr. Rochester is going to die? What about me? What about...what about this courtship I've been swept up in? Was he never going to tell me?"

I place a comforting hand on her shoulder. "It was so recent that he discovered this was going to happen, and by then, his feelings for you had been set. He doesn't know how to tell you himself."

Tears glaze her eyes, and she pulls her shoulders from under my grasp. However, it isn't sorrow she responds with but rage. "What a waste! Have you any idea how much favor I've spent on him? How much attention I gave him when I could have given it elsewhere? I wouldn't have looked at him twice if I didn't think he'd live long enough to marry me."

A surge of alarm runs through me. I thought she'd be more moved by this news, heartbroken. Instead, I'm losing her. Obviously, her love for Elliot isn't as deep as she first let on. I should have known better. I should have known it isn't *him* she's in love with, but the money and prestige he offers as a husband. At least that will make her final demise even sweeter when Elliot does away with her. Now it's time to throw my final hook and reel her in.

"I know you must be devastated," I say, forcing far

more pity into my voice than I feel. "If only it wasn't so hard to break his curse. Then perhaps the two of you could be together like you wish."

Her expression goes blank as she calculates my words. In the span of a second, her anger subsides. "You mean his curse can be broken?"

"It can, but it's so, *so* hard."

She snaps her fingers. "Well, come out with it. What must be done?"

I infuse my words with a romantic wistfulness as I say, "A human must care so deeply for him that they are willing to sacrifice that which they treasure most."

Her eyes bulge. "That's it? Someone must sacrifice something they treasure?"

"Their *greatest* treasure."

She turns around, arms hugged to her chest, and paces a few steps before stopping with her back facing me. After a few silent moments, she says, "It makes sense that his future wife should make this sacrifice."

I feign surprise, taking a few steps closer. "You can't possibly...are you saying *you* would break his curse?"

She turns to face me, expression resolute. "Yes, I shall do it. As soon as Mr. Rochester and I are married, I'll make this sacrifice."

The blood leaves my face. As soon as they're... married? But they aren't getting married. Ever. That was never part of the plan. "Imogen, I don't think you understand. Did you not hear me? He only has perhaps a week before the curse kills him."

"I've always wanted a quick wedding," she says with a shrug.

There won't be a wedding, you fool! I want to shout.

Instead, I keep my voice level and say, "Wouldn't it make more sense to break the curse first? Then you could spend all the time you want planning the wedding of your dreams."

She rolls her eyes, jaw shifting side to side. "Look, Gemma. Let's not act like we don't know the truth."

Panic seizes me. "What truth?"

"We both know I'm not getting any younger. Do you know how many seasons I've been out? It's a miracle I've found anyone at all, much less a fae royal—a fae *king*. More than that, I need the wealth. My family needs the wealth. We're running through my former stepfather's fortune, and it will be gone by the end of another year. If you didn't already know this, then you do now. I don't have the luxury of time, and clearly neither does Mr. Rochester. We will marry at once and I will break his curse." She lowers her voice, a flicker of sorrow clouding her face. "Besides, considering what I must sacrifice, it will suit me to marry before he can back out."

Her words combined with the desperation in her tone has the hair rising on the back of my neck. "What exactly are you preparing to sacrifice?"

Her lower lip quivers, and a tear rolls down her cheek. She wipes it away with a furious swipe. "My greatest treasure," she says. "Beauty."

I always knew she'd never value anything too deep, and beauty is certainly not something I'd consider of grave importance. But hearing her say it, *seeing* what it means to her, makes my blood go cold.

"How does the sacrifice work?" she asks, voice small. "Will I never be beautiful, or will what little beauty I do have be stripped away? Will it happen right away or take time?"

Her question drains all remnants of vindictive pride I've felt about scheming against her. Not even moments ago, I would have sworn she deserved what was coming. But hearing the fear in her voice, thinking about her actually making the sacrifice...

Several times, I've wondered how the sacrifice works. I've entertained what it would be like if I were the one to break the curse. Not because I considered doing so, but more out of morbid curiosity. Knowing I'd be giving up my freedom and independence, I've imagined I'd find myself locked in a cage, or perhaps trapped in my father's care for life. Or perhaps I'd be married to a controlling man. But would the change be instant? Would I find myself in one place one second, then chained to a stranger in the next? Or would this fate simply haunt me until it caught me in its grip?

I shudder and tell her the truth. "I don't know."

She sniffles. "I suppose it doesn't matter either way. I'm prepared to do it. Since he's fae, I'll require wedding vows that force him to love me and keep me for all of my days. He will not be allowed to abandon me. So long as our marriage vows keep him from casting me aside, even after I've made the sacrifice, then it will be done."

Revulsion sends my stomach churning. Marriage vows. That's what it will take to save Elliot's life. In all my scheming and plotting, never had it occurred to me that marriage would become a factor. I was supposed to trick her into falling in love with Elliot, not marry him.

Once again, I should have known better. I should have seen this coming. Imogen may be petty but she's desperate too. She isn't the sappy lovelorn fool I first took her for. No, she isn't like that at all. She's more like...like me. A desperate survivor. Hardened by her own experiences, determined to get what she wants at any cost. I may despise her and the way she treats others, including myself, but for the first time since I've known her, we see eye to eye.

She'll fight to get what she wants. Scheme, connive, and bargain her way to a better future. Even one where she loses a piece of herself to get there.

Unfortunately, so must I.

34

I feel empty as I walk Imogen back inside, and not another word is said between us, not even as we part ways at the ballroom doors.

We both carry the weight we must bear from this point on. She with the understanding of her impending sacrifice, and me with the news I must break to Elliot. News that makes my shoulders feel heavier with every step.

I'm grateful to find the ballroom has emptied out significantly since I was last here, telling me the festivities are coming to their much-needed end. What I don't find, however, is Elliot, not even as the final song plays. He isn't in the parlor, either, where a small group of guests recline and chat. Impatience flashes within me, bringing with it the sudden urge to shout at everyone to leave. I'm too exhausted, too drained to contemplate enduring this night even a moment longer.

Come to think of it, why should I? What reason do I have to continue this ruse, play the doting steward to these wretched people for one minute more? The ball has served its purpose—the trap has been set, the bait has been claimed, and there is but one way to go forward from here. A way that heats my blood and makes me want to scream.

I channel that rage into my outer persona and stroll into the parlor. "Our host, Mr. Rochester, thanks you all for coming, but the night has come to a close. The footman will see you out. Good evening." I don't wait to hear their complaints, to take in their bulging eyes and indignant protests. Instead, I make my way to the ball-room and relay the same message to every group of chatting stragglers. I'm relieved that Foxglove, Amelie, and Mr. Cordell seem to have already taken their leave, because I doubt I could find the grace within me to give them the kind goodbyes they deserve. Not with my vision blurring with red.

Lastly, I make my way to Imogen's party. Mrs. Coleman taps her foot impatiently while my father pretends not to see me. Ember offers a kind smile while Clara slouches, mouth open in a bored yawn. Nina is nowhere to be seen, so she must have been escorted home by her fiancé.

Imogen scans the now-empty room, arms crossed. "I suppose this is goodnight, then."

Father smirks. "What, no goodbye from your benevolent employer?"

I burn him with a glare, letting my anger seep into every word. "Mr. Rochester has retired early."

"Here I thought he was a gentleman," Mrs. Coleman says with a scoff. "He should at least have the decency to bid farewell to my daughter—"

Imogen tosses her mother a scowl almost as dark as mine. "Never mind that, Mother. He'll have plenty to say to me when I next come to call."

Mrs. Coleman's mouth falls open. "You're coming to call on *him*? Should it not be the other way around?"

"Perhaps it should, but not all things go perfectly to plan, do they?" Imogen's tone is sharp, bitter. "Worry not, though, Mother. Things will all work out in the end." Her eyes meet mine for a moment, lids slitted as she purses her lips over things she cannot say. I told her the curse prevents Elliot from straying too far from the manor, and made her promise to keep everything I've told her tonight to herself. If she wants his proposal, she'll have to come here to get it.

Another wave of rage burns inside me.

"Unconventional man indeed," Mrs. Coleman mutters.

"I wouldn't expect more from the fae," Father says with a cold laugh.

Mrs. Coleman turns up her nose. "Come along then. No need to dawdle."

They start off, but Ember lingers a moment longer. "Thank you for allowing me to play tonight. That was probably the most fun I've had in years."

I smile but know it doesn't reach my eyes. "I appreciate you providing music. You did my employer a great service tonight."

She furrows her brow. "Are you all right?"

The concern in her eyes nearly undoes me, sends all my rage flooding to my toes and leaving sorrow in its place. All I can do is nod.

"Ember!" Imogen hisses, snapping her fingers for the girl to follow.

She looks like she wants to say more, but I'm glad she doesn't. I can't take another second of her sympathy. Not when tears are already forming behind my eyes. She reaches for my hand and gives it a squeeze. "Thank you again," she whispers, then jogs to catch up with the rest of her party.

I remain in place, listening as the final guests are ushered outside.

WITH THE MANOR QUIET, ITS RESIDENTS ASLEEP, AND ALL our hired staff either on their way home or settling in the guest rooms we've offered for the night, I'm finally able to seek out Elliot. It proves harder than I expect, finding no sign of him in the gardens, the parlor, or the kitchen. I make my way upstairs, wondering where he's gone off to hide. With very little else to work with, I head toward the library. I don't dare seek out his private quarters, even though I know they're nearby, but I'm hoping he's yet to retire for the night. There's no way I can bottle in what I must say for even an hour more.

I make it to the library, finding the sconces alight with a soft glow, but the room is empty. My heart sinks. Where do I go from here? Did Elliot truly abandon me to finish the night on my own? A hint of irritation turns in my stomach, which helps burn away some of the residual rage and sorrow that continues to drag my steps.

With a sigh, I turn to the comfort of my silent

companions, brushing my fingers along the spines of books as I slowly pace the perimeter of the room.

"Ah, I should have known I'd find you here eventually."

I round on Elliot with a scowl. "Where the hell have you been?"

He smirks, as if amused by my reaction. "Looking for you. That and hiding." Still wearing his prosthetic, he's dressed down to his shirt and trousers, his cravat hanging loose around his neck, the top buttons of his shirt undone to reveal his upper chest.

I avert my gaze, fixating instead on the selection of titles on the shelf before me. "I take it you've done more hiding than searching for me, because I've been looking for you for the better part of an hour."

He walks into the room and makes his way slowly toward me. "I'm sorry," he says, tone genuine. "I couldn't take any more pretending tonight. My lips were going to split in half if I had to feign one more smile. Besides, I didn't see you even once after our dance. I was getting worried."

I cast him a quick glance. "I was around. And when I saw *you*, it seemed you were doing just fine pretending." I hate the bitter edge to my tone, unsure how it got there.

"Was Imogen convinced?"

I swallow hard, dread sinking my stomach. "She was. Which brings me to the reason I came to find you."

"Not yet," he says, pinching the bridge of his nose. "Give me some peace from Imogen Coleman."

I shrug. "You're the one who brought her up. And it's important we talk about—"

"Please." He meets my eyes, looking worn and empty.

An echo of what I feel inside. "Let it just be us for a minute."

I don't know what he means by that, but I force myself to hold my tongue.

He tilts his head back and closes his eyes, as if relishing the silence between us. When he straightens, a small smile lifts the corners of his lips. Then, slowly, he extends his hand. "May I have this dance?"

My pulse quickens, but I convince my traitorous heart not to join it. "The dance is over, Mr. Rochester."

"Humor me," he says, voice deep and rumbling. But there's another quality to it, one that's somehow tired and playful at the same time. "You forced me to dance and talk to people we both hate. It's the least you can do."

I fold my arms over my chest. "I thought the least I could do was dance with you the first time."

He says nothing, keeping his arm outstretched as his smile folds into a devious smirk.

It's a smirk that has my mouth fluttering in response, and I can't bring myself to ignore him. With a grumble, I put my hand in his and allow him to pull me closer. Right away, we close the space that we kept in public, his chest brushing against mine, his arm circling my waist to rest low on my back. Where our two hands meet, our palms press firmly together and his fingers lace between mine, something we never could have gotten away with when others were watching. In fact, we shouldn't be doing this now, but I'm too tired to care, too drained to argue or analyze what any of this means. All I know is it feels right to be this close to him, to rest my head on his shoulder while he takes us in a slow circle to the music of our beating hearts. We neither waltz nor polka, but sway to a natural rhythm, something I'm sure only fae do when dancing.

I find my free hand moving from the top of his shoulder to behind it, until it rests softly on the back of his neck. He gently nestles the side of his face into my hair, his breath warm against my ear. He pulls me closer, his hand roving up my back until his fingertips meet bare skin. There they rest, sending my pulse racing at the warmth of his flesh on mine. I can't help wondering how much warmer it would feel if his whole hand were pressed against my skin, not just his fingertips. And not just on my back, either...but everywhere.

He breathes in deeply, and when he speaks, his low voice echoes through my blood and bones. "Why do you always smell like mountain air and snow? Like everything I love?"

Love. The word sends my heart fluttering, and my fingers tighten on the back of his neck. I pull back slightly and meet his eyes. The tenderness in his gaze sends my heart skittering yet again, but with it comes a sudden self-consciousness. I'm painfully aware now—of him, of how close we are, of what I'm doing. Of what I *wish* we were doing, of how badly I want more of him. It's enough to make every inch of my body stiffen. He pauses, holding my gaze, eyes swimming with concern. His mouth moves as if he's about to speak. Before he can, I break away, taking a step back and gathering my composure. "I've humored you enough," I say, forcing my words to come out even. "It's time to talk about what comes next."

He looks like he wants to argue, but then closes his eyes. With a nod, he releases a resigned sigh and makes his way to one of the seating areas. Lowering into one of the chairs, he motions for me to sit.

I don't. Instead, I fold my hands at my waist and keep several steps away from him. The distance feels cold, but it's necessary. I clearly can't trust myself when he's so physically near.

This seems to concern him, trepidation filling his eyes, face going pale. "What is it?"

Steeling my heart against the words I must say, I tell him everything.

35

Elliot's expression is murderous by the time I'm done speaking. "Marry her," he says through his teeth. "I have to...marry her?"

"Yes," I say, forcing myself to keep my composure.

His fingers clench into fists as he meets my eyes. "In all our scheming, you never once mentioned I'd have to *marry* the girl. You said she'd break the curse and I'd never have to see her again."

"I didn't think you would have to." I try to come off apologetic, but instead, I sound as empty as I feel.

"Do you know what this means? She wants vows that will keep me from abandoning her. If I do this, I won't just be married by contract alone. As a fae, I'll be bound by the promises I state. I'll be tied to this human for life."

The way he says *human* sends a spike of annoyance through me, cutting through my apathy like thorns. I cross my arms and pop a hip to the side. "I'm sorry. I know marrying a human is the last thing you want."

"Marrying *her* is the last thing I want! You know this, and yet...you orchestrated it."

I throw my hands in the air. "What else would you have me do, Elliot? If I could have fulfilled our scheme any other way, I would have, but you're running out of time. I did the best I could. She wouldn't be convinced otherwise, no matter what I said."

He looks away, running a hand over his face, and leans back in his chair. The anger seeps out of him, dragging his shoulders down. "You're right. It isn't your fault."

I wring my hands, then pin them at my sides. "So... you'll marry her?" My stomach turns, my heart twisting, screaming in my chest.

His gaze slowly slides to mine, a pained look in his eyes. "You think I should?"

"I think you should do whatever breaks your curse, Elliot. This is the best chance you have or are likely ever going to get. That is, unless you break it yourself, but you've already said you won't."

He glances away from me, shifting awkwardly in his seat. "And you are all right with this?" The question is so quiet, it takes me a moment to comprehend it.

"Why should I not be all right?"

His eyes return to mine, and he opens his mouth only to snap it shut. "I don't know. No, I don't know what I was thinking." Shaking his head, he stands and begins to walk away.

I stalk after him, mind reeling. "Elliot, why should I not be all right? This is what you want. This is what you've been working for."

He rounds on me. "No, it isn't. Not if it means marrying that wretched girl."

"You were so desperate before, willing to coerce and trick anyone into breaking your curse. Now you've finally found someone who's willing to do it. Yes, she's coercing you right back, but why let that stop you? Surely, you can use that clever fae deception to work around marriage vows."

"No. I can't do it."

"Why?"

"Because it feels like a betrayal."

"Against who?"

"Against my heart." His words hang in the air between us, silencing me. There's pleading in his eyes. "How can you not see, Gemma?"

My body trembles from head to toe, a lump rising in my throat. "See what?"

"How can you not see what you do to me? You make me feel the way books do. Things I never had to feel as a wolf. Things I've only begun to feel since I met you." A look of desperate longing conflicts with the agony written in his expression.

"I don't understand. What is it you feel now that you couldn't before?"

He sighs. "The unseelie fae don't experience emotions the same way the seelie do. I told you how most unseelie have passions and instincts rather than deep emotion."

I nod, remembering the conversation we had the last time we were in the library.

"When I was first forced into this seelie form, I began to feel certain things for the first time. Horrible things. Guilt and regret. Every vengeful human death I'd caused no longer felt like a triumph but a sin. That's why I've resented this human body so much, why I've tried to punish it and rob it of comfort. Why I've felt so vile and hideous. When you came into my life, these pains only began to grow, and they grow deeper the more and more I get to know you."

My mind spins to puzzle through what he's saying. "So...you hate the way I make you feel?"

"No." His expression softens, and he takes a step closer. "Perhaps I did at first. I despised my attraction to you, and yes, it was there from the start. I hated the thought of you feeling the same about me. About this body. And yet, now...I may hate the way I hurt in this form. But with that pain comes deeper things. Things I don't think I can ever give up now that I've felt them."

"Like what?"

He closes the distance between us with another step and lifts his trembling hands to frame my face. His palms are warm on my cheeks as he stares into my eyes. "Gemma, I love you."

I feel like my legs will give out beneath me, like all the world will melt into that space beneath my feet. Tears well in my eyes, obscuring my vision of him as his words echo in my mind. *Gemma, I love you. Gemma, I love you.* Words I once thought I'd never care to hear again now feel like nourishment, as if my heart had been empty all along until it was filled with their warmth.

"Please say something," he whispers, bringing our foreheads to touch as he closes his eyes. "You don't have to say it back. You can tell me to freeze off, if you must. Tell me to never speak of love again and I will do as you wish. I'll marry that horrid girl and leave you in peace. Just...say anything, so long as it's true."

I want to say something, but words won't form. I'm

still reeling from everything I've experienced tonight—the euphoria of dancing with Elliot at the ball, the pain of knowing I'd have to let him go, the rage at what Imogen would ask of Elliot, the anguish over what she's willing to sacrifice for his hand. Then the apathy, the resignation, all culminating in the last thing I expected.

A declaration of love. Not only that, but the way my heart sings its return.

I can say but one word. "Elliot." My breath hitches from the weight of his name, for within it lies everything I can't bring myself to say just yet. My feelings, my desires, the yearning I've stifled for weeks now. I bring my hands to his torso, and he stiffens, as if bracing for me to push him away. But I don't push him away. I slide my hands up his chest, resting one at the base of his throat while the other glides toward his jaw, his chin. He trembles as I bring my thumb to his mouth, then slide it slowly over his lower lip.

All at once, we collide, lips locking together in a fierce kiss. My arms encircle his neck, pulling him closer. He presses in, and I feel my back come up against one of the bookshelves. I open my mouth and feel the slide of his tongue seeking mine. Our breaths grow sharp and heavy, and I tilt my head back to welcome more of him, more of his lips, his tongue, his breath. All these days and weeks I've denied my attraction to him have built up, wound tightly in a coil at my core. Having him against me like this, filling my senses, allows that coil to unfurl at last, and the rush of desire it loosens is almost too much to bear. His hand roves over the front of my dress, resting over the curve of my breast. I gasp, arching against him, wishing there wasn't a layer of lace and silk between his hand and my flesh.

His lips leave mine to trail across my jaw, then down my neck. My hands weave into his hair and his do the same with mine, sending pins flying to the floor as my dark tresses tumble free down my back. When his lips return to mine, I bring a hand to his chest, slipping it beneath the open collar to the firm musculature beneath. He stiffens against me, then pulls back slightly, muscles quivering with desire as he meets my eyes. That same desire echoes inside me, and I want nothing more than to act on it. But the brief pause is enough for me to hear the small voice in the back of my head, one that shouts something I shouldn't ignore.

I swallow hard, pulling back an inch, my head resting against the spines of the books behind me as I look up at him. "Elliot, I can't break your curse," I whisper.

He braces his arms on the bookshelf and lowers his forehead to mine. "No, my dearest Gemma. I will never ask that of you."

"Then...what will we do? What does this mean for us?"

"I know what I have to do." His words are firm, resolute.

My eyes widen. "You're going to...do it yourself?" I can hardly bring myself to elaborate. He's going to break his own curse. Sacrifice his unseelie form. Terror and awe and gratitude wash over me.

He nods.

Tears prick my eyes. "Are you sure?"

"I've never been so sure of anything in my life." He

leans in closer, and I claim his lips with mine. Desire returns, hotter than anything I've ever felt before, multiplied by the realization that he's willing to sacrifice the thing he values most...for me. For the unexpected love we've found between us. Before I met him, I'd given up on love. On romance. Even as I acknowledged my growing feelings while we danced the waltz, I'd resigned to let him go, knowing the wolf king could never be mine, even if the curse were to be broken. But now...possibilities I never could have expected span before me. He's mine. He loves me. He's going to break his curse.

My heart soars as it beats against his chest, radiating down to every inch of my being. Our kisses begin to slow, growing softer, more tender. He drags his tongue against mine in a languid caress, eliciting a moan from me. This is where it should end tonight, I know. We should ride the wave of this declining pace, take a step back, say goodnight.

As if he knows it too, he brushes his lips softly against mine but doesn't pull away. Not yet. My heart sinks in anticipation of him doing just that. I'm not ready to let him go, not even for a single night. Not with the desire that continues to burn in my veins, throbbing with every beat of my heart. "Take me to your room," I whisper against his mouth.

He stills, tensing against me. "Are you sure?"

My lips pull into a smirk, and I echo his own words back to him with just a hint of mockery. "I've never been so sure of anything in my life."

Matching my grin, he takes my hand in his and leads me out of the library and into the hall. A giddy excitement fills my heart as we move through the dark halls, making me feel younger, the way I felt the first time I fell in love. This, however, feels different. Elliot brings something new that I never felt before, a connection that was missing with Oswald and all my previous dalliances.

We reach a door not far from the library, and he pushes it open. Inside is a spacious bedroom with a neatly made bed at its center, plush rugs surrounding it, and a warm fire roaring in the hearth. He closes the door behind us, then faces me with a shy smile. It makes him look more youthful than ever, as if he too feels that echo of first love that has me so intoxicated.

"This is my room," he says, a hint of a blush in his cheeks.

"I figured." My voice comes out tremulous. Now that we're in his bedroom, the same sense of shyness creeps over me that seems to have taken him. But the desire remains, buzzing from my head to my toes. It's softer now, sweeter. I face him, bringing my hands to his shoulders as I meet his eyes.

I expect his lips to lower onto mine, but he hesitates. "I should tell you something," he says, his blush deepening.

I furrow my brow. "What is it?"

He grimaces, as if he dreads what he's about to say. "I've never," he clears his throat, "*taken* a mate while in my seelie form."

I stifle my urge to laugh, knowing it would only embarrass him more. Instead, I smile up at him. "First of all, you won't be *taking* me at all, but making love to me. Second of all, I can help you get...*acquainted* with lovemaking."

A mischievous grin tugs at his lips, and his body

relaxes. Bringing his lips close to my ear, he says, "Tell me what you like."

I kiss the corner of his jaw, then the lobe of his ear. "Undress me."

He pulls back to eye my gown, the one he so adorably had made for me. He quirks a brow. "I don't know much about dresses."

Slowly, I turn around so the closures at the back face him. "Good," I say. "I like it slow."

He brings his hands to my shoulders, then slides them down my back until they reach the low back of the gown where the clasps are. Despite him having little experience with undressing a woman, he undoes the closures with ease, working in silence while his breath stirs the back of my hair. Then, with the back fully open, he slips his hands beneath the fabric and runs them down my arms, taking my dress with it. With one more tug past my hips, the dress falls to the floor in a puddle of silk and lace. I angle my head to meet his eyes but make no move to turn around.

"What else do you like?" he asks, pressing a kiss to my neck.

My breaths quicken as I take one of his hands in mine, then guide his palm over my breast. His other hand splays over my stomach, and I guide it down to the sensitive place between my thighs. He presses in close behind me, lips moving down to my collarbone. I turn my head to give him greater access, then close my eyes as his fingers light a fire as they move against me, achingly slow.

My legs begin to tremble, my knees growing weak as a whine escapes my lips. His grip tightens on me, and I feel the softest graze of his teeth against my neck. "Gemma." The way he breathes my name, such a tender, musical sound, has my heart hammering against my ribs, flooding with warmth as pleasure burns my flesh.

I spin to face him and reach for his loose cravat, sliding it from his neck and tossing it to the floor, then begin working the buttons of his shirt. Once freed, I tug the shirt off him and slide my hands over the broad expanse of his chest, taking in the heat of his skin, the firmness of his muscles. I explore his torso like a treasure map, breathing in his woodsy scent. When my hands skate lower toward the waist of his trousers, his breath hitches. I pause and meet his eyes, finding vulnerability in them. "You're going to see me," he says, voice trembling. "All of me."

It takes me a moment to understand his sudden concern. Then it dawns on me—his leg. Keeping one hand on his hip, I move the other up his chest to rest over his rapidly beating heart. "I know, Elliot. You don't have to be afraid. I want to see you."

He releases a heavy sigh, then takes my hand off his heart, clasping it in his. With his sweet shyness returning, he leads me toward the bed. I stand naked before him while he sits at the edge, then slides down his trousers. My eyes lock on something that has my heart beating faster, and I guarantee it isn't his prosthetic. Lips pulling into a wicked smile, I meet his eyes. There's still hesitation in his face, but he seems encouraged by my reaction. Keeping his eyes on mine, he undoes the prosthetic. Once detached, he sets it softly on the floor, then sits motionless, a question written over his face. *Are you still fond of my body?* it seems to say. Or perhaps it's, *Do you still love me?*

I look him over, my eyes roving every inch of his flesh, then resting on his amputated leg. Ending at the knee, the skin is puckered with scar tissue in places, but is otherwise smooth. The sight doesn't unsettle me in the slightest. I find myself slightly fascinated, but the partial limb seems as natural as any other part of him, no less beautiful than his pointed ears, his wine-colored eyes, or his formidable stature.

I step closer, standing between his thighs. He runs his hands up the backs of my calves, my thighs, head tilted back. Lowering my face, I press a soft kiss against his lips. "You're beautiful, Elliot."

He releases a trembling sigh against my mouth, then moves his hands over my hips. Our kisses turn fiercer, and I part my lips to welcome his tongue. Then I settle onto his lap, straddling his hips. He grasps my bottom and scoots us back, until we're in the center of his bed. His hands wind into my hair as I move against him, eager to deepen our connection, to feel more of his warmth, his hardness. Slowly, I glide myself over him until he fills me, igniting a wave of sensation dancing within me, around me, mingling with the fluttering of my too-full heart.

"Freezing hell, Gemma," he says with a moan. "How did I ever live without this before? Without you?"

I devour his question with another kiss, and he shifts his weight until he's on top of me. Bracing himself on his forearms, we begin to move again in a new way. My arms wrap around his lower back, pressing him closer while my legs encircle his waist. Soon we find a familiar rhythm, as if we never stopped dancing in the library, pulsing against each other as heat floods my core. My eyes lock on his, taking in their garnet hue, the desire that spells my name with every beat of our hearts, pounding in tandem as pleasure unravels us both.

36

S weat-soaked and spent, we recline on Elliot's bed, the sheets pushed back, the room too hot for covers. I lay my head on his chest, my arm flung over his torso while one of my legs entwines around his. The music of his heart lulls me into peaceful relaxation as he brushes his hand along my hair. Every part of me that touches him feels like it's on fire, while the parts of me that brush only naked air are warmed by the glow of the hearth. I close my eyes, nestling closer.

Elliot presses a kiss to my forehead. "I've been alive over a thousand years, and yet never have I truly lived until now," he whispers. "Is this what it's like to open myself to the array of emotions and feelings and experiences humans have to offer?"

I prop my chin on his chest to look at him, tracing the line of his bearded jaw with my forefinger. "Is being in your unseelie form truly so different?"

"Yes, and I always carried pride about never having shifted into my seelie form."

"Are many fae like that? Remaining in their unseelie form their whole lives?"

He nods. "Long ago, that's all we ever were. There was no seelie or unseelie. We were all just creatures and spirits. We were more than animals but very different from humans. But when humans came to the isle, their presence began to change us. Some of the fae began to model themselves after humans, adopting their voices when they were taught human language, reshaping their bodies when they tried on human clothing. The ability to take seelie forms was born from that, and emotions and other human feelings came next. But not all fae considered it a gift. Those who maintained their original forms called themselves unseelie, and this divide led to unrest amongst the fae, fueled the wars we had with the humans. It pains me to say I spent my entire life fighting for whatever side pitted me against the humans. If I'd ever had my way, the humans would have been annihilated, or at least banished from the isle."

His words chill me. Remembering the trickster wolf I met when I first came searching for thirty-three White-spruce Lane, it isn't hard to imagine that version of him being as cold and cruel as he says. But it hasn't been long since he last expressed disdain for humankind. Could he truly have changed so much? Or is it only me he's come to value amongst my people?

He seems to read the concern in my expression and rolls to face me. "You've changed me, Gemma. Changed me in a way I never thought I'd want. I never thought I'd want pain or pleasure. I never thought I would choose both over the freedom that ignorance brings. And, yes, it's changed the way I judge your people. While I've yet to meet many I consider worthy of my respect or affection, I'm willing to believe your previous assertions are true— that not all humans are the same."

I bring my palm to the side of his face, and he angles his head to plant a kiss on my wrist. "You've changed me too, Elliot. You've reminded me what it means to trust, reminded me that pain in my past doesn't mean love can't exist in my future. It feels stupid now, realizing I nearly let one man close me off to the experiences of life."

"Does that mean you won't leave anymore?" A flicker of vulnerability crosses his face. "You can, Gemma. I know how much you miss your home country. I will not keep you here, no matter how much I love you—"

I press my forefinger to his lips. "I'm not leaving. I'm staying right here. Independence doesn't require running away and being alone. I can have freedom and still live amongst others. That doesn't mean I've forgiven human society, but I have a feeling there's more to Faerwyvae than what my experiences have shown me so far. And even if I were to discover every city on the isle is just as stifling as Vernon, well...I'll still have you."

"Yes, my love. You have me. So long as I live, I am yours." He kisses me, his hands roving my back, as if seeking undiscovered lands he hasn't already laid claim to. I do the same in turn, feeling his flesh, his muscles, his hair, tasting the salt of his skin. A spark of desire returns, and we continue to fan its flames late into the night, until we're too tired to move a muscle. Until we fall asleep wrapped in each other's arms.

～

WHEN I WAKE UP, I'M ALONE.

It takes me a moment to remember where I am, seeing the unfamiliar bedroom beneath the light of the rising sun creeping through the windows. Then it all rushes back to me, and I relax, images of last night's pleasure replaying in my mind, making me squeeze my thighs together. I roll onto my side, arm outstretched, seeking any sign of warmth left in Elliot's wake. But his side of the bed is cold, revealing only a slight indentation of where he was.

I wonder where he's gone off to, then sit upright as the answer comes. The curse! Surely, he's gone to break it. Throwing back the tangled sheets, I leap from the bed and hurry to the window. The view from here is far different from my bedroom. There is no sign of the garden, just forest trees and the tops of nearby mountains.

I leave the window to find my discarded gown and hastily climb into it. Then I leave the room, keeping an eye out for any sign of Elliot. The halls, however, are quiet and empty. I return to my room only long enough to don hose, boots, and a cloak, then dart downstairs and out the back doors to the garden.

Just as predicted, I find Elliot in the rose courtyard, sitting on the bench. He has his staff with him instead of his prosthetic, and he's dressed in nothing but trousers and a shirt—probably the same ones I took off him last night. The thought fills me with warmth, but it's quickly extinguished by his posture. When I came to find him, I'd hoped to see a triumphant grin on his face, or at least to find him buzzing with nervous anticipation. What I hadn't expected was to see him shrouded in his telltale aura of defeat.

Shoulders slouched and elbows propped on his knees, he holds a red rose petal between his fingers. Terror surges inside me, and my eyes dart to the withering rose, thinking the worst, but find it remains with a cluster of petals intact. I take a slow step into the courtyard. Elliot's eyes meet mine for the briefest second before returning to the petal in his hand.

My stomach sinks, pulse racing with fear no matter what I do to keep it at bay. Something isn't right. I clear my throat, attempting to keep my voice light and causal. "Are you going to do it?"

He meets my gaze again, his eyes wide and haunted. When he speaks, his voice comes out with a croak. "I can't."

A cloud of dread pummels me down, making me suddenly unsteady on my feet. Still, I force myself to maintain some semblance of composure. "You can't? Elliot, you said last night that you knew what had to be done."

"I thought I knew." He shakes his head, his voice rich with emotion. "But now...I can't give up what the curse requires. I will give up anything but that."

My blood runs cold, freezing my heart, chilling my bones. The world feels as if it's tipping upside down and I'm about to float into the sky only to crash onto the ground a second later. This is it. This is where it all falls apart, just like everything good in my life has before. Just like Mother's death. Just like Oswald's betrayal.

After a few trembling breaths, I find my voice over the lump in my throat. The words I say are an echo of ones

I've said in the past, a cruel reflection of a situation I thought I'd recovered from. "You lied."

"I didn't. I had every intention of doing it." There's so much conviction in his voice, I almost believe him. But I know better now, for it's almost the exact same thing the viscount said to me after our affair was made public. After he promised to fight for me.

"You deceived me. Last night—"

"If only I could go back to last night," he says, closing his eyes and tipping his head back. "To before I knew you loved me back. Erase all that happened after. At least then I could do this without losing the only thing that matters to me."

His words twist my guts, driving thorns into my heart. "You want to erase what we did last night? You regret it?"

He returns his eyes to mine, his gaze wild, looking more like the wolf I first met than ever before. "Gemma, you don't understand. Something has changed."

Shadows of the past threaten to invade my mind. The force of them is so strong, I fear they'll knock me off my feet. I breathe them away, hardening my heart against their attack, and channel all of my pain into the present. Crossing my arms, I let my sorrow turn to rage. "I know exactly what's changed. You got what you wanted and now you realize it was never worth it to begin with. You're just like Oswald. Full of promises in the heat of passion, but cold and afraid when reality sets in. I never should have trusted you."

He stands, securing his staff beneath his arm as he crosses the courtyard to me. "I don't know what else to do."

"So you're going to marry Imogen just to keep your

precious wolf form," I say with a sneer. He has the nerve to look confused, brows knitting together, but I continue on before he can interrupt. "I get it, Elliot. I really do. You value your unseelie form more than anything else. To you, it means freedom. I know that. But you didn't have to lead me on. You didn't have to tell me lies to get me into bed—"

"I didn't lie," he says through his teeth. "I'm incapable of it. Even if I were, I'd never lie to you."

I fix him with a seething glare. "*So long as I live, I am yours.* Do you remember saying that?"

"I meant it. Gemma, you have no idea how much I meant that and still do. I only wish—"

"What? That I could be your mistress? That you could lock me in a cave and only come visit me when you're bored of being a wolf? Or perhaps crawl into my bed after you perform your husbandly duties with Imogen? Well, that's not going to happen, I promise you." Each word that tumbles from my lips is another lash upon my heart, another gaping wound left bleeding in its wake.

"That's not what I'm trying to say." He advances a step closer, but I retreat back.

"Let me out of the bargain," I say, teeth bared. "I did my part, but I'm done and I'll participate in it no longer. You can finish our scheme all on your own. I don't want your money or your thanks or to ever see your face again. Just let me out so I can forget the last month of my life ever happened." My words dissolve into gasping sobs, but I swallow them down. Angry tears stream down my face, tears I wish I could hide from him.

Pain twists his face as he watches me unravel before him. Then his expression turns hard, a sudden realization dawning in his eyes. His voice comes out cold, flat. "You're right. This is the only way, isn't it? That we part now so you can forget about me."

"Can it be done? Can the bargain be dissolved?"

He nods, eyes closed.

"Then do it."

He stands trembling in silence for a few moments, then opens his eyes. Another flicker of pain contorts his expression, but again he steels it. "Gemma Bellefleur, I release you from our bargain. I consider it served and severed."

There's no rush of magic, no mysterious tingle. Nothing to denote a fae bargain has been dissolved. Or perhaps I'm just too numb to care.

Without a second thought, I turn on my heel and stride down the path.

"Gemma," comes Elliot's quavering voice.

I glance over my shoulder to see the plea in his eyes, but what it's begging of me, I don't know, and it does nothing to soften my heart. Instead, it fuels my rage. I wish I had a way to hurt him, to make him feel the pain he's inflicted upon me. But all I have are my words. Filling my voice with all the venom poisoning my heart, I say, "Fuck you, Elliot. I hope you and Imogen rot in hell."

37

My next days pass in solitude and silence. My bedroom at Father's townhouse feels like a tomb and my presence in it is weighted in defeat. I try not to count the days nor the petals I know are falling in the courtyard of a certain manor on White-spruce Lane. I try not to compare my cramped yet elegant bedroom to the spacious one I spent the last month in, nor the one I spent a single, pleasurable night in. Feigning illness, I take all meals in my room, refuse all visitors, survive Father's triumphant glares and Nina's pitying glances when I'm forced to be in their presence.

Despite all my best efforts to forget, when a week goes by, I know the exact tally of petals that have fallen and approximately how many remain. If my previous estimates were correct, then tomorrow is the final day before the curse is set to claim Elliot Rochester.

"I wish it would take him," I mutter without feeling as I lay reclined in bed, my eyes scanning the pages of a book. I can hardly call it reading, considering my lack of comprehension and joy over the words I visually digest. But it gives me something to do, some semblance of a distraction. It doesn't last, however, and I quickly find my thoughts returning to their previous musings. Elliot. The curse. The rose petals.

As much as I dread the countdown to the final petal, I welcome it with cold anticipation. For once that day passes, it will be over once and for all. There will be no wondering, no what-ifs. There will be no feverish, foolish urges to run back to the manor, wrap him in my arms, and proclaim that I will break his curse myself.

I scowl inwardly at the thought, at my reckless weakness when it comes to him. Even if Elliot deserved my affection, nothing could ever be worth sacrificing freedom for. That's never been truer than now.

Then again, I have no reason to believe the curse hasn't already been broken. He may have married Imogen by now, for all I know. It would be idiocy to wait until the last day, the last moment. They could have been married the day I fled the manor. Closing myself off in my bedroom, I've avoided as much outside communication as possible. I've certainly ignored every letter of Imogen's, every request to speak to me. There haven't been many, but she's come to call enough to make my feigned sickness almost feel real.

I shake the thoughts from my mind and return to my book. I give it a solid effort and have almost made it a full paragraph when I'm interrupted by a brief knock on my door. It's a knock I know well. Father.

Without waiting for me to answer, he opens my door. "Get dressed. Gavin Aston is coming for tea this afternoon, and you will see him." Just like that, he begins to close the door.

I lurch from my bed and race to the door. "What are you talking about? I can't have company. I'm unwell."

Father barks a cold laugh. "We both know that isn't true, and I'm done humoring your whims. It's time to do your duties as my daughter."

I stare blankly, feeling like I'm missing something. "Why is Mr. Aston coming to have tea with me?"

He purses his lips, jaw shifting side to side, making his dark mustache twitch. Then, in a rush, he says, "He's coming to ask for your hand, and you will accept."

He tries to close the door on his last word, but I grab the door handle. Terror and fury flood me. "He's going to what?"

"Do not try to argue," Father says, raising his voice. "He's already asked my permission and I've given it. Now that you are back under my roof, you will do as I say. You will accept his proposal and we will put this newest scandal behind us."

My mouth falls open. "What are you talking about? What scandal? Father, I took a job. My employment has now ended because Mr. Rochester will be taking up residence elsewhere."

He shakes his head, a bitter laugh on his lips. "You aren't fooling anyone, Gemma. Did you think you could come back here and return to your old ways, secretly sending off job applications and taking my hospitality for granted?"

I clench my jaw, having no argument against that. It is, in fact, exactly what I intend to do. That is, once I find the motivation to move about the house and interact with people again.

"Do you not know what they're saying about you?"

I throw my hands in the air. "What is so wrong about a woman like me taking a job?"

His face flushes crimson, eyes bulging. "You lived with an unwed man, spent who knows how many unchaperoned hours with him, and danced with him at a private ball while he was courting Imogen Coleman. Everything is wrong with that. I don't care if he's secretly the king, and I don't care if the rumors about you are wrong. The truth is, no one will hire you now, unless you plan on entering a brothel."

His words send shards of glass through my heart, puncturing the already bruised and bloodied organ. Still, I can find no word to use against him. Nothing. The disgust in his eyes has me shriveling before him, shrinking me into a speck of dirt. How did my father become this cold, cruel man?

"You're lucky anyone wants to marry you at all," he says. "You will accept Mr. Aston's company for tea this afternoon, and when he proposes, you will say yes. Otherwise, I will turn you out of the house tonight."

With that, he slams the door shut. In his absence, I lean against the wall, finding my legs too weak to support me. I blink, but no tears will come, for I have none to spare. They've long since dried.

∾

AN HOUR LATER, I DON MY FALSE PERSONA AND ENTER THE parlor. It isn't quite afternoon just yet, but I'd rather prepare for my doom now than wait until Gavin is being led upstairs to meet me. I go to the hearth, ignoring memories of another hearth in another parlor, and sit on a chair that looks nothing like one I've grown so fond of seeing occupied by a certain surly king.

My eyes unfocus as I watch the dancing flames, and I force my mind to empty.

Empty.

Nothing.

Too soon, the parlor doors open, sending my heart leaping into my throat. Every muscle grows tense as I squeeze the arms of my chair. But it isn't Gavin that enters; it's Nina.

I release a sigh, feeling my muscles ease as I lean into the back of the chair. Nina approaches and takes a seat next to me. I neither greet her nor meet her eyes but can feel the pity in them just the same.

We sit in silence for a few moments, until Nina speaks, voice quiet. "You aren't going to marry him, are you?"

I can't quite place her tone. Is there trepidation in it? Condemnation? "What do you want me to say, Nina?"

She leans toward me. "I want you to say no, that you'll refuse him."

I'm taken aback by this, and slowly meet my sister's eyes, finding them fierce and defiant. I wish they'd spark the same in me, but they don't. "Since when do you promote my disobedience against Father?"

"Since I watched you dance with Mr. Rochester."

My heart does a flip then sinks to my toes. I look back at the fire. "What is that supposed to mean?"

Nina leans closer, reaching for my hand. She takes it

in both of hers. "Gemma, I've tried to give you space and not question you, but something happened between you and Mr. Rochester, and I want you to tell me."

I pull my hand from her grasp. "Nothing happened."

She sits straighter, her tone sharpening. "You cannot tell me what I saw was nothing. I saw the way he looked at you. The way you looked at him. Anyone with eyes and a brain could see."

I scoff. "So very few."

"You loved him and he loved you."

I whirl in my chair to face her. "You don't know what you're talking about. The fae aren't capable of love like we are. Turns out that part of the fairytales is true."

"Then tell me what happened. Don't shut me out. I know you're hurting and I want to be here for you. I love you."

I love you. The words reverberate through my head, her voice mingling with *his*. It's too much, too soon. Too potent and painful. It shakes me out of my hiding place, dissolves the dark shroud of my outer persona. "He broke my heart, all right?" I hate the way my voice closes up as I deliver my truth.

"All right," Nina says with a calm and gentle grace. "Tell me about it. I'll listen."

"It's...it's not just my story to tell. There are things about him I can't share."

"Then tell me your side."

I'm silent as I ponder what to say, surprised at the relief that washes over me at the prospect of telling her even a fraction of all that I've bottled inside. When I speak, my voice is barely above a whisper. "I opened up. I trusted him. I gave him my heart and believed that things would work between us. Believed his promises that he was willing to do what was necessary to make it so. But just like with Oswald, when it came down to it, he couldn't fight for me. He couldn't do what he needed to do."

"What did he need to do?"

"Give up something that he cherished more than me." As I say it, guilt tugs at my heart, unearthing more that needs to be confessed. "I understand why he wasn't willing to give it up. If it was reversed, I wouldn't have made the sacrifice either. We both value freedom too much. Which makes us wrong for each other."

Nina doesn't ask me to elaborate, just says, "Did he explain why?"

"He didn't need to." But as I say it, my stomach sinks. He did try to explain, but I refused to hear him out. I put words in his mouth, words that are probably truer than whatever garbage he was about to spew. And yet, Nina has a point.

"Gemma, you do always tend to expect the worst of people."

"When have I ever been wrong? If I would have expected the worst of people from the start, I would have known not to trust Oswald."

"Somehow, you still managed to trust Mr. Rochester."

"Oh, and how did that work out?"

Nina releases a frustrated sigh. "What I'm trying to say is, you can't let one terrible man ruin your happiness forever. You managed to get over what happened with the Viscount of Brekshire enough to give Mr. Rochester a chance. Even if things didn't work out, that doesn't mean it wasn't worth a try. I saw how happy you looked when you danced with him, and I refuse to believe that, at least for a time, it wasn't all worth it."

Her words remind me of the conclusion I came to when I danced with Elliot at the ball. I'd been so ready to lose him, at peace with it even, knowing that having him in my life for a time had made it better. *Maybe it doesn't have to last forever to be real.*

Then he ruined everything, turned all my warm thoughts of him bitter. If only that last, beautiful night between us hadn't happened, then I could let him marry Imogen with nothing more than a bitter ache in my heart instead of this seething, venomous hurt.

As I think it, another echo weaves through my thoughts. *If only I could go back to last night...to before I knew you loved me back. Erase all that happened after. At least then I could do this without losing the only thing that matters to me.*

I shift uncomfortably in my chair, not wanting to unpack what he meant by that. Why would our night together have made it harder for him to sacrifice his unseelie form? Shouldn't it have been easier, knowing he had something tangible to sacrifice it for? It shouldn't have even crossed his mind before he knew I loved him back.

Nina must see the conflict on my face. "Maybe you should let him explain."

"It's too late," I say, my voice cracking. "Besides, you tend to think far too highly of others. There's nothing he could say to make this right. It's over, and I don't want to talk about him anymore."

"Then what about you? Are you really going to give

up on your dreams? I know you want to be more than just someone's wife. You want freedom and true love—"

"I don't want love."

"What you don't want is Gavin Aston."

A spark of anger ignites inside me, snapping me out of my apathy. "What else am I to do? Everything you warned me about has come to pass. Father will kick me out if I don't accept Mr. Aston's hand, and my job prospects are over in this town."

Nina rises from her seat only to sink down in front of my chair, taking my hands in hers. She looks up at me with so much love and adoration that it pains me to see. "You are clever and you are beautiful and you have never once stopped fighting."

I close my eyes, blocking out the sight of her. Her faith in me is too strong, too heavy. "I'm just so tired, Nina."

"It's okay to be tired," she says. "But don't give up. Don't let the spark die out. It's who you are."

I keep my eyes closed, listening as she rises to her feet and leaves the room. Once I know I'm alone, I open my eyes, and with that comes an avalanche of tears. Just when I thought I could cry no more, sobs erupt from my throat. This time, they feel not like an exercise in grief but a cathartic release. When it's over, the same feeling I felt at the end of my waltz with Elliot comes over me. The same thing I felt after I read the book about the boy and the dog.

A bittersweet peace that's as painful as it is warm.

avin arrives shortly after two in the afternoon. It's just me and him, and we gather around the tea table. He sits in a chair while I take my place on the couch. Susan, the maid, brings tea and cookies, and an awkward silence falls between us. I feel a strong urge to wrap my false persona around me, but for once I ignore that instinct. After my conversation with Nina, I've determined to face this head on as myself. Unguarded. Unarmed.

Just me.

Gavin reaches for the teapot and fills both our cups. Then, with shaking hands, he brings his cup to his lips and takes a sip. I do the same.

"Well, I suppose I should confess why I'm here," he says, replacing his cup on the saucer. "Although, I'm sure you've already guessed. I've made my admiration of you very clear, if not directly to you, then to your family and friends. You could hardly be surprised by my visit today."

"No, I am not surprised," I say, tone flat.

He seems encouraged by this, lips stretching into a smile as he stands and approaches the couch. Just as he takes a seat next to me, I rise and slowly make my way to the other side of the table. There I face him. Not with scorn or my well-trained haughty grin, but with open curiosity.

"Why do you like me, Mr. Aston?"

His brows weave together, and he stumbles over his words before he finds his answer. "You must know I find you very beautiful," he says with a blush.

"What else?"

He straightens his cravat and clears his throat. "Well, you're the smartest, cleverest girl in Vernon."

"How do you know? Have you spoken to every woman in town?"

"I need not acquaint myself with everyone to know your wit is unparalleled. Our few conversations were more than enough."

"And how do you know I'm smart?"

"I saw you holding my favorite book," he says. "The fact that you admire the same eloquent literature that I do—"

"Did you not see when I gave the book back to Mr. Cordell?"

He tilts his head, a ponderous look on his face. "Oh, yes, I suppose you did."

"Here's the thing, Mr. Aston. Your entire impression of me has been flawed from the start. I admit, it's a romantic idea to fancy another over mutual admiration of a book, but even if that had been true in our case, it doesn't guarantee compatibility, much less love. And the truth is, I have never read *Infinite Suffering in the Garden of*

Happenstance, nor will I ever, for one look told me it's the most dull and uninteresting thing I'd ever have the horror to behold. You see, the book was misshelved. In truth, I read romance novels. The kind with whirlwind love, passionate affairs, and happily ever afters. That is who I am."

He rubs the back of his neck, his blush growing deeper as he stares at the tea table. Then, with a short laugh, he returns his gaze to mine. "It's a funny story, meeting over a misshelved book. I'm quite amused, actually. Even more so that you feared this truth would make me think less of you or your intelligence. On the contrary, I only think more of it now."

I clench my jaw. "I didn't tell you this because I feared you'd think less of my intelligence. I said it to illustrate the fact that you don't know me. Not enough to make the declaration of love and marriage that you came here for."

He rises to his feet, fervor in his eyes as he rounds the table to stand before me. "You're wrong," he says, taking my hands in his. "I loved you from the moment I laid eyes on you, and I love you still. I'm more than willing to ignore the scathing rumors circulating town about you. That's how much I love you. I love you so much that I will save you from this scandal and make every gossiper regret the day they spoke ill of you."

"I do not need to be saved from this scandal." I pull my hands from his and take a step back, a slightly hysteric amusement creeping up my throat and drawing up the corners of my lips. "I don't need to be saved from it, because it's likely all true. I worked for Mr. Rochester, lived at his manor, and I spent many unchaperoned moments with him."

Gavin shakes his head. "I'm not so conservative as some of the others in town are. You are a grown woman in charge of her own mind. At least before you marry. I trust your judgment—"

"I fell in love with him," I say, cutting him off. "We went so far as to have an affair. A very physical one, just to be clear."

His eyes widen, throat bobbing as he swallows his defense of me.

"Before my family came here, I was involved in another affair, one with the Viscount of Brekshire. Rumors of that scandal are true as well, aside from the part that paints me as the instigator. In both cases I was in love and willing. In both cases, I don't regret exploring my passions. Only the repercussions of my lovers' false hearts."

Gavin goes a shade paler, a sheen of sweat coating his brow. "I...I would be a hypocrite to deny a woman's right to...to do as she wishes with her body, as men aren't expected to be chaste themselves." He swallows hard, as if keeping bile from rising in his throat, then lowers his voice to a whisper. "But a lady should never speak so freely of such things, especially not to a suitor. Just as a gentleman keeps his...romantic past discreet."

I take a few steps back, then lower into a chair. Sitting tall, I cross one leg over the other and place my hands firmly on the armrests. "Mr. Aston, if you came to me expecting me to be a *lady* by society's definition, then you are even more misinformed about my true character than I first thought. This is who I am. I read romance novels, I speak my mind, and I have no patience for gossip. I will never try to fit in to a town like Vernon, but I will go to great lengths to find just the right place for me someday. I guarantee that place will not be amongst human high society. In addition, I have loved and am still in love with Elliot Rochester. We will never be together, but right now I hate him and love him in equal measure, and I am not ready to heal from that."

My own honesty takes me by surprise, and with it comes another truth. "I will heal, though. Someday. But even when I do, I doubt you and I will be right for each other. You see, I want love from someone who knows me inside and out. Not someone who sees my past as a string of follies, but as building blocks that have made me who I am now. And the man who loves me will not ask me to hide, ignore, or keep any part of me or my past under lock and key. He will love me just as I am. Now, tell me, Mr. Aston. Does that sound like you?"

He's grown even paler during my tirade and seems to shrink in on himself with every second that ticks by. I hold his gaze, my expression neutral. This is his chance. His one chance to prove my prior judgments about him were wrong. Nina was right when she said I always expect the worst of people, so I'm willing to give him the benefit of the doubt. Maybe there's more to him than there seems now, just like there was with Elliot. Maybe there's common ground between us.

He takes a step back, and another, averting his eyes. Then, turning silently on his heel, he leaves the parlor, leaving his proposal unsaid.

∼

UNSURPRISINGLY, FATHER COMES NEXT. HE FINDS ME standing at the window, watching the busy streets crawling with people, buzzing with automobiles, and swarming with carriages. The light dusting of snow has already turned brown from today's traffic. I focus on the falling snowflakes as Father begins to shout. I find peace in their intricate patterns as they drift from the sky to the street. It brings me back to the quiet stillness of the mountains and helps me steel myself against Father's rage. I neither look at him nor interrupt him as he continues to shout. Then finally, it ends with a question, one I don't hear. Slowly, I turn to face him, and he repeats it.

"Why do you seek your own ruin?" Father's chest heaves, his face crimson.

I reply with my own question. "Why do you hate me so much?"

He takes a step back, eyes wide as if I've stabbed him. "I don't hate you, Gemma. Everything I've done for you has been out of love. But I can do no more, you've seen to that. You are too disobedient. If it seems like I love your sisters more, it is only because they obey. They give me no reason to be vexed by them."

I shake my head. "Obedience isn't love, Father. Forcing your daughter into an unwanted marriage isn't love."

"It's been enough for your sisters. Why isn't it for you?"

I turn to face him. "Because they were willing. They fell in love with their first prospects, and their suitors loved them back."

Father shakes a forbidding finger at me. "You could

have had what they have if only you hadn't set your sights on an engaged man."

I close my eyes, keeping my rage from rising to meet his. "I've made mistakes, Father, but they are not what you think they are. I'm done hoping you'll one day understand my perspective. I'm also done trying to be the daughter you want me to be, and I'm done fighting you. In the end, I don't know you and you don't know me. The father I loved died when my mother did, and the man that's left isn't worth my obedience, my anger, or my defiance."

His voice comes out with a hiss. "How dare you. You ungrateful—" He raises a hand but halts. As if struck by physical pain, he winces and takes a step back, shaking his head as tears glaze his eyes. When he speaks, his voice breaks. "You want to know why I hate you, Gemma?"

My breath catches, my lungs constricting painfully tight. All I can do is nod.

"Because you remind me the most of *her*. Of your mother."

His words sound so wrong leaving his lips. They should be tender, nostalgic, but instead are filled with disgust. It's enough to build a sob in my chest, one I choke back with all the restraint I have.

Father continues. "She was wild and defiant like you. And look where that got her."

"What are you talking about?"

"She was never content to simply be a wife. I gave her everything. Children, a home, horses to tame, and chickens to raise. Still, she wanted more than she had any right to. She insisted on inserting herself into my business too. She wanted to visit our employees in the mines, see to their welfare. She didn't have to be in the mine the day it collapsed. In fact, I forbade her from going when reports of instability in the deeper tunnels were reported. But did she listen? No. She wanted to check in with the workers herself, make sure they were well after she learned some had died of lung sickness. That defiance killed her."

Sympathy tugs at my heart, but it feels profane alongside Father's condemnation of Mother's actions. It makes me question whether he was ever the man I thought he was, even when Mother was alive. At least then he seemed kind. Happy. "You didn't have to let it harden you," I say, my voice trembling with suppressed tears. "You didn't have to give up on love and push the rest of us away."

He clenches his jaw. "I didn't give up, but I am now. Your disobedience will be the death of you, just like it was for your mother, and I won't wait around to watch it come to pass." With that, he turns on his heel and stalks to the door. Before he leaves, he pauses beneath the threshold. "Tonight is the last night I will allow you in this house. Be gone by morning. I don't care where you go."

39

The next morning, I rise with the sun and pack a bag of my belongings. This includes only a single book, the very first in the *Governess in Love* series. It's the book that made me fall in love with reading, and the one I've read more than any other. It will be a comforting companion in this next stage of my journey. Although packing just one book makes my heart ache with longing, it won't be long before I can buy more books again or have the space to store them.

I check my purse, counting the quartz chips I've collected during my employment under Mr. Rochester. Even though I relinquished my rights to the twenty thousand quartz rounds when I had him dissolve our bargain, the three thousand quartz chips I've earned will at least be enough to pay for several weeks at a hotel and transport to a new town. I'll stay a night or two in Vernon while I figure out where to go next and how to get there. Once I've relocated, I can begin looking for work. I'll likely have to lower my standards on what I apply for, but at least I'll be free from this town, the rumors, and the reminders of Elliot.

Free. Just like I always wanted. Maybe not in the *way* I wanted, but I shall be free nonetheless. It's a bittersweet comfort. A somber triumph.

Dressed in my warmest dress and cloak, I leave my room with my bag in hand. Nina is in the hall, her eyes wet with tears. "I'm sorry," she says. "I shouldn't have encouraged you to fight Father. I never imagined he'd truly kick you out."

I give her a sad smile and place a hand on her shoulder. "I'm glad you did, Nina. You reminded me of who I am."

Her face contorts with grief, and she wraps her arms around my neck, sobbing into my hair. "I don't want you to go."

A lump rises in my throat as I rub her back. "I know. But we'll see each other again. I won't stray too far."

"Where will you go?"

I shrug. Although I've given up on thoughts of moving back to Isola—mostly because I can't afford it—I've yet to settle on my next destination. "Maybe I'll wait until the Verity Hotel is complete, then visit my new friend Foxglove at Maplehearth Palace."

She pulls back, eyes red. "Promise me you'll be happy."

I nod. "I will."

She squeezes me one more time, then releases me. Side by side, we descend the stairs. A mix of terror and exhilaration washes over me. I have no idea what to expect. I've never traveled on my own before, much less *lived* on my own. But I know I can do this. I must. And just like I promised Nina, I will be happy.

We reach the bottom landing when frantic footsteps draw near. For a split second, I wonder if it's Father coming to see me off, or even to stop me from leaving. But of course, it isn't him; I know it even before Susan rounds the corner. "Miss Bellefleur," she says, somewhat out of breath, "there's someone here to see you."

A spike of alarm rushes through me. Could it be Imogen? Or Elliot? Both together? The thought is absurd but sends my mind reeling just the same. "Who is it?"

"I don't recognize her. She'll only say that she's a friend."

Relief and disappointment root me back to the ground, and after a few steadying breaths, my head stops spinning. I give Susan a nod. "I will greet her at the door, whoever she is."

Nina remains at my side, looking just as perplexed as I feel.

It's probably some random person I've met in passing, coming to make my acquaintance, I tell myself. *Or perhaps it's a detestable reporter, here to take my statement on the latest scandal circulating town.*

I steel myself against whatever confrontation awaits as we draw near the front hall, but nothing could have prepared me for the figure I find standing just inside my door. I stop short, eyes wide. "Bertha?"

The fae woman smiles wide and closes the distance between us. Before I know what's happening, I find myself wrapped in her embrace. My arms return the gesture before my mind catches up.

Once we pull away, I waste no time asking, "What are you doing here?"

"Mr. Rochester sent me here on business, but I can't stay long. I promised him I wouldn't."

A sliver of ice pierces my heart, and several more questions beg to be asked. *How is he? Is he back to being a wolf already? Are the children happy now that the curse is broken?* Pushing all these questions away, I focus on one I think might hurt the least. "What business could Mr. Rochester have regarding me?"

Without a word, she gestures toward the door and lets herself out onto the doorstep.

Nina and I exchange a glance, then follow her. My sister's fingers find mine and give them a comforting squeeze. I can't help the way my eyes prick with tears as a result.

We join Bertha on our front stoop, and I see two of Father's household servants hefting a large chest between them. They appear to have brought it from a coach that awaits along the sidewalk, one I've never seen before. I furrow my brow and look to Bertha. "What is this about?"

She waves a hand from the chest to the coach. "It's all yours, my dear. Courtesy of Mr. Rochester."

The chest suddenly makes sense, and I narrow my eyes. "I already told him I want none of his money."

She grimaces. "Well, I suggest you rethink that. He won't take it back, nor will he accept the coach to return. He has no need for it. It's in your care now."

I'm about to argue when Nina elbows me and burns me with a pointed look. Even without words, I know what she's trying to convey, and she's right. I don't have the luxury of being prideful when it comes to money right now. The coach provides an element of confusion, for it couldn't truly be *mine*. With that thought comes the horrifying realization that Elliot could have heard about my situation and decided to save me the indignity of walking to a hotel on foot. But how could word have gotten out so fast? And why would he care, anyway?

"Where do you want this?" one of the servants asks as they reach the bottom step.

"I suppose it should go back on the coach." My words come out slow, a new plan forming as I speak. Maybe I don't have to stay at a hotel in town after all. Perhaps I can head straight to a more desirable location at once. But where should I go?

The servants pause, then begin to turn around.

"You should at least look inside it first," Bertha says.

Again, the men pause and look to me for guidance.

I sigh. "Very well. Bring it just inside."

Nina and I step out of the way while the chest is brought inside. The two men leave it in the middle of the front hall, then take places near the wall, awaiting further instruction. A sudden trepidation washes over me as I approach the chest. Slowly, I lower to my knees before it only to realize I don't have the key.

Just as I think it, Bertha appears at my side, handing a brass key over my shoulder. I take it from her with trembling fingers and insert it into the keyhole. Once unlocked, I flip the latches. Bracing my hands on the lid, I pause, my pulse racing. Why am I so nervous to open it? I already know what's inside. Twenty thousand quartz rounds. Payment for a bargain I completed, despite the fact that I forced Elliot to dissolve it.

Nina crouches at my side and puts a soft hand on my back. "Go on," she whispers.

With a deep breath, I lift the lid. Inside, glittering orbs of smooth quartz greet me, far more dazzling than the small, oddly shaped chips in my purse. Even without counting, it seems like there are far more than twenty thousand rounds inside. But my attention is quickly drawn to what lies on top of the quartz. A letter.

I lift it and scan the script written in a hand I've only noted on a few spare scraps here and there—Elliot's handwriting. A lump rises in my throat as I read it.

> *Dearest Gemma,*
>
> *I am gifting you one hundred thousand quartz rounds. Do not try to give it back, I will not accept it. I also leave you this coach and four. Its services, care, and driver have been paid in full for a year in advance. I have instructed the driver to remain with you upon penalty of death. Yes, he now knows who I am and he will not defy me, so don't even try to send the coach back. You will not defy me either, for I leave you with one final request, demand, and gift.*
>
> *Go, Gemma. Be free.*
>
> *And know that, wherever you go, I will always love you.*
>
> *Elliot.*

I'm so torn and confused, for several moments I can only stare at the letter. Then I read it thrice over, puzzling out his words. Why would he leave me with so much money? Why remind me of his love when we parted on such bad terms?

Go, Gemma. Be free.

And why in the name of the saints did he write it with such a somber air, as if it were a will?

Seeking answers, I turn to find Bertha. But she's already gone.

WITH SEVERAL MORE BAGS NOW PACKED AND ALL THE books I own bundled up and ready to be loaded into my new coach, I face my journey with a new sense of possibility. I still don't know where I'll go, but I can at least ask the driver to take me to a new town while I decide on my final destination. The only thing that dampens my outlook is the dread that's settled into my heart ever since I read Elliot's letter. That, and the fact that Nina continues to remind me about it every spare moment she has.

"Are you at least going to stop by and thank him?" she asks, hurrying along at my side while I carry my final bag of possessions down the stairs and toward the front hall.

"No, Nina," I tell her for the fifth or sixth time. Every question has been about whether I'll write to him, thank him, or send *her* to thank him for me. And every answer of mine is the same. No. No. Absolutely not.

"But it was so kind of him, and he clearly still loves you."

We reach the front step, where I hand my bag off to Susan, who in turn takes it to the coach. Seeing as the front hall is now clear, that's the last of my things. I turn to my sister and force a smile. There's no point leaving annoyed. It's not like she can help being a hopeless romantic. I gather her in my arms. "I love you, Nina. Take care of Father while you can."

"Will you come back for my wedding?"

"Of course I will." We pull apart slightly, and I try not to focus on how my heart sinks. "I'll miss you."

"I'll miss—"

"What did you do?" The voice is so unwelcome and startling that it makes my skin crawl. Clenching my jaw, I release my sister to face Imogen standing at the bottom of the steps, hands on her hips. Her face is furious, blonde curls a tangled mess. She looks as if she hasn't slept in a week. Or perhaps she's been crying.

Narrowing my eyes, I descend the stairs and face her. "What are you talking about, Imogen?"

"What. Did. You. Do?" She bites out each word through clenched teeth.

I release a frustrated sigh. "I have no idea what you're talking about, and I have somewhere to be. Have a good life." I turn my back on her and make my way to the open doors of the coach.

"Are you going back to *him*?"

I pause and whirl back toward her, brow furrowed. "No, I'm leaving Vernon."

She lets out a bitter laugh and takes a few steps closer. "Sure you are. I know what's really going on. You've decided you'll be the one to break his curse."

My heart begins to hammer against my ribs. "Imogen, I have no idea what you're talking about." Then a question I dread to ask flies from the tip of my tongue. "Are you and Mr. Rochester not married?"

She throws her hands in the air. "No, Gemma. Don't play stupid. I know this was all your doing."

Nina hurries down the steps and storms up to Imogen. "Don't you dare talk to my sister like that."

Imogen rounds on Nina. "You should be careful before your reputation is tainted by her wicked ways."

Nina's mouth falls open, and she takes a step closer. If I didn't know any better, I'd think she was preparing for a fight. "How dare you! Who do you think you are?"

"It's all right, Nina," I say gently. "I can handle this."

Nina pins Imogen with a seething glare but takes a step back.

I face Imogen, my fingers curling into fists. "Now, I am only going to say this once more. I have no idea what in the name of the saints you're going on about. Speak clearly and say what it is you're so desperate to hint at."

Passers-by have stopped to gawk, but I pay them no heed. All I know is if Imogen doesn't explain herself in a matter of seconds, I'll shake the words out of her myself.

Finally, Imogen turns up her nose and speaks. "I've been waiting for him to propose like you said he would, but he wouldn't see me all week. I've come to call every single day, and yet each day it's the same. Mr. Rochester is busy, he'll see me tomorrow. I gave him the benefit of the doubt, assuming he was merely preparing for our upcoming nuptials. Then finally, he accepts my visit today. I find him outside in an unkempt courtyard of brambles staring at some horrid, withering rose. Minutes passed and he didn't say a word to me. Then finally, I threw all propriety to the wind and asked if he was going to marry me. You know what he did?"

She waits for me to answer, but I can't bring myself to speak.

"He shook his head," she finally says. "And when I

asked him why, he gave me a single word as his reply. Can you guess what that word was? It was *Gemma*. Your name is the reason he won't marry me, and he refused to say a word more, much less look at me. Why is that? What have you done?"

My eyes go unfocused, and a chill crawls up my spine. He didn't marry Imogen. Nor did he break the curse himself. That means...

Saints, no.

"Tell me what you did!" Imogen lunges forward and grasps my wrist in her fingers, squeezing hard.

I yank my arm back, but her grip is painfully tight. "Let me go!"

Nina tugs on Imogen's other arm. "Get away from her, you lunatic."

She ignores my sister's attempts to pull her away. "Not until you confess. Tell me the truth. Tell me you're just like Mother said. Just like your father said. You're a whore. A temptress. A seductress. You let me fall for Mr. Rochester, just to yank him away."

My stomach sinks with guilt; she's partially right. I orchestrated this scheme to trick her, to punish her for how much I dislike her, for the awful things she's said to me. And yet, it's clear she's hurting, funneling all her grief into rage. It's as familiar to me as a mirror. "I've wronged you," I say, speaking through clenched teeth. "And that I am sorry for. I never should have involved you with Mr. Rochester, and I never should have lied to you."

Nina's eyes dart from me to Imogen, her expression perplexed.

Imogen's eyes widen. "So you admit it! You're a shameless harlot!"

"Think what you will of me, I don't care. I meant it when I said I'm sorry, and I'll mean it for the rest of my days." I step closer, sharpening my tone. "But if you don't release me at once, I'll break your freezing arm!"

She holds my gaze for a matter of seconds before going a shade paler. Then she takes a reluctant step back and slides her fingers from around my wrist. Nina steps between us, burning Imogen with an angry scowl and forcing her to step back even farther. If matters weren't so dire, I'd have time to admire Nina's ferocity in my defense.

But I don't have time. In fact, I might be too late.

Nina seems to understand, even without knowing the severity of the situation. "Go," she whispers.

With that, I dart to the front of the coach. "Thirty-three Whitespruce Lane," I call to the driver. "Hurry!"

40

The manor is as quiet as a tomb when I reach it. I enter the front doors and am taken aback when I find the front hall crowded with wolves. Not the wolf-people I'm used to but *actual* canines. Some sit back on their haunches, heads hanging low. Others rest on their bellies or their sides. A few stalk from one side of the hall to the other, restlessness written in every move. I take a step inside the hall, and all stop to look at me, dozens of sets of eyes locking me in their predatory gaze.

That's when I realize—it's been nearly a month since I first came here and fell into Elliot's trap. A moon cycle has passed, and it is once again the time of the full moon. Time when the curse allows the wolves of the manor to shift into their unseelie forms.

Despite knowing the wolves are the same creatures I've spent time with over the past few weeks, I can't help but be unnerved by their silent, prowling presence. I swallow hard before speaking. "Where's the king?"

A wolf with tawny fur pads toward me, but a shaggy

brown—the first wolf I ever saw when I came here—leaps before me, a growl tearing through its mouth. "Who are you?" It speaks with Gray's creaky voice, filled with an uncharacteristic rage and suspicion.

"It's me...it's Gemma," I say, voice trembling as I lurch a step back.

"I don't know you," she says.

The tawny wolf bounds in front of Gray, trying to block her view of me. "Easy. We know her." This voice belongs to Blackbeard.

"I don't know her. I don't even know you."

My heart clenches. Gray's memories have been taken. Does that mean the curse...no. If Blackbeard still has his memories—or at least some of them—then the curse can't have come to claim them yet.

"It's all right," Blackbeard says, along with a low, almost soothing growl. "She's a friend."

Gray lets out a frustrated bark, then takes off down the hall and up the stairs.

Blackbeard pads forward, head low. "He's in the rose courtyard."

That's all I need to hear. I rush down the hall, past more wolves, hoping I'm not stopped by anyone else who's forgotten me. Desperation won't let me slow down or feel the fear I should be experiencing amidst these creatures. But as I reach the doors that lead to the back gardens, I pull up short. Four small wolves huddle along one of the walls, whimpering. At the sight of me, one lifts its head and comes bounding over.

"Why did you leave?" comes Micah's furious voice.

Another young wolf perks up at the sight of me. "Do...we know her?" It's Jenny's voice.

A lump sears the back of my throat. "I'm so sorry," I whisper. "I didn't want to leave you—"

"Then why did you?" Micah asks with an angry snarl. "You didn't even say goodbye."

He's right. In my haste to flee Elliot, I said my good-byes to no one. I simply got dressed and left on foot without even looking behind me. Guilt weighs me down as I recall the promise I made to Gray—the one stating I would take care of the children, should the worst come to pass. "I thought you would be taken care of. I thought the curse would break and you'd be wolves again, running free in the mountains by now. I never would have left if I thought otherwise."

Micah's shoulders heave as he continues to whimper. I slowly extend my hand until it makes contact with his soft head. He lets out a bark that sounds more like a sob, then a violent shudder ripples from his head to his tail. The fur dissolves and leaves Micah's seelie form in its place. He collides into me with an embrace. "I'm scared. I don't want to lose my memories. I don't want everyone to die."

I pull him close, breathing deep to keep from unraveling into sobs of my own. "I don't want that either."

He looks up at me, tears streaking over his face. "What will happen?"

I crouch down. "I don't know, Micah. First I need to speak with the king."

He sniffles, then reluctantly pulls away. With a trembling hand, he points toward the garden.

My feet feel heavy as I leave the children behind and enter the garden. As I approach the rose courtyard, my heart quickens and my stomach churns along with it. All I can think is, *what if I'm too late?*

I pause just outside the courtyard, finding Elliot in his wolf form, laying on his belly. I'm struck at once by how beautiful and sad he looks, his white fur as bright as snow while his powerful build sags with defeat. His head rests on his paws, his canine expression brimming with pain. My eyes flash to the rose. It droops from a cluster of twisting, twining brambles, its stem blackened. And at its center hangs one final petal.

Elliot lifts his head and lets out a low whine. "You weren't supposed to come back." His voice sounds so worn, so tired. "You were supposed to be well on your way to a new life by now. You were supposed to leave and forget about me."

With slow, cautious steps, I enter the courtyard, maintaining a wide berth around the rose, afraid a single step could cause the final petal to fall. When I speak, I keep my voice soft despite the terror, confusion, and sorrow that makes me want to shout. "Elliot, I don't understand what's going on here."

He eases onto his haunches as I approach. Then, with a shudder that rips through him, the wolf dissolves and the familiar man takes his place. He remains on the ground, neither his staff nor prosthetic anywhere to be seen. One leg is propped up and bent at the knee while the amputated one sprawls out to the side.

He shifts as if he's preparing to stand, but I sink down next to him. "Don't get up. Just tell me what's happening."

He looks from me to the rose. "The curse is coming to claim us."

"But...but you were going to marry Imogen. She was supposed to break your curse."

His face twists with pain as he meets my eyes. "No, Gemma. After the ball, I knew there was no way I could marry her."

A flash of anger ignites inside me as I recall what else happened after the ball. How he told me he was willing to break his own curse. I know he decided the sacrifice was too great to make, but I never would have guessed he'd reject Imogen too and choose death instead.

I ball my hands into fists. "So you're just going to give up? Let the curse claim you and all the residents of the manor? You're going to abandon the children to grow up without anyone they know?"

"The children will live," he says. "That's what matters most. And the others have made peace with their fate. They too are unwilling to lose any part of themselves to break the curse. It's all or nothing."

I remember what Blackbeard and Gray had said to me before, how they preferred death over a partial breaking of the curse. But...but...oh, for the love of the saints, these stubborn wolves! I throw my hands in the air. "What about you, Elliot? After everything you've told me about no longer hating my kind, is your wolf form still so important that you'd rather die than be stuck in a human body?"

His jaw tightens, but he holds my gaze. "If I could sacrifice my wolf form, I would."

"What are you saying? That it's too late? The morning after the ball, you said you changed your mind about making the sacrifice."

He averts his gaze, and it falls on a discarded petal.

Taking it between his fingers, he props an arm on his bent knee and watches the petal, eyes distant. "I came out here to break the curse that morning, just like I said I would. I had the stem of the rose between my fingers, and I paused long enough to reflect on what I was prepared to sacrifice. That's when it dawned on me."

The grief in his expression has my stomach in knots. Everything in me wants to lean forward, take him in my arms. Instead, I force myself to remain as still as possible. "What?"

"Do you recall the terms that allow me to break the curse myself?"

"Yes. Of the four things the curse will take from you, if you willingly sacrifice the one you value the most, you will be given the rest."

He nods. "Ever since the curse was placed over me, I've known my unseelie form was what I valued most. I cared for it more than life. And it remained that way... until something changed. You came into my life. I don't know when exactly my values shifted. It happened long before I confessed my feelings for you, I'm sure, but I think I could have at least convinced myself otherwise until that night after the ball. But once I held you, felt you, knew you loved me back...I now valued something greater."

"What? Which of the four things do you value now, and why is it so hard for you to sacrifice?"

As he meets my eyes, his are glazed with tears. He gives me a sad, heart wrenching smile. "It's obvious, Gemma. My memories. Before you, I couldn't have cared less if I lost them. I had nothing worth keeping. I knew I could survive off instinct, become a similar version of my former self even if I was forced to start fresh. There was a chance I'd lose my crown if I couldn't remember my past. There was even a chance I'd forget I was fae at all. I was all right with either situation, so long as I could live as a wolf. But now...*now*...if I lose my memories, I lose you. I lose everything we've experienced together. I lose the person I've become."

My breath hitches, and I feel a sob building in my chest. Everything is starting to come together, the words he said to me the morning I left becoming terribly clear. Words I took to mean something else. I remember the ones that hurt me most—how he said he wished he could take back our night together. How, if it hadn't happened, he could have broken the curse without losing the only thing he cared about.

Now I understand.

He must see the realization in my eyes, for he says, "If I hadn't had such strong memories worth saving, I could have convinced myself I still valued my unseelie form the most. I could have sacrificed it and kept everything else. But after our night together...there was no going back. There was no clever fae deception that could help me hide the truth. I saw it all as soon as I touched the rose. My memories had become that which I valued most, and if I sacrificed them, I would lose you. And I would lose myself."

Tears stream down my cheeks. "Why didn't you tell me? Why did you let me leave so full of hate?"

He reaches a hand toward my face and brushes a stray tear with the backs of his fingers. His touch is so gentle, so apologetic, it makes me feel like my lungs will collapse. "I almost told you, but I realized the truth would have put you in a position to consider breaking my curse yourself. And I will not allow it. You will sacrifice nothing for me, Gemma. I will not have you giving up what you value most. Freedom is too important, and I cannot comprehend what vicious plans the curse would have for you if you sacrificed it, nor am I willing to find out."

"But you will die," I say with a sob.

He leans closer, bringing both hands to my cheeks. "I will die happy and at peace, knowing that I loved you. Do you know I've never loved before? I doubt I've ever been happy, even. Every moment since the day I was born was driven by instinct and survival. When it wasn't that, it was passion, usually in the form of hate or vengeance. The happiest I ever felt was running free through the forests."

"Then take it. Go back to that. Sacrifice our memories and return to the forests. That can't be worse than death."

He brushes his thumb along my cheek, catching another tear. "No, Gemma. It would still be death, just of another kind. I didn't live an honorable life as a wolf. I wasn't kind and I wasn't happy. I had no idea what I was missing until you showed it to me, and now I can't go back to who I was before...or who I will become."

"I thought you hated this body."

"I did. For so long, I did. This body has caused me agony, opening me to new experiences and emotions. For the first time, I had to face everything I did as a wolf. The people I killed, and not only the hunters I was punished for, but the many others I've killed both during and outside of war. I used to relish it. Take pride in it. But in this form, I learned to regret, to feel what you called empathy. I scorned it for so long. But now...if I forget, I'll go right back to who I once was. Worse, even. I know it may not make sense to you, but I'd rather die with my memories intact than live out an eternity as a wolf who never knew you."

I lean closer, placing a hand on his chest, right over his heart. He places his hand over the top of it, the other still caressing my cheek. "We can start over," I say through my tears. "I can help you. We can rebuild all that you've lost."

He shakes his head. "As soon as my memories are gone, I won't know you. In my wolf form, I'd sooner eat you than love you. I won't be the same person I am now —or ever was—if I forget. I might become no more sentient than an animal, and I'm no longer content with that. Neither are the others. At least the pups will live full lives as human children. They may lose their memories, but there's still hope for them to find joy even if the rest of us are gone."

His words spear my heart. As much as I want him to live, I understand his reluctance to become a stranger to himself. What would I choose if the same choice was given to me? Who would I be if I forgot Elliot, forgot our time together? In the month we've spent together, he's changed me. He's taught me to believe in love again. To trust. Even when I thought he'd betrayed me, I maintained a kernel of everything I learned with him inside my heart. Nina helped me find it. Regardless of the pain involved, Elliot has made my life better.

But is it worth my life? If I could save myself and others, but at the cost of my memories with Elliot—

My breath catches in my throat, nearly choking me.

If I could save...*him*.

At the cost of my memories with Elliot...

Would I?

My stomach twists at the sudden realization that Elliot's values aren't the only ones that have changed. Mine have shifted too. I've come to value something greater, and maybe I always have. I will always fight fiercely for my freedom and independence, but neither of those things conflict with being in love...so long as that love is true, kind, and honest. At the end of the day, love is my highest value. And in this hour, in this moment, my relationship with Elliot is the very thing I treasure most.

I surge forward and wrap my arms around Elliot's neck, pressing my lips to his. For a moment, he's frozen in my arms, as if too afraid to reciprocate. Then he softens, his lips yielding beneath mine. I luxuriate in their warmth, their softness, knowing this is the last time I'll ever feel them. Tears continue to stream down my cheeks, but I keep kissing him until I'm out of breath.

Until I can finally bear to pull away.

I frame his face with my hands, locking his eyes with mine. "You might become a monster if you lose your memories...but maybe I won't. Maybe I can still learn to love again, even if I must lose you."

He furrows his brow. "What do you mean?"

I give him a tremulous smile, my lower lip quivering. "I read the book about the boy and the dog. Do you remember it? At the end, the dog dies. He sacrificed himself to save the boy."

He nods. "It's one of the ones I told you I'd read. One that made me want to throw it clear across the room after I finished it." He lets out a sorrowful laugh.

"I felt the same. And yet, it was a beautiful story, one that has stuck with me ever since. When we danced at the ball, and I acknowledged my feelings for you, I felt like the little boy in that story, knowing I was going to lose you. I was prepared to let you go. I knew it was for the best that you marry Imogen, even though it hurt."

He closes his eyes and presses our foreheads together.

"But I'm not the boy after all, Elliot. I'm the dog."

He pulls back slightly, eyes wide and panicked. "Gemma—"

"Never forget, no matter where you go, that I love you, Elliot Rochester."

Then, lurching to the side, I clasp my fingers around the stem of the withering rose and snap it cleanly in two.

41

A thorn pierces my skin, but I pay it no heed. All that matters is that the broken rose is in my hand, the final petal still intact. Then I close my eyes and rush to say, "I willingly and of my own volition, sacrifice my greatest treasure."

The last thing I hear is Elliot's cry of alarm.

Then there's nothing.

No, not nothing but a darkness that seeps into violet at the edges. I blink, trying to clear my vision, and little by little, the violet grows until it's eaten away at the darkness completely. What's left is an unsettling view of where I just was—in the rose courtyard. Except, I don't feel like I'm truly in it. I feel like I'm in a world between worlds, a time outside of time. My body feels both too heavy and too inconsequential. My mind feels slow and cloudy yet buzzing with activity at the same time.

Am I...dead?

The thought doesn't frighten me nearly as much as it should.

I look to the side, where Elliot last was. He's still there, but he appears frozen in time, hand outstretched toward me as if he were in the midst of trying to stop me from plucking the rose. I'm surprised I know it's him, for the more I study him, the more I realize his body isn't as it should be. Instead, it's nothing more than his shape made up of millions of buzzing violet particles of light. Come to think of it, everything in the courtyard is composed of the same swirling light, forming the cobblestone floor, the falling snow, the bench, the brambles. I look down at my hands and find they too are nothing more than purple light. The rose, however, is gone.

"You seek to break the curse," comes an ethereal, musical voice. I see no source for it, but it feels like it's coming from all around, singing through the violet particles of light. There's only one word for it. Magic.

It takes me several seconds to find my own voice, and when I speak, my tone is hollow, flat in my ears. "Yes, I am ready to sacrifice my greatest treasure."

Suddenly, the swirling purple light shifts and sways, and in its place is a scene that occurred minutes before. Or was it hours? Seconds?

Elliot and I are crouched on the floor of the courtyard, foreheads pressed together. Then, as if we're moving in reverse, I see him wipe a tear from my cheek. Next comes the moment I sank down next to him on the ground. The particles shift and form another time we were in the courtyard, fighting. My heart—or whatever is left of it in this strange place—clenches tight as I see the hate written over my face. I'm relieved when the scene disappears and brings me to the night before that, the night he told me he loved me. I watch everything in reverse, from our tangled naked bodies to our first kiss in the library. My only regret is that I hadn't told him I loved him then. At least now I finally have.

The play of light and memories continues, and I watch it all. Watch every moment I experienced with Elliot, all the way to a scene where I crouched down at a wolf's side and discovered he was smeared with tomato sauce. I remember how furious I was then, but now all I can do is laugh. And cry. The two are mingled now. Sweet and sorrow.

The voice speaks again. "This is your greatest treasure? Your time with the Wolf King?"

My heart sinks with the full weight of truth. "Yes."

The violet light shifts again, and I see a vision of myself, walking down the streets of Vernon. My smile is cold, cruel, and haughty. I make eye contact with no one. Handsome gentlemen stop to tip their hats, but I pay them no heed. I'm too wrapped up in my false persona to notice. Then Imogen is at my side and we are chatting on the sidewalk. Ember stands off just to the side and smiles at me. I acknowledge her with a smile of my own, but I know we'll never be friends in this version of reality. In this version, all I can focus on is scheming my way out of the conversation. I'll never open up to anyone, never tell a soul the truth about what the scandal in Bretton did to me. I'll only ever be fake. Protected. Afraid.

This is the person I return to being if I sacrifice how Elliot has changed me.

"This is what you are willing to trade your greatest treasure for?"

I already know my answer, but I take a few moments to consider it. Even though Elliot has made my life better —made *me* better—my life isn't over. If I found the ability to love and trust once, then I can do it again. Even if I can't, knowing what I know now, that Elliot and his wolves will be alive with their memories if I make this sacrifice...it's enough.

"Yes, I am willing."

The ethereal voice speaks one last time. "Then the curse has been served and severed."

The violet light disappears in a rush, flying all around me and away from me like a violent storm wind. Then it's gone, leaving me right where I was before in the rose courtyard.

Time comes unfrozen, and Elliot dives for me, nearly tackling me in the process. He fumbles for my hands but finds them empty. "The rose," he gasps.

I look over my shoulder, expecting to find it still there, to discover the last few moments in that strange, magical place was nothing more than a dream. A hallucination. But the rose is gone.

Elliot takes me by the shoulders, eyes swimming. "What did you do, Gemma?"

Words dissolve from my lips. I'm too afraid to speak, too terrified that if I do, I'll be whisked away to that reality I glimpsed. The one where we never met. The one where I forget him.

All I can do is stare, memorizing the color of his eyes, the shape of his mouth. The way his hair falls into his eyes. The sound of my name coming from his lips. The timbre of his voice, rumbling low in his chest. The melody of his heart.

Take it away, I think. *I'm ready.*

"Say something."

A flash of light, brighter than the sun, comes from behind Elliot. We both startle and face it, but no sooner than it arrives, the light goes out, leaving a shockingly beautiful female in its place. I know at once that she's fae. Even from several feet away, I can tell she's at least an inch or two taller than me, with a slim, willowy build, pale skin, and pointed ears. Her hair is a silvery shade that reaches just below her chin. It's smooth and straight, slicked away from her face in a style I've never seen worn by a female. Her clothing is most unusual, with tight black pants and a slim-fitting shirt that looks more like a waistcoat than a proper top.

Elliot scrambles to stand, rising on his single leg. As soon as he's righted, he opens his hand, and his wooden staff appears as if from thin air. He props it beneath his arm, then takes a forbidding step toward the fae. "Nyxia," he growls, "what the freezing hell are you—"

"Ah, so your memories have returned." Nyxia smiles at him, revealing a flash of pointed canines. Then she glances at his staff. "Your magic too, it would seem."

Elliot pauses, confusion tugging at his features. Slowly, I rise to my feet and make my way to his side. As I reach him, he throws his free arm out before me, eyes locked on the other fae. "Stay back, Gemma," he whispers.

Nyxia crosses her arms and pops her hip to the side, a look of contrived innocence on her face. "Why so tense?"

"I remember now," Elliot says. "You're the one who cursed me."

She shrugs. "I did. And, as the curse maker, I felt its

end and came to pay my regards." She turns her gaze to me, assessing. "You must be the one who broke the curse."

Elliot spins toward me. "Gemma, what did you sacrifice?"

I open my mouth, but I'm still too stunned to speak. Too confused.

Nyxia speaks before I do. "She didn't sacrifice anything, Flauvis."

I furrow my brow. Flauvis? Is that Elliot's real name? But that's not important right now. I face the fae woman, summoning my words from the oceans-deep shock that thrashes inside me. "You're wrong. I plucked the rose and sacrificed my greatest treasure...but why didn't it work? How did the curse break if...if nothing happened to me yet?" A flash of panic washes over me. Will my sacrifice be slow, like Elliot's loss of memories was over the course of the curse?

Nyxia throws her head back with a musical laugh. "The sacrifice worked, pretty human. You were willing and of your own volition to sacrifice your greatest treasure, just like my terms stated."

I stare at her with a blank look, waiting for her to elaborate.

She rolls her eyes. "The curse only required a human be *willing* to make the sacrifice. It said nothing about actually having to make it. It was right there in the wording all along."

"What?" I shout, indignation heating my blood.

A low growl reverberates deep in Elliot's chest. "You turned my curse into a riddle?"

She assesses her fingernails for a moment, completely

unperturbed by Elliot's anger. "I may be devious, Flauvis, but I'm not cruel. Why make a human suffer more than they should on your behalf? It's torture as it is that one must spend enough time with you that they come to hold you in any kind of regard. It would be pure evil to make them actually have to sacrifice their greatest treasure for you. You, of course, would have had to make a true sacrifice, should you have decided to break your curse yourself." She says the last part with a delighted grin, as if she's amused by her own words.

Elliot's chest heaves with rage. "This little riddle of yours could have been the death of me."

She pins him with a withering glare. "Trust me, that's a risk the Alpha Council was eager to take."

I bristle at that, feeling heat rise to my cheeks. I expect Elliot to lash out, and for a moment it seems like he will. Then he lowers his head and grumbles a string of curses under his breath.

"Can you blame us?" Nyxia asks.

He rubs the back of his neck and mutters, "Not entirely." He flashes me an embarrassed glance, then looks back at Nyxia. "We weren't on great terms, were we?"

She quirks a brow. "Are you talking about just you and me? Or you and everyone ever? Because the latter would be an affirmative."

"Freezing fae," he bites out. "I get it, all right? Now will you get off my damn property?"

Her mouth falls open in mock surprise. "Oh, so you mean, now that the curse is broken, you still consider the manor your property? Does that mean you've come to *like* human dwellings?"

"How long are you going to rub it in? Do you want a round of applause? A hug?"

She scoffs, then flips open a strange silver compact. "Bye," she says with a delicate wave of her fingers. The same glowing light from before bursts from the compact. In the blink of an eye, it takes the fae with it.

We stand staring at the place Nyxia just was for a few silent moments. Then slowly, I turn to face Elliot. My pulse races, mind whirling after everything I just learned and experienced. At the forefront of my mind is a flicker of trepidation, which only increases when I see the rigidity of Elliot's posture. I lift my eyes to his, finding uncertainty in his expression.

With the curse broken, have things changed between us? Elliot has his magic, his immortality, his memories. Even the ability to return to his unseelie form. Do I still mean as much to him as I did when he was cursed? Or is this where everything goes wrong again? Like it always—

No. I will not expect the worst. Not this time. If it comes to pass, so be it. But I will not fall victim to my doubts.

I open my mouth, but he speaks first. "Gemma, I don't even know what to say."

My heart lurches. Why does that sound like the beginning of a letdown?

"You...you broke my curse. You did the unthinkable. And I...I have my memories back. Things I didn't even realize I'd forgotten have returned to me. I feel like they're written all over my face."

I furrow my brow. "What are you saying?"

"Surely, you can see it all. You must have seen it in

Nyxia's eyes. I was not a good wolf, Gemma. But I promise to be better."

My breaths grow shallow, my mind reeling as I wait to see where he's going with this.

His lips pull into a frown as he reaches a trembling hand to my cheek. "Do you still love me? I understand if you don't, but...but I really hope you do."

My heart flutters with warmth while relief and annoyance fight for dominance within me. "Of course I do, you fool. Do you think I tried to sacrifice our entire relationship for nothing?"

His lips pull into a sad smile. "I just thought...after what Nyxia said about me and the Alpha Council...well, my point is, it will take a lot of effort to repair the relationships with the other royals. In the meantime, they'll talk. They'll speculate. They'll probably continue to hate me. I know you've been on the wrong side of gossip before, and I can't—"

"Elliot," I say, silencing him as I throw my arms around his neck, "let them talk. I don't care. If they say anything to my face, I'll have a few choice words for them myself, royal or no. All I care about is you. You, Elliot. The one I love."

His lips pull higher, and finally I see that genuine smile of his, the one I first glimpsed in his parlor so many weeks ago. "I love you too, Gemma."

He brings his lips to mine, tossing his staff to the side and gathering me in both arms. I pull him close, careful not to disrupt his precarious balance, reveling in the feel of him, the smell of him, the way his heart hammers against mine.

When we pull away, I feel like my grin will split my face in half. "So, your name is Flauvis? I suppose I should stop calling you Elliot Rochester."

"Honestly, I don't care what you call me," he says. "Call me Elliot, Flauvis. Anything. So long as I'm yours."

EPILOGUE

ONE YEAR LATER

At the top of the stairs, I call down the hall toward the children's room. "Dinner's ready."

I hear an excited whoop, followed by a bark, then three figures charge out the room and skid down the hall. Micah and Jenny are in their seelie forms, while Charlie pads over in wolf form.

My heart squeezes, noting Franklin's absence. The fourth child left the manor just last month when his mother finally came to claim him. I'm happy that he's been reunited with his original family, but I don't know if I'll ever get over the ache of having had to relinquish the pup I've grown to love over the last year. But I must bear it, for in time, all the children might be reclaimed by their parents now that the curse is broken. Until then, I will love them like they are my own with every beat of my heart.

"Who's eating what?" I ask when they approach.

Charlie barks, Micah says, "Bread!" and Jenny shifts from foot to foot, lips pursed. Then, with a shudder, she dissolves into a puff of black and gray fur and lets out an excited bark.

"All right," I say. "You know where to go."

They charge down the stairs, and I follow them at a more leisurely pace. Once inside the dining hall, Micah takes a seat at the long table, while the two young wolves begin playing at the other side of the room, tails eagerly wagging.

Bertha comes in behind me, carrying a platter of fresh bread in one arm and an enormous bowl of stew in the other. "Let me help," I say, taking the bread.

"Ah, thank you, my dear," she says, and we bring the dishes to the table, which is already laden with a generous spread. Once our burdens are set down, Bertha faces me and reaches into her apron pocket. "I almost forgot! You have letters from the post."

I take them from her, finding a few unexciting correspondences. Then at the bottom, I find an envelope sent from a familiar name—Ember Montgomery. Shortly after the curse was broken, Mrs. Coleman left Vernon, taking her daughters and stepdaughter with her. I can only assume that means her courtship with my father didn't survive, for he still lives in town. A town that is becoming more and more populated by fae and other interesting people I've been dying to get to know. Still, I haven't stopped thinking about my turquoise-haired friend, her beautiful piano playing, and her unfortunate living situation with her awful stepfamily. I begged her to write to me after she left, but this is the first letter I've received from her since.

My fingers buzz with anticipation, and everything in me wants to open the envelope at once—

"Where is everyone else?" Bertha asks, distracting me. "They know dinner is at six—ah, never mind. I hear them."

Just then, the sound of paws comes slapping over the flagstones in the hall. A few seconds later, several wolves enter the room. Two work together to carry an enormous deer corpse, which I shake my head at.

With a sigh, I tuck the letters into one of my dress pockets, promising myself I'll read Ember's letter first thing after dinner. For now, more pressing matters await. "Blood on the marble?" I call to the wolves with the deer. "Again? I hope you're on cleaning duty tonight."

The two wolves take the corpse over to where Charlie and Jenny wait at the far end of the room. When the children leap for an early bite, the wolves growl for them to be patient until the others arrive. More wolves file in, and some shift into their seelie forms to join Micah at the table while the others head toward the back. Finally, bringing up the rear, is my beloved white wolf.

With a shudder, he shifts out of his unseelie form into his human body and plants his leg beneath him. A second later, his staff appears in his hand, and he props it beneath his arm. While he's begun using his staff and prosthetic in equal measure, I think he's still fondest of the staff. I look him over, finding him dressed in his nicest trousers, but he wears no waistcoat or jacket, and his shirt is untucked. Luckily, tonight's dinner is the casual sort, so I don't have to force him to go get dressed.

He crosses the room to me, circling his hand around my waist once he reaches me. I place my hand on his chest then lean in for a kiss. His lips press into mine, and I breathe in his scent, noting pine and snow and the unmistakable lingering aroma of wolf fur—a smell I've grown surprisingly fond of. Just as I'm about to pull away, he deepens the kiss, pressing me even closer. A buzz of excitement flutters in my chest, heating my core. I yield to him, parting my lips to feel his tongue slide against mine. Not so much that those around us would notice...but I certainly do. When we manage to separate, he gently nips my lower lip, his arm still circling my waist.

I grin up at him. "You've only been out running with the wolves for a few hours, but you act like it's been days."

"What can I say? After the beauty of the woods and sky, I come home to you and am stunned by what you do to my heart."

I blush and lean in for another kiss. Again, it lingers far longer than it should.

"It's time for dinner," I mumble against his lips.

He lets out a frustrated groan. "Is it, though?"

I pull away, laughing. "Yes, Elliot, and my sister is coming too."

"Surely, we can sneak away to the bedroom for just a second."

My lips pull into a mischievous grin. "Trust me, when I get you alone tonight, we're going to need far longer than a second."

His grin mirrors mine, and I break away from him before he can reel me back in. My head feels light from our flirtation, my heart doing somersaults as I make my way to the table. Elliot takes a seat at the head of the table, his eyes burning into me while I help Bertha lay out the final dishes. I flash my mate a grin. "Stop staring, Elliot. When will you ever learn?"

"Never," he says with a wink. "You're just too freezing beautiful."

Blackbeard, who decided to keep the adopted name even after his memories returned, makes a mock-gagging sound and lowers into his seat. "Get a room."

The king throws a hand in the air. "She won't! She insists we must have dinner first."

Ellen, the wolf we used to call Gray, comes padding into the room in wolf form. "Did I hear dinner? Sorry, I was taking a bath."

"Finally," coughs Blackbeard. Ellen somehow manages to twist her canine features into a scowl, then joins the other wolves around the deer.

Bertha and I finish laying out the final plate just as our guests arrive.

"Gemma!" Nina runs to me, and I embrace her.

"How was your honeymoon?" I ask when we pull away.

A blush creeps up her cheeks, and her smile grows wide. Her eyes flash to her new husband, who shifts awkwardly from foot to foot as he looks from Nina to the dinner table, then to the pack of wolves. "It was wonderful."

I turn toward her husband. "James, it's great to see you again. I'm so glad you could come to dinner. Although, I do hope my sister warned you about us. We aren't a formal household."

He gives me a shy smile. "She has told me much about you and...and His Majesty." He bends into an abrupt bow, and I turn to find Elliot approaching.

"Oh, none of that," my mate says, then gives my sister a hug. To James, he offers a handshake. "It's just Elliot on casual occasions like this."

James stammers before finding his words. "Elliot? But is your name not Flauvis?"

The king grimaces, then smirks at me. "That's only my name when I'm in trouble. Isn't that right?"

I swat him playfully on the chest, then turn my attention to our third and final guest. "Mr. Cordell, I'm so happy you could make it."

"Oh, come now," he says as I pull him into a hug. "I know it's only because I brought with me the newest *Governess in Love* book."

My eyes widen. "No! It's out already?"

He pulls a cloth satchel from his shoulder and withdraws a rectangular package wrapped in brown paper. "You'll be up all night. Trust me."

"We're already planning on that," Elliot says, earning another playful swat from me. He then greets the bookseller, who has become a regular dinner guest of ours.

With all the greetings out of the way, I say, "Come, sit wherever you like. And I do suggest you choose a seat facing away from the wolves at the other end of the room. I know not everyone can stomach their choice of dinner."

James pales but Nina simply chuckles. I lead our guests to the table, and Elliot returns to his seat. I take my place to one side of him, opposite Blackbeard. Micah leaps from his chair at the other end of the table to steal the spot next to me instead. Bertha shakes her head with an amused laugh and sits on the other side of him. Nina, James, and Mr. Cordell take my advice and claim seats next to Blackbeard, backs facing the wolves and their unsightly meal.

"Let's eat," I say.

Everyone reaches forward and begins passing plates of food around. It takes James a moment to fall into the rhythm of our organized chaos, but Nina and Mr. Cordell help him. The table quickly erupts with chatter and laughter, not to mention playful growls and barks.

I scan the table, then the room at large, taking in the faces of the people and wolves who have become my new family, plus Nina, who has always been that to me. Even though linked through blood, we've grown closer this past year, as I've learned to open up in ways I never have before. She catches me watching her and smiles at me with a full mouth. I grin back, then slide my gaze to my mate.

He meets my eyes, and I find his glittering with a joy that reflects my own.

I return to my plate, but I'm almost too happy to eat, my heart full and warm in ways I never thought possible a year ago.

Back then, I'd convinced myself love wasn't real. Or that it had to last for it to have ever been real. But now I know love is more complicated than that. I didn't get it right the first time, and I almost messed it up the second time. And even if I had and went on to try a third, fourth, or thirtieth time...I think it would still be worth it. Love is worth it.

Whether I must be the storybook boy and lose someone important to me...

Or the dog and make a sacrifice for another's wellbeing...

Or the governess on the other side of a love that conquers all, with happily ever after spread out at my feet....

No matter what, love is worth believing in.

A warm hand falls on mine, and I glance again at Elliot. I turn my hand up, lacing our fingers together, and allow myself to get lost in his ruby gaze. No, not lost.

Found.

He leans toward me, and I do the same. His mouth moves to the side of my face where he whispers what has become our deepest expression of adoration. "You make me feel the way books do."

Before he can lean back, I turn my head and steal his lips with a long, lingering kiss. When we do finally break away, I whisper back, "As do you, my love. My wolf. My Flauvis. My Mr. Elliot Rochester. My everything. I love you too."

HUNGRY FOR MORE?
DON'T MISS YOUR FAVOURITE FAIRY TALES RETOLD IN THE 'ENTANGLED WITH FAE' SERIES

Each book in the 'Entangled with Fae' series features a different fairy-tale retelling, a different couple and can be read in any order as a complete standalone story. Journey back to Faerwyvae with these enchanting fantasy romance tales set in the same world as 'The Fair Isle Trilogy' and the 'Fae Flings and Corset Strings' series.

Happily ever after guaranteed!

AVAILABLE NOW

LOSE YOURSELF IN 'THE FAIR ISLE TRILOGY'

Return to Faerwyvae or begin your journey with these breathtaking fantasy romance stories set in the same world as the 'Entangled with Fae' and the 'Fae Flings and Corset Strings' series. This series is best enjoyed in order: *To Carve a Fae Heart* (book 1), *To Wear a Fae Crown* (book 2), *To Spark a Fae War* (book 3).

AVAILABLE NOW

The Lies That Summon the Night

From the art of liars, the monsters came ...

Ever since art gave life to bloodthirsty shadows, creative works
have been forbidden. The talented are sacrificed to the Sinless –
the immortal royals who feast on human blood.

Inana's secret storytelling nearly got her killed once,
and she'll be damned if she's ever caught again. With a bounty
on her head, she keeps to the city's dark underbelly where
she earns a meager living from thrill-seeking patrons
desperate to hear her illicit fiction.

Until a Shadowbane catches one of her performances ...

Dominic is a half-Sinless monster hunter as fearsome as
his prey. But the murderous shades he tracks aren't the only
creatures with bloodlust; Shadowbanes must consume blood
to survive. And to complete his hunt, he needs an artist to
summon the shadows. Inana is just what he needs.

Dominic delivers an ultimatum: serve him or he'll claim her
bounty. When survival is all Inana has left, the choice is clear.
At least until she can betray him and leave him for dead ...

As their tense alliance leads them into the heart of danger,
dark secrets unravel – about each other, their world and
the threats they face. But the greatest risk of all is the desire
growing between them. There's something more sinful than
lust at play, and it could bring the world to its knees.

COMING SOON

1

INANA

The first time I whispered a story to the wind, it was with the certainty that it would end in my death. I may have been a child then, but I understood the implications of the crime I was committing. To perform art is to lie, to lie is to sin, and to sin is to attract the shadows that haunt the dark. Still, instead of running from what I'd done, I waited with bated breath, safe in the sunlight, while my eyes were locked on the woods at the edge of my village. I hardly dared blink for fear I'd miss the telltale sign of movement darkening between the trees. Some indication that I'd stirred a shadow monster's hunger.

When an hour passed and no such danger presented itself, I wasn't relieved.

I was disappointed.

Not because I wanted to die; I wanted to feel alive. To quell the longing inside me, instilled not by sin but by holy scripture.

There is no lie greater than fiction,
No sin more beautiful than art.
Stray not unto these pleasures,
For the devil is their muse.

Gods, the way those lines moved me back then. Though they were meant to serve as a warning not to partake in the forbidden arts, they never sounded like one to me. They sounded like a calling. A challenge. Could I weave a tale so fascinating the devil would take notice? One so beautiful the Shades that plague humanity would seek my death?

That wasn't the last time I breathed fiction into the world. It was only the beginning, and eventually storytelling spelled my doom. Twice I was caught for my crimes.

The first time, it cost me the man I loved.

The second time, my freedom.

Yet it's funny how captivity is the place I've felt most free. On nights like tonight, at least.

A windowless room beckons me from up ahead. I keep my breathing steady as my companions and I proceed down the dim corridor toward it. We're silent save for the soft padding of our slippered feet, the air between us buzzing with a palpable blend of terror and anticipation. We know what awaits us, for none of us are new to performing at the Wretched Lair.

There are more than a dozen of us tonight, all of us artists and out-laws. At age twenty-six, I am neither the youngest nor the oldest. My colleagues range from a girl in her teens to a man twice my years. Most, like me, are indentured to Mr. Rockefeller, the well-dressed gentleman who leads our entourage. The rest have already earned out their contracts and are here by choice to make a living. In two years I'll be among them. Another year after that and I'll have earned enough to buy safe passage off this fucking continent.

I just have to survive until then.

A shiver crawls up my spine as the first strain of music reaches my ears, a lilting melody plucked on some stringed instrument. Such a chilling sound when all forms of imaginative art are forbidden. I should be used to it by now. After one year in Mr. Rockefeller's custody, one year of performances at the Wretched Lair, I've heard my share of music. Yet I don't think it will ever sound less haunting. Less enchanting.

The closer we draw to the doorway, the louder the melody grows, as do bursts of laughter and chatter. I brace myself for the sharp scent of liquor that floods my nostrils, hoping I don't smell the iron tang of blood along with it. If there are any Sinless in attendance tonight . . .

I swallow the ball of fear that rises in my throat. Mr. Rockefeller may hold enough sway over his fellow aristocrats to keep us safe from them, but he cannot promise the same with the Sinless.

At least all of us are masked, our identities further obscured by identical garb: silk robes in deep scarlet with ribbon closures from waist to neck and matching veils over the backs of our heads. No one will see my red-blond hair or freckled cheeks. They'll hardly notice my gray irises through the eye slits. All they'll see are the different designs on our masks—the only things that set us apart, save for our varying heights and builds. My mask is embellished with an elegant floral filigree and a halo of narrow spikes that resemble sunbeams, all of which trail bronze beads that rustle and sway with my movements.

We cross the threshold at last, the transition from the dark corridor to the brightly lit room temporarily blinding me. I blink to adjust to the glow of the glittering crystal chandeliers suspended overhead, their golden light made even more brilliant by the gleam reflected off the silver walls, floor, and ceiling. It's bright enough to send a throbbing ache to my temples, though I should be grateful. Silver and light are the two things that ward off Shades—shadow monsters that manifest from human sin.

That was the original purpose of this room, to serve as an underground emergency bunker. Sacred Cities like Nalheim are surrounded by towering silver walls as well as a dome of light cast by a Holy Brazier at the city's center. Bunkers like this one provide a haven for the aristocracy to flee to should Nalheim's primary protections be compromised. Yet instead of reserving his sanctuary for such a cataclysmic event, Mr. Rockefeller turned it into a social club for the upstanding city elite. A place to safely give his peers a taste of sin.

Rockefeller leads us to the center of the party, where we fan out to allow our audience a full view of tonight's entertainment. Despite the lack of windows, the room is what I imagine a parlor in a palace would look like, with velvet-upholstered wingback chairs and tables laden with decadent food. The silver walls are etched in a damask pattern, the silver ceiling is coffered, and the silver floors are polished to a shine. Such an extravagant display of the continent's most coveted metal.

A few sets of eyes dart our way, but most of our patrons are still engaged in conversation or deep in their drinks as they sprawl about on the furniture. They're dressed in their finest frock coats, top hats, and ball gowns in bright silks, laces, and brocades. Like ours, their faces are hidden behind masks, but theirs are featureless porcelain where ours are works of art, proof that they are not sinners like we are. They don't participate in the unlawful arts. They only watch. Judge. Bask in the splendor of the very thing they publicly condemn.

The melody shifts to a new tune, and I catch sight of the musician, seated in the lap of a slender male. She wears no mask, her eyelids heavy, pupils blown wide. Her fingers remain lithe and active on her harp despite her slumped posture, the bleeding punctures on her neck, and the roving pair of hands that climb up her petticoats and over her stockinged thighs.

My blood goes cold.

I recognize her. She only worked at the Wretched Lair on occasion, having earned out her contract with Mr. Rockefeller years ago. I haven't seen her in months. Now I know why, just like I know what kind of man sits behind her, even without looking at his face. It's written in the effortless grace that lines his posture, in how brightly he seems to shine, as radiant as the chandeliers and silver walls around him. But that's merely because he's the only person in the room who doesn't cast a shadow.

For the Sinless have no shadows.

Absolved of sin, freed from aging and death, the Sinless reign over humanity as the purest of us all. Since they are the only beings who don't attract Shades, they are above reproach.

My jaw tightens. I lift my gaze from the puncture wounds on the woman's neck to the bloodstained lips of the Sinless male. Like the musician, he wears no mask, revealing his sharp cheekbones and empty blue eyes, his golden hair that falls over his forehead. He has no reason to hide who he is or what he does. No reason to feed from his sacrifice in private. He can claim who he wants as his blood source and force them to consume his blood in turn, making them his obedient thralls.

Mr. Rockefeller welcomes his guests and announces the start of tonight's entertainment. Forcing my attention away from the Sinless and his thrall, I stride to an empty marble box, lifting the hem of my robe as I step up on it. Throughout the room, my companions do the same, some with musical instruments, others holding paintbrushes, sketchbooks, or other artistic tools. A few are empty-handed like me, though I won't remain so for long.

Clasping my fingers at my waist, I stand tall. Pretend to be fearless as I make myself a target of interest. Despite the anonymity my mask provides, I always feel naked during this part. Too seen. Too vulnerable. But I refuse to let it show.

Mr. Rockefeller weaves through the crowd, whispering temptations to our patrons.

The Blade juggles knives without drawing a single bead of blood.

The Bard has the scarred hands of a killer yet the voice of an angel.

The Lover waltzes like a prince from the forgotten faerytales of old.

The Harlot has thighs as smooth as silk and a pen that will draw you between them.

The Seamstress stitches a tale of horror and hope that will tug on your heartstrings.

None of us go by our true names, not even with one another. Long gone is Inana Westwood, replaced by the

Seamstress. Thanks to the gossip my master spreads, a small audience soon grows around me, hungry for the Seamstress's fare.

My patrons maintain a modest distance, bodies angled slightly away as if they fear they'll catch my vileness by proximity alone. If they were truly worried, they wouldn't have come to the Wretched Lair. In truth, their disgust is feigned. I can see the excitement that flashes behind their masks, the anticipation that dances in the shivers that roll through their beautifully clad bodies. They're as thirsty as the Sinless, though not for blood. As hungry as the Shades, though not for flesh.

The harpist's tune slows, and our patrons make their final selections. Some attendees keep to the walls to more convincingly maintain an air of indifference, like the Sinless male, who hasn't left his chair—thank the gods. I hazard a glance his way, a ball of tension easing from my shoulders. So long as he keeps to himself, I can give my performance my all. Otherwise, I would have to walk a fine line between entertaining my audience and remaining unmemorable. It's the most talented ones the Sinless seem to favor on their rare visits to the Wretched Lair.

My heart falls as I lower my eyes to the harpist once more. Her smile is so peaceful, her gaze so empty. What does it feel like to be drunk on a Sinless's blood? Is there a part of her that remains lucid, slamming helplessly against the cage of her mind? Is that the part of her that continues to play so well, her only act of rebellion while the rest of her body obeys?

I don't want to know. Only someone in her position could answer that question, and I would never wish her fate upon myself. Perhaps it's selfish to be grateful that

I'm not her, but outlaws don't survive this long by being selfless.

As the Sinless lowers his lips, pressing sharp canines to the gaping bite marks on his thrall's neck, his eyes lift and lock on mine. Or perhaps I only imagine they do. Surely he can't see my eyes from where he sits. I tear my gaze away. Just as quickly, the harpist's song cuts short. My pulse hammers in the wake of her silenced tune.

She might not be dead, I tell myself. She could have temporarily lost consciousness from blood loss. Not all Sinless drain their sacrifices to death. Some keep pets.

Not all Sinless stop at drinking blood, my darkest side whispers back.

I resist the urge to rub the scar on my chest, hidden beneath my robe, and remind myself why this is all worth the risk. Why I will choose to return here, even after I've bought out my contract.

Because this is my best chance at funding my escape from the continent.

And the one way I can satisfy my darkest longing.

Gathering a bracing breath, I lower my eyes to the audience that surrounds my tiny marble stage.

"Mine is a story of a woman who lost her heart," I say, my wistful tone barely carrying over the din that has risen as each performer starts to spin their craft. Unimpressed eyes droop behind their masks, my patrons second-guessing whether they chose the right performer. An intentional diversion on my part, as I loosen the top closures of my robe. Then I claw my fingers beneath the garment, letting the front sag open enough to reveal the puckered line of flesh that runs from my sternum to the upper curve of my breast.

My audience's eyes widen on seeing my jagged scar. Their interest is piqued.

I lower my voice to a harsh rasp.

"Mine is a story of a woman who lost her heart," I repeat, more sinister this time.

From beneath my robe I extract the still-beating organ in question.

"Mine is a tale of the treachery of love."

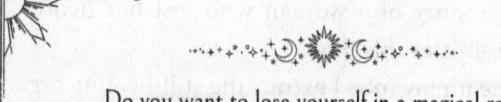